ISBN: 1-59129-433-9
PUBLISHED BY PUBLISHAMERICA BOOK PUBLISHERS
www.publishamerica.com
Baltimore

Printed in the United States of America

This book is dedicated in loving memory to

Joanne O'Brien 'Obie' Alger

Acknowledgements

One of the great fears I have in trying to write out acknowledgements is that there will be some deserving of recognition left off the page. To those, I apologize in advance.

There are many who helped shepherd me through the long and arduous process of writing a first novel. Many thanks are due to 'The Greg O'Brien Fan Club' (Nancy and Dick Bostdorff, Dave Hodel, Gabe Joseph, Noelle Allison, Wayne Melton, and all the ladies from Mom's work who peppered me with e-mails wondering when the next chapter was coming). Dave Ratto, Brent Richard and Sterling Morgan gave me help on the workings of technology beyond this humble weatherman's grasp. Ron Panzel helped keep me straight in the field of computer science. Special thanks go to Sheri Lynch and my father John Alger for their very extensive and insightful editorial suggestions. To Sue, Lynn, Mark and Steve… I am grateful for all the encouragement and suggestions from my 'bossy and overbearing siblings.' I owe a great deal to NYT best-selling author Dale Brown, whose pledge to 'encourage, cajole, shame and berate' me into finishing this novel was just the kick in the fanny I needed.

My mother, Joanne Alger, who sadly passed away before this was published, was chiefly responsible for my love of reading, and was probably my biggest support during this book's writing. If anything in it strikes your funny bone, you may hold her genes chiefly responsible.

To my children Mikaela and C.J.: thanks for being the inspiration of all that is good in Mary and Christopher.

And to my wife, Anita: Greg O'Brien is only the second luckiest man alive.

Finally, eternal thanks go to my Lord Jesus, who gives each our own story to tell.

Prologue

Riding the gentle swells of the Eastern Pacific Ocean, approximately 35 miles south-southwest of San Diego, the crew of the fishing trawler made a halfhearted attempt to tend to their nets. They rarely caught anything. The fishing wasn't so bad. But the tattered nets, cut or unraveled every third or fourth weave, nearly assured that any fish unfortunate enough to wander into their grasp would find it fairly easy to work its way free. A visitor to the boat's two large holds would perhaps understand the crew's cavalier attitude toward adding to their catch. Both appeared to be nearly overflowing with Albacore tuna.

Two sounds could be heard that night, for anyone who might drift by close enough in the nearly empty ocean. There was a constant low thrumming of the diesel engines, peppered by an occasional outburst of exhaust noises as the water covered, and then uncovered the outlet in time with the swells. Cutting through the engine noise was the somewhat tinny sound of music from a radio being played inside the main cabin. The radio played day and night.

The captain was a former skipper in the US Merchant Marines who lost his commission and briefly his freedom after a bout with the Maritime Court. A grizzled veteran of dozens of these fishing trips, he was awakened from a rum induced sleep by one of his crewmen. "*Mandy esta aqui,*" was the simple message the man passed along before returning to the deck.

"So the old girl finally decided to show herself, eh?" the Captain barked out to no one in particular, in a throaty voice made hoarse and raspy from too many shouted commands and too many pipes of cheap tobacco. "It's about bloody time. Those fish down there are really starting to stink."

Chapter 1

Oh dear God, please. Anything but that.
Anything but a knife.

In the predawn hours of a cold December morning there was little light,
but a faint beam from a lone street lamp glinted off the chrome steel blade
and reflected in my eyes, dilated with horror. The hand that held the knife
was as steady and emotionless as a cardiologist's, preparing for open-heart
surgery.

Knowing his intentions, it was an all too appropriate metaphor.

Please dear God…anything but a knife.

We all carry our own phobias throughout our lives, demons tucked away
in the recesses of our minds until something unlocks their cages and sets
them free. For me, I had always had an uncontrollable fear of being stabbed.
And the sight of that blade loosed the flood of terror that I had spent much of
my life suppressing.

It was that same terror I used to feel as a kid when my brother Paul would
pretend to stab me during a make-believe knife fight. In our constant war
games, I could handle guns, fists, laser beams, and even hand grenades. But
if he approached me with a broomstick sword or a willow twig bayonet, my
stomach would knot up in a ball as I imagined the "blade" finding a soft spot
between my ribs. At that point, the game lost all of its enjoyment for me. I
would turn and beat a hasty retreat, with Paul close behind, poking and
prodding my backside, until the combination of increased adrenaline on my
part, and laughter on his allowed me to put some distance between us. He
knew how to get my goat in those days, but I doubt that even he really
understood what a paralyzing fear his actions brought to me. I've had
nightmares about it ever since.

Only this time, the nightmare was real, and I had nowhere to run.

It was still snowing. I had come down to the Truckee River in Reno,

Nevada in the pre-dawn hours to help out the Dawn Donut Patrol. The Patrol was a volunteer group that met the homeless near the riverbanks at daybreak to give them hot coffee and donuts for breakfast, and a sack lunch before they lined up at the employment office. Some never seemed to break their pattern, showing up morning after morning with that same vacant look of despair in their eyes and the tang of Mad Dog on their breaths. But there were some success stories. Kurt Breeder, who drove down with me this particular morning, was a former recipient of the Patrol's services. At 6'6" and 285 pounds, Kurt looked every bit the ex-Canadian Football League linebacker that he was. Kurt had started to get established in Canada, and was about to get his shot at the NFL when a knee injury ended his career. Depression and a losing battle with the bottle had ultimately landed him on the streets. But things were turning around for the big guy. He was working steadily, and was with his family once again. Volunteering for the Patrol was his way of giving something back.

He and I were the first to arrive. We carted the big ten-gallon coffee machine down the path, through a fresh white blanket of snow to the picnic area at Rock Park. Since the park didn't open till dawn, and dawn didn't come until after 7 AM in mid-December, I had parked the car up on Rock Blvd. and we hiked in over the bank. As Kurt got the coffee going, I jogged back to get the food.

It was a clean, cold, wonderful morning, even to a guy like me who would rather see a dentist's drill than be awake before the sun rose. A thin mist lifted off the water, and the new covering of powder seemed to swallow up the sound of the river. I followed our footsteps back up to the car, parked at the foot of the bridge crossing the river.

That's when I heard it...an eerie, haunting sound. At first I mistook it for some kind of animal in distress. Perhaps one of the coyotes that was gradually losing its fear of the urban sprawl had cornered a cat. But when I heard it again all uncertainty left me. It was human. A human in pain. The low, moaning sound that came from the barely conscious. It gently echoed out from beneath the overpass, a favorite camping-out place for many of our homeless clients. Down there, hidden from the curious eyes of the outside world, being mugged for a bottle or a candy bar was a way of life.

I dropped the bags in the car, clambered down the bank and ducked under the concrete shelter. It was easy to see where the noise was coming from. A lone figure was huddled in the corner, wrapped up in a heavy coat, rocking gently and moaning softly. As I approached, something niggled in the back of my mind…something out of place. But there wasn't time to sort it out. He was obviously hurt, and in these sub-freezing temperatures he needed help.

I knelt down beside him and said hopefully, "Friend? You OK? Are you hurt? Hey Buddy…."

I was answered by more moaning.

I reached out and started to gently turn him over when I figured out what was wrong. It was the boots. While his coat was old and battered and smelled like a distillery, his boots were freshly polished, apparent even in the low light, and there were silver caps on the pointed toes. Just as I was trying to figure out how a street bum could've gotten a hold of a $400 pair of snakeskin boots *and* kept them this clean, my patient spun around and lashed out with a thin pipe he had hidden in his sleeve. The pipe crashed against my shin and my leg gave out from under me. I was too shocked to even cry out, and before I had gathered what little wits I had he was on his feet, around behind me, and had me in a chokehold that left me totally helpless. Not that I could have escaped anyway, with what I was sure was a broken shinbone.

He leaned in close and said with amusement, "Gidday, mate. Long time no see, eh?" His breath clouded in the freezing air, and in a detached sense of unreality, I could smell a faint odor of cinnamon gum. Dentyne, I believe. So this is what you think about when you are going to die. Here I was, my life about to end, but at least my assailant practiced good oral hygiene.

Then he pulled out the knife.

All thoughts of boots, teeth, gum or halitosis immediately fled, and my entire universe was focused squarely on the tip of that nearly ten-inch blade of carbon-hardened steel. My abdominal muscles immediately recalled my childhood phobia and started to spasm. I was totally, completely, and uncontrollably horrified.

Without any apparent effort he twisted my head and leaned in close so I could look straight into his eyes. There was no fury in those eyes, hardly any emotion at all…just…satisfaction. The deadliest man on the West Coast whispered in that high-pitched Australian accent, "Ya gotta understyand mate, it ayen't nuthin' *personal.*"

My feeble struggles grew weaker as his chokehold cut off my oxygen. Though my thoughts began to cloud, I became dimly aware that he shifted the knife. He placed the tip just under where my rib cage ought to be buried under the bulky parka I was wearing, and aimed straight for my heart. I closed my eyes and thought of Lauren and the kids.

Then he plunged the knife in.

My back arched violently. I tried to scream. All that came out was a strangled gurgle.

So this is what it's like to die. It's funny, after all that psychosis about being stabbed, the actual event felt no worse than a pin prick. A big pin prick, mind you, but I'd felt worse. Must've been shock, or loss of oxygen.

A surreal kaleidoscope of thoughts swirled through my fading consciousness. *My family...dear Lord, what about my family? Will they ever find out the truth? ...Strange, my shin still hurts...That should stop soon...Just give in to it...Before long, it'll all be over.* In my mind's eye, I tried to peer ahead through the mist, searching out the inevitable bright light that I assumed would soon be emerging.

I was nudged from my reverie by a sharp curse of frustration uttered by my assailant. He was tugging on something, and I took a moment to realize he was trying to pull the knife out and push it in farther. Oh, c'mon, one shot to the heart isn't enough? But something seemed to be wrong. In his frustration, he released the grip on my throat and tried to jimmy the knife out with both hands. It wasn't much, but the shock of cold air into my lungs brought me partly out of my fog.

I had been pretty limp there on the ground, but my hand found a good sized piece of river rock, and taking the best guess I could, I took a swing behind me hoping to hit a home run off his temple.

I managed a bloop single.

Glancing off the crown of his forehead, it stunned him so that he fell back momentarily. It was all I needed. I jumped to my feet and turned to flee up the embankment.

Pain shot up through my knee, into the hip, through my torso until it felt like a bomb had gone off inside of me. Stars blinded my sight. I'd forgotten about my leg. It collapsed, and I found myself down on the rocks again. As I wiped the tears out of my eyes the Aussie slowly got up, shaking his head to clear the cobwebs. He moved purposefully, planting himself between me and the only escape route out to the road. I tried to shout, but a bruised windpipe in 20-degree temperatures couldn't produce more than a mild croak, drowned out by the traffic of the early morning commute pounding overhead.

My adversary brushed himself off, took stock of the situation, and decided there was no rush. I was never going to outrun him on this leg, and he could easily cut me off before I could get into view of the road and any possible help. Bums get knifed down here all the time, sometimes in broad daylight. Often they're not found for weeks.

Speaking of knives, as I hobbled up on my one remaining good leg, I glanced down and saw the offending implement sticking out of my right side. It was weird; it still didn't hurt that much. My leg hurt a lot worse. It must've been real sharp. And how did he miss my heart? No time to think about that. But at least *he* didn't have the knife anymore. I started to think that we might be at a stalemate. As if it's really an even match between a one-legged, middle-aged, about-to-go-into-shock man with no fighting experience carrying a knife in his side, and a trained killer. The guy could've probably done me in with a pocket comb. He just gave me a bemused smile, reached into his boot, and pulled out what looked like…a pocket comb? What, was he trying to prove my point? Then he touched the tip of the handle.

A thin stiletto blade came flashing out.

Oh. Not a pocket comb. A switchblade.

Another knife. Not my day.

As he slowly backed me up to the river's edge, he cackled. "Didn't think Oy'd come weethout some backup now, didja?"

I picked up another rock as he drew toward me, but I knew it would be hopeless. I'd been lucky the first time when I caught him by surprise, but he was too quick, too nimble, and too strong. And I was too weak, too slow, and too hurt. I did the only sensible thing a half-conscious man with a knife sticking out of him would do on a snowy morning in December.

I turned, and with my one good leg, dove into the river.

My first thought was I'd have been better off if he had succeeded with the knife. Thousands of needles, driven by thousands of tiny hammers, plunged themselves into every square inch of my body. I broke the surface of the water, trying with all of my might to draw in a breath of air…but the air wouldn't come in. The Truckee River flowed straight out of the mountains, and the temperature of the water was barely above freezing. Every muscle in my body went instantly rigid. I flopped over and caught one last glance of the Aussie, who just stared at me as I floated away in the current. He probably figured that what he didn't do, the river would finish. At that point, I couldn't argue. The water was frigid, the current strong, and I was too spent to fight it. As I floated out from under the bridge I could see cars driving by. I waved my arms feebly, hoping against hope that one of them would see me, but as I rounded the bend I knew it was hopeless.

I gasped for breath, only to be rewarded with a mouthful of ice water. I had the ludicrous thought that I shouldn't worry about swallowing it. After all, Reno gets its drinking water from this river, so it must be safe. Oh, thank heaven for that, I might have really been in trouble otherwise. I gagged and spit it out anyway, and tried to hold my head above the surface, but I was quickly losing all the feeling in my limbs.

So this is what it's like to die. Twice in one morning.

I always was an over-achiever.

I tried one final time to make a push for the shore. I flailed my arms, only to have them flop uselessly around at my side. The same feeling you get when you wake up and your arm is asleep. Nothing but dead weight. At least the needles didn't hurt as much. After what seemed like an eternity, but in reality was less than ninety seconds, my muscles simply stopped working.

I had nothing left. As I started to drift off, and the icy water closed over my face, I thought I really could see the bright light. *I'll save a place for you, Lauren...*

I gave up and resigned myself to an icy grave. The only way I was going to get out of this was for God Himself to reach His strong hand out and grab me, and haul me out of the river.

Chapter 2

A strong hand reached out and grabbed me and hauled me out of the river.

And unceremoniously plopped me down on the gravel riverbank. After retching and coughing up a couple gallons of Reno's drinking water, I decided it was only appropriate to roll over and express my gratitude. Owing to that previous thought of God plucking me out of the current, I really rather expected to see the Old Man Himself.

Instead, my eyes beheld the bearded face and concerned eyes of Kurt Breeder.

It was almost as good.

In my panic, I had forgotten that I was drifting back down toward the picnic area. "Jeez, man…what in tarnation are you doing?" Kurt blurted. "I couldn't figure out what was taking you so long, and I was just about ready to head back. Good thing I waited, cuz I'd a missed you floating down river if I'd a gone back along the path. Then I sees you out in the water, and man, was it cold. Almost got swept away myself. Can't believe…" Kurt stopped suddenly as his eyes finally glanced down to my right side, at the protruding knife. "Holy…what happened? What's this? Here, let me get that."

Inside, my mind screamed for him not to touch it, that I would bleed to death if he pulled it out, but my mouth and voice didn't have it in them to produce more than a garbled flush of noise. And Kurt, bless his big and wonderful heart, is kind of hard to stop once he gets going. All I could do was brace myself for the inevitable jolt of pain as the blade scraped against the ribs on its way out. What I did not expect to see was what Kurt held up in front of my unbelieving eyes.

In the struggle in the river, the razor sharp edge of the knife had ripped a long gash in the padded parka that I was wearing. The knife came out quite easily. But instead of the blade being coated with my dripping blood, it was firmly imbedded into the middle of a hard plastic, ¾ inch videotape case. With a shaking hand, I silently took the knife, and its impromptu sheath, and turned it over and looked at the bottom of the case. The knife tip poked through about a quarter of an inch. Just a pinprick.

And here I thought I might be getting over my fear of being stabbed.

In all the excitement, I had totally forgotten that I had been carrying the tape case in one of the oversized pockets in the side of the parka. So that's why the Aussie seemed to falter after he shoved the knife in. The knife was one of those nasty things with a saw tooth cut along the top of the blade, opposite the cutting edge. All the better for sawing through bones while skinning the spoils of the hunt. But this time, the teeth got caught up in the plastic case and tape inside, and when he had tried to pull it out to take another shot at me, the tape got caught up in the pocket. I was incredibly lucky to be breathing, albeit not very efficiently at the time.

Kurt had started talking again, non-stop. "Whoa, would you look at the size of that thing. How did it get there? What were you doing? Lord, look at you, soaked from head to toe. Why, we'd better report this, or at least…"

I finally worked up enough feeling in my arms to grab a handful of Kurt's jacket, which blessedly quieted his diatribe. If I had let him go on, icicles would have started to form on my face. I pulled him close and croaked out the first intelligible word I had spoken since going under the road. "Car," I whispered.

Kurt got the message, and without a further word, picked me up like a rag doll and carted me off to the car. God bless the Canadian Football League.

As Kurt started up the Chevy Nova and turned up the heater to full blast, he only said one more thing on the way to the hospital. "Who was he, Greg?"

I didn't answer. But I knew. Because this wasn't the first time he had tried to kill me. And it wouldn't be the last.

But I didn't have all the answers.

I still didn't know why.

I sat in the emergency room at St. Mary's Medical Center, waiting for some attention from an overworked early morning shift. Two gang drive-by shootings, unusual this time of year, and a three-car pileup just hours earlier, combined with a skeleton staff, had St. Mary's looking more like a M.A.S.H. unit than a modern city hospital. After performing their triage, since I was breathing and conscious, I was apparently well down on their priority list. All the attending physician had time to do was to give a precursory look at the rapidly-developing, ugly purple mass on my shin and say, "I hope you iced this thing down after you banged it."

I looked at him with a touch of irony, pushed a still-wet lock of hair off of my forehead, and said dryly, "Yeah, Doc. It was the first thing I tried."

"Good!" he mumbled, and hurried off to attend to a sucking chest wound in surgery.

Subtle humor apparently didn't become him.

But the relative inattention was a good time to just sit and think without worrying about a knife slicing my carotid artery or another car trying to make me a permanent part of the pavement. The peace lasted all of about twenty minutes, after which time I was still no closer to the reason for my seemingly imminent demise.

My silent reverie was interrupted by a nurse, who after staring at me for about five minutes, finally screwed up enough courage to come over and ask that question that I have become so accustomed to. "Say, aren't you...the...um...."

"Yeah," I said. "The weather guy."

This is probably as good a time to as any to introduce myself. My name is Greg O'Brien, weather guy. I am a weatherman on Channel 3 here in Reno. Or, in my more ostentatious moments, KRGX-TV's Chief Meteorologist. Having served in such a capacity for the better part of ten years, it's tough to go anywhere in this part of the world and not be recognized. That is both the bane and blessing of my life. I enjoy meeting people, and it's an easy opening line for folks to talk about the weather, since that's just what folks do naturally. But it's hard to escape sometimes, and there are a lot of moments when I just want to remain anonymous. For instance, if I am feeling cranky, I don't have the luxury of showing it very often. A stranger having a bad day is quickly forgotten, but Greg O'Brien having a bad day sticks with someone for a long time.

But all in all, this town had been great to me, and I planned on making my life here.

Now if only I could figure out a way to make my life last longer than the end of the next ratings period.

Chapter 3

Life was treating Greg O'Brien pretty well about a month prior. I breezed into the KRGX studios on a Monday afternoon after the ten-minute drive from our house. I was feeling a lot perkier than most had a right to feel, starting a new workweek, but I'd had a pretty terrific weekend with Lauren and the kids. We had taken our annual trek over the mountains to pick apples at a place named, appropriately enough, Apple Hill. It was a cute little bend in the road just this side of Placerville, in California. We started doing this several years ago when Lauren wanted to try out a recipe for apple butter. Since it seems to take about a bushel of apples to boil down to about a quart of apple butter, we thought that picking them ourselves might save some money. We had such a good time scouting the dozens of apple farms and finding just the right types that we have made it an annual affair.

I had a freshly capped jar of apple butter, still warm, under my arm. I brought it into the News Director's office, and while she was busy trying to placate an irate viewer on the phone, I sat down opposite her, slipped the jar on her desktop, and covered it with the rundown from that day's 5:30 newscast.

I had worked for Channel 3 for almost ten years, and the last five had been under Jeanne Marshal's leadership. She continued with her phone conversation, her soothing, grandmotherly tones diffusing the apparent outrage on the other end of the connection, her snow-white hair and conservative gray suit showing, as always, no strand or thread out of place. She was a master at turning an angered "watcher" of our news into a faithful "viewer." She had mastered the art of tactfulness so well that she could tell someone where to go so nicely they actually looked forward to the trip.

She had decided that the benefits of living and working in this part of the world far outweighed the glamour and glitz of the big time. After "serving hard time," as she called it, in Washington D.C. as a White House Correspondent, she "retired" to Reno. Yeah, right. Arriving almost every day at 7 A.M. and rarely leaving before 8 P.M., she acted more like a hungry intern trying to break into the business. Of course, at the time she was breaking into the news business, I was still in diapers.

"That's right…uh huh…well, I'm glad you called, too, and I appreciate your concern, and you can be sure your suggestions will be taken to heart. Uh huh…yes… and thank you, too! Bye bye!" She set the phone back down on the cradle, and with an impish grin said, "Well, we must be doing something right. So far that's the eighth call we've had on our election race coverage, and as it stands, four think we are communists, and the other four are convinced we are skinheads." She chuckled softly before turning her attention to me. "So what's up, Sonny?"

I ever so slowly lifted the rundown up so she could peek at the jar underneath. "Who's your buddy, Boss?" I taunted.

Her eyes grew wide with delight when she spied the prize underneath. "Apple butter!" she squealed. "Yes! OK….What is it? Contract extension? Company car? Double your salary? Whatever you want. Gimme gimme gimme!" as she pawed at the quart jar. It was one of the few ways that I could get the normally stoic and elegant matron of the newsroom to start acting like a teenager.

I figured I'd better not press my luck. "How about getting engineering to fix the monitor in the weather office? I'm going cross-eyed trying to pick out which of the three images is the real one."

"You drive a hard bargain, but consider it done. Although, knowing engineering, the company car might have been easier." She claimed her prize and sighed contentedly. "So I see you made your Apple Hill run this weekend. How are Lauren and the kids?"

"Couldn't be better. Kids are growing like weeds in a compost pile, and Lauren's got us in apple butter for at least another month. I just thought I'd drop by and pony up my annual bribe before doing my radio spots." In addition to my television duties, I also provided forecasts for KOPP-FM, a local radio station.

Her eyes perked up. "So how's the radio gig going now, anyway?"

I shot her a quick grin. "Real good. They just got their Arbitron in, and the afternoon drive had its best numbers in years." The Arbitron is the ratings service for radio stations. It's similar to what we go through with our Neilson Ratings, but theirs lasts three months at a time, as opposed to four weeks for us.

"And I'm sure you pointed that out to their G.M. (General Manager), eh?" she said with a straight face. "What's his name, again?"

"He's a new guy. Um…Steve… Steve something…Richards. Yeah, Steve

Richards. Kinda hard to get a read on this guy. Seems friendly on the surface, but the one time I met with him, he would never look me in the eye. I'm still trying to figure out why they got rid of their last one. She was doing a good job, and I heard the station was finally starting to make some money."

"Hey, it doesn't have to make any sense. This is the media, right?" We both chuckled at the old joke, one that only made sense if you worked in television.

I rose to leave. "Well, enjoy the treat, and try not to finish it before the night's out, OK? We only have about three dozen jars left, and most of them are spoken for. I'd better get hopping. My first cut-in is in fifteen minutes."

I plopped myself down on my padded chair in the weather office. My office was built into the set in the studio, so that when we took a shot of the "Weather Office" while we were on the air, it actually *was* my weather office, instead of a mock-up like you see on so many newscasts. Something to do with journalistic integrity, or truth in advertising, or something like that. Anyhow, it was nice to be removed from the rat race of the newsroom, and it certainly made updating the forecast at the last second a lot easier. There were only a couple of downsides to the arrangement. One was I had to keep my workspace neat, a skill that I had never particularly developed in my youth, and which didn't seem to have improved with age. The second problem was, in an effort to counteract the effects of the hot studio lights, they kept the temperature of the place at a level such that you could leave a quart of milk out on the counter and it wouldn't go sour for weeks.

I flipped on my portable space heater, and got to reviewing the various computer models, satellite pictures, and numerical data that was automatically loaded into my computer workstation via a satellite downlink. This particular day, it was basically a no-brainer, with a persistent ridge of high pressure off the California coast blocking whatever storms might try to invade the area over the next several days. Satisfied that I was safe to stake my reputation on a sunny and mild forecast, I dialed up the afternoon drive disc jockey at KOPP-FM radio.

On the surface, Chuck Murphy and I couldn't be more different. Short and rail thin, with long hair, Chuck awoke in the morning talking, spent the day talking, and I was sure talked in his sleep. According to Chuck, silence wasn't golden; it was a waste of airtime. In our conversations, we clashed on everything from politics to religion, and Chuck felt no fear in breaking social taboos by bringing up either subject. But in the two years that we had spent bantering back and forth over the radio waves, I had come to a real appreciation of his quick wit and deceivingly gentle spirit. At least during those times when I didn't want to wring his neck.

"Radio Free Reno!" Chuck answered before the first ring ended.

"Hey Chuck!" I greeted him. "Ready to finally get some work done?"

"Well, look what the cat drug in! If it ain't ol' Mr. Greg 'I can say "sunny" sixty-four different ways in one forecast' O'Brien. I swear, I don't see why they don't just train a parrot to say 'Braaaaak! Sunny and mild! Won't rain or snow till hell freezes over! Braaaaak!' Would save the station a lot of money and would probably be just as accurate."

"They're considering that," I quipped, "but they want to see how that trained monkey they are going to use to replace you does first."

"No kidding, Sherlock," Chuck bemoaned. Actually, he didn't use the word "kidding," but since Chuck usually cusses like a stevedore, I have made it a point to mentally clean up his nomenclature a bit, in deference to the young who might read this. How the guy manages to avoid breaking every FCC obscenity rule on the air, I'll never know. "An ape could do this job these days. You ought to see the new playlist of songs that the new management handed down. It's the most ridiculous mish-mash of lousy, out of date, bubble-gum music you have ever seen." Of course, Chuck added some additional colorful metaphors of his own. The reader is free to use his or her imagination. "I mean, crimony, we are supposed to be an 'Adult *Contemporary* Format.' Since when is Barry Manilow Adult *or* Contemporary?"

"You're playing Barry Manilow?" I asked incredulously. Oh man, this was great! This would give me enough ammo to last me for months if I played it right. "I knew it, Chuck. I knew you'd come out of the closet eventually! Say it! 'I LOVE Muzak!' " I was beginning to enjoy this.

"That's it, kick a guy when he's down," Chuck mumbled.

I decided to save some of my powder for another day. "This a new management decision, huh? So how's the new boss working out, anyhow?"

"I'd say it was just more of the same old stuff, Greg, but this guy's worse. I don't trust him. He skulks around here at all hours of the night. Always peeking in on us during the songs. Heck, I can't even go out for a smoke anymore during the longer sets. I don't know what it is, but there is something mighty weird with this bozo."

This was nothing new coming from Chuck. He never had an overdeveloped respect for authority, and always believed that those in management were conspiring against him, or the world. You could bring Barbara Bush in to be his next boss and he'd have her involved in the JFK assassination within weeks.

"And now," he rambled on, "to make it worse, he's got this dag-burned (my translation) playlist that we have to stick to. And it's not just the songs, but the order of them as well!" A playlist was a list of songs that the radio DJs were allowed to pick from. Some stations were very strict about following it to the letter, while others allowed their on-air talent more flexibility.

"So, why is this any different?" I asked. "Why not just change the playlist to your liking? That's what you've always done before."

"Don't remind me," Chuck moaned. "I tried that once. Only once. The little Hitler came roaring in and, I swear, I thought he was going to pull out a gun and shoot me. Looked like he was going to burst a vessel. He had this wild look in his eyes, and said that if I ever, *ever* did that again, I was quote-history-unquote. He said that I would never work again. Here or anywhere. Anywhere! Guy thinks he runs the world!"

Chuck sighed. "What could be so important about a stupid playlist? Jeesh, you'd a thought I'd cost him fifty million dollars."

As it turned out, Chuck wasn't too far off.

Chapter 4

Playlists notwithstanding, the radio gig was a pretty comfortable one for me. I didn't get paid much for it, but it wasn't a real big drain on my time. I would call the station up on a standard phone line, but would speak into a separate microphone, which was fed through an "equalized" line. The result was an almost studio-quality sound which had most people listening believing that Chuck and I were in the same room. Since I had to prepare a forecast for the television news anyway, it was pretty fresh on my mind, and the radio show was almost like a practice run-through. Chuck and I had a good rapport on the air, and in radio you can be a little freer to chat back and forth.

On this particular day, since I didn't much feel like getting all sixty-four different ways to say "sunny" in this particular forecast, I finished it up early and tried to put a plug in for the upcoming Nevada Day parade down in Carson City. Nevada Day commemorates Nevada's entry into the union on October 31, 1864, and Chuck couldn't resist commenting on the appropriateness of Nevada's birth occurring on Halloween. "Now that's a scary thought, huh?" It was an old joke, and not all that funny, but that didn't seem to matter. After taping a few more weather spots that were to run later that evening, I signed off and turned my attention to developing a sixty-fifth synonym for "sunny" for the 5:30 TV newscast.

Ah, the trials we bear.

Leaving the station that evening, successful with number 65—"severe clear"—I couldn't help but be once again amazed at how lucky I was to be where I was. Reno is a wonderful place to live. Tucked at about 4,500 feet elevation in a valley between the Sierra Nevada Mountains and the Virginia Range, there is an incredible variety to the landscape and an almost endless choice of options.

If I went west I'd climb into the towering Sierra, resplendent with forests of Ponderosa Pines and huge winter snowfalls. If the Sierra Nevada is a jewel, then Lake Tahoe would be considered its centerpiece. One of the deepest and purest lakes in the world, and home in the winter to over twenty ski areas within an hour's drive, not to mention fishing and hiking in the summer, it just may be the most beautiful place on earth.

If I went east, I'd travel over semi-arid successions of mountains and valleys of the Basin and Range geologic province. Dry playa lakebeds and nearly bare peaks are a rock hound's paradise. Good place too, if you like solitude.

If one really wants to be alone, go north, past Pyramid Lake, home to one of the largest breeding grounds of the North American Pelican. Beyond the lake you would find your way to the Black Rock Desert. It's a bleak, bright-white, caliche-toughened flatland, which stretches for miles on end. The world land speed record has been set here, breaking the sound barrier.

But traveling south, I was heading to my favorite part of Reno.

My house.

That feeling was reinforced as I stepped in the side door to our very little mansion and was greeted by a whooping war cry from two renegade warriors who had been laying in ambush for me. Mary and Christopher broadsided me, took me down to the carpet, and proceeded to play "King of the Hill," with me, as usual, being the hill. It was a daily game that none of us seemed to tire of.

I looked at my two treasures and sighed contentedly. *Enjoy it while you can, fella. Blink twice, and they'll be teenagers. Nothing lasts forever.*

"Hi, honey, welcome home!"

I turned and saw Lauren smiling, peering around the corner from her music room, and I had to pause as all the colors of my world suddenly became brighter. She still had that effect on me. *No, I'm wrong*, I admitted to myself. *The way I feel about that woman will last forever.* Of medium height, with long, thick, wavy brown hair, her thin build showing only a hint of the effects of bearing the two prizes clambering on top of me, she had striking blue eyes that you could drown in. The years had added fine smile lines of character to them, which she dutifully fought with creams and lotions, but which I thought only made her lovelier.

She came over and shooed away the kids and accepted her "Boy am I glad to be home" kiss. "How was your day? Did Jeanne get her apple butter?"

I smiled. "Oh yeah. I figure my job's secure for at least another week. Assuming she doesn't finish it before then."

Later that night, the kids in bed, with pajamas, toothbrushes and Dr. Suess all having performed their nightly functions, Lauren and I settled back on our old, beat-up sofa. It was our time for connecting. Propped up against the thread-worn armrests, facing each other, with our feet planted in each other's laps, we caught up on the ins and outs of the day. With peppermint-scented foot oil, we kneaded and massaged each other's feet in what had become my favorite part of the day. It's pretty hard to feel too awful bad about anything when you are getting your feet rubbed.

I told her about my conversation with Chuck that afternoon. "Well, I guess that was to be expected," she quipped, referring to Chuck's paranoia about his new management. "Every time you have had a change in your news director or station management, you've had to go through some adjustment period."

"True, but this guy seems to be making micro-management an art form. He won't even let Chuck pick his own songs, and when Chuck tried getting around it once he went ballistic. Didn't just threaten to fire him. According to Chuck, he thought he was going to get violent."

"Well, consider the source, dear. Wasn't Chuck the one who was sure that they were hiding aliens at the Auto Museum?"

"He's scaled that back a little bit. Now he just thinks that some of the chrome work on that '26 Rolls Coach came from UFO parts, and is being used as an antenna for interstellar communications." I chuckled. Chuck's conspiracy theories were all the more entertaining because he really believed them. "But all that aside, I hope he lasts there. We have a pretty good thing going, and I wouldn't want to have to break in another DJ."

"Well, that doesn't seem likely they would get rid of him," Lauren countered. "You said yourself that your ratings have never been higher. Why would their owners get rid of a good thing? That doesn't make any sense."

I made a wry face. "Sense? This is the media, Sweetheart...."

"...It doesn't have to make any sense," she finished for me.

I strolled into work the next morning, expecting to be confronted with nothing worse than a few nasty-grams from the public because I had missed the high temperature from the previous day by four degrees. What I found in my in-box was an envelope from the radio station. I dropped into my seat and tore open the seal, muttering hopefully, "Maybe it's a raise."

Maybe it was my pink slip.

I stared at the tersely worded message:

"Dear Mr. O'Brien. The station has decided to take another direction. As of this date, your services with KOPP-FM will longer be needed. Final payment for your services will be sent to your home.

Steve Richards
KOPP General Manager"

I read it twice. Still said the same thing. Then it dawned on me. Chuck. Playing one of his games with me. Probably still mad at the trained monkey comment.

I chuckled and dialed Chuck on the hotline number.

"KOPP Radio." My heart sank. Chuck's voice seemed subdued, and I had never heard him answer the phone straight in all the years I had known him. Maybe it wasn't a joke.

"Chuck. It's Greg. What's going on?"

"Hey Greg. I assume they told you?"

"I was hoping it was just you playing one of your pranks. Tell me it was you playing one of your pranks."

"I wish I could, buddy." Chuck then let loose with a string of well-chosen invectives. "The Middle East makes more sense than this place. At least there, you know who your enemies are. What do they think they are trying to do? Man, we had a great thing going...the best numbers we've had in years, and now they do this? There's something fishy here."

I chuckled in spite of myself. Leave it to Chuck to still look for a conspiracy under every rock. "Aw, c'mon Chuck. They don't need a reason. No one said they had to be smart," I mentioned modestly. "I'm just curious why they want to make a change now."

"I don't have any idea. Buncha idiots! Or should I say, one in particular?"

"You think it's all the GM?"

"Who else? I told you he was bad news."

I pondered that. "Did he mention to you why he was letting me go?"

"Nope. Just came waltzing in here and said that you were no longer with us. When I asked him why, he completely avoided the question. Said something about 'a different direction' and walked out. I almost got the idea he was trying to keep something from me."

I shook my head. "You should have read the letter he sent me." I read it to him. It didn't take long.

"That's it?" he said. "No 'Thanks for all your hard work and professionalism'? 'Thanks for making Chuck Murphy what he is today'?"

I thought about it. "Hmmm.... Maybe that's why he canned me, now that you mention it." Sometimes all you can do is laugh it off. "Anyhow, it's not that big a deal. The money was barely enough to buy pizza for the family a couple of times a month. But it's the principle that really bugs me. The least he could have done was tell me in person."

"Oh, man." Chuck sounded about as low as I had ever heard him, even with his manic-depressive personality. "It just isn't any fun around here anymore. I'll poke around and see if I can come up with any answers."

"Yeah," I muttered. "So will I."

I wasn't being totally honest with Chuck when I said it wasn't a big deal. It was true about the money, there wasn't enough there to even worry about. So what was the rub? I had never been fired from a job in my life, but in this business it's bound to happen. I guess it was just the impersonal way it occurred. I'm still old-fashioned enough, or naïve enough, to think that even in the broadcast industry you can still handle people in a respectful way. I thought I deserved an explanation.

I picked up the phone and called KOPP's business office. "Steve Richards, please," I asked when the receptionist picked up the line.

After a wait of nearly three minutes, he picked up on the other end. "Steve Richards." I recognized the voice, as tense as ever. He always seemed on edge a bit, like he could never relax. He must have been a lot of fun on a date.

"Steve, this is Greg O'Brien."

I was met with a long silence. I could imagine him chewing out the receptionist for putting the call through. After about ten seconds (time it yourself, and just see how long ten seconds of silence *is* on the phone), I gave up waiting for him to make the next move. "Steve? Are you there?"

"Yes, Greg. What do you want?"

What do I want? I want to talk about the next election, you nimrod, what do you think I want? "Well Steve, I got this letter from you. I have some questions about it..."

"Was there something unclear in the letter? I thought it was very clear."

"Well...yeah, it was clear. But what I don't understand is why."

"I told you in the letter. The station is going in a different direction. That's all you need to know."

"Well, of course, that is your prerogative. But it just seems strange, since the ratings were the highest they have been in years."

"I hope you aren't so arrogant as to think that that was because of you?" He almost sneered.

I was stunned at his reply. No, I wasn't so arrogant as to think that. I *was* so arrogant as to think that I might have contributed just a wee bit. And, hey, if it ain't broke, don't fix it. But I could tell this wasn't going to get me anywhere. "I can see this isn't going to help either of us. I'm sorry to have taken up your time." I added, as a peace offering, "I've enjoyed being associated with your station, Steve."

I heard the line go click.

Chapter 5

I continued to hold the phone to my ear. After a while, I mumbled, "It's been nice talking to you, too," and let it slide back on to its cradle. In an industry where unusual methods of firing people have been raised to an art form, this one was a Rembrandt.

I recalled my comments to Lauren just the previous night. Well, I guess it didn't have to make any sense. This was broadcasting, after all. I spent the rest of the day convincing myself that I was better off severing my relationship with such a nutcase, anyway.

My spirits lifted considerably when I arrived home. If ever there was a sanctuary, this was it. It was time again for my usual round of wrestling with the kids. Sometimes, it would be like the old Pink Panther movies, where Peter Sellers would enter his home, only to be attacked by Kato, his oriental butler. If the kids saw me coming up the drive, they would find a new place to hide and pounce. This night, it was the coat closet. I walked right into their trap when I tried to hang up my jacket. It's a good thing I have a strong heart.

Lauren picked me up and dusted me off, and with a kiss asked me how my day went.

"Oh, not bad. Interviewed for a new intern, fixed that tricky monitor in the office, got fired from my radio job, gave a tour to a school group..." I ambled on nonchalantly.

"That's nice dear..." Lauren responded, before catching herself. "Um, you want to run that by me again?"

I gave her the whole sad story. "You know, the one I feel worst about in this whole mess is Chuck. He really is getting to hate it down there."

"Sounds like a perfect place for him, then," Lauren said. "He's never happy if he isn't miserable."

"Too true. But this may be even beyond his tolerance level."

"And this...this...manager guy, wouldn't even tell you why?"

"Nope. I guess he doesn't have to."

Well," she sighed, "I guess if this is the worst thing to happen to us, we can't complain."

I wrapped her up in my arms. "Sure can't. Time I put it behind me. What's for dinner?"

The next morning, I was running an errand in the car with the radio turned to KOPP. Habit, I guess. Just as I was about to switch to a news-talk station, I heard the morning DJ begin to give the weather. I was overwhelmed by a morbid sense of curiosity. This would usually be me.

"And now, for our 'Odds-on-Forecast,' you can expect a continuation of the sunny skies today, with an increase of high clouds overnight..."

I was shocked. They were still using the "Odds-on-Forecast" label. That was mine. They couldn't do that.

Perhaps I had better explain. Years ago, I had come up with the "Odds-on-Forecast" label to attach to my television weather reports. I was never crazy about it. I thought it sounded awkward, and a little too contrived. But the station management wanted something that tied in with the area's connection with the casino industry. Since weather predictions can be a bit of a crapshoot around here anyway, it was the best I could do. Anyhow, the label stuck. And it had become synonymous with "Greg O'Brien's Forecast." I brought it over to the radio station when I started with them, and they always introduced my segments that way. And while I suspect it may be a stretch to consider it "intellectual property," my agreement with the radio station didn't allow them to continue using it, regardless of how little intellect went into the creation of the phrase.

Maybe it was time to pay a visit in person to Mr. Steve Richards.

When one listens to the radio and hears "broadcast live from the KOPP studios!" one conjures up the image of a large, warehouse-type building in the industrial section of town, where the mysteries of Marconi's invention are only revealed deep within the bowels of a modern day fortress, with a towering antenna standing watch in the background. In actuality, most radio stations these days are housed in small office complexes or strip malls. KOPP's digs were on the second floor of a modest office building on Moana Lane and shared hallways with two dentists, a small CPA firm, and a guy who ran a string of candy and Coke vending machines around town. Far from having a thousand-foot antenna in the parking lot, their entire signal was microwaved from a small dish on the roof south to a tower on McClelland Peak, part of a mountain range between Reno and Carson City. This was where the real transmitter was located. From an elevation of over 7,000 feet, plus the additional one-fifty from the tower, KOPP's 50,000 watts of power could be heard not only all over western Nevada, but also with the right conditions, all over the western United States. Thanks to an "atmospheric skip," which occurred when the signal bounced off of layers in the upper atmosphere, it was not uncommon to hear KOPP in faraway places like Seattle, Albuquerque, or Los Angeles. One night, I even heard their signal while I was in Minneapolis on a business trip.

Usually, because of the increased noise that the sun's radiation produces, it would have to be nighttime to pick up any radio station more than a hundred or so miles from its transmitter. But because of KOPP's power and location, and due to the vagaries of geography and meteorology, there were little pockets several hundred miles or more away where their signal came in loud and clear. These nodes of amplified signal strength were surprisingly consistent. Once, a friend of mine who had been camping down on the Baja Peninsula told me that he listened to us all week long on his portable radio.

I was going to miss being heard by the fishermen in the Sea of Cortez.

On the drive over to the KOPP office, I tried to formulate a plan of attack. I am not a very confrontational person by nature, so a full frontal assault went a bit against my grain. But having received the response I did with Steve on the phone, I hiked up my courage and decided that I wasn't going to take no for an answer if I was told I wasn't allowed to see him. More than likely, his receptionist would run interference for him as he slipped out the back way. A little subtlety was in order.

I climbed the stairs to the KOPP office door and peered in. Missy, their pert, flaming red-headed receptionist (in the two years I had been there, I never did learn her last name, or find out if Missy was her real first name for that matter), was stationed at her normal watch post and unfortunately was depressingly unoccupied. It would have been impossible for me to slip in and get past her and through Steve's closed office door without her noticing. I suppose I could have barged right in over her protests, but if possible, I didn't want to make a scene. And after my earlier telephone call managed to slip through, I suspected that Steve had, in no uncertain terms, declared me *persona non grata* to Missy.

I decided to wait for a bit to see if any work might come her way to distract her attention, but when she, incredibly enough, started doing her nails, I knew it was a lost cause. And I thought they only did their nails in cheap detective novels.

As I pondered my dilemma, a UPS truck pulled up in the parking lot. A husky, sandy blond-haired driver in brown shorts…I swear they even wear them in the winter…hopped out and went into the first floor hallway with a couple of packages under his arm. I decided to make a little work for Missy. I pulled out my cell phone and dialed the station.

The switchboard ringing jolted Missy out of her cuticle controlled reverie. "KOPP Radio," she chirped.

"Uh, yeah, this is Dan with UPS down in the parking lot, and I got this package I, uh…need for you to sign for." I thought the longshoreman accent I was using was a bit overdone, but what the heck.

"Um…. Can't you bring it up? That's what they always do. I'd be glad to sign for it up here." Missy wasn't going to leave without a fight.

"Now listen lady, I got special instructions here. Sez I'm not supposed to take this out of the truck before someone signs for it. Some kind of electronic parts or something. Looks pretty valuable…"

"Oh, geez, those must be the new boards for the production room. Um…. Okay, I'll be right out." She craned her neck as she looked out the window. "Okay… I see your truck. I'll be right down. But I have to make this fast."

"I'll only need a second," I deadpanned.

I stepped back into the restroom door as Missy breezed by me on the way down the stairs. Wasting no time, I strode through the main doors and went straight to Steve's office. I glanced at the personnel status board, which shows which sales and management types were out of the office, and saw that the "IN" magnet was placed beside Steve's name on the board, so I figured he had to be in his office.

I paused a moment to knock on the door, but thought better of it. I doubt he would have invited me in. Recalling that ancient Chinese proverb, "Sometimes, 'tis better to ask forgiveness than permission," I opened the door.

Chapter 6

Having achieved my minor victory in gaining entrance, I wasn't sure what to expect upon facing Steve Richards face to face. I wouldn't have been surprised at anger, belligerence, shock, or disgust. What I wasn't expecting is what I got.

Fear.

I might not have caught it, except I had already decided to lock onto his eyes, stare him down, state my peace, and have it out with him, *mano a mano*. And it was his eyes that betrayed him. The unmistakable smell of fear. The kind that gives the green light to every growling dog from a Pekinese to a Rottweiler. I decided to take a few bites myself.

"Steve, you have no right to keep using the 'Odds-on-Forecast' label in your weathercasts. You can get rid of me if you want to, but if you persist on stealing my creative material" (OK, that might have been stretching things a bit) "then you'll have a lawsuit on your hands for copyright infringement faster than you can chew out your next board-op." I knew well and good that the "Odds-on-Forecast" label wasn't covered by copyright, but I figured, what the heck… in for a penny, in for a pound.

He still looked scared. I decided then and there his bark was considerably worse than his bite, and like most bullies, he was a coward at heart. Bolstered by this, I pressed forward. "And in addition to that, I want a check in my mailbox within five days for the severance payment that was agreed to in my contract. The full amount. That's one month's pay, to save you the trouble. And to save you the trouble of trying to weasel out of that provision by stating that *I* was the one who quit, I still have your letter, *your very terse and very clear letter*, that it was your decision alone to terminate our arrangement." Man, was I on a roll. The German Blitzkrieg had nothing on me. I leaned forward on his desk, bore into those yellow-bellied eyes of his, and said, "Well?"

The silence, to use an overworked cliché, was deafening. Steve's jaw moved up and down without effect a couple of times, barely emitting a gasp.

After what must have seemed an eternity, he stammered out, "…Okay."

Okay? I thought. *That's it? No "go stuff yourself"? No "drop the gloves, and let's get it on"?* I was almost disappointed. I hadn't expected to win quite so easily. I decided to give him one last good hard stare, for good measure. You know, just to make him really suffer. It was then that his gaze flickered to the right, drawing my eyes away from his for the first time since I entered the room.

We weren't alone.

A short, stocky mustachioed man with a dark complexion was seated next to the window, with the shades drawn. Nearly everything about him was dark. With the exception of a broad scar, perhaps from an old burn, above his left eye, he was strikingly handsome. Dressed immaculately in a navy blue pinstripe suit, cuff links, black polished shoes, and black tie almost painfully offset by a starched white shirt, he reminded me of a short Omar Shariff without his innate charm. The man seemed to swallow what little light there was around him.

Normally, I would have been embarrassed to be caught giving such a display in front of a stranger. But I wasn't really in character at the time anyway, and if he was a sales client of the radio station who decided to take his business elsewhere, well, I wasn't going to lose any sleep over it.

"I'm sorry you had to be here to see this," was all I could manage.

"I am sorry as well," the stranger said flatly, and without emotion.

Convinced I had screwed up Steve Richards' life enough for one day, I turned and breezed out of the room, gently closing the door behind me. Didn't even slam it. I wanted to leave a little powder in my arsenal. I passed a bewildered Missy on the way out who squeaked, "Wait…what…you can't…"

"Your phone's ringing, Missy!" I grinned on the way out. It wasn't really fair to her. But I was still pretty full of myself. Imagine. Steve Richards. Could I have really scared him that much? I chuckled at the thought.

One out of two ain't bad. Yeah, he was scared. Real scared.

But not of me.

* * * * * * * * * * *

The eyes that watched the door close were cold and dark, apparently devoid of any feeling or emotion. They left the doorway and slowly turned back to the cowering figure behind the desk in the General Manager's office of KOPP-FM radio. Silence settled into the room, a silence more terrifying to Steve Richards than the wails of the condemned from behind the gates of Hell. As the dark man's eyes bored into his, Richards could almost feel the emptiness behind them, a vacuum that sucked out the last vestige of self-confidence and arrogance he had within him. He wanted to say something… anything…to break the silence.

It was the dark man that finally spoke. "You…said…no one would see me here," he began slowly, in precise, measured tones, with just a trace of a Latin accent. "It was a simple request, really," he went on. " 'I must not be seen in conjunction with this radio station,' I told you. You said that would not be a problem. You said that there was no need for me to establish my own security team here, that no one would ever have a reason to see me here. And yet with no warning whatsoever, this man comes strolling in here, and in less than ten seconds, manages to accomplish the one…the ONE…thing…I had specifically asked not happen." The man sighed deeply, and Richards tried his best not to sink further into his chair. The dark man continued. "When we retrieved your sorry carcass from that hell hole in Cali, it was because I made an assumption that you could become more of an asset than a liability. Now I am doubting the wisdom of that assumption."

Richards licked his lips. "But Mr. Carillo, he doesn't know who you are. He can't identify you. He has no reason to connect you with anything that has gone on here. I'm sure…"

"What I am sure of is that after this failure on your part to uphold your instructions, you might want to reconsider whether it is wise to offer any advice to me, Mr. Richards." It was the first time the visitor had raised his voice at all, and the effect was immediate. Richards' wince couldn't have been more pronounced even if the dark man had reached out and struck him with the back of his hand. "And as if that weren't enough, you didn't even have the presence of mind to move…the document."

With a growing panic, Richards dropped his gaze to a worn, leather bound notebook, which lay open on the corner of his desk.

It was the reason that the dark man was there to begin with.

"Mr. Carillo, he couldn't have noticed it. I mean, even if he did, he wouldn't know what it meant." Richards wiped at the beads of sweat that had appeared on his upper lip, and then stammered, "I mean…look at it…if I didn't know the key, *I* wouldn't have any idea…"

"So now you are a mind reader as well?" Though he continued in his soft, precise diction, it was as effective as a shout. "How do you know what he saw? Do you suppose, for instance, he might have seen something a bit peculiar about your notes at the top?" He referred to a cryptic notation on the page header.

"Perhaps his mind isn't as limited as yours, Mr. Richards. Perhaps his has not been destroyed by years of abuse." He paused briefly. "Perhaps I don't want to find out."

A surge of foreboding settled into Richards' innards. "So what do you want to do?" he said, dreading the answer.

"I think it's time to give our Mr. Dunleavy a call."

"But he…O'Brien…he's too well known around here…"

"Accidents happen, Mr. Richards."

* * * * * * * * * *

Chapter 7

It had been a full week since my little run-in with Steve Richards, and apart from a few enjoyable flashbacks, it had pretty well become a distant memory. On this particular Wednesday morning, sunny and bright like so many we'd had lately during a stubborn Indian Summer, my mind was more concerned with the final climb out of the Virginia Highlands on the way to the crest of Geiger Grade.

Even though Reno is the center of population and commerce for Western Nevada, it wasn't always so. In 1859, weary of trying to grab on to a rapidly dwindling piece of the 49'er gold rush, Henry T.P. Comstock climbed the eastern slope of Mount Davidson in the Virginia Range, just southeast of present-day Reno. After digging around a bit and staking his claim, a strike that became known as the Comstock Lode was announced that kicked off a stampede which swelled the population of the newly formed town of Virginia City to over 20,000 people. This discovery, as you might expect, had a tremendous impact on the surrounding area...politically, environmentally, and technologically. Nevada's entrance into the union just five years after the discovery of the Comstock was almost entirely due to the Union's need for silver and gold during the Civil War. Environmentally, nearly every stick of usable timber was cut down in the forests on the east side of Lake Tahoe, twenty miles to the west, in order to shore up the mines, which in some cases dove over 3,000 feet under the ground. Mercury, or "quicksilver" as the prospectors used to call it, used in the refining process was allowed to drain into the nearby Carson River, creating our state's only "Superfund" clean-up site. It still hasn't been cleaned up, and you don't dare eat the fish. But perhaps the most lasting legacy the Comstock provided was in the field of engineering. As the miners dove down more than two thirds of a mile, in an area that was already geothermally active, hot water began to pour into the shafts faster than it could be pumped out. Temperatures of 150 degrees Fahrenheit made mining work an unbearable, and often fatal, experience. Adolph Sutro, a Prussian mining engineer, designed and helped build a tunnel into the side of the mountain 1,600 feet below the mines, an incredible feat at the time, although it proved to be a financial disaster.

Other projects included a pipeline that fed water from Marlette Lake, above the shores of Lake Tahoe, down across the valley below, and up to Virginia City, all driven by siphon power.

But the engineering escapade that was on my mind that beautiful November morning was the old Geiger Toll Road. Literally cut out of the rock and dirt on the side of the Virginia range, the Geiger Toll Road was built in 1862 by Davison Geiger and John Tilton in order to carry the huge amounts of timber and supplies eastward and Comstock ore westward. The highway historical marker, which I had just passed on the way up, described the tales of "unpredictable winds, snows, landslides and the everlasting danger of highwaymen, which could be told of this precipitous stretch of road." And while the original Toll Road was replaced back in 1936 by the present paved road under my tires, this new and revised version was no less precipitous. And the roadside crosses which mark the sites of fatal crashes prove that one must take care on this road, whether one is driving a "Concord stage, mud wagon, or ten mule freighter" as the historical marker said, or a four-wheel drive SUV today.

Or in my case, a bicycle.

It was my own personal war against aging. I figured that if I kept pretending I could do all the things I did when I was younger, then Age would somehow skip my address when it came by to dole out its yearly booty of more gray in the hair, wrinkles on the skin, or excess baggage around the middle. It hadn't worked real well for the hair and the skin. But while I had picked up a few hitchhikers above the belt line and lost a few steps in the 100-yard dash, I found I could actually ride my bicycle farther and climb higher than I could twenty years ago. I think that had something to do with nerve degeneration, especially above the saddle.

But for anybody who enjoys this kind of self-flagellation, Reno has some of the best bicycle riding around. Greg LeMond, three-time winner of the Tour De France, grew up in Reno, riding these very same roads. In fact, Geiger Grade was one of his frequent training rides. Heck, if it was good enough for Greg...well, we all have our fantasies. Starting at the intersection with Highway 395 south of Reno, Geiger climbs without ceasing nearly 2,500 feet in less than ten miles, to an elevation of just below 7,000 feet. The strain and pain to the body is offset by some of the most spectacular views imaginable. Sheer cliffs fall away to the valley below, only to rebound beyond to the 10,000-foot plus peaks of the Sierra Nevada Range. Kinda takes your breath away.

And at this point, breath was already in short supply. Meteorologically speaking, there is about twenty percent less air at the top of Geiger Pass than at sea level. I was convinced that someone had stolen most of the rest of it. Sweat dripped off my nose and forehead, constantly fogging my sunglasses. I had drained the last of my second water bottle a half-mile back, and my tongue was getting an agonizing dryness to it. After swearing for the umpteenth time that I was never going to try it again bottom to top without a rest, I crested the pass, slapping the road sign marking the peak. I probably should have rested to let my quivering muscles calm down, but I had to speak at a school that day before going into the station, and I was already behind schedule. At least it was downhill all the way. And if truth be known, as nice as the scenery is, it ain't half as much fun as that nine-mile glide to the bottom.

To begin the trip downward, the road follows a few gentle curves and then straightens out for a glorious mile to a brief leveling at the Highlands. This is the last level spot on the trip. It is also the last straight section. The rest of the way down is filled with treacherous curves, with solid rock on one side and the aforementioned sheer cliffs on the other. Here's where it got fun. And scary.

At 6'2" and weighing in at 215 pounds, I was provided with a frame by the fates that was much more efficient at going down than up. I wasn't going to let any of the potential energy I had stored up on the climb go to waste by putting on the brakes any more than necessary. My speed soon topped forty miles per hour, which was not so fast that I couldn't handle the turns, but was fast enough to keep ahead of any of the sparse traffic that might happen along that day. It was a thrill to feel and hear the wind whistling through the slots in my helmet.

It was because of that whistling wind that I didn't hear the low rumble behind me until it was nearly upon me. Glancing behind, I caught a glimpse of a motorcycle. A big motorcycle. A BMW 1200-C. I'd seen one about a month earlier at a show in the convention center. Fully loaded they tip the scales at nearly half a ton. They have an engine in them almost as big as the one in my Honda Civic. Well, if he wanted to pass me, there was plenty of room. It was the pickup trucks which had a nasty habit of passing on the corners that I worried about.

But he didn't seem to be in much of a hurry. He stayed on my tail for another half a mile before surprising me by pulling up on my right. Strange way to pass, I thought. But passing wasn't on his mind.

When he got abreast of me, I got my first brief look at the driver...or at least at what he was wearing. He appeared to be of medium height, with a solid build. He was decked out in full leathers, the inky black material broken only by silver zippers at the sleeves and ankles. He wore a mottled pair of cowboy boots, with silver caps on the toes. And even if I'd had the time to study him closer, instead of quick glances as I tried to keep away from the road's edge, I still wouldn't have been able to describe his face. He wore a black metallic-flake full-coverage helmet with a mirrored face shield. I could tell he was chewing gum by the constant appearance of his chin bobbing out from under his helmet. And even though I couldn't see his face, if body language said anything, he was definitely enjoying the ride.

I expected him to continue past me, but he seemed content to ride abreast for a bit. I didn't mind at first, since the curves here were relatively mild. But there was a sharper right turn up ahead, and claustrophobia was beginning to set in. If I'd had any sense, I would have slowed down and forced him to pass. But then, no one ever accused me of having an overabundance of sense. In the end, my pride wouldn't let me lose my momentum. In the end, my pride almost cost me my life.

As we approached the curve, when it became apparent that he wasn't going to go by, I did the only logical thing someone whose bike is powered by two legs would do when up against someone whose bike is powered by 1.2 liters of internal combustion engine...I tried to out-run him. I popped out of the seat as if I was sprinting to finish one of the legs of the Tour. Oh yeah, real smart. I heard a high-pitched cackle over the roar of the Beemer as the rider touched a minuscule amount of throttle and pulled even with me. By this time, we were entering the curve, and there was nothing to do but take it with him, and hope he held his line.

That was when the motor home appeared from around the corner, coming up the hill.

Struggling to keep from panicking, I leaned into the curve as tightly as I dared. At this point, I couldn't apply my breaks. The slightest brake pressure now would surely cause me to start to skid, and the tires of the behemoth headed my way would barely leave enough road kill for a couple of ravens' lunch. Tucked over so that my pedal was nearly scraping the pavement, I held my line.

Unfortunately, Mr. BMW didn't hold his.

As the motorcycle entered the curve, he gradually drifted to the left, surprising me since I would have thought he could have held a turn better than that. He gradually and painfully inched me across the solid yellow line. The sheer immensity of his motorcycle made my feeble efforts to turn back laughable. I saw to my horror that I wasn't going to make it. And by then I was close enough to see the shock in the faces of the two gray-haired occupants of the approaching motor home who were about to get a new hood ornament on their Winnebago. I had only one choice.

I broke sharply to the left, straining to get to the other side of the road before the front grill got to me. I missed the front bumper by a hair's breadth, although I took off their rear view mirror with my shoulder. So great was my terror, and so great was our closing speed, that I barely felt it. At least not then. But my momentary relief at not being strained through the motor home's grill was immediately replaced by the sight of the rapidly approaching guardrail.

The curve we were on was one of several with a small viewpoint. A gravel parking strip ended just ahead with a row of boulders giving way to a steel guardrail. It was on this gravel that I now found myself, hurtling along at fifty miles per hour. If you have never ridden a road bike off of asphalt and onto gravel, you can liken it to leaping out on to a dance floor covered with ball bearings. As I felt the wheels begin to slide out from under me, I ever so carefully straightened out the wheel. The parking strip had bought me a little more room, but I wasn't sure it was enough.

For the second time in less than two seconds (which felt like two lifetimes), I struggled to turn the bike sharply enough to avoid becoming a semi-permanent part of the roadside. At the same time I worked to keep the wheels from sliding out from under me, which would have turned me into hamburger on the gravel. Slowly…inch by inch…I began to creep back toward the pavement as the guardrail and the looming chasm raced toward me. As I teetered between disaster and recovery, my front tire just began to feel the bite of the shoulder pavement. For an instant, I thought I was going to make it.

Then I ran into the goat's head.

In this part of the world, there grows an unassuming little noxious weed that produces a thorny burr called a goat's head. No bigger than a pea, they have two or more horn-like spikes that protrude, which, when viewed from a certain angle, gives it the appearance of the head of a goat. Or a demon's head. These spikes are as sharp as needles and as tough as titanium, and are the bane of bicycle riders all over western Nevada. They easily slice through even Kevlar-reinforced tires, and if you pick one up on the driveway on the way home, you can be assured the air will be gone from your tires by morning.

If you hit one at the speed I was going, the air's gone in milliseconds.

When the front tire blew, it immediately slid back to the left and rammed into the guardrail. Guardrails are designed to keep vehicles from leaving the roadway and sailing into the canyon below. This one worked to perfection. My vehicle stuck to the guardrail, wrapping around it like a macabre pretzel. Unfortunately, it wasn't designed to keep me out of the canyon.

With arms flailing and a cry for help, I sailed over the edge.

Chapter 8

The previous two summers had been tough ones on the consolidated fire fighting units in and around Virginia City. Brush and weeds, left uncontrolled for years due to a lack funds and attention, had dried and created a tinderbox in the eastern hills surrounding the Truckee Meadows. Three major brush fires the previous year had finally gotten the attention of the residents of the county. The Storey County commissioners floated and passed a bond for the clean-up of the remaining brush, almost unheard of in this typically penny-pinching rural county. The homeowners were apparently swayed by the argument that saving a little extra property tax didn't make a lot of sense if their property was reduced to ashes.

All summer and fall long, crews had been working on the hills under the road clearing and thinning cheat grass, sagebrush, and small junipers and piling them into giant ten-foot-high pyres to be burned when the fire danger lessened. They were slated to be torched the next week.

When the laws of physics kicked in and gravity overtook my inertia, it was into one of these slash piles that I landed. Hard.

I had just completed a perfect one-and-three-quarters revolution when my back struck the pile. A sickening crunch reverberated around me, and I wondered just how many of my bones breaking had created that sound. Waves of pain shot through me as my jersey was literally ripped from my body, exposing bare skin to the branches and brambles below, which tore into my back like so many fishhooks. Bouncing off the pile like a demon-possessed trampoline, I landed in a twisted heap on a pile of rocks and tumbleweeds, my helmet bursting open as my head struck a large pillow-sized boulder. As I came to rest, with a cloud of dust settling over me and my head resting against the rock at what seemed like an impossible angle, I was too stunned to move. I was also too scared to breathe for fear of the onslaught of agony that ripped through my body like an electric jolt when I did try to inhale. As I stared blankly back up to the guardrail forty feet above me, a thin rivulet of blood traced a path down my forehead, across my temple, and into my ear.

Mind you, I wasn't complaining.

I suspect I would have been worse off if the fire crews had decided to touch off the slash piles this week instead.

As I pondered my good fortune, still staring blankly back up toward the road, the driver of the motorcycle pulled up, flipped up his visor, and peered over the side. I still hadn't gotten to the point of breathing yet, and I didn't even have the strength to swivel my eyes in his direction. At that point, I didn't really care. Let him think I was dead…serves him right. But instead of hearing a cry of remorse and a scramble down to help me, he simply nodded once, flicked down his face shield, and gunned the engine on his motorcycle. As the throaty roar of the bike trailed off down the road, I yielded to the needs of oxygenation and tried another breath.

It wasn't pleasant.

* * * * * * * * * * *

"Gidday, Mr. Carillo."

"Dunleavy…is that you? Where are you? What's all that noise?"

"Why, I just thought Oy'd take a bit of a walkabout on the old motorcycle. Beautiful day out 'ere. Kinduh reminds me of the outback." He spoke with a thick Australian accent through a mouthpiece mounted inside his helmet as the BMW sped down through the final stretch of Geiger Grade before turning on to Highway 395. Cellular phone technology. Next best thing to being there, he mused.

"I'm not interested in your leisure activities, Mr. Dunleavy. It seems to me that a considerable down payment has been placed in a certain numbered bank account, and I don't like to see my money wasted."

"Well, now, just the topic I was going to bring up. You may place the balance in said bank account now."

"You've completed the job? It's about time."

Dunleavy sighed. They never did appreciate art when they saw it. "Don't get a snout-on about it, Mr. Carillo. Accidents take time. You have to wait for the right opportunity. Oy'm right proud of this one actually. Do you want to hear about it? Bloody marvelous it was. Chap put up a pretty good…"

"Spare me the details, Dunleavy. Are you sure…the job is completed?"

"Oh, yeah…no one could have survived that kind of fall. Landed on a pile of rocks, he did. I took a peek at him afterwards, head split open, eyes fixed ahead and open, looked like the neck snapped, blood all over the…."

"That's fine, Mr. Dunleavy. And you are sure no one will suspect anything?"

"Mr. Carillo... Stone the crows! Oy'm hurt! No, no one will suspect a thing. You should be reading about another unfortunate victim of a very dangerous section of road. Might go up there and add a cross to the roadway myself."

"I don't think that would be wise, Mr. Dunleavy." The phone line went dead.

Chance Dunleavy chuckled softly. "A bit stiff, that one. Needs to get out more." He slowed down a bit as he spotted a Nevada Highway Patrol unit ahead. "Now, that wouldn't do, to ruin a perfect day like today, would it?"

He waved at the trooper as he passed.

* * * * * * * * * * *

Chapter 9

Reno Gazette Journal, Nov 12: "POPULAR WEATHERMAN HOSPITALIZED IN BIKE MISHAP" Reno (AP): KRGX-TV viewers will have to get their weather reports from another source for a while, thanks to a near-tragic bicycle accident on the slopes of Geiger Grade, Highway 341, 6 miles up from the intersection of highway 395. According to witnesses, KRGX Meteorologist Greg O'Brien lost control of his bicycle while descending the treacherous stretch of roadway, flew off the highway, and fell over 40 feet down a nearly vertical bank. "He came around that corner way too fast...barely missed our motorcoach," said Margaret Perry, 68, of Aberdeen, Washington. She and her husband, Augie, also 68, vacationing in the area, were the first to reach O'Brien. "Thought he was a goner for sure," Mr. Perry said. "When we got to him, he wasn't moving a bit"...

"No, and I really didn't appreciate you picking me up and shaking me to see if I was awake, either." I grimaced as I sat propped up in a bed at Washoe Medical Center. I noticed the newspaper didn't quote what I had said in response to the Perrys' bedside manner. Or was that cliff-side manner? Whatever. But then again, how would you spell a writhing, anguished howl of pain, anyway? Aw, heck, I shouldn't take it out on them. They were just a nice retired couple from Aberdeen who happened to be in the wrong place at the wrong time. I took another slow breath (they were starting to get a little easier to take...in moderation) and read on.

Doctors say O'Brien was extremely lucky to be alive, and that he was listed in stable condition at Washoe Medical Center. They describe his injuries as painful, but not life-threatening. O'Brien was unavailable for comment.
The Nevada Highway Patrol is investigating the accident. The Perrys are the only known witnesses to the incident, although there

are unconfirmed reports that a driver of a large, late-model motorcycle may also have witnessed the accident. No citations have been issued at this time.

Nor would there likely be any. There had been a brief interview at the scene of the accident by the Highway Patrol officer who arrived shortly before the ambulance. I wasn't in much shape to answer questions at the time, and in fact, can remember quite little from the exchange. I must have mentioned something about the motorcyclist in my half-delirium, because to my mild surprise, a plain-clothes officer arrived at my bedside the day after I arrived in the hospital. He had that unmistakable air of confident authority, combined with a certain lack of empathy which accompanies so many of the cops who have seen it all, and too often.

After a perfunctory flashing of a badge at me, he asked me to recount my experience on the road. Though things were still a little disjointed, I took him through my trip down the hill. When I mentioned the BMW rider, he stopped me. "Could you describe this man? Everything you can think of." Poor guy must have a cold. His voice was pretty raspy.

"Well, to be perfectly honest with you, I couldn't see him very well. In fact, not at all. He had about your height and build, as far as I could tell with him sitting on the bike, but between the leathers and the full-face helmet, I wouldn't know him if he had walked into this room."

He looked up at me. "You're sure you couldn't identify him if you saw him again?" His eyes bore into mine. I began to feel as if I was under suspicion for something.

"'Fraid not. His bike, maybe. But even that was a stock BMW 1200. Not all that uncommon a make. And I'm afraid I never saw a license plate."

With that, the officer sighed, seemed satisfied with my answer, muttered his wishes for a speedy recovery, and left the room.

While I was pleased to see the local gendarmes taking an interest in my misfortune, the whole scene began to bother me a bit. After a bit of unfruitful pondering, I decided it was probably because it got me thinking about my fellow rider coming down the grade.

I was still put off by the fact that the motorcycle rider had ridden away. Who knows why? Maybe he didn't have a license, or just got scared, although he didn't look scared to me. Whatever, there was still no excuse for leaving the scene of an accident. For all he knew, I was dead. I'd love to meet up with him again, I mused.

The anger at that made my impatience to get out of there all the greater. Lauren was due to come and pick me up in another hour.

Lauren.

My mind drifted back to the look on her face when she had first appeared in the emergency room. I was not a pretty sight. Split lip, nasty gash on my forehead, eye nearly swollen shut and already turning a deep shade of royal purple. She took a step into the room where the doctors were giving me the once-over and froze dead in her tracks when I turned to her. Her face went ashen, her hand came up to her mouth, and she choked back a cry of despair. We stared at each other for a moment, the rest of the room frozen out of existence. I'd never seen her so scared. I saw in her eyes that look of anguish that only comes when one's world comes within a hair's breadth of being destroyed. I also saw the first flickering of relief that comes when you stare death in the face, and then walk away. I didn't know what to say.

"Yo…Adrien…"

A tear slid down her cheek, as she stifled a half-sob, half-laugh. She walked over to me, touched my cheek gently with the backs of her fingers, and in a halting, raspy half whisper said, "Ya… could'a been a contenda, Rock…."

All the miracles of modern medicine couldn't hold a candle to that. It was going to be all right.

While incredibly painful, my injuries were surprisingly superficial. Besides three broken ribs, the only other orthopedic concerns were a dislocated finger and a hyper-extended knee, which was an aggravation of an old skiing injury. I'd stretched those tendons out so much that they should be on the mend in a week or so. It was the bruises and cuts that looked, and probably felt, the worst. Lauren stayed by me while the doctors sewed up the lacerations in my back. "How's it look, hon?" I asked her.

"Like you were runner-up in an ax-fighting contest."

Yep, she was going to be all right.

After a two-day stay in the happy confines of Washoe Med, Lauren finally arrived to spring me. Still in a lot of pain, I had convinced the doctors to let me out early for medical reasons. The hospital food was about to do me in. And besides, Lauren brought her own prescription for recovery.

"DADDY!!!!" Christopher and Mary bounded into the room, touched off their afterburners and made a beeline for the bed, preparing to launch themselves in a perfectly synchronized swan dive onto my broken ribs.

I had experienced a lot of fear in the past couple of days, but none that compared to that moment. When I was sailing over that cliff, I could only imagine how it was going to hurt when I landed. I *knew* how this was going to feel. It looked like Kato was finally going to kill the Pink Panther.

"NOOOOOOOOOOO!" The pain tensing my muscles was nearly as bad as what I was trying to avoid by keeping them from jumping.

The kids stopped just short of the bed. Mary, hands on hips, looking a decade older than her eight years, eyed me pityingly. "Sheesh, daddy. You didn't really think we were going to jump, did you?"

Christopher piped in. "Yeah. Mom thought it would be kind of funny."

"Serves you right, you big galoot, for giving us such a scare." Lauren strolled over, grinning, and planted a gentle kiss on the less painful side of my face.

Somewhere in the recesses of my body, my internal EMTs had put the paddles on my heart and somehow gotten it going again, and now we were working on starting up the breathing. The kids gently crawled into bed with me, and Christopher ever-so-gently kissed the Owie-Boo-Boo on my forehead. "Does that hurt, daddy?"

There are times when the best medicine has some side effects, but it still remains the best medicine.

"Not anymore, son. Not anymore."

Although I doubted I looked very graceful leaving (the hospital always insists on patients departing in a wheelchair), it sure beat the alternative— being wheeled out in a box. Which is what the docs had said would have been my fate if that slash pile hadn't been there. Someone was looking out for me.

As much as I had wanted to avoid attention, a reporter from the newspaper met me at the door. They're like lawyers. They show up everywhere. "Can you tell us what happened, Greg?" The questioner was Peter Neely, their Life section writer, and in all fairness, a pretty good guy.

There has always been the same kind of natural affinity between the print and broadcast media that dogs and cats have. Most of it stays fairly lighthearted, but beneath the surface, there are petty jealousies on both sides. They crop up every now and then in the form of gentle, or not so gentle, digs at the other's expense on the air or in print. Newspapers have always had the advantage in this respect, because television news rarely ever reports on something that newspapers do, while newspapers, by their nature, have several formats that can allow dirt to be spread about the public and private lives of television personalities. Many print "journalists" never miss out on the opportunity to print letters to the editor complaining about the "just gosh-awful glasses that girl wears on the air," or chortling over the ratings misfortunes of a particular station. So it is a natural reaction to respond very cautiously to an approach by any newspaperman.

Lauren was already keyed into this and tried to shield me from his approach. "It's ok, hon," I murmured to her. "I'll talk to him."

In reality, Peter Neely was the exception to the rule. The Life section of the paper was typically responsible for covering the "TV Beat." In my ten years of dealing with him, he was always fair, being critical when warranted and offering praise in print when he saw something he liked on the air. He also had that rare sense of judgment of newsworthiness that is so often missing in some papers. If there weren't a story, he wouldn't make one up.

"Hey, Pete." I tried a grin, which looked a little lopsided due to the swelling on the right side of my face.

"So how are you feeling?"

"No worse than anyone else who got caught in a paper shredder."

He chuckled and wrote that down. "So what's the scoop here? What happened?"

"Pretty simple story, Pete. Went too fast, tried to set a record in the long jump. Think I did, too. Fortunately, I landed in the best possible position. On my head. Didn't threaten any critical organs that way." I reached around in the carryall that was hanging from the wheelchair handle and pulled out the two pieces of the bike helmet that ER nurses had saved for me. They never did find the third. "If I ever wasn't a believer in bike helmets, I am now. Maybe this will encourage some kids that wearing one is a little more 'cool' than they thought."

"What about this motorcycle the cops are looking for? They're being pretty tight-lipped about him."

I had already given this some thought. I wanted this whole issue to go away. Any more mention of a mysterious motorcyclist would just add fuel to keep the story alive longer than it deserved. To be honest, I wasn't sure how much he was at fault. If I hadn't been so bull-headed, and had hit my brakes instead of my pedals before going into that curve, I'd be back at the station right now instead of playing invalid in front of the papers. Sure, he got in the way, and he wasn't going to win my vote for humanitarian of the year, but the blame fell mostly on my bruised shoulders. I decided to downplay it.

"Pete, there was this guy on a bike, but I'm not sure that he could add anything to the story. The fault was mine, pure and simple."

"Simple as that?"

"Simple as that."

I'm not sure he bought it completely, but he seemed satisfied. He flipped up his reporter's notebook and swung a 35-millimeter camera off of his shoulder. "Smile for the folks back at home, Greg."

Oh, great. Getting me while I look my best. I endured a couple of clicks before Lauren and the kids wheeled me to our waiting minivan. The climb into the passenger seat was no harder than climbing out of the canyon two days earlier. "Babe…can you give me a push?" I pleaded.

"Is this what its going to be like thirty years from now?" she teased.

"Oh no, I ought to be feeling a bit better by then."

That night, with the kids tucked in, Lauren and I, propped up on the couch and facing each other with feet planted naturally in each other's laps, were able to connect again. Foot rubs. If Ariel Sharon and Yasser Arafat would just meet every other week and do this, there would be peace in the Middle East. Well, maybe not. But it did wonders to soothe my soul. Or is that sole? Even though my bum finger limited my effectiveness somewhat, we spent ten minutes in companionable silence, working out the knots and gravel around the arches. Lauren, as usual, knitted her eyebrows in concentration as she worked around my big toe. I, as usual, just looked at her.

"You know what I was thinking as I was going over that cliff?"

Lauren looked up and paused. "No, what?"

"I was thinking that it would be a shame if I could never sit on this couch and do this again."

Lauren was silent for a bit. "Greg."

"Yeah, hon?"

"Is there more to this? Did you just get going too fast?" She had the extremely annoying gift of insight.

"I don't know, luv. I've taken that curve and that road dozens of times, at faster speeds than that." I had told her in the hospital about the motorcycle rider. "Obviously, if that guy hadn't been there, there wouldn't have been a problem. We just got into a childish game, I guess. Neither of us wanting to back off. I still think if he had had a little more presence of mind, he could have given me more room, but I guess he froze. Pretty dumb of me, huh? Trying to take on a man and machine five times my weight."

"Just don't do that again, OK? Because as much as I want my children to grow up with a father, if I have to go through all that again, I might just finish the job myself." She grinned.

I grinned back. She was kidding.

I think.

Chapter 10

Thanks to Lauren's ministrations, and a marked level of restraint on Christopher and Mary's part (they didn't jump me once in two days…I could tell it was driving them nuts), I was able to return to work on the following Monday. Even though I was still in a lot of pain, an intense rehab program had jacked my activity level up to at least that of your average octogenarian. Jeanne Marshal had called to let me know I could stay out as long as I needed and to not feel that I had to hurry back. "Bert's doing a great job filling in for you, Greg," she chirped, all too cheerfully.

She can be cruel at times.

I didn't doubt that Bert was doing a good job. Bert Gooding, our weekend weathercaster, was young, energetic, good looking, and what made things even worse, talented. He has never made any bones about the fact that he has wanted to be a 5-day-a-week, main weather anchor. Jeanne Marshal, of course, knew this. She also knew that every anchor, be they news, sports or weather, has just enough insecurity to get just a little uncomfortable when some up-and-coming young buck has designs on their position, and I was no exception. Uneasy lies the head that wears the crown. So, before the body got to be too cold in the grave and the public grew too attached to the young and dashing Mr. Gooding, I hauled my aching bones into the station.

I poked my head into Jeanne's office on my way in. "I want you to know that I didn't buy a word of it. Pretty underhanded thing to do to get me back on my feet."

"*Qui, moi?*" she asked, with a wide-eyed look of innocence. The world lost a great actress when she decided on a news career. "Greg! I'm surprised to see you back. Are you sure you feel strong enough?" she asked coyly. After playing with my mind the way she had, she knew good and well I'd have crawled through broken glass to get back.

"Sure. Just don't ask me to go live from any roller coasters." I grimaced.

"I want you to know that I never would let you come back if it weren't for the book." November was one of the four months throughout the year when we were in one of our ratings books. Called a "book" because a small group of viewers actually fill out a book, or diary, of the shows they watch. Getting them to write us down is the golden ring of our business.

"I wouldn't have missed it for the world. Say, I was thinking. Maybe I should use the wheelchair for a while. Go for the sympathy vote."

"Sounds like a great idea! I'll get promotions on it right away!" She reached for the phone.

My eyes grew wide. She was taking me seriously, I thought. "Boss," I protested, "I was kidding."

"I know. Gotcha!" She grinned back. "You *were* shook up in that fall, weren't you? You never used to be this easy. Hardly a challenge now."

I threw back an embarrassed grin and chuckled as I limped out the doorway and plotted my revenge. It was good to be back.

I got to my office and went through what I considered the fun part of my job. Computer models, charts, air soundings, weather station reports, and good old-fashioned intuition were just some of the elements that came together as I tried to play soothsayer and predict what the weather was going to have in store for us over the next week or so.

The atmosphere is such a complex organism that no one will ever get it right all the time. In many ways, I wished I could have been around when maps were hand-drawn, and a person used slide rulers to calculate some of the atmospheric characteristics. At least then you had more excuses when you were wrong. In the early 60's, with the advent of weather satellites, there was a tremendous leap in one's ability to see storm systems come in. But even if forecasts were then right 70% of the time, instead of 60%, that didn't make the public any more forgiving when they woke up with three inches of "partly cloudy" on their front lawn.

Then came computers. While the actual equations that go into computer modeling of the atmosphere can get awful complicated and convoluted, the basic theory is pretty straightforward.

If you know the speed, direction and mass of a particular bit of air at any one time, using simple Newtonian Physics you can make a pretty good prediction of what that bit of air will be doing in, say, 24 hours, as long as there's nothing else to run into it. Obviously, though, there are plenty of other bits of air to get into the way, some of which are traveling in different directions. Of course, those same mathematical equations that predict what will happen to an unimpeded chunk of air can also be used to calculate what will happen to the two bits that bump into each other. Just envision the old high school physics lessons that used vector arrows when two billiard balls came together. Every time you sink the eight ball in the corner pocket, you are, perhaps unconsciously, using vector physics.

But the problem becomes more complicated as you throw more billiard balls onto the table. It becomes even *more* complicated when your two-dimensional pool table becomes a three-dimensional atmosphere. Then toss in the thermodynamic consequences of temperature and pressure changes, heat transfer properties of water in the atmosphere, which all affect the outcome, and instead of 15 cue balls on a pool table, you're talking about sixty billion gazillion (a scientific number meaning "a whole bunch") air molecules, and all of a sudden you have what must be described as a pretty complex system.

Prior to the advent of computers, weather maps were drawn by hand. Some attempts were made to predict the weather from a "modeling" standpoint, but hand calculations had to be grossly simplified in terms of the input. The old slide rules just couldn't move that fast. The first computers were a tremendous boon to forecasting, but they too proved to be limited by their processing speed. If you tried to input all the data that goes into today's computer models into one of the old Univacs, it would take weeks of processing to come up with a result. Not too practical when you are trying to forecast for tomorrow.

But now we have Cray supercomputers that can crank out calculations at a rate of 60 billion per second. That's pretty impressive, and powerful enough to draw a much more accurate model of the atmosphere. The forecasts from these models have become a lot more accurate as well, second only to Great Aunt Ida's bunions. And, if truth were known, my forecasts live and die in large measure with the accuracy of these computer models. But 60 billion is still a lot less than 60 billion gazillion (about 1/gazillionth), and in the end, even with the most powerful computers, there are still too many unmeasured subtleties, and lest I ever get too proud, God still has the final say.

Besides having to come up with a forecast, I also had lots of "public relations" responsibilities to take care of. Because I had been out for much of the last week, my voice mailbox was stuffed pretty full. "You have 17 voice mail messages," intoned the androgynous voice from the speakerphone. There were three requests to speak at schools, two luncheon speaking requests (alright…free food!), one wondering where I got my hair cut, seven wondering where I had been the last week and if I'd been fired. So they DO care! There were three that fell into the miscellaneous "anonymous G&C (gripe and complain) file"...and one somewhat cryptic message from Chuck Murphy.

"Greg...Chuck. I...have something that you might be...interested in. I... you...well, just call me. I've figured it out. We need to get together." The line went dead.

I had often been the recipient of Chuck's late night e-mail and voice mail messages, which contained a somewhat mysterious edge to them. Without fail, they all turned out to be phantasms of his more-than-adequate imagination. So why did this message sound any different than any of the rest? I thought about it for a minute. There was something there.

I was about to drop the subject when it hit me. In the past, whenever Chuck came up with a new conspiracy theory, it was always accompanied by a sense of joy at the discovery. Like when he called claiming the new cellular phone tower outside his apartment was really a cover for Pentagon mind-control experiments. He was like a kid in a candy store. "I've got those SOB's dead to rights now!" he chortled. Of course, nothing ever came of it. I never took him seriously. I never told him that... it would have ruined the fun. We all get our jollys our own way and I suppose this was his way of blowing off steam harmlessly.

But there was no joy in his voice this time.

Not wanting to strain his already-tenuous relationship with his management, I decided against calling him on the hotline at the radio station. I made a note to ring him up later that night at his apartment after he got off his shift. I half suspected, and hoped, that by the time I reached him, he would have forgotten what it was all about and would be on to his next crisis.

I went back to work. Our fair and unusually mild weather the last several weeks had been caused by a very stubborn and strong ridge of high pressure which had built up from the south a couple of hundred miles off the California Coast. This effectively acted as a block to the polar jet stream, just like a concrete bulkhead blocks waves from the ocean and sends them crashing over the top, protecting the shore. Because of this, the jet was kicked well up to the north, carrying winter storms into British Columbia. But I began to notice a weakening at the base of the high, a slight buckling of the flow before it was redirected north. It was almost as if our bulkhead was being undermined. I had seen this happen a few times in the past. If the high builds up a little farther north, then the jet would punch through underneath it and make a beeline for the coast right in our direction. Some of our most violent winter weather gets started this way.

It looked like a storm was headed my direction.
I couldn't have been more prophetic.

Chapter 11

It was good to be back on the air after my little vacation. My co-anchors, Mark Dudding and Sue Ann Stevens, publicly made positive comments on the state of my fitness, while privately arguing about the virtues of the heavier-than-usual make-up I was wearing to cover up the still-healing bruises and cuts. As we went to a commercial break after my forecast, they didn't waste time.

"Personally, I wish you would have left the make-up off," Sue Ann piped in. "It kind of gives you that rugged individualistic look."

"Hey, it worked for Freddie Kruger," Mark added unnecessarily.

I groaned. "That's all I need. For children to go screaming to their mothers whenever I come on the screen."

"Hey, why should it be any different now?" Skip Walker, our sports anchor, had just entered the studio.

I was beginning to feel picked on.

"Hey Skip, good to see you too." I pretended to do a double take as he sat down. I leaned forward and stared at his hairline, which had been on a slow but steady march to the north for the last couple of years. "Geez, Skip, I thought you had been having some success with that Rogaine. Did you stop taking it? Looks like you've lost some of your harvest."

"Awww, no! You're kidding. Do you think so?" Skip, whose anxiety about his hair loss bordered on psychosis, grabbed a mirror and scanned his forehead. "I thought I'd made some real progress."

"Yeah, you're looking more like Michael Jordan all the time," Mark offered.

"Hey, he has his like that by choice," Skip moaned.

"What you need is some real way to keep track of the old shoreline," I offered. "Here, lemme mark it with this." I approached him with a black indelible pen I used to mark up my weather charts. "I'll just draw a line where the hair ends now…"

"Fifteen seconds out," chimed the floor director.

"You come near me with that thing and your adoring public will be wondering why you decided to get a tattoo on your nose." It was an idle threat, although at 6' 10" and 275 pounds, the former power forward in the Continental Basketball League wouldn't have had much of a problem backing it up.

"Ten seconds."

"What do you think, guys? Sounds like a lot of talk to me. I think he's gone soft in his old age." This was getting fun.

"Five…"

"C'mon, you want a piece of this?" Skip snarled.

"Four, three…"

"Bring it on, old-timer."

"Boys, boys…." Sue Ann chirped happily.

"Two…one…"

The red tally light on the camera flicked on. "Skip Walker joins us now with the latest from the world of boxing," Mark smoothly tossed across the desk. "Or should I say, professional wrestling?"

"Sometimes it's hard to tell, isn't it?" Skip caught the pass and went with it with a smile on his face that would disarm Saddam Hussein. "Today, Mike Tyson continued his bid…."

Visitors to the studio during the airing of a show are always taken aback at the banter that goes on during the commercial breaks. "How can you switch gears so easily?" they would ask. "Don't you need to concentrate on what's coming up?" What they don't know is all the hard work goes on before we take our seats in front of the camera. Reviewing scripts—or in my case, the forecast—has to be done ahead of time. But success in the television business depends on the presenter being relaxed and able to connect with the viewers. The preparation is intellectual, the presentation is emotional. Our little scenes during breaks are our ways of staying loose. It works well for us. It takes a while to develop the relationships to make the chemistry work, but it is worth the effort.

Skip and I had known and worked with each other for 7 years now, unusual in such a transitory business as television. But we both had a lot in common, having decided to forgo the lure of the bigger market in favor of a nice place to raise our families. As we were both on the wrong side of 40, age was a constant theme in our good-natured fencing. And although he could probably halt the charge of the Light Brigade with one look at his imposing frame, inside was a heart so soft that he'd go a block out of his way to avoid stepping on a caterpillar.

After the show was over, Skip came over and clamped a hand on my shoulder and gave it a squeeze. I winced. "It's good to see you back, Greg. You gave us all quite a scare. I can't let you out of my sight, can I, without you getting yourself into trouble? Next time, you had better take me along."

I chuckled. I knew the odds of him getting on a bike ranked right up there with me pitching relief for the Giants the next year. "Don't worry, Skip. The most strenuous thing I have in mind consists of a lot of time in the steam room at the club. After about a week or so of that, I ought to be in fine shape. That is, if my kids don't put me back in the hospital."

Skip chuckled and slapped me on my back with no more force than your average bull elephant in heat and ducked his head as he went out the door.

"Thanks, Skip," I gasped when my head cleared.

Remind me never to get on your bad side.

After dinner that night, I tried to give Chuck a call at his apartment, but no one was home. I left a message on his phone recorder, knowing well and good that the odds of Chuck ever returning one of my messages was even worse than Skip riding a bicycle with me. Since probabilities were a part of my profession, I put it about the same as being struck by lightning the next year—one in 600,000, according to government statistics. I'd keep trying to reach him.

I was beginning to finally fall back into a comfortable schedule. I poked my head into the kids' room before I left to go back to the station to work the 11 PM newscast. I was greeted by that reassuring buzzing of kiddie snoring at which Mary was especially adept. When they were first born, I was continually checking on them at night, just to make sure they were still breathing. Years ago, I had a close friend who lost a child to Sudden Infant Death Syndrome, and the fear of this kind of tragedy hitting our family always preyed on my mind. Even though the danger almost completely passes after a child's first year, I guess I never grew out of the habit of checking up on them. I walked in, kissed each of them, and just stared for a bit, their bedtime prayers still echoing in my ears.

"Heavenly Father," Mary always liked to sound grown up when she prayed, "I pray that you help Daddy feel better and place your angels around him as he goes back to work."

Christopher, while lacking some of the verbal flexibility of his sister, nonetheless made up for it in efficiency. "God," he prayed, "keep daddy on his bike next time."

Amen.

Part of my self-imposed rehabilitation consisted of going to the Sports West Athletic Club for some light stretching, which was agonizing, and some steam, which almost made up for the stretching. While on my temporary hiatus from work, I made a couple of visits during the afternoon hours. But I had gotten into the habit, before the accident, of keeping a sports bag packed in the car and venturing to the Virginia Street location just south of the downtown area late at night, after finishing the 11 o'clock show. I much preferred these late-night trips to the 24-hour club, where I could have plenty of room to stretch out. I could have the steam and locker room to myself, and was less likely to feel intimidated by all the Schwarzenegger wannabees who seemed to come out of the woodwork whenever I tried to hit the weights. Of course, at that time, lifting weights was the furthest thing from my mind, although I'm sure I could have used a little firming up. After lying on my back for the most of the last week, the only things in my body that were firming up were my arteries.

So after putting the late news to bed, and prior to putting myself to the same, I looked forward to the relative isolation of the almost deserted club at midnight. I limped in, presented my membership card, and was pleased to see that apart from an elderly lady pushing a vacuum cleaner and the college kid sitting the desk with his nose buried in his anatomy and physiology textbook, I had the whole place to myself.

I took my time with the stretching. A lot of time. There were still muscles that had lived a life of contented anonymity prior to the accident, which now expressed extreme displeasure at the slightest challenge to their rigidity. I had been negotiating with them for several days now, and while we still were not the best of buddies, it did appear that an armistice was on the horizon.

After 45 minutes of painful progress, I actually felt cocky enough to do a little exercising. I considered the stationary bicycle for only a moment. Christopher's prayer notwithstanding, it still brought back too many painful memories. I also bypassed the treadmill in favor of the lower impact nature of the stair-climber. Putting it on the slowest speed possible, I climbed the equivalent of, oh, about a three-story office building before exhaustion overtook me.

I was making real progress.

I only put up with the suffering because of a promise that I would treat myself to an extra 15 minutes of the steam room. As far as I was concerned, the invention of the steam room ranked right up there with the telephone, penicillin, and foot rubs. As I hauled my weary bones to the deserted locker room, the thought of losing myself in a womb of hot, thick steam, and feeling the effects as it seeped deep into my muscles and lungs was almost too much to bear.

The locker room, like the exercise room, was deserted, with the exception of a lone cleaning/maintenance man. He looked new, but that wasn't unusual. Working graveyard while cleaning swimming pools, hosing out showers and disinfecting toilets makes for a lot of turnover.

"How's it goin tonight?" he said when he saw me come in.

"Uh, fine... thanks," I stammered. It was the first time in over two years of belonging to the club that any of the late night crew ever said anything to me, and I was a bit taken aback. Without exception, all the rest had been at best uncommunicative, and at worst sullen. This was understandable, given the late hours and low pay. But this chap was downright cheery. I wondered how long that would last. "Got a busy night tonight?" I said with a smile.

"Yup! In fact, I'm gonna have to close down the whole locker room 'bout now, cuz I got some major league overhaul I'm doin' to the plumbing in here."

My face fell. Visions of a nice long steam bath began to fly out the window. "OK," I said with more than a hint of disappointment in my voice. "I'll get dressed and out of your way."

"Wouldn't hear of it. Take your time. I'm just closing off the entrance now, but I won't be breaking into any pipes for another hour or so. You have the whole place to yourself."

"Ahhhh...thanks!" I grinned. Nice fellow. I hoped we kept him around for a while. "What's your name? Mine's Greg."

"Awww, I know who you are, Mr. O'Brien. Call me Bobby. Or Beau. Or Bubba, if you prefer. Just don't call me late for dinner." He cackled as he turned and started putting up barriers in front of the door.

I had to smile, in spite of the old joke. I wondered where he was from. He had the dark complexion and the thick black hair that made me think he might have some Mexican in him, but his face didn't show it. Talked with that likable bumpkin lilt that is almost a parody of southerners. I watched him go off, whistling an unknown tune, content to be there. Nice attitude.

I turned and set to the arduous task of stripping off my clothes. I paused for a moment, and considered for a second slipping on the Speedo and swimming a few laps. Fortunately, the feeling didn't last very long. I wasn't hit *that* hard on my head. So I tossed a towel over my shoulder and limped into the shower room, acutely aware of the rapidly tightening muscles. Man, that steam was going to feel good!

As I came around the corner into the shower room, I rear-ended Bobby/ Beau/Bubba as he was backing up, pulling a line of hose out of the maintenance closet. He slipped, reached out to catch himself, knocking against my thigh in the process. Pain shot through me like an electrical jolt. He had inadvertently found one of the deepest bruises.

I froze for an instant, trying not to let my face betray the pain I was feeling. I don't think he bought it.

"Oh, man! I am so sorry! Did I hurt ya? Ya wanna sit down?" Concern oozed out of his electric blue-gray eyes.

I steadied myself, took a deep breath, and tried to smile. Came out a grimace. "Don't worry about it. I wasn't watching where I was going. I'll just put a little heat on it."

"Hey, good idea." Poor guy was practically fawning over me. "Lemme run a hot shower for you."

My mother stopped running my showers for me when I was 12. "No, that's OK. I'll be fine." I eased my way into the shower room.

The pain in my thigh began to moderate to a dull ache after stepping under a hot jet of water from one of a half-dozen showerheads lined up along the wall. I felt the cares of the day begin to melt away as I washed off the little sweat I had worked up.

At first I thought I was running out of hot water. I usually take showers just on the tolerable side of scalding. But the water was rapidly losing that heated edge that was there just moments ago. Thinking I might have inadvertently knocked the knob on the shower to the cool side, I turned to check.

In slow motion.

And getting slower.

I stared at the knob. Still pointed to the H. What was wrong? I twisted agonizingly around. It seemed to take hours. My first thought was I might be having a stroke or popping an aneurysm as a result of the accident. But I was still *thinking* clearly. I just couldn't move.

Bob/Beau/Bubba watched me with keen interest.

I felt a tremor in my leg. I forced myself to lock my knees in a losing battle to stay upright.

"I....What....is..." I tried to speak. Even speech was leaving me.

I started to waver. I felt myself begin to pitch forward. Using every last ounce of will, I pressed my toes into the tile to stop my forward progress. It worked too well. Feeling like a man sitting atop a tree that is too skinny to support my weight, I stopped toppling forward only to head backwards. No stopping it this time.

A loud crack reverberated through the shower room as my head met up with the wall, breaking a tile in the process. It hurt. A lot. My knees gave up the battle and buckled underneath me. The pain in my skull was replaced an even sharper one as my coccyx ended up taking the brunt of my fall. Once my fanny was down, there wasn't much left to fall, and I ended up slumped up against the wall, feet splayed out at awkward angles, head lolling to one side, a pitiful Raggedy Andy doll discarded by a bored toddler.

The shower continued to pour out on me.

I was paralyzed.

Or was I? I could still *feel*. I had my eyes shut, trying to discern which pain was worse, the one in my head or the one in my butt. I could feel the water pounding on my bare skin. I could even begin to feel the heat from it again. I just couldn't *move*. What was wrong with me?

I let my eyelids creep open. At least they still worked. I noticed Bob/Beau/Bubba standing sideways in my view, casually leaning against the wall. He didn't seem concerned, and there was even a hint of amusement on his thin lips. I tried to call out to him. Nothing. Even the voice was gone now. Why didn't he come over and help? I knew he must have seen what had happened.

I stayed there, unblinkingly staring at him, because quite frankly, there was nothing else I could do. After what seemed to be an eternity, he casually strolled over and shut off the tap. He picked my towel off the nearby hook and methodically dried his hands. Tossing the towel over his shoulder, he squatted down, lifted my chin so I could stare into those piercing gray eyes. Gone was the easy-going, aw-shucks, bumpkin demeanor.

"Gidday, mate. It's about bloody time you showed up." Also gone was the good ol' boy accent. It was replaced by one from Down Under. "Oy was gettin' real tired of cleaning stalls all night long."

I wanted to ask, "Who are you?" I wanted to ask anything. But my vocal chords felt as if they were filled with peanut butter. A quiet gurgle is all that came out.

"Now, you jist relax, mate. That's what the steam room is for, ayen't it?" He seemed to be enjoying this. "Course," he chortled, "you already look to be pretty relaxed, now, eh? See this 'ere?" He held up his left hand and showed me a wedding band. What was I supposed to do, congratulate him? He twisted the band around, revealing a tiny barb on the underside. "Sorry about the slap on the thigh." He didn't seem sorry at all. "Terrific stuff, this. Shuts down all the communication from the brain to the muscles from the neck down, without affecting the heart and lungs. Sort of a beefed up version of the paralysis darts we used to use in the outback for tagging wild game. Won't be able to talk or move a muscle for 5 hours or so. Well long enough for my purposes. Borrowed some from a couple mates in the Mossad. They use it in case they want to snatch someone. Little poke in the thigh or the arm, and 30 seconds later the poor lad looks like he's had a stroke. Whisked away in a conveniently near ambulance…works like a charm."

Kidnapping. So that was his game. But why? I didn't have enough money to appeal to the most desperate extortionist.

He must have seen the unasked question in my eyes. He smiled. "Kidnapping? Naw…you don't have to worry about that. Oy'm not here to kidnap you.

"Oy'm here to kill you."

Chapter 12

I believed him.

If the shock and horror of his statement reflected in my face, he didn't seem to notice. He stated his intentions with no more apparent guile or malice than if he had just told me he was going to throw another shrimp on the barbie.

If I'd known exactly what he had in mind, I might have appreciated the irony of that comparison.

Although he wasn't a particularly large man, 5'10" and maybe 170 pounds, his frame hid surprising power. He hoisted up my completely flaccid body and threw it over his shoulder with no more concern than if I were a sack of flour. The muscles across his shoulders felt like boulders, as hard as the tile that I just left.

He carried me across the shower room and stopped only briefly to open the steam room door at the end of a short hall. Steam room? What in blazes could he do to me in there that he couldn't do out in the abandoned shower room?

As if he could read my mind, the "Aussie," for lack of a better name, plopped me unceremoniously down on the upper platform of the steam room. He lifted my chin so I could look into his eyes and cheerfully stated, "It would be too easy jist to snap your neck out there. Would look a bit suspicious, as well. But your well-known love for the steam is jist the ticket. But first, will you join me in a quick one?"

He reached into his back pocket and pulled out a hip flask. He unscrewed the top, parted my lips and forced a mouthful of what must have been rum down my throat. A light drinker even in the wildest days of my youth, I was completely unprepared for the burning river of fire that poured down my gullet. Apparently, my stomach was unprepared as well, as it immediately rejected the liquid, and it came flowing out of my mouth and dribbled down my chest, as clear and as untainted as when it had entered. Thanks to the paralyzing effects of the nerve agent, it was probably the most docile display of vomiting in medical history. I couldn't even toss my cookies right.

None of this seemed the bother the Aussie. He sprinkled a bit into my hair, and then, in what I suppose was a cheap challenge to my masculinity, took a full swig himself, tossing back a shot without even having the good graces to tear up afterwards.

"Not bad...not bad at all. Never beat a schooner of Fosters, though."

Funny guy.

The steam room, like the shower, was fully tiled from bottom to top. The Aussie had placed me in the far corner on the top of two benches, which ran along two sides of the small room, so that my head was no more than a foot and a half from the ceiling. I was still in the dark as to what he had planned for me. He left me slumped against the corner, crossed to the far end, and picked up the hose connected to a spigot near the floor. He turned to me and paused, raised an eyebrow, and gave me one more chance to figure out what he was doing.

With a mounting sense of terror, I figured it out.

This steam room, like all steam rooms, had a thermostat mounted on the wall. When the temperature of the room dropped below a pre-subscribed level of about 80 degrees F, the steam would kick on, and the room would rapidly heat up to about 105 degrees F, after which an electric signal from the thermostat would trip a solenoid, shutting off the flow. This kept any occupant from getting par-broiled.

In order to kick on the flow of steam, a hose attached to a cold-water spigot was provided. Turning on the faucet and splashing a little water on the thermostat rapidly cooled it, starting the flow.

A small hook for hanging towels was mounted on the wall slightly above and a little to the left of the thermostat. As the fates would have it, the hose's diameter was just slightly more than that of the hook. The Aussie slid the hose into the hook's crook, which held it tight, and adjusted the length so the open end of the hose was positioned just inches above the thermostat. He turned on the water, satisfied that the steady stream completely covered the open vents of the thermostat.

Only moments later, the roar of the steam filled the room.

The Aussie sauntered over to and reclined on the lower bench, just ahead of the billowing steam cloud. Leaning back so he could look up at me, he grinned and shouted over the cacophony of the steam, "There yaw, mate! Jist what the doctor ordered. A bit o' steam, and all those aches and pains will go away. Permanently!" He shrieked a high-pitch cackle, overcome by his own sense of black humor.

I struggled once again to move. Nothing. Nada. I remember watching one of those wildlife shows where they hit the unsuspecting elk with a paralyzing dart. While the game wardens and scientists tagged, poked and generally fussed about the then-immobile beast, I was drawn to the look in the great creature's eye. It was unable to move a muscle, and there was still an unmistakable mark of terror and confusion reflecting off its iris.

I wondered what an impassive observer would see in my eyes.

The cloud of steam enveloped us. In just seconds, his dry, bleached white shirt and jeans were soaked through. Moments later, drops appeared on his forehead, rolled down and fell off his nose. I wondered how long he would stay.

Not long.

"Oy was thinkin' of having a bash at staying with you for a while, but Oy don't want to bob in on your fun. Sorry to have to shoot-through like this, but this air's starting to remind me of Darwin. Always hated that place. Too 'umid for my tastes. Gidday."

And with that he got up, checked to make sure the hose was securely in its cradle, and walked out the door. A brief rush of cool air accompanied the opening.

It didn't last.

Noise.

The constant assault on my ears was almost as bad as the rapidly rising temperatures. Even at that, the roar from the jets wasn't enough to cover up the drumbeat of my heart as I tried to calm myself down and take stock of my situation. While it is all nice and good to tell yourself that panicking will only make things worse, reality sometimes makes the best theories impractical. Especially with about 100 decibels grinding away at my tympanic membrane. The temperature was already well above the normal shut-off level. The superheated steam was beginning to become uncomfortable to swallow. Soon, breathing itself would become agonizing, blistering the lining of my esophagus.

I prayed that somebody might come along and discover my dilemma, and realized the incredible odds against that happening. As the fates would have it, my left wrist rested awkwardly across my lap, but within the line of sight of my slumped head. I still had my watch on, and noticed it was nearing one o'clock in the morning. I morbidly thought that by the time anybody got impatient enough with the closed-off locker room, it would be daylight, and I would be ready for de-boning. And I thought the Aussie's humor was black.

Once discovered, I can imagine what the cops would say. "Poor guy fell asleep in the steam room. Wasn't content with the normal amount of steam, had to juice it up a bit by setting up the hose that way. Besides, did you get a wiff? He'd obviously had a few before he came in." My adversary had obviously thought way ahead.

Strange as it seems, I was more confused at why the Aussie had gone to such elaborate steps to do me in instead of wondering why he wanted to do the dirty deed to begin with. I was probably still in denial about that.

The temperature was climbing. I was like the proverbial Boy Scout who always came prepared; my watch had a built-in thermometer. No self-respecting meteorologist would be complete without one. Although the watch face continually fogged up, drops of water coming down from the ceiling periodically cleaned it for a moment if I stared at it long enough. Of course, I didn't have a lot else I could look at.

125 degrees and climbing.

I considered briefly whether the extreme heat might overcome the flow of water and cause the thermostat to switch off. I discarded that thread of hope just as quickly. The hose was turned on full steam (poor choice of words, I know), and the cooling effects wouldn't be overcome until well after the steam became fatal.

134 degrees. Death Valley. 1913. North American record.

136 degrees. El Azizia, Libya. 1922. World record. Uncharted territory.

I couldn't leave bad enough alone. I watched the temperature on my watch climb and thought about the Heat Index.

Temperatures of this magnitude, while certainly not healthy, are still survivable, if they are found in a dry desert environment like Death Valley or Libya. That's because the body has its own form of air conditioning which takes advantage of one of the physical properties of water. When a drop of water evaporates and changes from a liquid to a vapor, it absorbs energy (heat) in order to make the phase change. When a drop of water is on your skin, that heat is drawn from your body, cooling it down. So whenever the brain senses the body is getting even a little too hot, it sends a signal to the sweat glands to start wetting down the skin, which evaporates and gives you relief from the heat. Kind of like a built-in swamp cooler. As long as you drink enough water, your body can control its temperature.

There are two instances where this marvelous air conditioning unit might not work. If a person gets exposed to extreme conditions for too long of a time, heat stroke can set in. When a person is suffering from heat stroke, the sweating response quits operating altogether, and a person's body temperature can skyrocket...causing seizures, and often death, if it's not treated soon.

The other fly in the cooling ointment is when there's no place for the sweat drops to evaporate. When the air is very humid, there is less impetus for the liquid water to turn into vapor, and so the evaporation is greatly reduced. The slower the evaporation, the less cooling. That's why 85 degrees in Biloxi, Mississippi is sweltering, and 85 degrees in Reno is comfortable. Because of the differences of the "feel" of the same temperatures due to humidity changes, some bright guy came up with the Heat Index. 100 degrees with a 70% relative humidity has a Heat Index of (feels like) 141 degrees.

In the end, it's a simple way of saying that the muggier it is, the worse off you are. And there ain't no muggy like steam room muggy. Almost 100% humidity.

145 degrees. Without the heat index.

Breathing was becoming almost unbearable. I pursed my lips and slowly sucked air in through my teeth to try to cool it as much as possible before it blasted into my lungs like a blow furnace. Hot water poured onto me from above, as the steam condensed on the ceiling and flowed off like a devilish hot spring. I wasn't sure if I would die from the heat or by drowning.

155 degrees.

So this is what hell is like.

It became almost impossible to keep my eyes open, as the steam seemed to burn holes in them, but a morbid sense of curiosity prompted me to take another peek at my watch.

The watch face was black. The liquid crystal had vaporized and burst through the barriers that held it in.

Remind me to never buy the cheap brand, I thought futilely.

As the agony wore on, I could only guess how long I'd been in that nightmare. But I knew that it was coming to an end. I no longer dared to open my eyes, and my mind began that initial stage of wandering, a journey that would soon announce its arrival in a different world. As I resigned myself to my fate, the pain lessened, my breathing slowed, and one by one my senses began to shut down, like the end of those cartoons I watched so many years ago, where the black closed in from all sides, forming a circle around the last scene. At the end, the picture shrank to a pinprick of light before blinking out altogether. And just as the music was always the last to turn off, the roar of steam that had become my last soundtrack gradually faded away, until it too was gone, and there was nothing.

Chapter 13

Silence.

Thirst.

Like rising from the murky depths of a muddy pond, these were the first two sensations I discovered. If I was dead, the silence was believable.

But thirsty?

One by one, other sensations began to reappear as if the fog in my brain was burning off under the morning sun. The tenderness of my broiled skin began to register once again, as did the burning of my lungs. And when I built up enough gumption to open my eyes, I discovered to my amazement that the fog had cleared in the steam room as well.

Oh, that's nice, I thought. *I think I'll go back to sleep.*

Sleep. When I slept, all the pain had gone away. Sleep was good. Sleep was pleasant. Sleep was escape.

But from deep within, a voice called out, trying to campaign against such thoughts. Lauren's voice. Pleading, prodding, begging me to wake up.

"Aw, sweetheart, just lemme sleep for a bit. Jus' a nap...." I mumbled.

But there was a tremor of urgency in the voice that would not go away. Sleep was not good. Sleep was death. Get up. GET UP!

I opened my eyes. Silence? Not quiet. While almost soundless in comparison to the barrage that the steam had made on my ears, a steady stream of water still poured out of the hose and covered the thermostat on the opposite side of the room.

And I could see it.

The steam had stopped.

It took a while for that to sink in. The steam had stopped. Something happened. What was it? The hose didn't slip. I could see that clearly now. But the steam had stopped, and, hallelujah, it wasn't as hot in the room. I guessed that something must have broken in the steam generator. It couldn't have been meant to run that hard for so long. A breaker must have tripped. It wouldn't start again until someone came and reset it. I watched with detached interest as the water poured out on the opposite wall and ran down the drain.

Water. Thirsty.

While the steam had been attacking, my body was continually pumping out water in a useless attempt to counteract the heat. As a result, I was severely dehydrated. The cold, clear water was just 10 feet away, but it might as well have been on another planet. Water, water, everywhere, but ne'er a drop to drink.

Or was there? I had become so accustomed to the incessant dripping off the tiled ceiling that I almost ignored it. A steady drip, drip, drip plopped on my forehead just over my left eyebrow. By virtue of inconsistencies in the ceiling's surface, a low spot in the runoff was positioned right above me. I tilted my head up fractionally and opened my mouth.

Although it was mixed with the scum and sweat of weeks of use by countless other bodies, no nectar of the gods could have ever tasted so sweet. A moan of pleasure gargled out through my lips. I won't say that I drank my fill, but with every drop, I could feel my head clear. It was during this gradual return to lucidity that two thoughts struck me forcefully. Good news, and bad news.

First the good news. I had moved my head to get to the water. I heard myself moan. The effects of the nerve agent were beginning to wear off. Not completely, mind you. I still couldn't move my legs, and any attempts to budge my arms barely resulted in a quiver. But at this point, any port in a storm would do.

I wondered how long I had been there. What was it the Aussie had said? "Should last 5 hours or so"? Have I been here that long? A glance to the side wall gave me the answer. A clock on the wall, out of my previous line of sight, and apparently somewhat more steam-proof than my watch, showed the time to be just after 2:20 AM. Not even two hours since I first found myself in this position. How can it be wearing off so soon? The Aussie didn't strike me as the type to make such an error. I was sure he'd seen it used many times before.

But not in a steam bath. The rapid de-watering my body had undergone must have flushed some of the toxins out. I guessed in another hour or so, I might to be able to haul myself out of there.

That was the good news.

The bad news was I didn't have another hour. I had less than 10 minutes.

As the drops from the ceiling slowed, and then finally stopped, my gaze returned to the clock. 2:22…almost 2:30.

2:30. What was it about 2:30? And then it hit me like a cruel joke. The timer.

It was the cause of a running argument I had been having with the club's management for months. In order for the cleaning crews to come in and hose out the steam room, which they never did anyway, the generator was put on a timer to shut it off once a night. The timer was set to turn it off at 1:30 AM, often the time I wanted to use it. Whenever I asked any of the cleaning crew about it, none of them was even aware that the timer existed. When I finally worked my way up the authority ladder and talked to one of the club managers, just before the mishap on my bike, they finally agreed to switch the time to 4 AM.

I will never again complain about corporate lethargy. If they *had* changed the time, I would be dead.

But that was faint comfort. The timer only turned the steam off for one hour. In eight minutes, my trip from the frying pan into the fire would be complete.

I tried to will my limbs to move. Nothing. Panic began to set in. I couldn't go through this again. I almost wished I hadn't awoken the first time. Tears of frustration formed in my eyes.

I tried to take stock, forcing the rising tide of terror downward. I rechecked my inventory. I had little that I didn't have the first time around. I tried to scream, but it was barely above a whisper. I could make noise, but not enough to attract the attention of an attendant on the other side of the building. I could move my head a bit now. Apparently, movement came back from the top down.

I tried rocking my head back and forth, lifting it and sliding it to the left, and then pressing it back and pushing to the right as I attempted to wriggle my body toward the door. It may as well have been a mile away. It felt like my back was Velcroed to the wall. I heard my hair squeak as it slid along the tile in a desperate attempt to gain traction.

2:28.

Just as I was about to give up, there was an imperceptible movement of my shoulders along the tile. Barely a millimeter, but movement. Emboldened, I tried to pick up the pace, but a ridge in the tile seemed to stop my movements.

2:29.

Stuck again. My shoulder blade wedged into a minuscule valley between tiles, but it may as well have been the Grand Canyon. The friction from my back was too great to overcome. I stopped to regroup. Just the small movement of my head had me close to exhaustion once again.

2:30.

2:31.

Maybe I was wrong. Maybe the steam generator really did break.

A heavy clunk sounded as the solenoid closed once again, and the roar of the steam filled the room. In moments, the thick, evil cloud re-enveloped me.

Oh, my Lord, not again.

Beads of water immediately formed on my skin. It was because of this, that the contact of my back and the tile became slightly lubricated. In a panic, I tried to drag my head across the tile one more time.

Like the sneeze that starts an avalanche, I felt my body begin to topple.

Up to that point, my only concern was with moving. I rapidly realized that I had no plan as to where that movement would take me. As I slid down like a pile of oranges at the supermarket when you remove one from the bottom, my still-useless legs twisted with the rest of my body and dropped onto the lower bench. The rest of me followed, and as the top half of me picked up momentum, it cascaded over the legs like a giant slinky, and I ended up in a heap on the middle of the steam room floor.

I still couldn't move. I had hoped to at least make it to the door, but there was no gravity to help me anymore. So close.

In all the commotion, I hadn't noticed where my hip had landed: on the drain.

The cold, life-giving waters began backing up, filling the low depression where the drain set. The water level rose about three inches before spilling out the steam room door, but it was enough. The cold water running from the hose and pooling up along my side was just enough to offset the steam, which wasn't as hot near the floor anyway. I found I could turn my head and drink fresh water.

I was going to make it.

It took another 45 minutes before I was able to get enough movement in my arms and legs to drag myself out. I might have been able to sooner, but I was deathly afraid that if I moved my butt off the drain, the water would disappear and I wouldn't be able to plug it up again.

As I pulled myself out of the door, into the shower room, I drew in my first breath of dry air in what seemed to be an eternity. I lay on my back, letting the coolness of the floor tiles seep deep into my flesh.

And I slept.

Chapter 14

My experience at the Reno Police Department was somewhat less than satisfying. For some reason, the overworked officer assigned to hear my complaint was decidedly lacking in sympathy to my story. His lack of sympathy appeared to be in direct proportion to my lack of credibility.

"Lemme get this straight. You say a guy, a janitor down at Sports West, drugged you with some exotic nerve agent, slipped you into the steam room, and rigged the steam to go on and stay on, with the direct intention of killing you?"

"That's correct officer."

"So why would a janitor want to do you in?"

"Well, he wasn't really a janitor..."

"Oh, I see. So you are changing your story?"

"No... I mean, yes. What I mean is I think he was just posing as a janitor...cleaning guy... maintenance man, whatever."

"So if he wasn't a janitor-slash-cleaning guy-slash-maintenance man-slash-whatever, then just who was he?"

"Well, I don't know. But I think he does this for a living."

"Wait, you just told me that he wasn't a janitor-slash-cleaning..."

"No! Wait! Not that for a living. I mean, I think that... he... kills...people." I knew it sounded weak as soon as the words began to tumble out.

"I...see." I could tell he didn't see at all. "So you believe that this chap was a professional hit-man?"

"Yes. Yes, I do."

"And now for the 64,000 dollar question. Why would this professional assassin, with, if you are to be believed, worldwide connections with counter intelligence agencies"...I had mentioned his comment about the Mossad earlier... "want to do you in? You mess up the forecast for some Mafioso daughter's outdoor wedding?" He thought this last line extremely clever.

"As I said, I don't know."

"Mr. O'Brien. You have placed me in a very uncomfortable position. If your story is to believed, then there has to be a good reason why someone would go to the obvious expense and trouble to permanently end your career. In my experience, professional hits happen between parties who are *both* treading on the wrong side of the law. If this story you have told me is the truth, then either 1: you don't *know* the reason behind it, which is very unlikely, or else 2: you won't *tell me* the reason behind it, because you might not be the Polly Pureheart that you pretend to be.

"Of course, there is another explanation," he went on, building up momentum. "When I interviewed the attendant who found you, passed out on the bathroom floor, he told me there was," he checked his notebook, "an 'unmistakable odor of alcohol' on you. He also said that other members in the past had rigged up the steam room to make it hotter in there, because they thought the temperature never went high enough."

This was true. Most of the time, for those who wanted it a bit more intense, a wet paper towel was wrapped around the thermostat, which insulated it somewhat from the steam, allowing the temperature to get up into the 120's. Management frowned upon it, but usually turned the other way.

"He thinks you are one of those guys who likes it hot. So here's what I think. I know how you TV guys are. A quick stop at the bar at Famous Murphy's or some other joint after the show, a little hair of the dog before showing up at the club, combined with a dose of steam, and bam, you're out cold. Now, it wouldn't look too good for a big shot TV celebrity like yourself... family man, churchgoer, all that... if it got out that you were having problems with the bottle. Especially after your little mishap last week up on the mountain. What would the public say? So, the quick thinker that you are... all you TV guys are fast on your feet, aren't you?... you come up with this Looney Tunes story that just might pull your fat out of the fire."

I wished he had used a different cliché, all things considered.

He continued. "So you want my honest opinion?" I didn't, but telling him that probably wouldn't have scored me any additional points. "Get yourself some help. Check into a program somewhere. Ya got a nice wife and kids out there who are worried sick. They've got a long haul ahead of them. Don't put them through any more."

I was beginning to suspect that he perhaps wasn't my biggest fan. In any event, I was also beginning to see that it was unlikely Reno's finest were going to drop everything to search for my assailant. In all fairness, I wouldn't have believed me either.

I sighed deeply, slowly rose to my feet, and shuffled out the door. Lauren and the kids were waiting for me out in the precinct room. *Don't put them through any more.* If I only knew how.

Lauren was trying to be tough. But how does one react when for the second time in a week, one is called and told her husband has landed in the hospital? Especially when she was awakened at 5:30 in the morning, expecting to find the subject of that phone call asleep in bed next to her? And then how does one react when one finds out they weren't accidents, after all?

The kids thought it was a great adventure. As soon as they saw that there were no obvious signs of injury, apart from a ruddier-than-usual appearance, they got caught up in the fun of being in a real live police station.

At least my stay in the hospital was a short one. Apart from sore kidneys and a screaming headache, the doctors didn't seem to have any reason to admit me. Ironically, my sore muscles actually felt better. Terrific therapy. Highly recommended.

Most of the evening was spent in relative silence between Lauren and me. I needed time, and she knew it.

Lauren. Rock steady Lauren. She was the perfect compliment to my little eccentricities. In the past, whenever we were faced with a crisis of some sort, she was the one who maintained a calm manner, with a rational and thoughtful approach that often offset my more emotional one. All this without losing a playful side that could always make me smile. We were a good team. She was the Bud Abbott to my Lou Costello. And I needed her strength now. But how could I expect that kind of strength from anyone?

When the kids were finally put down for the night, I knew it was time to talk. I just didn't know what to say.

"They didn't believe me. They think I'm trying to hide a drinking problem, or else I am mixed up in something illegal. They think I am hiding something from them." I stopped. For a moment, I was afraid that Lauren might be entertaining some of the same thoughts. I knew her better than anybody on the face of the earth, and we enjoyed that rare sense of telepathy that only comes with the joining of two souls that trust each other implicitly. But we were on unexplored grounds here. I couldn't read her eyes.

"Babe..." I went on, almost pleading, "I really don't know what's happening. I want you to know that I am not mixed up in anything shady...."

"You listen to me, mister. If you think for one moment that *I* thought for one moment that you were caught up in something illegal, you've got another thing coming. For heaven's sake, you're a choirboy. You haven't got it in you. Give me some credit." There was a familiar spark of fire in her eyes now.

"I…I'm sorry. It's just… I don't know. I don't even know what to believe anymore. Why is this happening to me? This doesn't happen to normal people. I mean, I wouldn't have believed that cock and bull story I gave to the cops. Why should I expect them to? For that matter, why should I expect *you* to?"

Her eyes softened. "Because you've never lied to me before, and you're too old to change." In the midst of all that had happened, she still allowed a small smile at the use of "old."

"There has to be a reason for all this," I said. "Maybe it's some crazy stalker, getting his kicks trying to make a name for himself." I discounted that as soon as I said it. "But the problem with that idea is he didn't *seem* crazy. He knew what he was doing every step of the way." I thought for a moment. "Even on the hill coming down from Virginia City."

Lauren's eyes widened. "So you think that was him, too?"

"It had to be. And if not him, then somebody working with him."

"I know this is grasping at straws, but you don't think that one of the other TV stations…?"

I almost laughed in spite of the situation. "Trying to gain the upper hand by bumping off the competition? No, I can't flatter myself that much. And besides, while it's a cutthroat business, it isn't *that* cutthroat. No, it has to be something I… we… haven't thought of."

"Greg," she said abruptly, "Let's leave. Pack up and go." Her voice, usually so calm and assured, began to crack. "Nothing is worth this. You can work somewhere else. Please."

I had already given some thought to this. I couldn't leave. I couldn't run. It had nothing to do with a misplaced sense of machismo, or of honor, or least of all of bravery. Quite simply, it wouldn't help. "This guy is a hunter. A professional hunter. He must have spent weeks trailing me and learning what my habits are. Look at where he tried. On the road: I ride there regularly. At the club: I'm always in the steam room. He learned all about me. And there's one thing more. For some strange reason, he wants it to look like an accident. On the road, he could have just as easily shot me. The steam room…why go to the bother of setting up such an elaborate way of doing me in? If I leave, it will be like flushing a rabbit out of its hole. Away from here, where I'm not on my home turf, I might just make the job easier for him.

"But there's more. If I run now, I'll always be looking over my shoulder.

Always wondering if the friendly person who is filling up my car with gas is really slipping a grenade in the tank. Hon, we'll be prisoners. A life sentence. I can't do that to my family. It's no way to live."

Now I had to face the hard part. "But as for you and the kids…"

"No, way. No way, no how. I am not leaving you." She wasn't having any of it.

"Sweetheart, please. I'm worried about you."

"And you don't think I'm worried about you? Forget it. 'For better or worse….' I meant it then, I mean it now."

I had the good sense not to finish for her, "Till death do us part."

I knew that I wasn't going to get very far. So far, the Aussie wasn't showing any signs of threatening my family. But how could I be sure that wouldn't change? I would have to come back to this topic again, I knew. For now, I gave it a rest.

Lauren wanted to hire a bodyguard. I resisted, but said I would look for one. In the meantime, I would stay out of places where I might get caught alone. And when I did go out somewhere, I would bring a friend. A big friend. Like Kurt Breeder, my ex-Canadian Football League buddy from church.

Thanksgiving came and went without any more attempts to shorten the life span of Meteorologist Greg O'Brien. Something to be thankful for. But there were two very disconcerting events that kept me from overflowing with the holiday spirit.

The first was my inability to get a hold of Chuck Murphy. I called his apartment several times, always getting his answering machine. I didn't think too much of it, since he had been tough to get a hold of in the past. But I also noticed that he wasn't on the air during his regular time slot. I called the station, pretending to be a listener, and asked when Chuck would be back on the air. The new receptionist…I don't know what happened to Missy…told me coldly that Chuck was on a leave of absence, and she didn't know when he would be back on the air. *Leave of absence?* There's no such thing in our business. Either you are on the air, or on vacation, or you're out of work. They don't give sabbaticals in broadcasting.

I swung by Chuck's apartment several times. Each time I found it as before, door locked and lights out. I also noticed his mailbox was overflowing. Wherever he was, he hadn't been there in a while.

I thought back to his cryptic message to me. What was it he said… "I've figured it out." Brother, if there ever was a time I needed something figured out, it was now. The odds were still that it had nothing to do with my situation, but the short hairs on the back of my neck stood up as I recalled the tension in his voice. And now he was gone.

But where? Vacation? Not likely. The station would have said so. There would be no reason to lie about that. Off on one of his crazy conspiracy investigations? Doubtful. In the past, he always told me about those, and he never was gone for more than a couple of days. Usually to hike out to one of the mountain peaks overlooking Area 51, an alleged top-secret military base in Southern Nevada, which is rumored to contain everything from super stealth technology projects to frozen alien cadavers. He'd be back by now.

Hiding? On the run? I remembered the strain in his voice. Whatever he thought he had, he believed it to be real, and he believed it to be big. For the first time since I'd known him, I began to think that Chuck might have really stumbled upon something.

It's amazing how a simple thing like a couple of attempts on your life by a trained assassin can change your perspective.

The second unnerving event occurred when I tried to do a little investigative work myself. Figuring the police weren't likely to knock themselves out on my behalf, I called the Highway Patrol to see if they had made any progress in locating the mysterious "motorcycle man."

"What motorcyclist?" came the unenthusiastic reply.

"It should be in your report. Your man interviewed me in the hospital, and he seemed interested in following up on locating him."

"Our man? Let me check." I listened to the background sounds of radio chatter and typewriters clacking for about 5 minutes. When he returned, my impatience was only outweighed by a growing sense of unease.

"Sir, I'm sorry. I do see here in this report that when you were interviewed at the scene, you made mention of a motorcyclist who might be a witness, but no one has followed up on that."

My hackles began to rise. "Wait a minute. I want to make sure I understand you. You didn't send an officer to my hospital room?"

"No, I don't believe so. What was the officer's name?"

"I don't know. He showed some sort of identification, but I didn't pay attention."

"Well, I just talked to the officer who made out the original report. He said you made mention of another fellow on the road driving a motorcycle, and he has that in his report. But since this wasn't a criminal matter, no follow-up has occurred. We sure didn't send anybody to the hospital."

"What about Reno P. D.? Or Washoe County Sheriffs?"

"You'd have to ask them, sir, but I can't see why they would. This was in our jurisdiction, and we haven't made any requests for assistance."

I thanked him and let the phone slip back onto its cradle. It threw an uncomfortable wrench into the mix. Up to this point, the only advantage I felt I had was that at least I knew what he looked like. OK, not exactly the Wall of China in terms of defense, but at least it was something. Now I had to consider the distinct possibility... no... *probability*...that the Aussie wasn't working alone. He had a partner. Maybe more that I hadn't seen. It was enough to depress a fellow.

It was also enough to make a guy paranoid.

During that period of time, I don't imagine that my performance on television was anything that would win me an Emmy. Being relaxed in front of the camera is critical to getting people to watch you. If you're relaxed, the viewers are relaxed. If you are tense, the folks at home are tense as well. The way I must have appeared, I suspect the gastric specialists' caseload of ulcers in the Truckee Meadows must have taken a sizable leap.

It did make for some interesting television at times, though. On the Tuesday after Thanksgiving, I was standing in front of the camera, right in the middle of performing the somewhat mindless task of reading off some of the forecast temperatures around the state. Since I can do this without tying up too much of my limited gray matter, my mind inevitably began to wander toward thinking about all the unpleasant surprises the Aussie and his minions might have waiting for me around the next corner. One of the overhead studio lights had the bad graces to pick that exact time to burn out and explode, resulting in a loud popping noise. This was not a rare experience, and the usual reaction when it did occur was a sudden jump on the part of the unfortunate anchor that happened to have a camera trained on him or her.

In this case, the viewing audience was treated to the sight and sound of Northern Nevada's Most Popular Weatherman immediately dropping from view, concurrent with a piercing cry of alarm, followed by about 15 seconds of silence until the floor camera operator could convince Northern Nevada's Most Popular Weatherman that he was trying to take cover from a light bulb.

It was not a good week.

Chapter 15

* * * * * * * * * * *

Chance Dunleavy turned down the volume on his phonograph. The phone's ringing was interfering with the Brandenburg Concerto. He picked up the receiver.

"Mr. Dunleavy."

"Oy, gidday Mr. Carillo. How are you this morning?"

"I would be much better if I didn't possess an irritating notion that I was wasting my money employing your services."

"Ahhh, c'mon, Jorge. I know you think that time is money, but don't get your knickers in a knot. You put some very specific requirements on this job, and that means planning. Planning takes time…"

"It seems to me that all your 'planning' has resulted in is a lot of bumps and bruises to the object of our attention, without a satisfactory conclusion. Those 'requirements' were meant to avoid any undue official attention being directed our way. Now I hear he has been to the police with a description of you."

Dunleavy chuckled. "Oy wouldn't worry too much about that, Jorge. Oy took some precautions to make it look like he had a nip too many. Would 'a worked too, but how was Oy supposed to know the bloody machine was timed to go off in the middle of the night? But anyway, the coppers think that O'Brien must be havin' a bit of the battle with the bottle and that he made the whole thing up. And as for giving them a description…" He grinned as he stroked the fair skin on his freshly shaven head, leaving him as bald as a bandicoot. "If they ever do look for anybody, they'll be looking for a dark complexioned chap with a full 'ead of 'air."

Jorge Carillo sighed. "I do hope you are accurate, Mr. Dunleavy. I needn't remind you that I am not the only one who is concerned with this operation. Some of my friends aren't as patient as I."

Now it was Chance Dunleavy's turn to sigh. "Oy'm sure your friends understand that a rushed job means a botched job, and a botched job can leave a trail. We don't want any trails, do we? Let's not sacrifice quality for quantity."

There was a moment of silence. "Speaking of quantity," Carillo finally spoke. "It appears that the balance sheet on the value of our esteemed General Manager has begun to sink into the red. Someone broke into the station last week. I'm not sure what, if anything, was missing, but who knows what might have been copied. It appears that Mr. Richards has failed again to provide the necessary security that our operation demands. That's two failures in less than a month. I am afraid that I have never become enamored with the rules of this country's national pastime. In my book, two strikes and you're out. I think it's time we offer Mr. Richards early retirement."

Dunleavy had to laugh. It was the closest thing to a joke he'd heard out of the normally humorless Carillo. "Sure thing, boss. And just to show you my heart's in the right place, this one's on the house."

"Let's hope you have better luck than with O'Brien."

The line went dead.

Dunleavy allowed a mirthless smile. "Richard's will be easy," he thought. "Picked before he was ripe, that one was. Has all kinds of habits that Oy can take advantage of. Take no more than a week. Then Oy can get back to work on O'Brien…

"O'Brien," he murmured to himself. "Kind of a pity about him. Sort of a fair dinkum fella." But now he'd become a rock in Dunleavy's boots. Missed twice. "*Twice*, for crimony's sake. That hasn't ever happened before.

"Well, third time's the charm."

* * * * * * * * * * *

Sometimes in my line of business, you hear about so much tragedy and destruction that it ceases to affect you. It was because of this that I almost missed it. I was sitting in the studio during the broadcast of the 6:30 news, typing in the current temperature, wind speed, and other weather conditions when Mark Dudding read the following story, accompanied by dramatic pictures of a house in flames.

"Police and fire officials have now released the identity of the man killed in last night's three alarm blaze in Southwest Reno. Steve Richards, General Manager at KOPP-FM radio here in Reno, died in the inferno that reduced his home on Lakeside Drive to ashes. Because of the condition of the body, forensic officials had to use dental records in order to make a positive identification. There were no others in the house at the time of the fire.

"Fire investigators now say they believe the fire was caused when Richards fell asleep while smoking in bed.

"The coroner's office is conducting tests to see if alcohol or drugs were a factor."

Sue Ann Stevens took over. "Chief Phil Walker of the Reno Fire Department says this tragedy points out the need to once again review some simple, but essential fire safety rules. KRGX reporter Mike Kneeland is standing by live with the Chief to explain. Mike…"

I didn't hear any more. Didn't need to. Didn't want to. Although I'd never remotely liked Steve Richards, his death still shook me to the core. An "accident." There were coincidences and there were coincidences. As of late, I ceased believing in them.

As I sat in stunned silence, my mind reeled in its efforts to make some sense of it all. It was bad enough trying to account for the attempts on my life. Then Chuck disappeared. Now this.

The answer still wasn't known. But at least now there in the mist appeared a hazy connection.

KOPP.

I still didn't have the vaguest idea what it all had to do with me, or where the Aussie fit into all this. I certainly didn't have anything I could go to the cops with. Not that they'd listen to me anyway, after the last time. It was like one of those connect-the-dots puzzles. I had just enough to begin to form the outline of a hand.

But I had no idea what the hand was attached to. Or if, instead of a hand, it was really a claw. Or what the head looked like. I just hoped I could stay breathing long enough to connect a few more dots.

As time went on, the dots stayed unconnected. The next several days passed uneventfully. Boring, really, to the idle observer. I never thought boring could be so beautiful. Even though I had developed a habit of walking backwards nearly as often as forwards, watching my 6 o'clock, as the navy pilots say, nothing untoward happened to me. I even began to fantasize that the murder…and I was sure it was a murder, the Fire Marshal notwithstanding…of Steve Richards might have been a sign that whatever dark forces were behind all this might be cutting their losses and leaving me alone. I became so bold as to quit making excuses to avoid some of my outside activities. I started giving school talks again. I appeared at a Rotary Club luncheon. Not once was there a sign of the Aussie. For the first time in nearly a month, I could begin to think of something else other than how I would like my remains handled. I was still as in the dark about the origin of the attacks as I was before. But seeing as how curiosity killed the cat, an unsolved mystery was a small price to pay.

I finally came to the conclusion: It's over. Whatever it was, it's over.

The first snow of the season continued to fall outside our window as Lauren and I huddled under an afghan on the couch. We had even gone so far as to start up our foot rubs again. Sort of our version of whistling past the graveyard.

"Do you really think it's safe?" Lauren asked, when I told her of my plans for the next morning.

"I think so, sweetheart. I am tired of feeling like a prisoner in my own home. All I want is for our lives to return to normal. Maybe it's time to test the waters. Get out and do something useful."

Lauren tensed at the thought. "Not yet, hon. It's too soon."

I considered this. "It will always be too soon. But I have to start somewhere. I have been signed up to go work the Dawn Donut Patrol for weeks now. I can't keep giving excuses. It's not fair."

"Are you going to go alone?"

I wasn't *that* convinced. "No, I thought I'd take Kurt Breeder along."

The lines of tension in her forehead began to lessen a bit. "Kurt... isn't he that...."

"Big guy, that's right." I smiled in spite of myself. Although I wouldn't have admitted it, a lot of my boldness was sown in that giant football player. "Honestly, would you bother somebody if they had a friend like him? Nobody would dare!"

Another blown forecast.

Chapter 16

As described at the beginning of this little epiphany, the trip down to the river on behalf of the Dawn Donut Patrol didn't exactly turn out the way I would have preferred. As I leaned up against the counter at the hospital's pharmacy waiting for my prescription of Tylenol and codeine to be filled, I tried to get rid of the last of the hypothermic shakes from my untimely dip into the Truckee River. Fortunately for me, Kurt Breeder had an extra pair of well-worn but dry work clothes stashed in his trunk. I also tried to reassess my situation.

My father once told me that it was a good idea, whenever faced with a challenge, to stop and evaluate the positives and negatives of any situation, in order to approach it more rationally. Apart from the fact that I was getting to be on a first name basis with the emergency room personnel all across the valley, there were few silver linings in the snow clouds that had settled into the valley that cold December morning. But with a bit of an effort, I managed to find a few bright spots.

Although very unsightly to look at, and tender to the touch, my shinbone somehow miraculously escaped being fractured. Apparently, the pipe had caught enough of the outside front area of my foreleg so that my bicycle-toughened muscles were able to absorb some of the blow. I gingerly touched the welt, and found a furrow had been carved into the muscle. It would be a long while before I would be winning any "best legs" contests.

The knife wound, if you could even call it that, turned out to be so small as to only require a Band-Aid and a tetanus shot.

But perhaps the brightest spot was simply that I was still alive. Might not be next week, but at that point I was beginning to develop a philosophy which states any day above ground is a good day.

Of course, all this was weighed against the fact that:

I had a homicidal maniac trying to kill me.

My body had been through more in the last few weeks than a professional wrestler would have endured in a year, even if it were real.

And I still had no idea what this was all about.

Pretty hard to tip the balances to the positive side. But somehow I managed to.

It was optimism stretched to an unrealistic level, I suppose. Much like the story I'd heard years ago about an old man who lived in a desert region in Africa, who was known throughout the villages for always being able to find the positive in every situation. Resolved to prove him wrong, a witch doctor from his village, who had developed a sour outlook on life, took him out into the desert. A crowd followed, much to the delight of the cranky old pessimist. He led the group to a rotting and decaying carcass of a wildebeest killed by a pride of lions and now left to the flies and the occasional hyena.

"So, old man," the Witch Doctor said, "tell me how there can be any good in the pain and suffering of this creature before you."

"He has fed the pride, and the hyenas, and even the flies," the old man answered.

"That's all well and good for them," the pessimist said, "but how can you say anything positive on behalf of the wildebeest. Look at him, his flesh is in tatters and rotting, his bones broken, and his blood spilled. He is a gruesome sight," he finished triumphantly.

"Ah," the old man replied. "That may be so. But look at how white his teeth are."

I'm not sure if I ever understood that story before, but I resolved to never take that next breath of air for granted.

All misplaced euphoria aside, as Kurt drove me home, I thought about the apparent change in tactics by the Aussie. This time, it would have never been ruled an accident. But was it a change after all? How would any competent investigating officer have viewed this? Even though it would never have been viewed as an act of God, or an act of negligence, like my other mishaps, life among the homeless is filled with peril. Muggings along the banks of the river are quite commonplace. It inevitably would have been written off as me stumbling into a bad situation and getting rolled for the money that was on me, all $14.36 of it. It certainly wouldn't have them looking for any deeper motive behind the crime. And if what I thought of the abilities of the Aussie was even close to being accurate, it would be way too much to think he would ever be tracked down. It looked like business as usual.

During the ride home, I gave Kurt a brief synopsis of my adventures during the last month. He was, as I expected, quite sympathetic to my situation. But in all honesty, this was a little out of his league as well.

"Why don't you just go to the cops, Greg?" he asked.

I explained that I had tried that, and didn't get too far.

"Are you going to try again? I mean, I can be a witness for this morning."

"A witness to what? What did you see?"

"Well… I saw you floating down the river…" He let the words trail off.

"You see what I mean?" I asked. "As far as they are concerned, I probably just fell in. All that proves is I was either clumsy or inebriated."

"But the knife! What about the knife?"

"What about it? Doesn't prove anything. Especially if it didn't really do me any harm. After the reception I got a couple of weeks ago, they probably just think I am trying to pull a publicity stunt or something. Of course, if the knife had found its way buried to the hilt all the way into my rib cage, then they might have found that more convincing…."

"Yeah… too bad about that." Bless his heart; he said it without any guile.

"Thanks for the thought, Kurt."

"But dang it, Greg, I know you didn't just fall in the river. You would think you could get someone interested in your case down there. I mean, what's the matter with cops these days?"

"You can't blame them for this one, Kurt. Put yourself in their shoes. Everything that has happened to me so far could easily be explained away by something other than a hit man out on my trail. That's the beauty of this guy. He is always one step ahead of the game, so if anything goes wrong, I've got nowhere to turn to for help."

"Yeah you do." His normally cheerful, happy-go-lucky face had taken on a seriousness that I hadn't seen since that night after his first Al-Anon meeting. For all of his apparent simple-mindedness, when he made a decision that was important, there was no one more tenacious. Must have come from eating quarterbacks for breakfast.

"Hey buddy, I appreciate the offer. But this guy doesn't play by the Marquis de Queensbury Rules, you know. You've got a wife and kids to think about."

"Oh, and I suppose you don't?"

I couldn't argue with that. "OK, OK. I appreciate the help." And I did.

The rest of the trip was spent in companionable silence, each of us left to our own thoughts. "Are you sure you don't want me to go inside with you to check out the house?" Kurt asked as he dropped me off. He was already getting into this bodyguard thing.

"Thanks for the offer, pal, but I don't think there's any reason to worry for a bit. He always takes a while to plan his next move. Shoot, he probably still thinks that I'm feeding the fish down river." Besides, I needed some time alone with Lauren.

Kurt didn't sound too convinced. "OK," he finally conceded. "I'll come by tomorrow and take you to work, if you want."

"I'll give you a call."

As it turned out, I wouldn't need my friend's services.

As I limped up to the door, I tried to think of what I was going to say to Lauren. In a way, I was almost more afraid of what the news of that morning would do to her than of what it almost did to me. Maybe she was right. Maybe we should just pack up, pull up stakes, and try to hide. I knew, after what happened, the subject would come up again.

At least, if the past were any indication, we would have a little breathing room. I wondered how long it would be before the Aussie tried again.

I walked into the side door of the house and into our great room. Lauren was seated on the couch, and immediately I knew something was wrong. Her shoulders were hunched forward, hands clasped tightly together, and when she looked up at me as I came in, I could see the strain on her face. "Greg…" she began haltingly.

"Honey, what is it?"

She didn't say anything, only turned slowly and focused her attention across the room.

So intense was my concern for her, I hadn't noticed the man who was in the room with her, seated comfortably in a recliner chair, legs crossed and fingers steepled under his chin.

"Mr. O'Brien," the man said evenly. "It's good to see you up and about."

That voice. It was familiar. So was the face. It took a moment or two for me to remember where I had seen him before.

The hospital. In my room. The phony inspector.

One of the Aussie's boys.

Chapter 17

I was already in somewhat of a foul mood. I guess it had been building up for a while. In the past month, I had been run off a mountain road, steam-cooked, shish-kabobbed, nearly drowned, been made to look like a fool (not that that was ever exceedingly hard to do), and had lost a pretty nifty radio gig. To top it all off, it now appeared that my family was being dragged into the fray. So I hoped I could be excused for taking a "shoot now, ask questions later" approach to the situation as it presented itself.

Without waiting to ponder the implications, I launched myself at the man while still halfway across the room. I don't know if the fierce cry from my lips, which filled the room, was a result of inexpressible rage, or intense pain from my still wobbly leg, but at the time, it didn't matter. I had met the enemy, and he was in my easy chair.

Although I had no doubt this guy was more experienced at this than I was, my unexpected charge did place the element of surprise on my side. As Lauren cried out in alarm, my body became an airborne battering ram, which found its mark just above the stranger's solar plexus, sending the chair toppling over backwards. Our bodies came crashing down in a tangled pile of arms and legs, coming to an ungainly and short-lived rest under the dining room table.

Having the wind knocked out of the man gave me a few precious seconds to regroup. I clambered on top, rising up quickly to gain leverage, in an effort to try and get an effective swing at him. In theory, a good plan. Until one realizes we were still under the dining room table. My head smashed into the solid oak table bottom, sending a meteor shower of stars through my field of vision.

I'll say this for him...he bounced back quickly. While I shook my head to clear it, the man managed to leverage his elbow under my ribcage and push, sending a wave of nausea surging through my gut. He then followed with a short jab to the chin, which popped my head up into the table once again. I began to hate that table.

Lesser men would have quit right there. And I would have, if the image of Lauren's fear-stricken face weren't burned into my mind's eye. I was no longer fighting for myself. This was our turf, our sanctuary.

I was like the black swan that used to make its home at a pond in Eugene where Lauren and I used to live. Whenever anyone or anything would approach the nest where its mate sat covering their brood, that bird would charge, hissing and spitting with its wings outstretched with such an intensity that it would drive away even the largest and most aggressive challenger. I once saw it drive away a pair of rottweillers which had wandered into the park. Although physically it was no match, the swan had motivation on its side.

And so did I.

His next two short jabs to my chin seemed to have a little less behind them as the man fought to regain lost oxygen from my initial charge. The third shot, still coming in quick succession, I managed to parry with my forearm. I countered with a short roundhouse, which missed its mark and glanced off the crown of his forehead. I think it did more damage to my hand than it did to his head, but at that point, I was nearly immune to the pain. I was also immune to Lauren's cries for me to stop. She didn't understand. This man was here to finish what the Aussie started, and she and the kids were in danger as well. I blocked out her cries and looked for a weapon, any weapon, I could use.

In the tumult, we had somehow managed to roll out from under the dining room table. "Wait…listen…" the man tried to croak out, but my initial attack had taken enough of his breath away that speech was nearly impossible— not that I would have listened anyway. If there was one thing I had learned from the Aussie, it was that words could sometimes just be a distraction.

The stranger, wiry, quick and agile, tried to disentangle himself from me and get a little room to maneuver. It was a move I knew, if successful, would be my downfall. He knew what he was doing in a fight. I hadn't traded fisticuffs since Will Parker split my lip open in the seventh grade.

I managed to lock my legs around him, which both kept him from getting away and shortened his punches enough so they caused little permanent damage. But at the same time, my feeble attempts at inflicting any harm to his well-conditioned frame were almost laughable. I might be prolonging the inevitable, but inevitable it was.

A shot to the eye. A quick hook to the ribs. With each successive punch he landed, I could feel my already low reserves dwindling. I could feel the grip of my legs weakening.

"Greg!" Lauren cried out again. "Stop!"

She didn't understand.

My opponent managed to wiggle out just enough to get his legs underneath him, and I knew I was out of time. I looked again frantically for a weapon to use. Finding none, I realized that while he had strength, speed, ability and health on me, I did have one thing on him.

About 40 pounds.

As he rose to finish me off, instead of trying to hold him down, as I had been the whole time, I suddenly reversed directions. Fueled by a rage that would have made that black swan proud, I thrust up under him, lifted him up on my shoulders, arched my back, and in my best Hulk Hogan fashion, turned over and drove him into the floor.

I didn't give him a chance to recover. Stunned by the body slam, he could only offer faint resistance at first as I wrapped my hands around his throat and tried to cut off his air supply. Squeeze. Just squeeze.

For the first time in my life, I was ready to end another man's. I had never served in the military, where I suppose they teach you about that kind of thing. I had been conscripted into my own war, and there could be no truce. But the horror of what I was doing hammered at me as persistently as Lauren's confused cries. Tears began to flow from my eyes as I felt the man weaken further inside my grip. But I had come too far to stop now. They brought the battle to me.

His leg shifted beneath me in what I assumed was a feeble attempt to gain some leverage, but he had nowhere to go. I watched as the strength in his eyes began to fade. My hands began to shake. I didn't know if I could do this, even with all that was on the line.

A loud click and the sharp pain of the barrel of a Colt 38 revolver being shoved into the base of my sternum made my deliberations moot. He had pulled the gun out of an ankle holster, and as weak as he was, I still had no doubt that his finger pressing down on the trigger would end my life in far less time than any further attempt on my part to end his.

I was frozen in indecision. We stared at one another. Then in a hoarse voice, he haltingly whispered, "If you would… kindly… relax your grip… it would save me the unpleasantness…of having to shoot you."

Defeated and resigned to my fate, I slowly released his throat and slid off him. I looked at Lauren, who was frozen in fear and uncertainty. Dear Lauren, I'm so sorry. I couldn't protect you or myself.

I turned back to the stranger, who was slowly getting into a seated position. "So what will it be this time…another accident?" I asked him.

The man raised one eyebrow. "Accident? I don't think you understand."

"Understand what?"

The man gently lowered the hammer on the revolver. "I'm one of the good guys."

Chapter 18

Lauren gently placed an ice pack over my nearly swollen shut right eye, which had taken quite a peppering from the stranger's jabs. "I don't suppose you could have told me any of this before you used my face as a speed bag?"

The man looked at me with irony and winced as he shifted uneasily in the easy chair, once again turned upright. "Have *you* ever tried to talk after receiving a cannon ball in your chest? If you could have stopped your bombast for just one moment and asked, I would have been glad to enlighten you. I'm just glad *I* had the gun." He massaged the welt on the side of his forehead. "By the way, you aren't bad at wrestling, but you need some help with that right cross. You're going to break a knuckle if you keep trying to hit that way. It's a good thing for me you don't know how to throw a punch."

I sighed deeply, pressed back into the couch, and closed my eyes. "I'm a lover, not a fighter."

Lauren nearly choked on that, caught in that maddening state of being unsure whether to laugh or cry, and wanting to do both. It wasn't the only time that hour when she had been rocked with uncertainty. "I didn't know what to do. One minute he's telling me he's here to help us, and the next you come in and you're trying to kill him. I wasn't sure whether to stop you or to help you. I didn't know he was the one who interviewed you in the hospital room."

"Yeah, well, sorry about that," the stranger commented. "I had to know how close you were getting to the organization."

"If you had been straight with me from the start, it might have saved us both a lot of discomfort," I added unnecessarily.

"I'm afraid in my line of work, lack of candor becomes an occupational hazard."

I allowed the ice to sink deep into my bruises while he told us his story. It was a long story. We had plenty of time.

His name was Bryce Hudson. 41 years old, 170 pounds solidly built around a 5 foot, 10 inch frame, and formerly employed by Uncle Sam as a special agent with the Drug Enforcement Administration. I say formerly because he no longer drew a salary at the taxpayer's expense.

Coming from a family that had a long history in law enforcement, Hudson always figured he would follow in his father's footsteps and become a beat cop in Detroit. But after attending the University of Michigan, he began to set his sights higher. Graduating Cum Laude in Criminology, Hudson had his pick of spots at various agencies, including the FBI, the State Department, and the Department of Alcohol, Tobacco and Firearms. But an experience with a college roommate in Ann Arbor changed the direction of his life.

"Rich Jenkins was my best friend, though we could hardly have been more different in upbringing or personality. He was real bright, the first one in his family to go to college, on a full ride yet, and he was also one of the nicest kids you could ever want to meet. Straight from a corn farm in Nebraska, Rich had spent most of his life sheltered from the more urban temptations that I had grown up with. When I first met him, I thought they had roomed me with Opie from Mayberry. The kid had never even gotten drunk before." He paused, and continued with regret in his voice. "Wasn't long before I changed that.

"As often happens when someone gets his first taste of the lifestyle, Rich kind of went off the deep end. He started becoming a real party animal. It was too much, too fast. From beer he went to hard liquor, then to smoking pot. He wanted to try it all. I started to get a little worried, but he just shrugged it off. He was having too much fun. Who cares that his grades began to suffer? He would get back to business after just one more party.

"One night I came back to the dorm room and found him staring at the ceiling, eyes bulging with terror, sweat pouring from his face. His breathing was shallow, and he was barely conscious. 'They're after my eyes! Keep them away!' he kept whispering, over and over again." Hudson had a faraway look in *his* eyes as he recalled the episode, and his voice took on an eerie, low monotone as he chanted the words. " 'My eyes… keep them away…' " Hudson paused a moment, then resumed. "I couldn't get any more out of him. After a while, he started clawing at his face, gouging at his eyes. It was all I could do to keep him from plucking them out. I got him to the hospital, but he never was the same after that. He dropped out of school later that month. He never came back.

"I found out later that someone had gotten him to try a mixture of angel dust and magic mushrooms. Whoever it was who gave him the stuff hauled him back to his room when he started to wig out. Never even bothered to check on him after that.

"It took me some time, but I found out later who it was that fed him that poison. Kid by the name of Jimmy Daniels. Son of a state senator. Rich wasn't the only poor sap that had gotten messed up by this creep. Apparently, he got his jollies by experimenting with different drug combinations, but would always check them out on others first, just in case there was a bad reaction like the one Rich had. A regular prince, this guy was. Anyhow, I went to the cops with what I found out. They were sympathetic, but couldn't just go and arrest him on what I had. Especially considering who his old man was. I finally talked them into letting me wear a wire."

He chuckled. "It was my first 'sting' operation. I cut my hair, put on some glasses, stuck a plastic pocket protector in my shirt, and weaseled my way into a little party he had at his apartment. There were a few more people there, including a freshman girl who couldn't have been much over 17 at the time. She was passed out in the corner when I got there. I wanted to blow the whistle right then, but he could have denied giving her anything.

"I told him I was an engineering student from Des Moines, and left no doubt that I was a world class nerd, and that I was desperate to lose that image. He looked at me like the wolf looked at Little Red Riding Hood. Putting his arm around me, like the caring big brother I never had, he started telling me that to be really 'cool,' I should learn how to party like a man. I said 'Groovy,' or some other dim-witted response that even back then was about 10 years out of date, and asked him what the stuff was. He wouldn't say exactly, but did us all a big favor by assuring me that it was from his own private reserve, and he usually sells it to people, but since I was his newest best friend, he was giving me some for free. The idiot even put his arm around my shoulder and leaned over and whispered it right into the microphone, which was under my collar.

"He gave me three pills, which turned out to be a peyote button, an LSD derivative, and some speed, the combination of which would have like as not killed me if I had actually taken it. I was able to palm the peyote and the speed, but he was looking right at me when he gave me the LSD, so I popped it in my mouth and slipped it under my tongue and pretended to wash it down with a shot of Mad Dog.

"I could slowly feel the pill beginning to dissolve. Have you ever really tried not to swallow? It's like trying to not think of pink elephants. Saliva was pouring into the back of my throat. He was staring at me, waiting to see what kind of reaction I was going to have. I was beginning to wonder what more the cops on the other end of the wire wanted to hear when the door came crashing in, and they took the place down. I spit out enough of the pill for a chemical analysis and tried washing out my mouth. I don't think I really swallowed any, but I still had a buzz that lasted all night.

"But it was all worth it just to see the look on that moron's face. Even with daddy's money and influence, he was sent away for a long time.

"I knew I had found my life's work."

Hudson sighed and leaned back and took a sip of the coffee that Lauren had provided. Always the perfect hostess, that one. For a minute I thought that his story was finished. He seemed unwilling to go any further.

"Um... so how did you end up here with a pistol stuck in my sternum?" I queried.

He smiled mirthlessly and held up his revolver. "This little ol' popgun? I just keep it for sentimental reasons. It was my first issue at the academy." He settled back and resumed his tale. But I sensed it was leading to something unpleasant.

"After I graduated from UM, I applied for and joined the D.E.A. That's the Drug Enforcement Administration."

"Thanks," I said. I already knew that, but I didn't want to seem like a know-it-all. I kept my mouth shut and listened to the rest of his story.

He rose pretty fast in the ranks, making Special Agent in record time. He started out by chasing shipping on the West Coast. Tough assignment, that one was. An awful lot of coastline between Mexico and Canada to cover, and drug smugglers had this nasty habit of neglecting to include illegal drugs on their manifests. After a couple of years on the docks, he busted up an operation running pot out of the National Forests in Oregon and Washington. Doesn't sound like much, but some of those guys could get pretty nasty. They would set up a few gardens out in the middle of nowhere, put together a solar-powered irrigation system, and leave it alone until it was time for the harvest. Nice and innocent. Just a bunch of hippies growing some weed for the folks back at home. Certainly nothing for the big bad DEA dudes to concern themselves about. But as soon as word got out that the THC content in Oregon marijuana was about a third higher than classic Aculpoco Gold, it started to get a little competitive. The hippies started to get organized.

And protective. Worried more about competitors than the cops, the pot farmers came up with some creative methods of booby-trapping their acreage. One of the first DEA agents to descend on one of the farms tripped a thin wire connected to a pipe bomb filled with buckshot and old razor blades. "He lost both legs. Would've died if the rest of us hadn't been there. Sort of explained why there were an unusually high number of reports of missing hikers and hunters in the area."

Hudson found out he was good in this kind of field operation. He spent three weeks camping out, with three other agents, waiting for the farmers to come and claim their harvest. When it appeared like the bust was likely going to be a bust, the other agents called it quits. But Hudson couldn't let go. Returning to the site on his own, he struck pay dirt. Four armed goons, who looked like they would be more comfortable in a biker bar than in the wilds, were in the process of threshing the last of the ten-foot-high plants when Hudson calmly strode up and informed them they would be detained at the pleasure of the United States Government. One of them made the mistake of arguing the point by reaching for his automatic rifle. A slug through the knee from the very same Colt 38 I had the pleasure of being introduced to convinced him and his friends that they might just want to be a bit more agreeable to Hudson's hospitality.

"Blasted foolish chance. The book says go for body shots, and don't stop at one. But there were four of them, and six rounds in my service revolver. If they had all decided to come at me at once, I never would have stopped them all with body shots, especially as big as they were. But a knee shot drops you right away, and there is nothing like the agonizing cry of pain of your buddy to put a damper on your enthusiasm.

"I learned then that the battle is usually won by crushing the enemy's morale, before crushing his army."

I gently touched the welt over my eye, wishing he had started on my morale first.

"Before long I was riding a desk in San Francisco. Agent-in-Charge of West Coast Operations. They told me I had a real future in the Agency. Might make a top spot in D.C. some day. But after a while, the office work started to get to me. I requested and got a transfer back into the field."

He paused for a moment, as if deciding how he was going to tell me the next part. I had time. I waited.

He sighed. "Actually, there was another reason for requesting the field transfer. My kid brother, Jeff.

"Jeff decided he wanted to be like big brother. After hearing all about my exploits in the service, Jeff applied for the DEA himself. He was six years younger but a lot brighter than I was, and got accepted easily. I decided that

I wanted to keep an eye on him.

"Although it went against Agency policy to have any members of the same family on the same field assignment, I managed to bend the rules a bit and get us both sent on a joint operation with the Colombian Drug Enforcement folks. We weren't allowed to participate in any substantive way because of international treaties, but were to act as observers only. In other words, we were about as useful as an udder on a bull. But it made the bureaucrats back in the home office feel good, and it gave the President some fodder when it came time for his spin doctors to say how much we were doing to get drugs off the streets.

"That's how we came to find ourselves in the middle of a remote field outside of a town called Tejada, about 40 kilometers from Cali."

Once again he stopped his story. His eyes bored through the floor, focusing on a small, ramshackle warehouse through an opening in a thick jungle forest, in the foothills of the Andes. Even though four years had passed, he was instantly transported back to a scene that he had unsuccessfully been trying to wipe from his dreams since. When he finally spoke again, it was without emotion. He'd walked this road too many times before.

"The building didn't look like much from the outside, pitted and rusted, like you could knock it down with a couple of well-placed whacks with a sledge hammer. Only one road in and out, with a crude airstrip off to the side, but we had a tip that it was a major processing plant for about 1,200 kilos of snow a month."

"Snow?" I said, trying to imagine snow in a rainforest.

"Cocaine," he snorted (no pun intended). "Drug of choice for a whole new generation."

"Oh, of course." I felt foolish. I'd led a pretty sheltered life, and besides, I tended to view snow in a different context. Occupational hazard.

"Jeff and I were accompanying a small strike force that the Colombians had put together. Looked like a slam-dunk. Only minimal firepower showing outside the warehouse. What we didn't know at the time is we'd been sold out.

"Someone high up within the Colombian government's drug agency was also on the payroll of the Cali Cartel. Whoever it was told the Cartel we were coming. When we made our move on the building, we found it nearly empty inside. While we were going in, they pulled a back door maneuver on us and came up on our rear. We never stood a chance."

Hudson took a deep breath. "They wiped out our strike force in less than a minute. They didn't even give us a chance to surrender. They just gunned them down. I thought that Jeff and I had bought it as well. We weren't even armed. Went against the rules, you know," he added bitterly. "But instead of gunning us down, they blindfolded us, tossed us in the back of a flatbed, and drove us to an abandoned warehouse in Tejeda. And that's where I met him."

He was silent. "Him?" I asked.

"The leader of the operation that wiped out our task force," he spat out. "One of the most ruthless members of the Cali Cartel. A man directly responsible for the deaths of hundreds of people, and indirectly untold thousands more. And the reason I am sitting here today."

He looked at me for the first time since he began his story. "His name is Jorge Carillo."

His eyes then looked past me. "He's also the man who killed my brother."

Chapter 19

Perhaps fearing that if he stopped he would never begin again, Hudson forged ahead with his story. Lauren and I listened on in silence.

"At first I couldn't figure out what Carillo wanted from us. The fact we were both still alive told me that he had some use for us, but I was in the dark as to what it might be. They took us separately into a small room and roughed us up, but never asked us any questions, not that we had anything to tell them that would have been much use for them. I would have expected with all the money he had he would have hired some goon to administer the beatings, but I was surprised that Carillo did all his own dirty work. He seemed to enjoy it. Some of the idle rich take to tennis, some to sailing. He apparently preferred strapping on leather gloves and working up a sweat by using us as human body bags. He certainly indulged himself with gusto when he tried to rearrange my features." I had wondered where he had gotten that scar tissue buildup around his eyes, wrongly assuming he had been a boxer at one time. It marred a face that was undoubtedly good-looking in days gone by. I supposed Lauren would have considered it "ruggedly handsome." Some guys have all the luck. On me, it would have made me look like a pug.

"After three days of this, three times a day, I found out what he was after. He had just finished a particularly aggressive work out, and then took the chair opposite me. He was sweating profusely, but seemed completely calm and unemotional. He fixed his gaze on me. His eyes were black and cold, almost lifeless. I could barely see him through the one eye that wasn't swollen shut. He just sat and stared at me for a couple of minutes before his inky voice spoke.

" 'Your country has committed an act of war on our country, Mr. Hudson.' I was surprised he even knew my name, but I realized he must have known someone on the inside. 'You are a spy, and as such, will be tried for espionage. The international community will rush to the United Nations and call for an end to this subterfuge. As for you and your brother, you will be shot at dawn. That is, of course, unless you cooperate. I am prepared to offer you what you call in your country 'a plea bargain.'

"So the shoe finally dropped. He wanted us to sign a 'confession' and appear on camera, after the bruises healed, saying we were agents of the United States illegally performing counter-espionage in Colombia. It would have caused an international uproar and would have forced our country to pull way back on its efforts to stop the flow of coke into the States. It would have created a political backlash that would have destroyed any cooperation between our country and the Colombians. The cooperative efforts were in their infancy as it was."

"There's something I don't understand," I interrupted. "If you were the guests of the Colombians, how could this 'confession' have any credibility? Wouldn't the Colombian government back you up?"

"You are right, you don't understand, do you?" Hudson said, but not unkindly. "There's a lot about Latin American society, and especially politics, that is completely foreign to us gringos.

"You have to understand, any government official down there, either elected or appointed, keeps one eye looking forward and the other looking over his shoulder. There's always someone, a political enemy, waiting in the wings to take advantage of a slip-up. If this 'confession' of ours were to be made public, those responsible for getting us there in the first place would have dropped us like a hot tamale and disavowed any knowledge of us. If they didn't, their butts would have been left hanging out there, just waiting for enough anti-American sentiment to boil over and run them out of office. Lord knows, we're not that popular there anyhow. And besides, I am sure that Carillo had several members of the politicos bought and paid for, and they would have loved the idea of getting some mileage out of all this. No, we were all alone on this one."

"So what did you do? Did you sign the confession?" I asked.

"Oh sure. I might as well have signed our death warrants," he spat out bitterly, and then winced as he thought of his brother. He went on. "If we had gone along with their scheme, as soon as they got done with parading our faces around and setting back drug prevention efforts a decade, we would have been fertilizer for the rain forest. All we could do was to stall for time.

"Jeff was in rougher shape than I was. I told Carillo we would do it, but I insisted that he put us together so I could tend to his wounds. Wouldn't do to have the world see us looking like the last scene in Rocky when we went before the camera. He kept a couple of guards on us while I tended to Jeff's wounds, and then left us tied up during the night.

"After a week, the night before they were going to bring the cameras in and film our mea culpas, I decided we had better try and make our move. Carillo's men figured with our hands tied behind our backs, we didn't need to be watched too carefully. I had spent the previous week becoming more apathetic and docile, resigned to my fate, which seemed to bolster their over-confidence. What they didn't know was I have a trick shoulder and am able to pop it out of joint whenever I want to. Came from dislocating it back in college."

"Football injury?" I asked.

"Frat party," he answered. "Had too much to drink one night and fell off the sleeping porch balcony. Anyhow, by popping out the shoulder, it gave me enough slack so I was able to slide my tied hands under my butt and get them out in front of me. With my hands where I was able to see them, I was able to untie Jeff, and then he freed me. It took us most of the night, because even though they weren't being as stringent with their security since we had seemed to come over to the fold, they still tied some pretty good knots.

"At daybreak, we could hear them down the hall setting up the video equipment. A guard came into the room to get us. With our hands free, it was pretty easy to jump him, knock him out, and get his gun. We didn't kill him."

He was silent for a moment. "I won't make that mistake again." I felt the hairs on the nape of my neck stand up. He continued.

"We started sneaking out the hall toward the alley, when the guard came to and sounded the alarm. We made it to the stairway and were on our way out when Carillo and a couple of his bodyguards came on the scene. We made a run for it. We were half way down the alley when they started firing. I had just gotten around the corner when I noticed that Jeff wasn't with me anymore. By the time I turned and looked back into the alley, Carillo had Jeff in a headlock with a gun to his head. Jeff was bleeding from taking a hit in his hip. I still had the guard's gun. I pointed it at Carillo. 'Mr. Hudson,' he said. 'Please don't do anything foolish. I don't want to hurt your brother. Put your gun down.' He said all this with about as much emotion as if he were ordering at a restaurant.

"I was about 20 yards from them. I didn't have a very good shot, but Jeff thought it was worth a try. 'Blow him away, Bro!' he shouted."

He looked down at the floor. "Blow him away, Bro..." he repeated softly. "He always had too much confidence in me." He paused again, and then said sadly, "Now, I wish I had given it a try."

I could sense what was coming. It wasn't going to be easy, even after all these years. We gave him time. He took it.

"I couldn't take the shot," he said after a while. "Even though I knew in my mind that if I laid down that gun, we would probably both die, I couldn't take the shot. The black-hearted coward was hiding behind Jeff, and I didn't think I could risk shooting. I laid my gun down slowly. Carillo just smiled."

Another pause.

"Then he shot Jeff." Pause. "Just gunned him down like he was a dog in the street." The words came out woodenly, almost without emotion, but rose out of the depths of a soul that hadn't seen peace since that nightmarish morning in a back alley in Tejeda.

Lauren involuntarily squeezed my hand, and I saw a tear slide down her cheek. "I…am so sorry, Mr. Hudson…" Lauren said tenderly. "I…" Her voice trailed off, lost in the wilderness of words too inadequate to bring comfort or healing.

"I know," he said. "Thank you." He tried to smile. "And call me Bryce. Please."

We all sat surrounded by our thoughts for a long while, before Hudson finally broke the silence. "So maybe you can see now why I have some added motivation to see Mr. Carillo brought to justice."

"I guess I do," Lauren said slowly. "But I still don't see how all this involves Greg."

"Jorge Carillo is a man who places value on only one man's life, and that is Jorge Carillo's," Hudson explained. "If he even suspected that you or anyone else might become the slightest inconvenience in his life, he would shoot first and ask questions later." Hudson showed a faint reaction to his own unfortunate choice of words. "Somehow, Mr. O'Brien, you have found yourself on the wrong side of the self-interests of one Jorge Carillo, businessman, entrepreneur, and ranking member of the Cali Drug Cartel."

It was to Lauren's credit that her cry of alarm was nearly silent, but she nearly broke a couple of my fingers as her grasp tightened.

I was bewildered. Scared. But most of all, confused. The scene began to take on that misty air of complete senselessness that occurs right before you wake up from that dream in which you are walking naked through the hotel lobby at the Hilton. I closed my eyes. For a moment, a huge sense of relief swept over me as I actually expected to wake up to the kids bouncing on my bed, and face nothing more stressful than wondering if my forecast high for tomorrow was right or not. I opened my eyes.

No kids. No bed. Just Hudson, looking grim, and Lauren, ashen-faced, looking lost.

Sometimes, reality sucks.

"I just don't get it, Bryce," I stammered. "What could I possibly have to do with a druglord a half a world away?"

"I'm not totally sure," he replied. "But I can give you a hint. You heard how I described Carillo as not just a member of the Cartel, but also as a businessman? Organized crime figures almost always mix legitimate businesses into their portfolio. Not only looks good on their resume, but it also provides a nice outlet to launder their dirty money. Well, Carillo must own about 30 or more businesses all over the globe. In most of those, he just acts as a silent partner, albeit with a majority interest. Well, lately, he seems to have taken an unusually active interest in a new business venture. You might be interested in a recent filing and ruling by the FCC."

"What's that?" I asked.

"It seems as of September 15th of this year, our friend's application was approved by the Federal Communications Commission to take over ownership and control of a certain media property."

"So?" I said.

"Jorge Carillo is now the owner of KOPP Radio."

Chapter 20

Finally. A connection. Not much of one, but a connection all the same. I sat and pondered the revelation for a moment.

For two moments.

I still wasn't any closer to knowing why a Colombian druglord would want to hang my hide on his mantelpiece. But somehow, just knowing there was a face to the evil I had been living gave me a small sense of empowerment that I hadn't felt since this whole insane period started. At least I had a target to fight back at.

Of course, empowerment is one thing. Comfort is another. And in this case, a little knowledge didn't go very far in making me feel much better.

"OK. So now I know there's a connection. But what does it all have to do with me? What'd I do, blow a forecast and ruin one of his advertiser's ski holidays? I mean, I've worked for some pretty tough management before, but this does seem a bit of an over-reaction, doesn't it?"

"I don't know, Greg. That's something I am still trying to find out. You must have seen something, been in the wrong place at the wrong time, stumbled onto something."

"But how could I have? I don't even work down there. I just phoned my work into their station. I've never even met the guy. I don't even know what he looks like."

Hudson answered. "He's about 5'8", well-built, dark hair, mustache, always well-dressed when he's not beating your face to a pulp, very proper and educated manner. Perhaps most noticeable about him are his eyes. Kind of hard to describe exactly. But they are dark…"

"So dark they seem to suck the life right out of you," I finished the sentence for him. I continued, staring off at the distance, words coming mechanically. "Eyes that reveal a soul that hasn't seen the light of joy or goodness for years. I wondered what it was about him that bothered me. I thought it was just the circumstances." I snapped out of my reverie and looked at Hudson. "I *have* met him…or at least I have seen him." I told him about my surreptitious foray into Steve Richards's office. "I just assumed that he was a client. You're telling me he owns the station?"

"Bought and paid for. Probably one of the fastest license transfers in the history of American broadcasting. Tells me he bought more than a radio station. He probably owns someone in the FCC as well."

"That still doesn't help me understand how I could have gotten on this guy's black list. And it also doesn't tell me how you came to have such an interest in me. If you don't know why Carillo's after me, how did you know he was?"

"I followed his dog." Hudson smiled.

"His dog?" I asked, confused.

"Yes. Carillo doesn't ever do anything in the light of day, as it were, if he doesn't absolutely have to. Although there is a trail of death and ruin following him everywhere he goes, he almost never gets his own hands dirty anymore. That would be too risky," Hudson scowled, "although I suppose he would say it would be beneath his dignity." He stopped, and then went on sadly. "The last time he dirtied his hands was with my brother."

The room went silent. "So he has taken to using intermediaries to do his somewhat less-than-socially-acceptable tasks. And since he is a man of considerable means and connections, he has quite a rogues gallery to choose from." He looked at me and almost smiled. "You should be honored, Mr. O'Brien. In your case, he has hired one of the best."

I didn't like where this was going. "The best?" I hated to ask.

"Fellow by the name of Chance Dunleavy. One of the top paid assassins on the globe."

Lauren visibly shuddered. It was to her credit that she was able to maintain any composure at all up to this point. I wondered if everything didn't have such an eerily unrealistic aura about it, if she wouldn't have broken down completely. I'm not so sure I wouldn't have joined her.

"Was he the one on the motorcycle?" I asked resignedly.

"I'm pretty sure he was. By the way, that was a neat bit of riding on your part. If you hadn't aimed for that trash pile, we wouldn't be having this conversation."

I didn't want to tell him that I didn't see the life-saving pile of brush until I landed in it. I wanted to retain at least a scrap of self-respect.

Hudson continued. "Dunleavy specializes in 'accidents.' Apparently, Carillo doesn't want too much attention drawn to the loss of a local television personality." I winced. "Sorry about that," he said, noticing my reaction.

"Anyhow, he has been using Dunleavy a lot lately. In order for me to follow Carillo, I just follow his dog, Chance Dunleavy.

"Do you recall that high administration official who was killed in that plane crash a while back?" I nodded. "Dunleavy's work. Apparently, he was in Carillo's pocket and was stricken with a severe case of conscience. He was in the process of negotiating a deal with the feds when his little 'accident' occurred. Somehow Dunleavy got on the plane without being shown on the manifest. I'm not sure what he did next, but I can assume that he immobilized the crew, perhaps by using some kind of nerve gas, and reset the altimeter so the plane would fly through the next mountain top, thinking it was flying over it. Dunleavy parachutes out, and voila...no high-level official, no investigation, and Carillo stays out of the limelight."

I considered what Hudson had told me. "So where does this leave us? I don't imagine I can call on this Jorge Carillo and just say 'Gee, I'm sorry, but there must be a misunderstanding. I really didn't see anything, and I really don't know anything about you being one of the most evil criminal minds in the Western Hemisphere, so it's OK now if you call your hired assassin off.' And then I'm sure we'd sit down at La Hacienda, let bygones be bygones, and split a plate of nachos."

Hudson actually smiled at this. "No," he said, "that might put an end to it, but not in a way that would be very satisfactory to you and your family." And then he turned serious. "Speaking of your family..."

That got my attention real fast. "What about them?" Then it occurred to me where he was going. "You don't think...?"

Hudson took his time, choosing his words very carefully. "I have been following the activities of Chance Dunleavy for a while now and have tried to build a personality profile on him. As strange as it might seem to you, I don't believe he is an immoral man. In many ways, he's much worse. He's amoral. He doesn't have feelings one way or the other about right or wrong. And he's proud, proud of his 'work.' By managing to stay alive this long, you have hurt his feelings. Sort of violated his sense of professionalism. This has never happened to him before, and it is likely to stick in his craw. He hasn't had a history of going after anyone but his intended target, but as we saw in the plane crash, he doesn't lose any sleep over 'collateral damage.' I suspect he's getting just a little weary of failing with you and might just be looking for a way to get some leverage."

His words sent a chill to the very core of my marrow. I looked at Lauren. Up to this time, I had been most concerned avoiding making her a widow. I closed my eyes. Now my thoughts imagined a possibility much, much worse. And the kids. I thought of them now, at school, and how I used to worry about them hurting themselves on the monkey bars. Oh, dear God. *The kids.* If anything happened to them...

I looked up again at Lauren. "Babe..." I began.

Even through the fear and the anguish that she had suffered in the last few weeks, a glint of steel shone through her blue eyes. "I am not leaving you," she said with resolve.

"Lauren," Hudson spoke tenderly for the first time. "Please listen for a minute. I know this is hard, but I'm going to ask you to stop and think. None of you deserves this. You could all go through a hundred lifetimes and not have to deal with the hell that you are being asked to endure now. But these are the cards you were dealt. And all you can do now is to try and do what is best.

"Greg is being pursued by a very dangerous man right now. Two very dangerous men. I wish I could promise you that I could keep him out of danger, but I think you know it would be an empty promise. But you have to remember one thing. These *are* just men. They may be the personification of evil, but they bleed just like we do." Hudson's eyes looked off in the distance. "I can testify to that. And because they are just men, we can fight back. I don't know how yet. But in order to be able to do that, Greg needs to have his wits about him. He *has* to know that you and your children are safe. If he has one eye on you and the other on his back, he won't be able to protect you or himself." He looked straight at her. "You have to make a tough decision, but it's the only one. Right now, as much as you want to help him, to be by his side, your being here is dangerous...to you, the kids, and to Greg."

He was right. It wasn't fair.

Lauren was reeling with indecision, but in the end there wasn't a choice. In our years of marriage, we had always tackled problems side by side. "Babe," I said softly, "Do you remember what you said to me 17 years ago?"

She looked at me, her cheeks wet with tears. "What?" she answered.

" 'I am your lover, your helpmate, and your friend...' " I began.

"And 'I love you with a love that is more powerful than yesterday, though less than tomorrow,' " she finished. The final words of our wedding vows were almost choked off by sobs.

"Honey, I need your love now more than ever. And what I need to know most of all is that you all are safe. Please, take care of our kids."

In the end, there was really no other decision she could make. "Where should we go?" she finally asked.

I thought about it a moment. "Let me call Karen." Karen was my sister, in Conroe, Texas. She was a bit bossy and overbearing, but she knew how to keep a secret. And I could trust her. And besides, the kids would get to play with their cousins. It would make it easier to explain to Mary and Christopher. Since they were due to be out of school for Christmas break next week anyway, the sudden trip would make more sense. "We'll make a big deal about going to your folks in Minnesota, just in case Dunleavy tries to find out where you went. I'll make sure Karen knows that your visit has to be on the Q.T. Maybe I can talk her into taking you all out to her summer place at Taylor Lake."

Lauren sat despondently. Finally she said, "O.K."

Probably the toughest words she ever uttered.

Chapter 21

I had to give my sister Karen credit. She didn't ask too many questions, but she understood there was a real need for Lauren and the kids to find a safe place. I didn't want to overstate the problem (like somehow I was going to make things sound *worse* than they really were?), so I opted to just tell her that there had been some threats on my life, and I wanted to get my family out of the way. I tried to make it sound like it was one of those things that we TV people had to deal with every now and then. I already had enough people I loved worrying if the Christmas church service would be a celebration or a memorial. I didn't want to add to the list.

"So are the police taking care of the situation?" she asked.

I wasn't sure how to tell her that the police weren't exactly breaking their overtime budget on my behalf, so I just said, "The police have committed every resource at their discretion to wrapping this up." I didn't add their discretion was to just forget the whole matter.

I told her I would call her back with the flight information. I spent the rest of the afternoon making travel arrangements, and Lauren started getting the kid's things packed up. We were lucky. We found three seats on Southwest Airlines to Houston for the next morning. I guess that was lucky. I was already beginning to feel the ache of their absence.

Hudson agreed to spend the night. When the kids got home from school, I introduced him as a friend of ours from college. They accepted that, and him, and then whooped with joy when they were informed they would be getting out of school a week early and going to Texas. Only Mary looked at me a little funny. I think she knew something was up, but wasn't sure what to say. She always had a frustrating sixth sense about that kind of thing.

Because of all the hustle and bustle of the last minute arrangements, it wasn't until the kids were tucked away in bed and Hudson was tucked away on the couch that I realized we never found out how he had escaped the situation in Colombia. I would have to ask him later.

Meanwhile, I was just beginning to come to grasp with the full impact of what the next days/weeks/months (?) would hold, for both Lauren and me. In every other crisis in our lives, from the loss of my father to cancer four years earlier, to Christopher's bout with meningitis, to my own recent trips to the hospital, we always faced them together. Lauren was always there. Then Jorge Carillo forced us apart.

Damn him.

I have never been a person who drew strength from anger. Far from it. Anger in my life usually was destructive and unproductive, and as such, I did my best to avoid being swallowed up in it.

In this case, I decided I would make an exception.

On that night, as we lay in bed, I held the wife of my youth in my arms with the quiet desperation of a man who might never get this chance again. I tried to remember every touch of her skin and every sound of her breath with the same intensity of a condemned man savoring the taste of his last meal. I tried my best to avoid the condemned man analogy, but with no success. I was unjustly accused, convicted, and sentenced to die by a man I never knew, whom I never wished ill upon, and whose path I crossed only by fate and not by choice. An innocent man on death row.

I wondered if this was how Christ felt.

Lauren and I lay quietly bound together, both afraid to say anything, and both afraid to go to sleep for fear of wasting a moment. After a while, I decided to abandon the pity party I had been dwelling in, and instead turned my thoughts to what Lauren was going through. It was at that point the anger began to boil deep within me, building up like the first winds ahead of a mid winter snow storm. Not usually one to resort to profanity, I cursed Jorge Carillo, cursed Chance Dunleavy, and swore vengeance on what they brought to the ones I loved.

Without realizing it at first, something changed in me that night. Up to that point, I was the hare being pursued by the hound, surviving less by speed than by luck, but always the prey, never the hunter.

I didn't know how, but that was going to change.

The illuminated dials of the bedside clock flicked over to read three AM. Sleep had still not come. We had spent nearly all the time in silence, together in our thoughts and prayers. Up to that time, fear had kept sleep away. But sleep was needed, for both of us. I put my lips to her ear and said softly, "Babe?"

"Yes?" she answered softly.

"Tomorrow, you will take our children and travel to Texas. I don't know how long you will have to be away. But you will come back." I fell silent for a moment before going on, with a conviction in my voice that I didn't know was there. "And I *will* be here when you do. I promise you. You have to know that."

There was half a minute of silence. Then, with a catch in her voice, she answered, "Yes, I believe you will."

We slept.

We live in a pretty great neighborhood, but as with most things, there are little annoyances that we have had to deal with. Dave Brown's streetlight was one of them. Citing the need for more security, Dave, who probably could have made a living selling snowboards to Australian aborigines, somehow managed to talk the county into installing a street light off of the telephone pole that bordered his property. Would make some sense on the face of it, except this particular telephone pole was wasn't on the street. It was in his back yard. Not wanting to waste any of the valuable light on the street, most of it illuminated the real estate behind his house. The power and phone lines ran along the common boundary between our two pieces of property, so the light which emanated from this new street lamp provided Dave with increased security, the street out front with nary a lumen of light, and me with a constant, though minor, aggravation.

As the fates would have it, the light lined up perfectly with the crack that often occurred in the curtains over our bedroom window. And the fates being what they are, the photons of light, which passed through the curtain opening, found their final resting place at the exact spot where my head found its resting place on my pillow. Rather than make a big issue about it, which would put a damper on my neighbor's coup d'etat over the county engineers, I usually made it a point to make sure the curtain was closed all the way.

Circumstances being what they were, I had neglected to double-check the curtains that night. Exhaustion overcame my usual sensitivity to light, and I managed to sleep in its presence. But not in its absence.

At first I wasn't sure what it was that woke me. Blinking in the single beam of light, I tried to clear my head. Then, for the second time, the light was blocked as something once again passed by my window.

There was someone outside.

I quietly slipped out of bed, sure that the pounding of my heart could be heard across the neighborhood. I crept to the window and peered out the side of the curtain, hoping the light outside and the darkness inside would prevent whoever it was from seeing me. He didn't see me.

But I saw him. The Aussie. Chance Dunleavy. Had to be. I couldn't see his face, but he was the right height and build, and I was long past believing in coincidences. He was twenty feet away by then. His hand reached out and felt something on the side of the house. It took me a moment to realize what he was touching. It was a window. He was trying to open a window.

Christopher's window.

Shocked and frozen for a moment in indecision, I was on the verge of storming into Christopher's room when he pulled his hand back. I resumed my breathing, barely, and whispered a quick prayer of thanks that my son had finally remembered to lock his window. Dunleavy slowly made his way down the side of the house, away from me. He was obviously looking for a quiet and easy way into our home. To finish his job. To kill me. Maybe my family as well.

But I could see him coming, and although a real and palpable terror still rose up in the pit of my stomach, I resolved that this time the hunter was about to become the hunted.

As long as he thought we were still asleep, I reasoned, he would move slowly and stealthily. That bought me a little time. I looked for a weapon and settled on my graphite-ceramic tennis racquet. So intense was the swirl of emotions inside of me that I never thought to go get help from Bryce, who was sacked out at the other end of the house. I also didn't bother to put on any shoes or a coat, such was my desire for stealth and speed, even though there were three inches of new snow outside.

I crept into the bathroom away from where Dunleavy was moving. I slid open the small window, and gently removed the screen cover, and tossed the racquet outside, which fell silently in the snow. It was a narrow window that I'd never tried to get out of before, but I judged that if I turned sideways, I could just squeeze through.

I nearly judged wrong. Once I climbed up enough to get my head and shoulders through the window, my feet no longer had anything on which to push off. My hands fell just short of reaching the eaves, so I didn't have anything I could reach out and grab to pull myself through. Stalemate. I couldn't get out, and I couldn't get back in. My hands and feet flailed in midair, trying to gain some leverage that would change my situation. Stuck in that ridiculous position like an abandoned teeter-totter, my panic grew as I realized that now Dunleavy was free to take his time to get into the house, or worse yet, if he found me here, my only defense would be to hope he died laughing.

Abandoning stealth, I started to rock back and forth, the bottom of the metal window frame grinding mercilessly against my waist. Like a fish flopping on a dock, I managed to bounce up and out, my hip landing squarely on the window track, sending shock waves of pain through my torso and down my legs. But after a few of these oscillations, my center of gravity gradually shifted to the exterior of the house, and my upper body dropped down to the point where I could reach the hose bib near the foundation.

I hooked the faucet with a little finger and began to pull myself down. Knowing it was going to hurt, I yanked. The window frame caught the waistband of my pajama bottoms, which was all I had on at the time, as the rest of me tumbled out the window, plopping ungracefully into the snow, with the pajamas now down around my knees. Barefoot, bare-chested, and now bare... well, you get the idea. Abandoning all hope of retaining any degree of decorum, I scrambled up and dug out the tennis racquet and tried to prepare myself for what might come next.

What came next was an explosion. Of laughter.

Not really expecting Dunleavy to succumb to a fatal case of the guffaws, I reeled around and raised the racquet, only to see Bryce Hudson slumped against the house, holding his sides, roaring with laughter at the sight of me.

"I was outside here checking to see if your windows were all locked," he said between chuckles when he finally caught his breath. "I heard this window open and got back around the house just in time to see your exit." Even in the low light, I could see the tears of laughter streaming down his face. "I gotta hand it to you, Greg, you never let anything get boring around you, do you?"

Red faced, all I could say was, "Um... do you think we could go back into the house?" I picked up my racquet and what little was left of my dignity, and with already freezing feet, trudged back into the house.

The Great White Hunter.

Chapter 22

The next morning came too fast. A swirl of emotions spun inside of me before I put Lauren and the kids on the flight to Texas. I gathered the kids in my arms and held them as if it were the last time. I tried not to think of it in those terms, but the fear of it turning out to be true was so real I couldn't escape it.

"Daddy…why are you crying?" Christopher asked. I hadn't even realized I was.

Almost afraid to speak, for fear my voice would betray me, I said huskily, "I just wish I could join you all. I'm gonna miss you." It was weak, but it was all I had.

"I wish you could too, Dad. I'm gonna miss you. Are you going to come out and join us?"

"Daddy doesn't know for sure, son. Hopefully I will…soon."

"Better make it quick. Christmas is only two weeks away."

How I wished it would be soon.

Mary still looked at me in that uncertain way, reading the underlying turmoil that I was so desperately trying to hide. Wise beyond her years, she kissed me and said simply, "I love you, Daddy."

I buried my eyes in her soft hair, trying to hide the flow of tears those simple words created. "Baby, I love you," I croaked. "I always will. Remember that, will you?"

"I will."

With puffy eyes made worse by the lack of sleep, I finally released the kids and stood to hold Lauren. "Dear God," I prayed. "Don't let this be the last time I can do this."

Lauren, who was holding up better than I was, read my mind. "Remember your promise," she whispered.

Her words settled deep in me, where they took root and germinated. I found strength in them. "I will be here."

She gathered the kids up, and with an effort of will far stronger than my own, she smiled at them and led them down the tunnel into the waiting jet bound for Houston. She turned just once to look at me. I placed two fingers to my lips, kissed, and waggled them at her.

I watched the plane take off from the large window at the end of the terminal, eyes fixed on the steadily disappearing speck in the sky, unwilling to even break off that tenuous connection with the life I had come to love. When I could no longer see the plane, I still stared at the sky where it had vanished.

An hour and a half later, I finally turned away.

Reno is a beautiful place to live, especially when there is a fresh blanket of snow. But on that day, during the drive home, the landscape seemed bleak and lifeless. The colors seemed dull. Instead of refreshing the soul, the sun shining off the fresh, new snow served only to irritate the eyes. It is amazing how one small woman and two tiny children can change the very essence of a landscape by their mere absence.

I tried to snap out of my maudlin state by the time I got home. Hudson was gone by then. I was expecting that. He had given me a pager number to get a hold of him and asked me to call him later that evening.

"We need to make some plans," he told me before I left with Lauren and the kids. I wasn't sure I liked the sound of that, but I was now trying to play in his league in a game I had just taken up, and this rookie needed the best coaching he could get. I found I was impatient to make contact with him again. And besides, I still hadn't found out how he had managed to get out of Colombia.

In the meantime, I did have a job to do, and I had decided that Bert Gooding had already had enough of my airtime under his belt.

I called Jeanne Marshal at the station and told her I would be coming in to work that day. After my episode at the river, she said that Bert could fill in for me until I felt up to coming back. I told her I felt like coming back.

"Are you sure?" she asked. "Bert told me he would be glad to fill in for as long as you needed."

"I'm sure he did," I answered, trying to keep it lighthearted, and not really succeeding. Then I thought to myself, a bit morosely, "Bert, ol' buddy, just stick around, and you might be filling in for longer that you think."

Jeanne picked up on something in my voice. "Greg, are you sure you're all right? Seriously?"

I smiled in spite of myself. "You mean apart from being in mortal danger with every step I take? Couldn't be better."

"That's good," she returned, thinking I was just referring to being accident-prone as of late. "We'll see you this afternoon."

I hung up the phone. "I hope so," I muttered to the walls.

Heading out of the driveway on my way to the station, I absentmindedly stopped at the mailbox. In amongst a couple of bills, there was the bimonthly envelope congratulating me for winning millions of dollars. Of course, upon closer inspection of the brightly colored announcement's small print, with the aid of a 20-power microscope, I would only win *if* my number happened to be the one out of 250 million issued that was the *winning* number. Kinda like congratulating someone for winning an Olympic gold medal in the 100-meter dash, and then saying, "By the way, all you have to do to claim your prize is to run faster than anyone else on earth."

This misleading method of getting people to buy your magazines or seeds by pumping them up with visions of untold riches has always irked me. I don't mind sweepstakes, but they seemed to be bordering on fraud as of late. I had heard of numerous occasions of elderly recipients, without the aid of the above-mentioned microscope, who were overjoyed at their newfound windfall. They then proceeded to write thousands of dollars of checks to their friends and family, only to find out that their money was as illusionary as their dreams of what they could do with it.

I couldn't help but think, in my situation, I probably had a better chance of holding the winning number than I had of living long enough to spend it.

It was a measure of my annoyance at the sweepstakes game and the pessimism that I was trying so hard to battle, that I only gave a cursory glance to a package in a small, 5 by 8 padded manila envelope. It had my name and address written in sloppy block lettering with no return address. I tossed it onto the car seat along with my impending gold mine and drove to the station.

I made it into work unscathed, although I found it hard to keep my eyes on the road ahead. They kept involuntarily glancing at the rear view mirror and out the sides of the windows, expecting at any minute another attack from Chance Dunleavy. All it served to do was to make me a threat to public safety. After I ran a stoplight and narrowly avoided hitting a telephone pole, I reflected on the irony if I finished the job that Dunleavy started due to my own carelessness. Would certainly make it hard to prove *that* wasn't an accident. I wondered idly if Carillo would ask for a refund.

The day hadn't started real well. It was about to get worse.

I walked into the station to a smattering of muted hellos from the staff. It was as if they knew something that I didn't, and they didn't want to be the ones to break the news. I wondered if this was just a symptom of my over-developed sense of paranoia. I decided that I had better get busy, so I avoided my usual beginning of the day bantering session with Jeanne Marshal and went straight to my office. Without thinking, I reached for the phone to call in my radio forecast. The phone got halfway to my ear before I caught myself.

I was staring at the phone, dwelling on the radio station's connection with my present situation, when Skip came in and sat down quietly next to me. He immediately picked up on my brooding.

"Greg?" he started slowly. "I'm sorry. I know this must be tough on you."

It took me a second. How did he know what was going on? He must have heard that I sent Lauren and the kids away. I turned slowly and looked vacantly at him. "How did you find out?"

"Hey…you know. It's our business to find out about these things," he said without the humor usually associated with the old line.

Now I started to get confused. And without meaning to, a bit peeved. He probably thought Lauren and I were having marital problems. Why should they go prying into our private lives? "Skip," I began, trying to maintain my ragged temper, "it isn't what you think. We are going to be all right, and this is only for a little while." I started getting louder.

Now it was Skip's turn to look confused. "Wait a sec, Greg. Maybe we are on two different wavelengths here. I came in here to tell you, but when I saw the long face, I thought you had already heard."

I almost shouted. "Heard what?"

Skip spoke softly. "The police found Chuck Murphy. He's…dead, Greg. I'm sorry, I thought you knew."

The words shocked me into silence. The room tilted a bit. A stabbing pain took hold of me, nearly doubling me over. Chuck. Gone.

"How…?" I finally managed to say.

"Drug overdose. They said he'd been dead for a couple of days when they found him."

"Drug overdose? How did they know that? Have they already done an autopsy?"

Skip looked uncomfortable. The big black man, who was one of my best friends in the world, wasn't used to passing along bad news. He was always content to leave the stories of mayhem and disaster to the "newsies," and the worst tragedy he usually dealt with was a losing streak by the University basketball team. He didn't want to add insult to injury. "They…well, they found a bunch of needle marks. Toxicology won't come back for a while, but that's what the cops apparently are putting this one down to. I usually wouldn't know any of this kind of stuff, but it's been all over the newsroom."

I sat stunned by the news. I tried to sort out the implications. What had Chuck stumbled onto? My mind rewound back to his last cryptic phone call that he made to me… when was it? Maybe two weeks ago? It seemed like a lifetime. What did he say? "I've figured it out." Figured *what* out? I internally agonized at my failure to get in touch with him. What difference would it have made? What could he have told me? And for that matter, could I have warned him of danger? I was numbed by the implications.

Skip knew enough to be quiet while I tried to absorb the information. He looked keenly at me, and somehow, intuitively, knew there was more to the story than I was letting on. He waited until I spoke again.

"I don't buy it, Skip. Chuck didn't OD. At least not this way."

"What do you mean, Greg?"

"Chuck and I had a lot of arguments on the whole issue of drugs. He was pretty Libertarian about the whole thing. Thought they should be all legalized. It wouldn't surprise me to find out he dabbled in them. But he didn't die this way…at least not on his own."

"Why do you say that?" Skip eyed me curiously.

"Because he was deathly afraid of needles. I met him once at one of those radio blood drives. I thought he was going to have a coronary right then and there. It took him about an hour before I could get him to sit in the chair, and he almost passed out a half a dozen times. He'd face a room full of snakes before he'd ever put a needle into his own arm."

Skip thought for a moment. "Maybe you should pass that along to the police."

I internally blanched at that, but said, "Yeah. Maybe I should."

Skip couldn't keep it in any longer. "Little brother…what's going on here?" His eyes bored a hole in me.

I looked at the big man. I was caught in a conflict of emotions. On the one hand, I needed all the allies I could get. And there was no denying when you need friends, 6' 10" and 275 pounds can buy a lot of comfort. But I'd already lost one close friend, and I wasn't about to put anyone else in the line of fire. "Skip," I said haltingly, "I wish I could tell you. But this is something that you don't want to get involved in. It's something that *I* would give anything not to be involved in. But if I told you, it could be dangerous for you, and I wouldn't want that on my conscience."

"Dangerous?" he snorted. "Man, do you know what it was like growing up in Watts? Drive-bys every other day?" He actually smiled. "I was kinda starting to miss the excitement."

I didn't buy it for a minute. We had often talked about how Reno seemed a safe haven for Skip and his family compared to his humble beginnings. The last thing he wanted to do was to return to the days of dodging bullets in the streets of the projects. "Buddy, I appreciate your concern, but I'll be OK," I said with a lot more conviction than I felt. "Maybe I can tell you about it later."

What I was really thinking was, "I *hope* I can tell you about it later."

Chapter 23

It wasn't the best weathercast I have ever given, but under the circumstances, I took it. I have always been curious to know if the viewing audience could tell if I was having a bad day, or if I had gotten to the point where I could just "flip the switch" and go on without revealing the turmoil that was brewing beneath. I suppose this would have been a great test of that. I'm still glad that our audience research project, which quizzed the public about what they thought of us, wasn't due for another nine months.

I drove home after the evening shows, dreading entering the empty house. With the kids fifteen hundred miles away, I mused that the only Pink Panther attacks on me this time would be for real. But I feared the emptiness more than the danger. I gave the house a quick once-over to convince myself there weren't any boogiemen lurking in the hollows and dejectedly plopped myself down into the easy chair. The same easy chair that I had unceremoniously caused Bryce Hudson to vacate the night before. The thought of that reminded me that I needed to give him a call.

I dialed the number for his pager. An androgynous voice told me to leave a message, which I did, telling him I was home. I left the number and hung up.

I idly wandered to the fridge and looked inside. Lauren, always prepared, had stocked up with all kinds of treats a couple of days earlier, but try as I might, I couldn't muster up the energy or the desire to eat anything. Great way to lose weight.

The phone rang. It was Hudson. "First of all, I think you probably ought to lock up the house and find another place to stay. It will be too easy for Dunleavy to arrange an accident at home. Faulty heater...electrical fire...knock you out, jack up the car, and drop it on you..."

"OK, OK...I get the picture. I'll go get a room at the Truckee River Lodge." That was a nice place along the river that was the only smokeless hotel in town.

"Good. Don't use a credit card, and try to avoid letting the whole world know you are there. Only stay there for two…three days tops. Then we'll move you somewhere else. Go now, and I'll meet you there in an hour. We have some talking to do." I heard the line go dead.

Trying hard to overcome a frustrating sense of inertia, I packed a few things, and then went through the process of closing up the house. I turned down the heat, left a few lights on, and locked the doors.

I hated leaving that place. It had always been my sanctuary, and now Dunleavy had made it a place of danger, almost a prison. The anger, which I had begun to feel the night before, was rekindled and took flame. As I drove out of the driveway, I took one last look at our home, wondering if I'd ever return.

I drove to the Truckee River Lodge, stopping by an ATM to get enough greenbacks to foot the hotel bill. It was a few blocks west of Casino Row in downtown. I parked my car in their lot and walked in, hoping to pay cash and to sign the register under a different name. The clerk dashed those hopes by greeting me upon my arrival with, "Good evening, Mr. O'Brien. How are the passes tonight? Has this latest storm closed the roads?" And then, noting the bag in my hand, "Would you be wanting a room tonight?" So much for anonymity.

I told him that the roads had cleared up nicely, and that Cal-Trans had even lifted the chain and snow tire restrictions from travel over Donner Pass, the main mountain route on Interstate 80 between Reno and Sacramento. And that, yes, I would like a room, since I was having some work done on the house which made it uninhabitable. And would he mind keeping this to himself, since I didn't want it advertised that my house was sitting vacant and vulnerable to easy pickings by burglars and vandals?

He assured me that mum was the word, gave me a room key, and was about to call for a bellboy, when I assured him I could show myself to my room. I left a message for Bryce to come up. "He is to be the only one to know I am here," I told the clerk.

"Of course, Mr. O'Brien," he responded, happy to receive the $20 tip I left him.

Hudson arrived about ten minutes after I got settled in. "You have a lot to learn," he said after I opened the door to him.

"What? What did I do wrong?" I queried.

"You opened the door without so much as looking through the peephole. How did you know it was me here?"

My face burned red. "I was expecting you. I guess I just assumed…"

"Assuming is a luxury that you can't afford anymore, Greg. Never open a door until you know who is on the other side. If you don't have a peephole, stand to the side and ask who it is. And make sure you have something solid in your hand in case whoever it is on the other side decides to take out the door. The only assuming I want you to make is to assume the worst. If I knock on your door, it will be two quick knocks, followed by one, followed by two."

Properly chagrined, I returned to sit on the bed. "So, you wanted to meet tonight and make some plans. So… what's the plan?"

Hudson smiled stiffly and pulled up a chair. "I wish I had one all laid out. We have to somehow get more information about what Carillo is using that radio station for. He never does anything without having a purpose behind it. The station is a key to the whole operation, somehow. All we have to do is find out what that might be. So far, I am guessing it has to do with one of three things."

"What's that?"

"The cartel drug operations are very self-sufficient while they are in Colombia in terms of production and consolidation of their operations. Especially when there's cooperation between the members. But once they try to get the stuff into the states, into their 'market,' they run into three challenges.

"The first is importation. That's what I was mostly dealing with during my days in the DEA. While it is easy to move the drugs within Colombia and to get them out of the country, Uncle Sam at least makes a spirited effort to keep them from coming in. Even more so now. Since Nine-Eleven, the Feds have really started to crack down on their patrol of the borders. Most of the big busts, the ones that are damaging to the cartel, are made as they try to bring the snow into the country. After that, the stuff is cut up into so many little units that it's like trying to retrieve all the cash in an armored car that spills its load on the freeway on a windy day. You might get little bits and pieces, but you are going to lose the majority of it.

"The second challenge for the cartel once they get a load into the country is distribution. While it may be hard for drug enforcement to keep track of it all once it's across the borders, it's almost as hard for the cartel to keep a line on it as well. A huge number of distributors, middlemen, dealers and ultimately, customers all have to handle the drugs going one way, and the money going the other. It takes an incredibly well-organized network with some very sophisticated communication capabilities in order to make sure that none of it is bleeding out along the way."

My ears perked up at the use of the word 'communication.' *Radio communication.* Is there a link there somewhere? Could the station be used somehow in the distribution network? I voiced my thoughts to Bryce.

"I've been thinking that as well. It makes some sense on the surface, but I still don't know what the tie-in might be. But is does raise an eyebrow, doesn't it?"

I gave it a little more thought but couldn't come up with anything else to support the hypothesis. I gave up. "What's the third obstacle they have to overcome?"

"Laundering," he answered. "Drugs are a big cash crop. It creates huge amounts of currency. Fives, tens, twenties, even hundreds. Now, cash is wonderful stuff, but it becomes a hindrance when you are talking about a multi-billion dollar business. The feds just might take an unhealthy interest if Carillo waltzed into your local Wells Fargo branch with a couple of million dollars in small bills stuffed into a duffel bag. He needs a way to funnel the cash into legitimate businesses, which wash the money, so to speak, and then make paper or wire deposits, all clean and neat. The incredible cash flow which is created by drug traffic is probably the biggest limitation to the cartel's expansion efforts here."

"So do you think the radio station might be a way to launder Carillo's drug money?"

Hudson shook his head. "I don't think so. Maybe. But it would be an unusual way to do it. First of all, you can't just carry your duffel bag of cash in and buy a radio station either, so the station would have had to be bought with money that was already laundered. Through a wire transfer, most likely. Secondly, a radio station doesn't conduct a lot of cash business. Usually, you look for businesses that deal in a lot of paper money on a daily basis. Race tracks, casinos, amusement parks, even large supermarkets would all be better for laundering that a radio station. Banks wouldn't blink an eye if a casino made a million-dollar cash deposit, but a radio station? Day after day?"

I could see his point. "So what's your gut feeling? What's Carillo doing?"

Hudson pondered the question. "If I had to guess, I'd say he is using it in the distribution process somehow. From what I understand, radio stations employ a sales force. Maybe they are a cover for his other 'sales'."

"But wouldn't he have to have replaced the entire sales staff with his own people? The only change in personnel I noticed was replacing the general manager with Steve Richards. And apparently that didn't turn out to be a very wise career move for the good Mr. Richards." I told him about Richards' "accident," but he had already heard.

"Who knows?" I added. "Maybe Carillo is just a music lover. Who would have picked him to be a fan of adult contemporary music?" I smiled thinly, and then the smile faded when I thought of the last time I talked about the station's format. It was with Chuck. The thought of him sent a stab of sorrow into my gut. "Actually, he didn't even leave the format alone," I muttered bitterly under my breath, remembering Chuck's frustration with being forced to stick to an inane playlist.

"What's that?" Hudson asked.

"Oh, it's nothing. I was just thinking of another casualty of this insanity." I told him what I had just learned abut Chuck, and of how he tried to tell me that something was going on at KOPP. Now, it appeared, he might have been on to something, but unless he could talk to me from beyond the grave, I would never know what it was he found.

I had his interest. Hudson stared at me, listening keenly to what I was saying. After a while, he said, "I'm sorry about your friend. I truly am. But if he was on to something, maybe he *can* talk to us from the other side."

Now it was my turn to stare at him. "So what's next? We go consult a psychic?" I said with a weak attempt at humor.

"Nope," he answered. "First, you go back and do the 11 o'clock news." I looked at my watch in a panic. It was after 10 and I had completely lost track of time. "Then I want you to come and pick me up here, and we'll go to his apartment afterwards. Let's see if Mr. Murphy left us a trail to follow."

I left the hotel and drove quickly back to the station. I wondered what we could possibly find out from a dead man. "Talk to me, Chuck," I said under my breath.

Chapter 24

Chuck didn't talk to me on the way back to the station. He was silent through a forgettable weathercast, and there wasn't a peep out of him as I drove back to the hotel.

I knocked on the room door using our pre-arranged code of two quick, then one, followed by two quick. It was all I could do to stop myself from giving it the old "shave and a haircut" knock, but I didn't think Hudson would appreciate the humor.

"So just what are we looking for?" I asked as we left the Truckee River Lodge and climbed into my Honda. I swept the mail off the front seat and threw it in the back to make room for him.

"If I knew that, we probably wouldn't have to go looking," Hudson answered. Sometimes he could be annoying. "But we can assume that he found something of value. He told you he had something." He paused for a moment, before going on. "And apparently, Carillo agreed."

We spent the next couple miles in silence. Hudson's was thoughtful, mine was melancholy. He spoke first. "I just hope they haven't already found whatever it was."

We arrived at his apartment at about a half an hour past midnight. It was in a large complex of one and two bedroom units near the Meadowwood Mall. I checked his mailbox on the way in.

Empty. Not a good sign. It was overflowing the last time I was there.

Chuck's apartment was on the second floor in a corner unit. "I don't have a key," I whispered as we came to the door. "I don't know how we'll get in."

Hudson looked at me as he would look at a small child who had said something real cute, and for a moment I thought he was going to pat me on the head. Instead, he said nothing, and brought out a narrow leather wallet, which looked to contain a manicure set. Pulling out a pair of thin, needle-tipped tools, one of which had a hook on the end, he got to work. His initial cocksure attitude began to erode when after a couple of minutes he still wasn't able to spring the lock.

"I don't understand this. This should be a simple Schlage lockset. I can open these in my sleep."

"If I know Chuck," I responded, unaware that I was still referring to him in the present, "he probably did a few modifications to it. He is pretty paranoid about anyone, from the CIA to the Moonies, trying to get into his place."

Another minute of poking and prodding produced nothing but a few colorful metaphors from my new friend. As he pulled out a third tool from his wallet, I suggested, "Why don't we just break down the door?"

"I don't want to attract the neighbor's attention," he said through gritted teeth.

"At this point, I don't think it will be any louder than your swearing…"

The door clicked open.

As soon as we walked inside, it was apparent we were too late. While Chuck would have never received the Good Housekeeping Award, even he wouldn't have left the place looking like this. Cupboards opened, couch overturned, cushions and mattresses slashed, debris everywhere… it looked like the aftermath of a force 5 tornado. Hudson cursed softly under his breath. "I was afraid of that. They've already been through the place. And they didn't seem too concerned about the shape they left it in, either. Unless he had some special place for hiding things, I don't think we are going to find anything useful." He turned to me. "Did your friend ever confide in you about a hidey-hole of any sort?" I shook my head. He sighed. "Well, we might as well give it a going over, anyhow. Although we are probably wasting our time."

He was right. We were wasting our time. After an hour of prying up carpets, looking behind pictures, inspecting toilet tanks, and disassembling drains, we had nothing to show for our efforts but some skinned knuckles and a firm conviction that if a killer bacteria ever wipes out the human race, it will originate in the s-trap of a bathroom sink.

We were in the process of replacing the last bit of plumbing when Hudson calmly grabbed me and pointed out the window. We could see reflecting off two neighboring windows the red and blue flashing lights of a Reno Police Department cruiser, which had just pulled up into the parking lot, followed by a back up unit. "Lights, but no sirens. Standard response for a burglary in progress."

It took me a moment. My eyes widened. "You think they're coming here?"

"Did Chuck's death make the news?" I nodded yes. "Then I think we can expect visitors real soon. These walls are paper-thin. We haven't made a lot of noise, but maybe one of the neighbors heard about your friend's death, and knew there shouldn't be anyone in here."

I groaned inwardly. I already was pretty low on the list of favorite people for at least one RPD detective. I could imagine how this would look. I decided I didn't want to be found without a key, in an apartment that wasn't mine, with a dead man's belongings strewn from one end to the other. I got up and started for the door.

Hudson grabbed me. "Too late for that. They'll be coming up the stairs by now."

"Where do we go?" I asked, a touch of panic rapidly creeping into my voice. "Out the back?" I said, referring to the balcony beyond the sliding glass door.

"Maybe," he answered. "Stay down and follow me."

We crept to the glass door, slipped out on to the balcony, and silently slid it closed behind us. We peered over the pony wall. What I saw chilled my blood. The apartment buildings formed a closed courtyard, with only one way out to the parking lot area. Making their way cautiously into the opening and heading right for us were two uniforms, their guns at the ready. There was no way we were going to make it off of that balcony without being seen. Another spicy epitaph slipped softly past Hudson's lips. "Just what I was afraid of. The back-up unit always covers the rear door."

My heart raced. We were trapped. I was about to head back into the apartment when I heard muffled voices outside in the hallway. An authoritative voice told someone to please stay back. *Probably the cop talking to the neighbor who called it in,* I thought. The front door opened slowly. "This is the police. Anyone in this apartment, come out with your hands empty and above your head. I'm not joking. Do it!" I think he meant it.

I was frozen in indecision when Hudson gently grabbed my arm and directed me to a door on the side of the balcony. It was a small storage closet, and the door was fortunately opened a crack. In my panic, I hadn't even noticed it. We slipped inside and closed the door just enough to make it appear shut, but without letting the knob click into place. Our friends down below the balcony would have heard that for sure if it had.

"Now what, Sherlock?" I asked so quietly, I could barely hear the words myself.

Hudson put his lips to my ear. "We hope they don't check in here," he whispered back.

I didn't hold out much hope in that. "And if they do?" I wasn't sure I wanted to hear the answer.

"I'll try not to hurt them too badly."

Oh great. What's that worth? Ten to twenty at the state pen in Carson City, at least.

I had just about made up my mind to give myself up when my hand touched something in the dark. It was a barbecue grill. And right next to it, a bag of charcoal briquettes. An idea formed.

My hand slipped into the bag of briquettes and as quietly as possible plucked two out. I cracked the door open just enough to get my hand out, praying that the hinges were well oiled. They were silent. I then waited for what I hoped would be coming next. I didn't have to wait long.

The door to the hallway burst open, and I could imagine one officer entering the room, gun drawn, while his partner covered him. It was the distraction I needed.

As soundlessly as I could, I pitched the chunks of charcoal up and over the roof, hoping I threw them far enough to get over the ridge, but not so far as to clear the roof altogether. I heard a satisfying clunk and rattle as the briquettes rolled awkwardly down the tiled roof toward the front of the building.

The neighbor's voice burst through the back window. "They're on the roof! I can hear them. On the roof, in the front of the building! Get 'em! They're right above me!"

I barely had enough time to get my hand back inside the closet door when one of the officers came crashing out onto the patio. At first I thought he must have seen me make the throw, but he leaned over the balcony wall and called to his back-up. "Can you see anyone up on the roof?"

"Not on this side of the ridge," a voice from below answered.

"They're on the other side, I tell you. I heard them walking on the roof," an excited, high-pitched voice came from the neighbor's window.

"Get around to the front, fast!" the officer on the balcony told his back-ups. "If they're up there, they won't go far. It's a twenty-five-foot drop." He then ran back through the apartment and into the hallway, followed by his partner.

Hudson chuckled in spite of himself. "Not bad, Ace," he said. "Let's go."

We slipped out of the storage closet, checked once to see if the back up units were really gone, and climbed over the edge of the balcony. We dropped onto the lawn, Hudson accomplishing the task smoothly. I slipped and tumbled, but popped up no worse for the wear. As we made our way out through the opening in the courtyard, I looked both ways and made ready to make a run for it. Hudson restrained me again, saying, "There will be more back-up units arriving any minute. They might look a little suspiciously at someone running *away* from a scene of a burglary."

"So what do you suggest?" I asked.

"Let's go see what all the excitement is all about, shall we?" he said with a twinkle in his eye.

I thought he was crazy. When he turned and walked toward the flashing lights of the police unit, I knew he was. I stumbled after him. We walked up to the black and white, leaned against it and waited, and heard voices calling back and forth as the officers tried to pin down the location of the burglars on the roof.

It was all I could do to keep from running when another unit came driving up, lights ablaze. "What's going on here, officer?" Hudson asked in a bewildered voice.

The new arrival glanced briefly at us while keeping an eye on the roof. "We got a call about a possible prowler on the roof." He looked at us again. "Do you live here?" he asked.

Hudson spoke up before I could say anything. "Not in this building. We live over a couple of units down. Don't get this kind of excitement very often."

"I'm afraid I'm going to have to ask you to leave the area. I don't know how safe it is here."

"Oh…OK." He sounded disappointed. "Whatever you say. Hope you get who you're looking for." We turned and walked away.

I hoped the officer hadn't noticed the grass stain on my knees.

Chapter 25

Hudson couldn't stop chuckling on the way back to the hotel. "That was fun. We'll have to do it again sometime."

"Fun? That's your idea of fun?" Exasperation had taken the place of panic. I couldn't believe it. He was actually enjoying this. "Remind me to leave you off the guest list at our next dinner party."

He looked at me and grinned. "Hey, you did all right. That trick with the charcoal was a thing of beauty. You might have a future in this business after all."

I groaned inwardly. "Right now I'd settle for having a future, period."

We pulled into the parking lot. "Let's go back up to the room and put our heads together on this thing," Hudson said.

"Sure," I answered dejectedly. "It's done us a lot of good so far, hasn't it?" As I got out of the car, I noticed the pile of mail on the back seat. "I might as well get my bills paid off," I told Hudson as I grabbed the envelopes. "I want to make sure I leave a clean estate," I added under my breath

Hudson slapped me on the back. "Have faith, friend. Something will turn up."

I looked at the sweepstakes envelope in my hand. I thought about windfalls and gifts from heaven. "Yeah, right," I said without conviction.

I was at the small desk, opening bills and setting them aside for payment. Hudson lay prone on the bed, hands behind his head, planning our next move. "OK, we struck out on your friend's place. Somewhere, there's a key to this whole thing. All we have to do is to go and get it."

"Where would you suggest?" I asked as I tossed the sweepstakes entry into the trashcan and reached for the remaining item in the pile. It was the padded five by eight manila envelope without a return address. As usual, whoever sent it had gotten carried away with sealing it up, and I spent a minute trying to tear the fiberglass strapping tape away from the opening. I almost gave up and tossed it in with the sweepstakes entry, but curiosity got the best of me, and I dug out a cheap miniature pocketknife I carried on my key chain and went to work on the stubborn seal.

"Well, the way I see it, we have only two choices. We either break into KOPP, or we break into Carillo's house."

I blanched at that. "After tonight, I'm not wild about either. Especially KOPP. I'll bet they have some security there, and the place is probably wired as well. If I get a vote, I say we try Carillo's place. But I don't know where he lives." I finally managed to get the knife blade under the tape, and I began prying it up.

"I know where he lives," Hudson answered.

I looked up. "You do?" I swallowed hard. "Then I guess we ought to go visit him next, huh?"

Hudson shook his head. "It isn't that easy. If you think the security around KOPP would be bad, you ought to see Carillo's place. He's got one of those spreads down in Washoe Valley off of Franktown Road." Franktown Road, about ten miles south of Reno on the west side of Washoe Lake, is one of the most exclusive and expensive areas around. "Nice place...about ten acres. He just picked it up a few months ago, right after he bought the radio station, and it's already like a fortress. Infrared beams around the perimeter, armed guards, all hidden, and worst of all, dogs. Doberman Pinschers. They've had their vocal chords removed so they don't make a sound. I just barely missed getting nailed by them when I did a little recon on his place. You have to go through all that just to get to the door. Lord knows what else he has inside." He shook his head. "Breaking into the center ring of the Pentagon without credentials would be easier."

He blew out his breath. "I just wish your friend had left us something to go on."

"It looks like he has," I said, staring at the contents of the envelope. "You son of a gun, Chuck. You *are* calling us from the other side, aren't you?"

"So what do you think might be on that?" I asked Hudson, as he took the 3½ inch floppy disk from me. "The note here doesn't seem to help much." I read the hastily written scribbles on a half a sheet of yellow notebook paper. 'Greg, keep this safe. Hide it. Don't tell anyone. IMPORTANT! Chuck.' That was it.

Hudson asked to see the envelope it came in. It was a standard 5x8 manila envelope with a bubble wrap lining. "He probably got it from the radio station," I told him. "They use them to send out tapes and CDs."

He was more interested in the postmark. "He sent it out book rate. This thing could have been floating out there for a week or more." He tossed the envelope onto the bed and held up the floppy disk. "Well, let's see just what your friend is trying to tell us, shall we?"

The nearest computer of any use to us was back at the television station. It was a quarter to three when we got there, and I let us in the back door so the overnight producer wouldn't see us come in. As we walked through the studio past the news set and sat at my desk, I wondered if the eerie feeling my surroundings gave me was a result of the circumstances or the fact that I was almost never there when it was completely dark like it was then. It was probably a combination of both.

I had three computers that had a 3 ½" floppy drive, but one was networked into our newsroom computer, and only worked on an old style DOS operating system. The other two were Windows- based operating systems. The first was a graphics computer that displayed the weather pictures behind me while I gave the forecast, and the second a workstation computer that downloaded the raw data and weather charts I used in creating my forecast. Since my workstation computer was hooked up to a printer, I slid the disk into its floppy drive.

"OK Chuck, you've been quiet for too long… talk to me," I whispered, hoping that he wasn't a Macintosh fan. Mac files wouldn't be recognized on my PC.

I clicked on the "My Computer" icon on my screen and opened up the "A" drive. What appeared were two files. Their names didn't do much for me: "pl-tran.xls" and "cd.doc."

I asked Hudson, "Do those mean anything to you?"

"One's a spreadsheet. The 'xls' tag on the end of that 'pl-tran' file is the extension that is used for Microsoft Excel files. The other is a simple 'Word for Windows' word processor file. Do you have those programs on your computer?"

"I think so. I have a suite of programs that I hardly ever use, but I think it includes Excel. I know I have Word."

"Try opening the 'xls' file first then."

I clicked on the file and, true to form, a spreadsheet opened up. I was far from being an expert in spreadsheet programming, but I expected and hoped to see some kind of financial report. *Follow the money*, the old maxim went. But instead of anything that marginally resembled a financial accounting, it appeared to be a database of some sort.

"OK. It's a database. But of what? Where does it say 'x number of pounds of cocaine in inventory'?"

"That might be a bit too much to hope for," Hudson said. "It looks like more of an inventory of music. Hard to find anything unusual in that."

The spreadsheet was a fairly simple one. Under the first heading was simply "Song 1." Beneath that, a list of songs, numbered, interestingly enough, from 0-3: Bruce Springsteen, "Born in the USA," was next to the zero; Pat Benatar, "Shadows of the Night," next to the 1; Kool and the Gang, "Celebration" by the 2, and so on. "I'm no expert on contemporary music," I began, "but I doubt they are going to stay on the top of the ratings with this selection."

"What's wrong with these songs?" Hudson asked. "I like them. Look at these. Elton John, Jackson Browne, even a little John Lennon."

"You like them?" I asked with a grin. "That just proves my point. Most of these songs are pretty old. Not ancient, like the Beatles or the Stones..." Hudson blanched at calling the Beatles and the Stones "ancient." He probably thought they were still in vogue. "But every one of these came out at least a couple of years ago. In the world of radio, they are just a few years from belonging in an 'oldies' format. Chuck was complaining about this, right before..." I paused, and then went on quietly. "Just before I talked to him last."

This piqued Hudson's curiosity. I related Chuck's frustration at having to adhere strictly to a playlist that he didn't like, and of Steve Richards' reaction when he varied from it. He thought about that for a bit. "Do you think that's relevant?" I asked him.

"I don't know, but it is information. Sometimes you just have to wade around through a lot of trash before you come up with anything useful." He looked at the computer screen. "Let's hope this isn't just more refuse."

The spreadsheet was pretty extensive. There were ten categories, beginning with the aforementioned "Song 1" and going to "Song 10," and beneath each category, a list of songs, each numbered. Curiously, the numbering started with 0 and then went up from there. Most of the categories had 10 songs in them, with the exception of Song 1, which only had 4; Song 3, which only had 3; and songs 7 and 9, which only had 6 each. Seventy-nine songs in all. A lot of them I recognized. David Lee Roth's "California Girls." Bob Seger's "Like a Rock." Billy Joel's "Uptown Girl." Even Michael Jackson's "Beat It." But nothing that appeared to have anything to do with the distribution of drugs. It looked like a dead end.

"Let's try the other file," Hudson suggested.

I was rapidly losing optimism. I clicked on the "cd.doc" file. As the word processing program kicked in, I muttered, "With a name like 'cd.doc,' it's probably just a list of compact discs that the radio station has."

"Let's see," was all Hudson said in return.

But when the word processing program opened the file, all that spilled out on the page was a mess of ascii characters and symbols, mostly squares. These went on for several pages. Every once in a while a word came out that was legible, but it was buried in a cascade of unintelligible garble. "Oh, great," I muttered. "What is it? Is it in a code of some sort? Maybe encrypted?"

"I don't think so," Hudson answered. "How old is your software?"

"Mine? I don't know. Probably a couple of years old. That's how long I've had this computer."

"Did your spreadsheet software come in a package with your word processing software?"

"Yeah. I'm sure it did."

"And you haven't upgraded either?"

"Nope. No need to. I don't use either of them that much anyway. I only use the word processing to write letters back to viewers that have written me, and I can't remember ever using the spreadsheet before. But it was a suite of programs that came with the computer."

"Interesting."

"What? What does that tell you?"

"It tells me that these two files were probably made on two different computers. If my hunch is right, the 'cd.doc' was written on a newer version of your Word program. You see those rows of squares? I think that's formatting code that your older version doesn't know how to handle. Microsoft is always upgrading things, ostensibly to put in newer features, but I think it's to create a 'planned obsolescence.' While you can open your older files inside of the newer software, you can't view the newer files with the older software. Encourages the customer to upgrade their programs. For a price, of course."

"So how does this mean the files were made on two different computers?"

"Well, it doesn't mean it for sure, but it suggests it. Your older version spreadsheet opened the 'xls' file just fine. That means the software on the computer that created that file was as old or older than yours. But the 'doc' file may be from a newer version of software than you have. Most people don't upgrade their word processing programs before they get a whole new computer." He sighed. "We'll know better if we find a computer that can read this file." He looked at me. "Why don't you print out this spreadsheet? Anybody else in the building have a newer computer system?"

I thought for a moment. "Our controller has a new system. He seems to get one about every six months."

"Lead the way."

The halls of the station were still dark in the early morning hours as we walked past the sales offices. I didn't expect the occupants of this end of the building to arrive for another few hours, so I assumed we would be alone, but all the same I still felt uneasy about our furtive excursion to the controller's office.

When we got to the office, it was, of course, locked. I rolled my eyes skyward as Hudson pulled out his lock-picking wallet, but this time he acquitted himself admirably and had the door open in less than 30 seconds. Grinning smugly, he opened the door, bowed low, and said, "Age before beauty. After you."

We slipped inside and closed the door before turning on the lights. As expected, a new, powerful Pentium IV computer sat prominently on his desk. I switched it on and waited for it to boot up.

"I still can't help shake the feeling we are just fighting windmills here," I muttered. I had immunized myself against any terminal cases of optimism.

"We've got to just keep shaking the trees and see what falls out," Hudson answered. "When I was back in the DEA, 90 percent of all the leads we got ran into dead ends. Just takes patience. Something will turn up."

I slid the floppy disc into the drive and tried to open the file labeled "cd.doc." This time, instead of gibberish, a clean document appeared. It was legible, but instead of answering any questions, it just posed some more.

"Sure seems to be a smaller document than it appeared on my computer," I observed, as we were now left with just a half a page of text instead of the dozen or more pages of garbage we saw on the other computer.

"Yep. That goes along with my theory that it was made on two different systems. It certainly means that this was produced with a newer version of the software." He stared at the screen. "Now all we have to figure out is why your friend thought this was so important."

I read along with him. There wasn't much to read:

Key: Mandy

1-2: Dt
3-4: Tz
5-10: Lat

That was it. "Who do you suppose this 'Mandy' is?" I queried Hudson. "She appears to be the key, whatever that means. Do you suppose that is a code name for someone?" There was something about that name, but try as I might, I wasn't able to place it. I tried to think what the other notations might mean. Dt? All I could think of was Deuteronomy, and I somehow doubted that these were Bible study notes. Tz? That was an abbreviation for "tease," which was a quick insert in a newscast about an upcoming story, which was still no help. "Lat" made me think of "latitude," but "5-10 latitude"? I wasn't getting anywhere.

Hudson was silent. If he was having the same struggles that I was, he didn't show it. He finally said, "Let's get this printed as well. I don't know what it means. But Rome wasn't conquered in a day. Let's sleep on it."

I checked my watch. Almost 5 AM. I was so wired, I didn't know when sleep would come. But the crew should already be setting up the studio for the 6 o'clock morning news, and I had already spent too much time that night in places I didn't belong. I punched off the computer after the printer spit out the paper, turned out the lights, and we snuck out the back door into the winter darkness.

Chapter 26

I was right. Sleep didn't come easy, even though it was after six in the morning before my head finally hit the pillow. Hudson left me at my door, and he disappeared down the hall. I didn't know where he was staying, and he didn't seem eager to volunteer the information. I realized there was a lot about the man that I didn't know, or understand. I still hadn't found out how he got out of Colombia. Under normal circumstances, I probably would be asking him about it every few minutes, but I had other things on my mind.

I thought about trying to call Lauren and the kids, but even though it was after 7 in Texas, they had had a long trip the day before, and they might still be sleeping. It didn't help that I was worried about them. I wanted them to fly under assumed names, but in our post-terrorist world the airlines were getting pretty strict about checking IDs on passengers, and I wanted to make sure they got on their flight. They'd planned on flying into Houston, and were to be picked up by Karen and driven the 50 miles to Conroe. I hoped that paying cash for the tickets and just using Lauren's maiden name was enough to cover their tracks. I know they would have lost me if I tried to track them, but I was pretty naïve when it came to this kind of thing.

But I wanted to hear their voices. I wanted to know they were all right. After almost picking the phone up a half a dozen times, I decided I would try to get some sleep and call them later that morning.

But as I lay down on the ultra-firm bed and tried to get comfortable on the pillow that was stuffed so full my neck was at right angles, my mind refused to lose its grip on consciousness. Even though I had abused my sleep cycle the night before Lauren and the kids left, and my tank was so low I was running on vapors, feelings, words, sights, and fears kept attacking my mind with such ferocity that I became reluctant to close my eyes. The sight of the airplane reaching its vanishing point south of the airport… feeling I would never hold my wife again while I was in the river… the bone chilling, paralyzing fear I felt when I thought it was Dunleavy outside my son's window. As soon as I banished one image from my mind, another would come and take its place.

I decided to try and occupy my mind with a more fruitful exercise. I got out the printouts we had made from the station and stared at them, willing them to reveal their secrets. I didn't get anywhere with the spreadsheet. It simply seemed like a standard playlist of songs. I couldn't see anything significant in the groupings. The numberings were a bit of a curiosity, only because they began with 0 and not with 1, but apart from that... I began to fear that it was just an innocent list of songs in the radio station's arsenal. But I couldn't help feeling that there had to be something in this piece of paper that explained Chuck risking... and losing... his life.

I gave up on the playlist and moved on to the more cryptic document. "Mandy...key..." I muttered. Who was this Mandy? A 'key' personnel? Was she a contact? Maybe she was an intermediary in the distribution of the drugs. She is the key? Is that what it means? I started to get dizzy. Without knowing who Mandy was, I wasn't going to get any further with this.

"Dt." Dt? That didn't do anything more for me now than it did before. Neither did "Tz," or "Lat" for that matter. Try as I might, I couldn't free up my brain enough to see anything more in those abbreviations, if indeed that's what they were, than I did the first time I saw them.

I decided that maybe I was looking too closely, that the trees were obscuring my view of the forest. I dropped the pages on the bed and looked at them together. Even though they were in all likelihood created on two different computers, perhaps by two different people, it's possible they were meant to be seen together. At first glance, I couldn't see any similarities. Even the numbers didn't seem to match up. A column of four here, then ten, then three, then a list of tens. A lot of tens. What did that mean?

I stepped back a little farther. Was there anything to connect them? Tens. Tens...why did that ring a bell?

I looked at the spreadsheet, the "playlist," again. There were ten "song" categories. But not all them had ten songs under them. Then my eyes drifted to the other document. 1-2, 3-4, 5-10? Ten again? Did these numbers correspond to the ten "songs" on the spreadsheet? Does "1-2" correspond to "songs 1 and 2"? I thought I might be on to something there.

Let's see. Songs 1 and 2 somehow gave a value for "Dt." Was "Dt" a number? I still didn't know what the heck "Dt" meant, but if it corresponded to a number, then it must be a number that was less than forty. Since the choices for the first digit (song 1) were 0,1,2 and 3, and song 2 went up to 9, the highest number would be 39, and the lowest, I supposed, would be two zeros...0. 39 sure didn't ring any bells, especially next to "Dt." Or did it? Something briefly flew through my brain. But it was too fast for me to catch it, dissect it, analyze it, or even identify what it was. I pounded the pillow in frustration, but try as I might, it was gone before I could retrieve it.

I went on to the next numbers. "Tz" corresponded to 3 and 4. Another 2-digit number? If that were the case, using the logic from the previous example, "Tz," would have to be a number between zero and 29, since its first digit was 0, 1 or 2, and its second was 0-9. 29 didn't sound any more familiar than 39, and this time there wasn't even a fleeting sense of recognition.

If I thought that was tough to figure out, I didn't know what to do with songs 5-10. A six digit number. Well, sort of. The third and the fifth numbers couldn't be over 5, but still, nearly a million different combinations possible there. I might as well dig my sweepstakes entry out of the trash. Whatever it was, it appeared to correspond with "Lat." What did "Lat" stand for? Latitude? That was my first impression, but I didn't see anything that even closely represented "Lon" for longitude. Latitude without a longitude is like a kiss without a squeeze...doesn't do you much good at all. What else could it stand for? Lateral? Latent? Latisimus Dorsi? I wasn't getting anywhere with this.

I looked at the clock. It was almost eight. Lauren and the kids would have to be up by now. I reached for the phone and began dialing. I was just one digit from completing the call when I stopped. I dropped the phone into its cradle. If Dunleavy ever traced me to this hotel, and I had no doubts that he would eventually, I didn't want to leave a trail to my family.

I threw on a coat and plunged out into the bright morning sunshine. The light hurt my eyes. I walked a few blocks and went into the lobby of the El Dorado Casino, stopping first to get a roll of quarters from a sleepy-eyed slot machine attendant. I found a bank of pay phones, dialed Karen's number, and started dropping in quarters in deference to the sterilized, recorded voice of the operator.

After the third ring, a knot began to twist in my stomach.

After the fifth, panic very nearly set in.

"Come on... answer," I pleaded.

After the seventh, ready to hang up and make a mad dash to the airport, I heard Karen's voice answer with a chipper "Hello?"

"Where have you been?" I shouted into the mouthpiece. Several heads in the lobby turned and looked at me questioningly. I turned away, my face reddening.

"Where have I been?" my sister answered calmly. "Let's see. I've been sipping mint juleps under the cabana. But I suppose you meant your family. Well, Lauren has run off with the starting five of the Houston Rockets, and your kids are down at the river playing with cottonmouths. Where do you think they are?" She sighed with exasperation. "We've been having brunch out in the back. I didn't hear the phone at first, until Lauren told me it was ringing. Honestly, Gregory, you've got to relax and quit..."

"Hey, sis, man, I'm sorry. I didn't mean to snap at you like that. It's just that..."

"Greg? Is that you?" Lauren's voice cut in on the line, and an overwhelming sense of relief flooded through my very being. "Greg, are you OK?"

I blew out my breath for the first time since dialing. "Yeah, babe. I am now."

The call didn't last long. Even a $20 roll of quarters gets eaten alive on a pay phone from Reno to Conroe. But it was like a healing balm to open sores. I related a bit of what had transpired over the last 24 hours, dropping the unnecessary details, such as nearly being arrested for breaking and entering, or worse. But I tried to build up the significance of our discovery of the computer disk. "At least we are making some progress."

After that, we talked about anything but the problem at hand. The kids came on the line, and I was glad to hear that instead of playing with poisonous snakes at the river they had instead been chasing lizards in the back yard. Definitely a non-poisonous species, I was assured, although Christopher remarked, "You mean there are *poisonous* lizards too? Cool! Where do we find them?"

After promising to call again that night, we said our good-byes, and I hung up the phone. Instead of feeling the expected depression, I felt lifted and energized far beyond what a middle-aged man working on four hours' sleep in forty-eight should feel. I walked back to the hotel with a lighter step than that with which I had left.

I had a visitor when I got back to the hotel. Hudson was sitting on the bed as I let myself in the door, and I nearly jumped out of my skin when he greeted me. I was going to have to get used to him appearing out of nowhere.

"Don't you ever sleep?" I asked him, as my newly-gained sense of well-being slowly began to dissolve.

Hudson smiled. "Sleep's for sissies. We've got work to do." He was tapping out commands on a laptop computer.

"What's that for?" I asked, looking over his shoulder.

"Well, my friend, we are going to try to break in to the KOPP studios and do a little exploring."

I groaned inwardly. "I thought we decided security would be too tough to risk it."

"Too tough for you, yes. And for that matter, I would have reservations trying to get in myself. But not too tough for Max."

"Max?"

"Yes, Max. Mr. O'Brien, meet Mad Max."

He turned the screen of his laptop toward me. All I saw was a series of digits and letters arranged with numerical headers on the left side of the screen. It looked to my uneducated eye like a programming code of some sort. I told Hudson so.

"Give that man a Kewpie Doll," he said. "Max is a little creation of mine. I created him to go on the occasional search and destroy mission. We're still working on the destroy part, but he's gotten pretty good at searching. All we have to do is to put him on a flight into the radio station."

"How are we going to do that?" I asked.

"By using God's gift to computer hackers. Does KOPP have an Internet home page?"

I thought for a moment. "I think so. I've never seen it, but I think I remember hearing them mention it on the air for writing in with suggestions."

"Well, let's see, shall we?" Hudson picked up the laptop and set it down on the desk by the telephone. He unplugged the phone and connected the computer up to the jack. He dialed up his Internet Service Provider (ISP) and did a search for KOPP Radio.

"Here we are," he said with satisfaction. A colorful homepage popped up on the screen, extolling it to be "Reno's best stop for Contemporary Adult Favorites" that was the staple of its music library. There were links to a request line and a comment section, as well as links to bios of their on-air talent. I was surprised to see that Chuck's link was still there.

"OK, we're in to their homepage," I said. "But I could have done that. I don't see any links to drug trafficking or 'Click here to break the secret code.' How do we see any more than they want us to see?"

"That's where Max takes over," Hudson answered as he began entering a series of quick keystrokes. "One of the least understood aspects of the Internet is that while it opens up a whole new world to people, it can also open up a lot of your personal life to the whole world."

"I'm not sure I understand."

"You might think of being on-line as kind of a voyeuristic experience, when you can peek through digital windows without anybody noticing. And for the most part, no one does notice, because no one is looking. But whenever there is a computer connected to the Internet by a phone line, it is a two-way connection. It is possible for someone to get into your computer while you are on-line, and if they are smart enough, or mean enough, take a look around. Max is both smart and mean."

"But I thought when I looked at a homepage, all I was actually seeing was just some space on a hard drive at some ISP's location, and not from the actual computer that originated it."

"Ah, yes, well, here's where we have to be a little patient, or lucky. I am assuming that the radio station has a dedicated computer line to the ISP, and that it is open all the time. Even if it isn't, every time the station wants to update their site, they will have to dial it up. Max just hangs out at the gateway, monitoring all the hits on the site, and looks to see which communication line sends any info through that changes the home page. Since it is probably the 'home' computer which will change the home page, Max sends a cookie back up their phone line."

Now I was really getting confused. "A cookie? Isn't that a program of some sort?"

Hudson was pleased. "Close, but not quite. A cookie is generally a simple text file that your computer can receive from another over the Internet. They are usually designed to speed up the interface with the particular site's graphics or to aid in identifying a user to the site."

"Don't I have to manually accept the cookie every time it is sent to me?" I asked.

"You can set your browser to refuse cookies, but most don't bother. You probably have a whole bag of cookies floating around in your computer right now if it's hooked up to the net."

"But if this is a sensitive computer we are trying to hack our way into, wouldn't it probably refuse the cookies?" I asked.

"If it held sensitive data, yes. But we're not trying to get into Fort Knox yet. If my guess is correct, the 'home page' computer has a low security concern for them. But it may provide a door to the rest of their system." Hudson pointed at the screen. "Atta boy, Max. Step one completed. It seems as if Max has found our linking computer back at KOPP." I looked at the screen. If Max had found the Fountain of Youth, I wouldn't have known. It all appeared as a flush of indecipherable data to my eye. I took Hudson at his word.

"So just how does this cookie get us into their computer system?" I asked.

"It doesn't, at least not directly. Real cookies can't do anything on their own, since they aren't programs. But this one is bigger than normal and will make a little room for an applet."

"An applet?" I queried. "All this talk about food is beginning to make me hungry." Which wasn't hard to believe, since I hadn't eaten since the previous morning. "What's an applet?"

"It's a program that will allow Max to sweet talk the computer into believing we are long-lost friends. I send it over in bits and pieces, and the computer thinks it is just the cookie it's already accepted. Each bit of the program attaches itself to the others, and pretty soon enough of it is together to get the computer to do one important task."

"And what's that?"

"Why, to invite Max in, of course."

"And when it invites Max in?" I asked.

Hudson's grin bordered on sinister. "Then it's mine."

Chapter 27

"C'mon Max, you silver-tongued fox. Say the right words." Hudson's coaxing of his program's progress had me actually imagining the little paramour on its knees, courting the station's PC. "Bring her some flowers. Whisper sweet nothings... Bingo!" Hudson shouted triumphantly. "Max, you devil, you. You've got her eating out of your hand."

"I take that to mean we are 'in'?" I asked.

"We are not only 'in,' as you say, but have been given the keys to all the closets."

"OK, but if, as you say, this computer you just hacked your way into—breaking Lord knows how many Federal Statutes in the process—is probably only used for the web site, what possible good can that do us?"

"Well, here's where we have to get a little lucky. I told you I was making a couple of assumptions. The most important assumption is that the station has a network, such as a LAN, set up. If these computers are all on a LAN, then ol' Max can just hop onto a virtual subway into all the other computers on the network. A quick check of the hardware on this machine ought to let us know if it has a network card or not."

Hudson's hopes were confirmed. "Yep! There it is. Max, old buddy, kiss your new sweetie there on the cheek, and tell her you'll call her later. Time to do a little traveling." I caught myself feeling sorry for the jilted computer. I hoped Hudson treated the women in his life better than Max treated those in his.

I watched Hudson work his magic, marveling at not only the skill, but also the youthful enthusiasm he had for the job. His personality seemed to change from the serious, no-nonsense field agent into a giddy adolescent, trying to save the earth from a video game-induced invasion from outer cyber-space. I mentioned it was a good thing he wasn't twenty years younger, because he would probably be spending his nights in a college dorm room, hacking his way into the CIA's computers.

He chuckled. "The CIA? Heck, Max has already left a trail of broken hearts throughout the company's computer network."

I didn't want to hear any more about it.

I watched in silence for the next hour while Hudson and Max traveled through the electronic nooks and crannies of the KOPP computer network. Occasionally, Hudson would utter a few indecipherable grunts of frustration, to be followed by an exclamation of satisfaction every time Max was able to steer around the ever-increasing encryption obstacles they encountered. Finally, he leaned back, interlaced his fingers behind his neck, and let out a long breath. "Interesting," he said slowly.

"What did you find?" I asked hopefully.

"Well, we were right about some things. Those two files your friend sent you did come from two different computers. One of them, the 'doc' file, apparently came from the computer of the departed General Manager's PC."

"Steve Richards?"

"Yes. I was lucky to find it, because it had been erased from his hard drive."

"Erased? Then how did you find it?"

"Erased files can be recovered as long as nothing is written over them. The file is still magnetically on the hard drive… you just can't access it, unless you have the right tools. Fortunately, Max's tool bag is very full."

"What about the spreadsheet? The one with all the songs on it? Did you find the computer that carried that one?"

"Yes I did," he answered smugly. "I sped up the process by asking Max to find the computer in the system that had the toughest security measures imbedded in it. This one was pretty sophisticated, and the directories that held this file had an additional password encryption wall around it. Did me a big favor. It raised a red flag that made finding it a lot easier."

"So what have we learned from all this?" I asked hopefully.

"Not a lot," he admitted. "But I did find something else that might be relevant. I asked Max to do a search on the same song titles that were on the spreadsheet to see if they pop up anywhere else. I couldn't find any other document or spreadsheet which had all of the songs listed, but I did find one that had some of them." A few keyboard strokes later, another document appeared on the screen.

"I've seen one of these before," I said. "This is just a standard playlist insert. Sometimes the program director, or even the corporate management, will want to run a contest of some sort. They will play a special list of songs, and then ask listeners to call the station. They select one of the callers at random, say the 7th one, and if he or she can tell the D.J. what the 4th, 6th, and 9th or whatever song was of the set, then they will win a prize of some sort." I looked at the playlist. "But I don't see what this might have to do with our situation."

"Ah, but I think it does. Two things to consider. Has KOPP been running any contests like the one you described lately?"

"Not as far as I know. They did one last summer, but I haven't heard of one since." Then I reconsidered. "And it doesn't necessarily have to be a contest. I remember Chuck getting aggravated at all these special playlists that Steve Richards was making him run. So maybe it's not a contest playlist."

"OK. How many songs in all do you think the radio station has in its collection?"

"Oh, gosh…thousands, I would imagine."

"Then it would stand to reason that if this was a just a random selection of songs, it would also include songs from the rest of their repertoire. The odds of all ten songs on this list coming from that spreadsheet, without any of the thousands of other songs showing up, is well beyond coincidence."

I did a double take at his mention of ten songs. There was that number again. I related my earlier musings about the songs somehow translating into a numerical code.

He listened intently. "You just might be on to something there. I should have noticed that myself." I allowed myself a moment of self-congratulation. "One thing I am becoming convinced of is this is all supposed to mean something to somebody. Somebody who isn't here."

"Back to communication, again?"

"Exactly. I'm now quite sure that all this is a fairly elaborate code of some kind. That's good news and that's bad news. The good news is, like any code, this one can be broken. Some are tougher than others. But with enough time and patience we'll be able to crack this thing."

"And what's the bad news?" I wasn't sure I wanted to know.

He looked at me squarely. "Time is a luxury that's in short supply."

We poked and prodded the computer network of KOPP for another hour without finding anything else of any great use. "Time to come home, Max," Hudson sighed. He turned to me and said, "He can usually sneak around without being detected for quite a while, but if anybody is keeping a close eye on the system, they might hear a twig snap as Max creeps by. If they were real savvy, they might, just *might,* be able to trace him back through the line and to here." He turned and looked at me. "We wouldn't want them to know who was poking around in their network, now would we?"

I returned his gaze and said dryly, "Certainly not. I wouldn't want them to get mad at me."

Hudson chuckled and tapped in a couple additional commands. "We'll just let him leave their system a couple of presents."

"Presents?"

He grinned. "A back door."

I nodded. I had heard of these kinds of programs. They would allow us to get access back into their computers, bypassing all the security walls. "So you think Max might just want to visit again with his new honey?"

Hudson shrugged. "Who knows? But if we ever want back in, this will save us a lot of time and effort. Max won't have to go through the hassle of having to decode encryption, and it will make him a lot less noticeable."

"What other present will Max drop off?"

A devilish glint appeared in Hudson's eyes. "A neutron bomb."

I knew I shouldn't ask. But with the same irresistible force that draws your eyes to the head-on collision on the side of the road, I asked, "OK, what's a neutron bomb?"

"Oh, one of my own little inventions. It just sits idle in a hidden file until I give it a command. Then it immediately wipes out everything on the computer network...files, operating system, kills everything but leaves the hardware intact. It even alters the ROM BIOS so the computer can't be brought back with a boot disk. All that appears is a simple message that can't be changed without replacing all the hardware."

Now I was getting uncomfortable in earnest. "Bryce, do you think that is really necessary? I mean, I certainly don't have any love for this man who has brought me...brought *us*...so much pain. But aren't we just shaking the hornet's nest here? Do we really want to give him any additional incentive to come after us?"

He looked at me with a mixture of sadness and determination. When he spoke, gone was the hacker's enthusiasm for creating mischief. "Greg, listen to me. You may not want to shake the hornet's nest, but believe me, the hornets are already out of the nest and are gunning for your fanny. You have to understand how a man like Carillo operates. Once he makes up his mind to do something, and he's apparently made up his mind that he doesn't want you around, he then does it. His decisions are cool, calculated, and unemotional. And he doesn't do things half-way. And when he can operate in that kind of environment, when he is in control, he makes very few mistakes. That's about as dangerous as it can get for you.

"If we can rattle his cage...get him off balance...disrupt his life a bit, then we have a chance of getting him to slip up. Right now, that's our only chance of coming out of this alive." I felt it was generous of him to say "*our* chance" instead of "*your* chance," but I didn't say anything. He went on. "You don't play by the rules with these guys, Greg. You may not be able to fight them face-to-face, but you take every opportunity you can to throw sand in their eyes. If you don't, they'll eat you alive."

I considered that. Though it went against my personality, I couldn't find fault in his logic. I sighed. "Well, in for a penny, in for a pound."

He smiled and clapped me on the back. "That's the spirit."

"So, just what is the message that your neutron bomb leaves?"

He told me.

I smiled.

Chapter 28

Having retrieved Max, none the worse for his trip into the KOPP's cyber-world, Hudson shut down his laptop and made ready to leave.

I was getting tired of hearing myself ask what was next. "So what's next?" I asked.

"We watch and we listen," he answered flatly. "And we try to find out who in the world this Mandy is. I have a feeling she is the contact person to this whole operation. I'm going to call in some markers I have with an old friend at the DEA. They might have her, whoever she is, in their database somewhere."

"What? I'm surprised you aren't going to let Max traipse through *their* database for a while," I said, only half joking. "It's not like you to ask permission."

Hudson took it well, but his tone was serious. "A family of wolves will never pee in their own den. I never know when I might need a friend over there."

"So you still keep in touch with your old outfit, eh?"

A hint of sadness crossed his face. "The old outfit?" He shook his head. "No, not the outfit. Just a couple of friends."

"You never did finish telling me what happened in Colombia."

"Later," he said as he opened the door. "Some other time. Try to get some rest, and I'll see you tonight."

Watch and listen. I didn't have anything to watch, and it took me a while to figure out what to listen to. I clicked on the bedside radio and dialed in KOPP's frequency. I didn't have any idea what I was supposed to be listening for, but part of the plan was to listen, so I listened.

Listening made me thirsty. I got a glass of water out of the sink, then lay back on the bed and tried to make some sense of the whole thing, with the net result equal to my last two dozen attempts. Zilch.

The new DJ chattered away between songs. He was young, and even under better circumstances, I don't think I would have liked listening to him. His banter was mindless, and his humor always seemed to contain off-color undertones.

It made me think of Chuck. Though in person his language could sometimes peel paint off the wall, he always had a respect…almost a reverence…for his job. He never succumbed to the temptation to employ "shock jock" tactics, and I always respected him for that. "You never know who might be listening," he used to say when I complimented him on his restraint. "Even though I doubt too many kids are listening, who can tell? Maybe they are getting ready to consider this kind of music 'retro.' Anyway, I don't need to hold an audience by being crude."

I wished his replacement felt the same way.

The music finally drowned out his monologue, and I closed my eyes and tried to think if this song being played was on the list. I didn't recognize it, so I doubted it. But I still listened, and soon my thoughts drifted from music, to Chuck, to hospitals, and inevitably to my family.

The door opened. A loud creaking, as if the hinges hadn't been oiled in years, caught my attention. I turned my head to see what it was. What I saw sent a shock wave of paralyzing terror throughout my body, almost at once freezing my heart, then sending it pounding against my ribcage at break-neck speed.

Chance Dunleavy stood in the doorway. He was casually leaning against the doorjamb, chewing a wad of gum, looking down at me, eyes gleaming.

He was smiling.

"Giddaaaaaay, mate," he said in a strange, slow, drawn-out voice. "It's so good to see you again."

I tried to roll off the bed, hoping to go fast enough to get to the chair before he got to me.

But I didn't roll off the bed. I didn't roll anywhere. Like an insect buried in the sap of a maple tree, my limbs were very nearly frozen in place by my side. I swung my head back to Dunleavy, fighting through the dense, viscous ooze that seemed to cover my body. *Oh, no. I've been drugged again,* I thought. I immediately realized he must have put his nerve agent in the water. I felt even more helpless than I had in the steam room.

Dunleavy continued to smile at me, his eyes narrowing. Then a soft cackle began from his lips, which peeled back to reveal sharp points and yellow stains. This time there was an evil glee in his manner, blacker and more bloodthirsty than before.

152

He held something in his hand. It was a rope, two ends trailing out the door. "Oy've got a little present for ya, mate," he said slowly, as he tugged on one of the rope ends.

My initial fear was nothing compared to the sheer terror that struck me as I saw what the rope was attached to.

Lauren.

Bound by the ropes, with her mouth taped over and her eyes filled with horror, Lauren struggled to free herself. With almost no effort, Dunleavy pulled her to him, his arm clamping vice-like around her waist. Lauren's attempts to scream were reduced to a muffled murmur behind the tape.

His smile became even more demonic, and he laughed louder as he pulled on the other end of the rope.

Mary and Christopher. Bound like their mother, eyes pleading for help. "Daddy, do something," they seemed to say.

I threw every fiber of my will into a single command. "Get up!" my mind screamed at my muscles. I managed to raise my head ever so slightly, but I knew it was hopeless. A cascade of agony swept through me, as I knew I had failed, and there was nothing I could do to save my family.

Dunleavy's laugh grew louder and even more sinister. He swept up Lauren in one arm and the struggling kids in the other with no more effort than if he were hefting a couple of sacks of groceries. "There's a nice river outside. Nice day for a swim, dontcha think?" He winked at me and said, "Now don't you be going anywhere now. Oy'll be right back for you. Oy've got a spot of business to take care of first." And over the muffled cries of my wife and children, he walked out the door, throwing his head back and, straight from the deepest recess of the darkest room in hell, let loose with a howling, cackling scream which continued as he walked, echoing off of the hallway walls.

I shot up off of the bed and sprawled onto the floor. The last of the scream died reverberating off the walls of the empty hotel room, but it wasn't Dunleavy's scream that I had heard.

It was my own.

I looked at the bedside clock. I'd been asleep for almost three hours.

So much for getting some rest.

The dream's unsettling effect still lingered even after I hung up the phone. But it was a vast improvement on the state of my mental health from fifteen minutes earlier. Bathed in sweat and nerves on fire, I didn't even bother to put on a coat as I ran back the three blocks to the pay phone at the El Dorado. Out of breath, barely daring to breathe, I nearly broke down when Lauren's voice came on the line at Karen's. "I just had to hear your voice again," I explained when she asked what was wrong. "I…had a dream. I…just had to hear your voice." I felt like my kids did when they walked into our bedroom in the middle of the night after waking from one of their own nightmares. How I wished I could just crawl under the covers and have her hold me and make it all better. But for now, this would do.

"Do you want to tell me about it?" she asked.

"No…not now. I'll tell you about it some day. This is what I need now." And it was.

If she thought I was going over the edge, she didn't say it. If she had voiced that diagnosis, I would have been hard pressed to disagree with her. But mankind hasn't designed a therapy to equal her handling of my frayed nerves. It would have been better if the kids could have come on the line, but they'd gone out with Karen to watch one of their cousin's Pop Warner football games.

When I asked her why she hadn't gone herself, she replied simply, "I thought I'd better stay by the phone."

Imagine that.

I told her I would call her that night and reluctantly dropped the phone back onto its hanger. I walked back to the hotel room oblivious to the December chill, showered, changed, and drove to work.

No one, real or imaginary, tried to kill me while I was at work. It was a nice change.

The chance to occupy my mind on another problem, namely determining the path that the polar jet stream was likely to take during the upcoming week, helped clear my mind out a bit. After the newscast, I drove past the north end of the airport on Mill Street toward downtown. I switched on the radio. Watch and listen. The first two songs were unfamiliar. Then, one of the songs I remember being on the list began to play. "Goodie Two Shoes" by Adam Ant. I sat up in my seat. Like Hudson, I had the unmistakable conviction that this song was meant to tell someone something. But what was it? I drove past my hotel so I could listen carefully to the rest of the song. Was anything changed in the song? Some hidden change that someone else could decipher? If there was, I couldn't pick up on it, and I knew this tune pretty well.

I waited for the next song, hoping it was another from the list. My hopes were dashed when the annoying voice of the new DJ piped in, "And now, straight off their newest release, destined to go platinum, let's hear…" and started a song from a new group that I knew wasn't on my list. Deflated but determined, I forced my mind to focus on the task of trying to figure out the code.

I never had much of a mind for figuring out abbreviations. Our family had a game we would play in the car of trying to be the first to decipher the meaning of vanity license plates. Even the kids were better at it than I. Especially Christopher. I would just begin to set my mind on the first two letters of the plate "2THDKTR" when Christopher would chime in "He must be a dentist, Dad. His license says 'Tooth Doctor.'"

"How did you do that, Son?" I would ask with incredulity.

"Aw, dad. That one's a piece of cake. I just looked at it and it said 'Tooth Doctor.' You're thinking too hard."

Oh, for the pleasure of an uncluttered mind. If mine had been a little less occupied, I might have seen that the headlights behind me, made more noticeable with one parking light burned out, hadn't changed since I passed my hotel.

It was time to make another phone call. I didn't know if it would make a difference, but I decided to play it safe and call Karen's place from a different location. By then I had circled back toward the airport and decided to pull in to the Reno Hilton. Originally the MGM Grand, the Hilton is one of the more noticeable landmarks in the valley. Finding the main parking lot filled almost to capacity, I steered around to the right of the building and found my favorite, though unofficial, parking spot. When the management of the Hilton built a large outdoor concert arena a few years before, it covered the majority of the lower parking lot. But around back tucked up against the hill, below the bus entrance, the fence around the stage area took a sharp bend, leaving a couple of spots of the now abandoned parking lot. Unless there was a concert, these were almost always empty, and it was a lot closer to the entrance. I pulled in, turned off the car, got out and locked up. It was only then that I realized I had effectively steered into a box canyon. The hill and the fence formed a U-shaped enclosure with a narrow opening I had to walk out of to get to the front entrance unless I wanted to try to scale the hill. Six inches of snow and the street shoes I was wearing made that a very unappealing option.

I was relieved to see no one followed my car into the recess where I parked, so I hiked up my courage and walked back out toward the opening.

My mind began to settle back on the problem of the code. The unlit entrance to my little cul-de-sac was bordered on one side by a couple of mini vans, with a large trailer used for concert security operations on the other. As I passed through, a noise behind me and to my left snapped me out of my daydreaming. My nerves being what they were, I whipped around, immediately ready to fend off an attacker. But the noise wasn't an attack on me.

In the shadows, between the minivans, I could barely make out two men locked in a struggle. One was large, the other much smaller. I overcame my initial impulse to high-tail it out of there and cautiously approached.

The smaller man was holding his own quite well. In the close quarters they had found themselves in, the big man had a tough time landing any punches. Short, peppering jabs from the smaller man found their mark but didn't have a lot of effect.

The larger man apparently grew tired of trying to keep it a boxing match. He pinned the smaller man's arms to his side, picked him up as if he were a child, and slammed him against the side of the minivan. Then he did it again, just for good measure.

The force of the blow took a lot of wind out of the smaller man's sails, but it didn't stop him altogether. I saw him lift his knee in what I thought was going to be an attempt to kick out at his larger foe, but he didn't have an angle for that. Then I saw his hand drop toward his ankle, and realized he was reaching for something protruding just below the cuff of his pants.

As he was about to pull out his gun, I walked up, put my hand on his wrist, and said calmly but firmly, "Don't shoot him, Bryce. He ain't much of a sportscaster, but he is my friend."

Chapter 29

"I just figured you needed some looking after," Skip Walker said over a quesadilla half the size of Nebraska. "So I followed you. I knew that you were having some kind of problem, and you were too dang-blamed proud to admit it or to ask for help." He washed down the cheese and sauce with another swig from an enormous Diet Coke. "But I gotta tell you, little brother, when you get your bloomers into a bind, you don't mess around, do you?"

Skip, Bryce, and I were in the Reno Hilton, sitting at a back table inside Chevy's Restaurant. I had spent a tense minute or so out in the parking lot convincing each of them that the other was on the side of the angels. At first the two eyed each other with some suspicion, but progress on détente had begun when they found a mutual fondness for Mexican food.

The classic "guy who was following the guy who was following the guy" scenario had caught them both. Unbeknown to me, Bryce was tailing me, watching my rear. Skip, who was also watching out for me, noticed Bryce following me. Bryce was about to walk up behind me in the parking lot and chew me out for not noticing the tail, when Skip decided to intervene. I had to admit it felt good that both of them were looking out for my best interests. But I still couldn't resist a quick jab at Bryce for not noticing Skip on *his* tail.

"I must be getting old," was all I could get in response.

At first, I hesitated to tell Skip anything about my situation, still not wanting to get him involved. But I realized he *was* involved already, and instead of him blindly following me around, where he might stumble into danger, I had better fill him on what I was up against.

So I told him the story. The whole story, from start to finish. The "accidents," the drug connection, even some of Bryce's history, who sat quietly through the discussion.

Skip listened and asked intelligent questions at the right time. Throughout, I worried what I was getting him into. I worried I might be responsible for him getting hurt, or worse. I was hoping he might get scared off when he found out who and what was behind all this. Well, sort of hoping. I guess that if I were truly honest with myself I would have to admit I really wanted some more players on my team.

When I was finished, I wanted to give him an out. "Skip, you don't have to get involved with this. I know you've lived through some pretty tough times when you were growing up, but you should stay away. These are bad people. And it isn't your war."

He looked at me for a moment. "It is now," he said simply.

I showed Skip the readouts from the computer disk and told him about our foray into the KOPP computer. "I knew that radio station was evil from the start," he commented. "Anybody who would play the kind of music they play has to be without a soul." Skip's musical tastes, heavy on the bass and light on melody, which blared continually from two large speakers in the sports office, were well known throughout the station. And into the next county, I daresay. None of us knew how he ever got any work done in there.

Not wanting to get into another argument on what constitutes music, I drew the conversation back to the problem at hand. "What we have to figure out next is what these songs mean to whomever they're meant for, and what these abbreviations mean." I showed him the document with the "Dt," "Tz," and "Lat" notations. "Mean anything to you off the top of your head?"

Skip could fool you into thinking he was a fairly simple individual, but topping that imposing physique of his sat a quick and perceptive intellect. But he shook his head. "Can't think of anything right now. Let me mull it over for a while." His eyes brightened. "Maybe over dessert. They have a great fried ice cream here."

"You two get some," I said with a smile. "I have to go make a phone call."

I left the two men at the restaurant while I bought my roll of quarters and found some phones near the elevators. My mind was still going over the problem figuring out the code when Lauren answered after the first ring.

For a moment, I could imagine everything was all right in the world. I told her of the occurrences of the rest of the day, including Skip's entry onto the scene. She sounded worried for Skip, but I could also detect a note of relief in her voice as well.

I read her the two computer printouts to try and get a fresh perspective. As with me, the abbreviations didn't light any bulbs over her head. "I'm afraid I'm just not very good at this game," she answered.

Game. That gave me an idea. Even though I knew the kids were already in bed, since it was after 10 PM in Texas, I said, "Honey, go get Christopher up. I want to ask him something."

Lauren hesitated, always reluctant to wake the kids, but realized these were not normal circumstances. After a couple of minutes, the soft voice of my son came on the line.

"Hi, Dad," he said, his voice slurred by sleep. I could imagine him on the other end of the line, with tousled hair and puffy eyes. "Wassup?"

"Son, I need you to play the license plate game with me."

"Now? Can I do it tomorrow?" He was unusual for a six-year-old. He actually *liked* going to bed.

"Just play once with me, Bud. If you figure it out, I'll buy you a present." If he figured it out, I'd buy him a car at this stage. I decided to try just the first two codes, since they only had two digits in them. "Let's say I have two numbers, okay?"

"Okay."

"Each number has an abbreviation after it. You remember what an abbreviation is?"

"Daaad…" Whenever Christopher got exasperated with me, he would drag out the 'a' sound in 'Dad.' "Of course I remember."

"Alright, son, I thought you did. So pretend there's a license plate, but instead of numbers, it has two abbreviations."

"Okay."

"Okay. The license plate says 'Tz' and 'Dt.' Guess what that means."

"Time and date, Dad. Can I go back to bed now?"

I was stunned. Time and date? 'Date' made sense, but… "Time and date, Son? How do you get 'time' from 'Tz'?"

"Daaad…. You're the one who told me about Time Zulu."

I stood red-faced. Of course! What an idiot. Time Zulu, another word for Greenwich Mean Time, the universal time clock set up so that all of the world can have one reference time to follow. Back when the British Empire ruled the seas, Greenwich, England became the center of world travel. With the advent of different time zones, it became apparent there needed to be a single worldwide reference time. That has become especially necessary for the meteorological industry. All the weather balloons go up globally at the same time—midnight and noon, Greenwich Mean Time. Mariners, pilots, and even more pointedly, meteorologists, lived by Time Zulu.

"Dad?"

"Yes, Son?"

"Can I go back to bed now?"

"Yes, Son. Sleep well. I love you, buddy."

"I love you too, Dad." He paused. "Dad?"

"Yeah, tiger?"

"Did I do good?"

"You did good, Son. Real good."

"Of course!" Bryce's palm slapped against his forehead. "Time and date. How could we have missed it? How did you figure it out?"

"I hired a consultant."

I had returned triumphant from my phone call after saying my goodnights to Lauren. She was as encouraged as I by the discovery. I enjoyed seeing the look on my friends' faces when I passed along Christopher's revelation.

"Okay, 'Dt' means date, and 'Tz' means time. Where does that leave us with 'Lat'?" I asked. "If this has to do with the distribution of the product throughout the country, I still don't see what it all means." I felt my initial euphoria begin to slip away.

Bryce was thoughtful. I could tell he was putting the pieces of something together. I waited.

"It's not distribution."

I was surprised. "It's not?"

He smiled. "No. It's importation." Then he positively grinned. "And that's good news for us. No wonder he's so testy about all this."

Skip gave up trying to follow. "What are you guys talking about? What's this distribution and importation all about?"

I brought him up to speed about the three possible uses for the radio station in Carillo's plans, and how we had been thinking it might be used to help in a distribution network once the drugs were in the country. "But now our esteemed Mr. Hudson seems to think it is being used in the importation of the junk into the country." I turned to Bryce. "And just why is that good news?"

His eyes gleamed. "Because now, we can hurt him."

We decided to go back to my hotel room and talk it all out. Bryce said he still needed to figure out a couple of things on the way, and the drive would help him get his thoughts together.

As we got to our cars, Skip stopped and asked, "Before we go, I need to know one thing."

"What's that?" Bryce queried.

160

Skip grinned. "Who follows who?"

"Cute."

I did a little thinking of my own on the way back to the hotel. In the midst of the fear and the tension of the last few weeks, I couldn't help but wonder at how lucky I was to have gotten this far. Or was it luck? It certainly wasn't due to any great survival skill on my part. Somebody was watching out over me. A slash pile on the mountain road, a timer in the steam room, even having a river to dive into...why were they all there at the right place at the right time? It was as though I was being given a second chance at life. Actually, if my count was right, I was working on the fifth chance. While not yet ready to laugh in the face of danger, it did help lift the feeling of hopelessness that I had been in danger of falling into.

I remember fishing for salmon in the bay where I grew up. About half the time I'd hook a salmon, and the other half some kind of bottom fish like a cod or a dogfish. I could always tell what I had on the other end of the line. Even a large bottom fish when hooked would put up a brief struggle, and then, resigned to its fate, would just let me haul it to the surface, eyes bulging, awaiting the gaff or the net without protest. But salmon...the salmon was a different story. A salmon half the size of a bottom fish would reel off line from the time it was hooked. Never giving in to defeat, if it couldn't throw the hook, it would try to break the line. If it couldn't break the line, it would try to chew through the leader. And instead of succumbing to the inevitable, the sight of the net would send the exhausted creature on yet one more desperate run for freedom.

The salmon didn't always win. But he never gave in.

I rolled down the window, letting the frigid air embrace my face. "I ain't in the net, yet, Jorge," I spoke into the night.

The three of us sat around the table in my hotel room. The radio played softly in the background. Bryce said, "Okay, let's get our ducks in a row. I'll bet the purpose of this whole thing is to help facilitate the importation of cocaine into the country. Thanks to Greg's discovery, I think I have figured out how this code works. Well, at least most of how it works."

"Do tell," Skip said.

"All right, class. We know that 'Dt' means date, and 'Tz' means time zulu, or Greenwich Mean Time."

"Are we sure of that?" I asked. "I mean I know that's what I said earlier, but how can we affirm that?"

"It almost has to, Greg. Remember the 'Dt' abbreviation was a two-digit number between zero and 39? A date, if you only use the day of the month, has to be between zero and 31. Two songs on that list are played, and the corresponding numbers form a date. You recall the first digit in the 'Dt' column could only be 0,1,2 or 3. The second song could correspond to anything from 0 through 9. Those are all the numbers needed to count from 1 to 31."

"Okay, that would give us the day of the month, but how do we know what month?"

"If it is what I think it's for, that's all you need to know. When whomever this message is intended for gets it, he has less than a month to act on it. Probably much less than that. I think it can be assumed the date is within the month."

"And the time?" I asked. "Wait a second. I think I see what you mean." I looked at the spreadsheet again. "The time, 'Tz,' at most has 29 different choices. Are we thinking 24, perhaps?"

"Exactly," Bryce exclaimed. "24, for 24 hours on the clock. The second set of songs will tell someone when the delivery is to be made. A 12 would be at noon, Greenwich Mean Time, for instance."

"That would make it 4 AM our time," I calculated. I began to see the light. "So, depending on what songs are played, you think it sends a message to someone that they are supposed to deliver a load of cocaine at a certain date and time?"

"Yes. So we have a time and date. What's missing?"

"Location," chimed in Skip. "Knowing when a load comes in doesn't mean a lot if you don't know where to deliver it."

"Bingo!" smiled Bryce. "That's where 'Lat' comes in."

"Latitude?" I asked. "That was my first impression."

"I'm pretty sure of it. It would give you all the pieces to the puzzle. And it fits in other ways as well. You can see the 'Lat' code has 6 digits in it. On a worldwide scale, you need to take a latitude out that far to give an accurate position."

"Wait a minute," I put in. "I hate to rain on our parade, but a latitude won't do us much good without a longitude. You have thousands of miles along any one latitude line."

He smiled. "That's the beauty of it all. Not only did Steve Richards help us crack this code by writing it all down so he could remember it, he also unwittingly told me how the drugs are delivered."

"Now you've lost me," I said.

"Okay. There are only really two ways to move large amounts of cocaine into the country. What do you think they are?"

"By plane... and by boat, I would guess. And by truck too, I suppose."

"Right on the first two. But since Nine-Eleven, the Feds have really clamped down on any large vehicles crossing the border, so trucks are out now." He thought for a moment. "The extra border security is probably why Carillo dreamt up this whole scheme in the first place, now that trucking routes are basically worthless. That leaves planes and boats. And the way this code is set up, he's told me which it is. Which way do you suppose?"

Skip caught on before I did. "By boat," he said, the light of understanding flashing in his eyes.

"Very good."

I was still being slow. "How do you know that?" I asked, feeling dumb.

Bryce was patient. "It only becomes effective to bring drugs into the country once you are on land, so whether by plane or by boat, the snow is off-loaded on land, right?"

"Right."

"A plane can land anywhere inside the borders of the country, so you would need both a latitude and a longitude to pin them down. But a boat..."

It finally dawned on me where he was heading. "But a boat stops once it hits land. Since our coastline, at least on this side of the country, basically runs north-south, once you have a latitude, you just follow it to where it intersects the coastline."

"Exactly. So depending on what songs are played, you have a date, a time, and a location."

Skip was troubled. "Wait a moment. Why go to all this trouble? Why don't they just arrange a pick-up before they leave Colombia?"

"Two reasons for that. One, I'm sure they have dozens, maybe hundreds of possible landing sites all up and down the west coast. Carillo has several of them checked out right up until before delivery to see if any of them is being patrolled. He would want to wait until as late as possible to let the ship know where to land in case he had a bad feeling about one of the sites.

"But a better reason would be lack of trust. A man like Carillo plays his cards pretty close to the vest. And a secret in Colombia is about as secure as it is in Washington DC. He doesn't want any chance of the delivery location making its way to the DEA or the border patrols. This way, he can make the decision late enough to almost eliminate the possibility of the good guys getting wind of it."

"So why doesn't he just radio the location to the ship?"

"Two reasons for that, too. One, there's no such thing as secure communications anymore. One of the biggest pushes the DEA is making is to intercept so-called *secure* communications. All along the coast, the airwaves are being monitored to see if anything fishy turns up. Cell phones, radio phones, even encrypted satellite links are getting busted by some of the latest spy techniques." He grinned. "A peace dividend of the cold war. Carillo must know that and can't take a chance that any of his calls would be picked up.

"But another reason is even if we couldn't intercept the calls, we *can* tell if any communication is occurring. If we thought that a fishing boat off the California coast was making a satellite call *somewhere*, that alone would raise a red flag. We wouldn't bust it, but you can be sure we would track it."

Skip wasn't convinced. "Isn't a radio station a pretty expensive way to just act as a message boy?"

"Expensive?" Bryce snorted. "Cheap at twice the price. How much do you suppose the station cost him? Five... ten million dollars?"

"Maybe," I said. "No more than that, I would guess."

"He would make that with one shipment and have change to get half a dozen more. Depending on the size of the boat, we're talking over 50 million dollars a run."

Skip still wasn't quite convinced. "Okay, one last problem. How can the boat hear a radio station in Reno? I mean, they are out in the ocean."

I had the answer to that one. "It's the skip, Skip."

"Huh?"

I told him about the range of the station, and how fishermen in Baja could pick it up clear as a bell. "I'm sure with 50 thousand watts and a transmitter on the crest of the Sierra you could probably hear it all up and down the coast, out for hundreds of miles. And who would suspect a *Reno* radio station would be sending messages to drug runners in the Pacific? It's ingenious."

I thought about the implications. "So here's a secure way to communicate to a boat, with a code that can't be cracked, because no one knows it's a code?"

Hudson smiled. "But *we* do."

Chapter 30

I hated to rain on anybody's parade, much less my own, but there was still a problem. Two problems, actually. "Okay, so we know it's a code. But *when* is it a code? I heard one of the songs on the list earlier this evening, but it wasn't followed by any of the others. That either tells me that something else is needed to kick off the code, or else we're way off base here."

"The key," Hudson said, half to himself. "You're right. There is another piece to this puzzle. Mandy. We have to find out who this Mandy is." He thought for a moment. "Or what she is."

"What she is?" Skip asked.

"Sure. How do we know Mandy is a person? Maybe it's the name of a boat, or a corporation, or who knows what else he/she/it might be?"

"A boat. I like that idea," I said. "After all, haven't we pretty well decided this is a code for deliveries by water?"

Bryce dwelt on that for a bit. "I don't know. Something doesn't fit there. If this 'Mandy' is supposed to be the *key* to cracking this code, it wouldn't make sense that it would be the boat. The boat, wherever it is, is the recipient of the information, not part of the delivery of it. But let me check into the shipping registry records and see what I can come up with." He pulled out his laptop computer again and plugged it into the phone jack. "I'll start with Lloyds of London and do a search on any ships named 'Mandy.'" He booted up the computer and sent Max back to revisit some of his old flames. With the ease and speed of his entry into some of the databases, I could only assume that Max had made this trip several times before.

"This might take a while," he said. "I'll stay here and work on it. Don't you two have to be somewhere soon?"

"Huh? Where...?" Then in a panic, I looked at my watch. 10:20. The 11 o'clock show started in 40 minutes. "Holy Cow! Skip, we've got to get back to the station."

Skip had lost track of the time, just as I had. "It's a good thing I had that intern set to update the basketball highlights," he said as we breezed out the door. "We'll just have time to make it." He looked at me. "How about your forecast? Any storms headed our way?"

"More than you know, brother. More than you know."

There was a pretty good storm brewing out in the Pacific. A cold low dropping down the coast of British Columbia was just then nearing the tip of Vancouver Island. Within two days, the Sierra Nevada were almost certain to get a pretty good shot of snow, and even the valleys could end up with a few inches out of the deal, although not near the amount as the higher elevations. That was due to an effect known as a "rain shadow," a drying of the airmass as it sweeps down the lee side of a major mountain range. It's the reason Reno only gets about seven and a half inches of precipitation a year, while the mountains just 35 miles to the west can get ten to twenty times that. It's a phenomenon that the Chamber of Commerce loves since it provides more sunshine in an area, and weathermen hate since it screws up forecasts.

But for once, an approaching storm wasn't foremost on my mind after the late news. A girl named Mandy was. I hoped Lauren wouldn't get jealous I was spending so much time thinking of another woman. I think she'd understand.

I tried to get Skip to go home after the newscast, but he refused. "I think I'll just tag along for a while," was all the response I could get out of him. I didn't mind the company.

When we walked back into the room…giving the proper door knock this time, I'm proud to say…we found Bryce still surfing the waves of cyber-space, looking for any references to a ship by the name of "Mandy." The radio, still tuned to KOPP, played in the background.

"I haven't had a lot of luck so far," Bryce said when I asked him for a progress report. "But I do have a couple of things that I want to check out. There are two ships that might meet the criteria listed through various registries. There is a 'Mandy' and a 'Mandy B' that have a Panamanian registry, but unless they are a lot better at covering their tracks than I am in uncovering them, one's in dry-dock for a total overhaul, and the other's in the Atlantic. I found three more ships with 'Mandy' in their names, but they are all too big to consider."

"Too big? Drugs don't come in on big ships?" I asked.

"Not in this kind of operation. Remember that we are looking for a boat that has the ability to off- load in remote, isolated places. I'm assuming this code communicates one of perhaps several hundred possible landing sites up and down the West Coast. The boat may even just nose onto a deserted beach somewhere." He pointed to his screen. "A freighter the size of, let's say 'Mandy Barnes' here, would require docking facilities that you will only find in the major ports. That wouldn't be consistent with what I think we've stumbled onto. No, it has to be a smaller ship. Besides, you don't need a large boat. You can pack an awful lot of snow onto a 50-foot fishing boat."

We were all silent for a while, the only sound being the music playing in the background. Bryce slapped his thigh in frustration. "I can't help feeling that I'm just wasting my time, though. The boat, if it is named 'Mandy,' probably isn't registered under that name. Or for that matter, Mandy may be the English translation of another name in Spanish. What's 'Mandy' in Spanish?" Skip and I looked at each other and shrugged our shoulders. "But the odds are that I *am* just wasting my time, and the name doesn't have anything to do with a boat. There has to be some other connection with this 'Mandy' and the code. I've got to think." He buried his face in his hands, massaging his eyes and his temples, which were overworked after two hours staring at the computer's screen. "Turn that noise off, will you?" he asked, referring to the radio.

I walked over to the radio and started to switch it off when something stopped me. There was something about the song playing which struck a chord. "*...Shadows of a man, a face through a window cryin' in the night. The night goes into morning just another day...*" I tried to place the song, but it wouldn't come to me right away. I continued listening, and turned up the volume a bit to get the words. "*Happy people pass my way...looking in their eyes...*" And then like a burst of fireworks, it dawned on me.

"Will you please turn that off?" an irritated Bryce nearly shouted.

"Shhhh!" I said. I grinned broadly, and said, "Listen!"

"I don't want to listen, I want to..." and then he shut up as I held up my hand for silence and turned up the volume another click.

The voice of Barry Manilow came crooning out of the speaker:

"I never realized how happy you made me,
Oh Mandy, you came and you gave without taking,
But I sent you away, Oh Mandy...
You kissed me and stopped me from shaking..."

We looked at each other with astonishment on our faces. Looks of shock grew into smiles of triumph as Bryce knocked both sides of his head with his fists and exclaimed, "Of course! Mandy isn't a boat, or even a person. It's a song! The *key* song. This is what starts the ball rolling. Get something to write with and take down the next ten songs they play."

I grabbed a pen and pad, and feeling a new hope, waited for the song to finish. Overjoyed at the breakthrough, I started to hum along with Barry as he made his way toward the chorus again. *"Caught up in a world of uphill climbing..."* Skip began to hum along with me. *"The tears are in my mind..."* Hudson joined in the humming, getting louder as we approached that magical chorus. *"And nothin' is rhyming..."*

No longer content with humming, we all burst into song along with Barry: *"Oh Mandy...you came and you gave without taking...but I sent you away."* What we lacked in musicality, we made up for in volume. *"Oh Mandy! You kissed me and stopped me from shaking."* We stood together, put our arms around each other's shoulders, and nearly lifting the acoustic tiles off of the ceiling, broke into the most horrendous three-part harmony heard since before the Gregorians intoned their first chant: *"And I neeeeeeed youuuuuuuuuu!!!!!!!"*

Fortunately, the management of the hotel didn't come and evict us. In any other situation, the cacophony would have been frightful enough to make a train take a dirt road. In this case, it was the sweetest music I had ever heard.

After our outburst, tension crept back into the room, as we crowded around the radio to hear if our deciphering of the code was correct. Bryce had the spreadsheet as the next song came over the radio. "Bingo!" he cried. "Pat Benatar, 'Shadows of the Night.' "

I scanned the spreadsheet. "That's number 1 on the sheet."

"That's the first number of the date, right?" Skip asked.

"Yep," Bryce answered. "That was easy. Now we just have to listen to the next nine songs."

Skip moaned. "Hey, little bro. When I volunteered to help save your skin, I expected to have to face guns and knives. I didn't know I would have to listen to this kind of music. I may have to rethink this."

I filed away in the back of my mind to get Skip an album of *Yani's Greatest Hits* someday, but decided to keep it to myself. "Just sit back and relax, boys, and enjoy the music."

The next song played was Janet Jackson's "Escapade." "That's 9 on the list," I said.

Bryce picked up on it. "So that means their next delivery will be on the 19th, if we aren't completely out to lunch on this."

I thought ahead. "That's this Sunday."

"Okay, let's see what time."

It was somewhat of a tedious process. For one, from a listening standpoint, there was no flow to the music at all, and it looked like it was going to take the better part of an hour to hear all the songs.

But then, I had nothing else to do.

The third song was Billy Joel's "Uptown Girl," and the fourth was "You Give Love a Bad Name" by Bon Jovi. Skip winced every time a new one came on. But it told us the next part of the puzzle.

"A 1 and another 1," I said. "11 o'clock Zulu. That's 3 AM West Coast time."

"Well, now we know the how and the when, let's find out the where."

That took another six songs, a little over a half an hour when you threw in all the commercial breaks. But it was worth the wait.

Bob Seger, "Like a Rock": 3

Asia, "Don't Cry": 7

Adam Ant, "Goodie Two Shoes": 5

Marty Balin, "Hearts": 3

Bruce Springsteen, "My Hometown": 3

Finally, Mick Jaggar and David Bowie, "Dancing in the Streets": 6

Much to Skip's chagrin, we listened to the next song just to be certain it wasn't on the list. It wasn't.

"Okay, here's what we have. If we understand this, our dear friend Mr. Carillo's next shipment will arrive this Sunday at three in the morning, on the coast at 37.5336 degrees latitude." Hudson looked at us for confirmation.

"Almost," I said in return. He looked questioningly at me. "I think the latitude is 37 degrees, 53 minutes, and 36 seconds."

There are two different ways to give a longitude and latitude. Both use degrees as the largest unit, but then to fine-tune it, you can either divide each degree up into a decimal fraction, which was coming into vogue, or else do it the old-fashioned way. Each degree is divided up into 60 minutes, and each minute is divided up into 60 seconds. It makes a big difference which way you read it. 37.5336 degrees would be about 25 miles to the south of 37 degrees, 53 minutes, 36 seconds.

"Remember the spreadsheet. Columns 7 and 9 only had 6 numbers in them. Has to be the old way of giving coordinates."

Bryce couldn't find any fault in that reasoning. Turning to his computer, he inserted a CD into the drive and pulled up a program. "Okay, so it's 37 degrees, 53 minutes, and 36 seconds." He made a few keystrokes and a map appeared on the screen. "We'll just slide along the parallel until we intersect land…and…. ah!" Hudson seemed pleased. "Perfect. Just perfect," he said with a smile.

"What?" Skip asked. "Have you figured out where the drop will take place?"

"I sure have."

"Where?" we both asked in unison.

"Bolinas."

Chapter 31

"Bolinas?" I asked. "Where's that?"

"It's a sleepy little hamlet near Point Reyes on the California coast, north of the Bay area, that never really grew out of the 60's. It has a small bay and a lot of shoreline. A perfect place to make a drop. Not only because of its location, but the inhabitants of this area, for the most part, wouldn't exactly go out of their way to stick their nose into the business of other 'entrepreneurs.'" He thought for a moment. "If there was anything else I needed to confirm that we're on the right track, this is it."

I hated to ask the next question, but I couldn't find any reason for delaying the inevitable. "So…now that we know what we know, and when we know, and where we know, what do we do with this information? Go to the cops? To the DEA?"

"Nope, not yet." I was afraid of getting that answer. Bryce went on. "That may come at a later time, but what are we going to give them? First of all, who would believe us? From what you tell me, Greg, you haven't had the best of luck getting your local gendarmes to buy your side of things around here. And it isn't their jurisdiction anyway. Secondly, what proof of anything do we have? I know we've convinced ourselves that this is all legit, but if I know the fine folks at the DEA, they will need a lot more than what we have in order to commit their resources to a raid. And even if they did, and they confiscated a boatload of stuff, I'll be willing to bet they would never be able to make a case against Carillo. He would just go into hiding and resurface somewhere else." He looked squarely at me. "But he wouldn't forget who bollixed up this operation, Greg. And as hard as you might want to try to keep anonymous, he would find out it was you who blew the whistle. And then getting rid of you wouldn't be just to protect him. It would be for revenge. And Cartel justice doesn't stop with the offender. It includes the family as well."

His words hit me like a shot to the solar plexus. Lauren, Mary and Christopher. I would spend the rest of my life wondering if my family was safe, even in the unlikely event Carillo was put behind bars. It was blackmail, pure and simple, with no way out. At least none that I could see. "So just what can we do?" I asked helplessly.

He looked at us both, and I saw a devious glint in his eye. "Got any plans for this weekend?"

At that point, the only plan I had for the weekend was to be breathing by the time it arrived. I felt I had just about used up all my luck at the Truckee River Lodge, so I moved my worldly goods to The Ormsby House in Carson City. It was about a 40-minute commute to work, and I spent most of the drives back and forth continually checking my rear view mirror, but I decided that getting out of town for a while was worth the trade-off. I would move to another place after the weekend.

The drive back and forth was made tougher with the appearance of the storm, arriving right on time. It was a good one, and while the mountains did pile up the lion's share of the white stuff, getting over three feet in some of the prime locations, we made out pretty well in the valley as well. Six inches of snow in Reno and up to nine inches in Carson City slowed the commute through Washoe Valley to a crawl at times.

I hate it when I'm right.

On Friday morning, I left The Ormsby House early so I could check out our house. On the way, I took a quick detour along Franktown Road.

I wanted to get a look at Jorge Carillo's house. Bryce had described it to me, and it was easy to find tucked in a corner behind the Lightning W Ranch Golf Course.

I'm not sure why I wanted to see it, but as I passed the richly adorned mansion with its expansive grounds behind chain link fencing, I shuddered to think that such evil could hide behind such beautiful digs. I took Bryce at his word when he said it would be futile to try and infiltrate his home, but somehow it felt like I was fighting back by visually invading his turf. I blew a raspberry out the window as I continued to head north and out of sight.

That showed him.

Even though the little detour and the driving conditions slowed my trip north, I still had time to check out our house. Plowing through the fresh snow, I drove up to our mailbox, remembering the last time I pulled out its contents. The thought depressed me, as I thought of what Chuck must have been going through when he tossed the floppy disc and the hastily scribbled note into the envelope. It seemed a desperate move. Did he know they were on his heels? Did he really understand the significance of his own discovery? I resolved to make sure his efforts weren't in vain.

I drove up to the house, punching the remote control on the garage door opener. Nothing happened. I drove the nose of the car right up to the door and tried again. Nothing again. "Must be the battery going bad," I thought in frustration. I got out of the car with the remote in my hand, pushed the button, and pointed it accusingly right at the door. The door stared back at me in mock silence.

Sighing, I returned the remote to the car's visor and slogged through the snow, blown around by a brisk north wind, to the front porch. I put the key in the lock, twisted, and pushed on the door. It opened a bit and caught. "Sticky door," I thought and grabbed the knob harder to give it a firmer shove.

An alarm in the back of my mind sounded.

It wasn't a loud alarm. Just a distant clanging, trying to get my attention from far away.

My hand slowly released the knob. I stepped away and looked at the door. I couldn't see anything unusual. So what was sounding the alarm? A remote alarm. Remote?

Remote. As in *the* remote. The garage door opener. I had just replaced the battery two weeks earlier. It's possible it might be a bad battery, but in the past the little nine-volt had never given out before a couple of months minimum. Coincidence? It could be, but it could also be someone not wanting me to enter by the garage. With the motor hooked up to the garage door, I couldn't open it up by hand without getting inside to disengage the locking mechanism on the drive. The front door would be the logical place to get into the house.

I stepped up to the front door for a closer look. I scanned the seal around the perimeter. There was nothing obvious there. I took out my wallet and extracted a credit card. Don't leave home without it. I bent the end of the card ninety degrees and inserted it into the jamb around the doorframe. I slid the card around the door's perimeter, a task made easier since the door was partly ajar. I was just about to the point of deciding that it was all a result of an over-active imagination when the card stopped against something jammed into the upper left hand corner of the door. I attacked it from the other side. Once again, the card hit what seemed to be a small piece of metal. I clumsily hit the object with the card, and the piece shifted, nearly dropping out. The door shifted a fraction, emitting a single loud creak.

I froze.

Even in the cold, a trickle of sweat began to drop down the back of my neck, and started to roll down my spine. I slowly stepped back from the door. I still wasn't sure what was jammed in it, but I had a pretty good idea, and it wasn't a nice one.

I looked around for telltale signs of activity. The top layer of snow seemed undisturbed, but subtle waves expressed on the surface suggested someone might have been walking on the first couple of inches of snow during the beginning of the storm.

I tried to think. I wasn't sure how close I had come to knocking that metallic piece out of the door, but it seemed like it must be barely hanging on. The wind had continued to rise and was beginning to put some pressure on the door to open. If what I feared was really happening, I had to do one of two things, and I had to do either of them quickly. I either had to turn around and run very fast far away from the house, or I had to get inside and try to fix it. If I ran, I would be abandoning our home. If I tried to get inside, I might be abandoning my life.

Although it might have been foolish, I decided to fight back. Dunleavy wasn't going to rule my life, and I sure wasn't going to give him the satisfaction of driving me away. If I had thought it through, I might have realized the only satisfaction Dunleavy was going to get was to read my obituary, and I was only increasing the chances of that by going in the house.

I walked around to the side of the house to look for a window I could get through. I passed on the master bathroom window, thank you very much. The next window around the corner was the window into our bedroom. It was larger, lower, and thankfully unlocked. I paused before opening it. Would Dunleavy have rigged the windows as well? I wouldn't have thought so.

As a man who makes his living making predictions, I let it all ride on this one. I braced myself and slid the window open.

Nothing happened.

I climbed in this window with a great deal more aplomb than I exited the last and made my way carefully through the bedroom, out into the great room, and to the front door.

What I saw took the sweat trickling down my spine and froze it into tiny ice cubes.

A metal clip the size and shape of a small door hinge was hanging by its corner, jammed loosely now into the doorframe. A thin wire ran down to what appeared to be a small transistor radio. Sitting next to the radio was a duffel bag filled with something I couldn't see. But what caught my attention was the buffeting the door was taking from the wind, and little streams of blowing snow were coming inside through the half-opened door.

Without thinking about how little I knew about the device, I ran to the door and gingerly wrapped my hand around the clip. It was spring loaded, and the door being closed was the only thing keeping the clip closed. I squeezed both my hand and my eyes shut, and gently tugged. The clip came out of the door.

The house did not go up in a ball of flames.

The next puff of wind blew the door open.

My hand ached.

I had been sitting on the living room floor for nearly thirty minutes, trying to decide what to do, and my hand had a death grip on what I was sure was a triggering device for an explosive. I didn't know how strong the spring on the clip was, and I didn't want to test it.

I did look at the set-up a little closer. I noticed the wire running to the small radio-like device didn't end there. Coming out the back of the instrument, the wires appeared again, and they in turn ran into the duffel bag, which was zippered shut around them. I didn't need to be an expert to imagine what was in the bag. I *did* need to be an expert to know if the whole thing was rigged to go off if it was moved. And while I may have thought I knew a lot of things, I didn't know diddly about explosives.

But I had learned a thing or two about Chance Dunleavy, who I was certain was responsible for this little surprise. And I couldn't imagine he would have left this kind of apparatus rigged up without a secondary plan, in case I came in through the back door.

I did finally get up enough nerve to kick the front door shut. The wind had blown a small drift of snow into the room, and that began to melt into the carpet as I stared at the duffel bag and pondered my next move.

Overcoming mental lethargy, I finally came up with two possible options. I could try to move the whole apparatus across the living room and get to a phone. I was nervous about doing this, because as I mentioned, I didn't know if the explosives or the little radio device had a mercury switch or something like that. If it did, and I jiggled the stuff, it would make my holding the spring-loaded switch a moot point.

I knew about mercury switches. I'd read a lot of spy novels.

My other option would be to try and disarm the apparatus myself.

I hadn't read enough spy novels for that.

By default, I decided that I would make a try for the phone. I only had about 7 feet of wire between the clip and the radio, so I had to move the whole unit just less than ten feet before I could make a call.

What should I do? Should I try to slide the objects along the ground? If it was a hardwood floor, then that might be an option, but the friction of the duffel bag against the carpet made a smooth slide unlikely. I realized I had another problem. I had three objects to move and only two hands. I could have probably picked up the radio and the clip in one hand, but the muscles in my right hand were so cramped from squeezing the clip that I didn't dare release any pressure. It looked as if I was going to have to do this by stages.

There was only about two feet of play in the wire between the duffel bag and the radio. Gingerly reaching down with my left hand, I drew a deep breath, and as slowly as I could, lifted the device.

A thundering roar and a blinding flash, mercifully, did not occur. Trying desperately and somewhat unsuccessfully to keep my hand from trembling, I moved the device toward the phone. I set it down carefully and released my hand. Nothing. If the device had a hair trigger, at least the hair had some body to it.

Next, I turned my attention to the duffel bag. This might be trickier. If there were a switch inside that reacted to any imbalance on the bag, I would have to lift the bag straight up, without tilting it. Without any stiff reinforcement of the duffel's bottom, lifting by its handles would cause the ends of the bag to droop to the outside. I was quite sure the thin canvas material had no such support at its base.

Stuck for a moment, I considered other options. My eyes wandered to the bookcase next to the door. On the bottom shelf, three large children's books were placed near the end closest to me. An idea germinated.

I pulled the books out. They were all bound by large, stiff cardboard covers, with a smooth and shiny finish. The kids hadn't read them for years, and it was only due to a combination of nostalgia and laziness that we hadn't either given or thrown them away.

I placed the first one on the ground. *Read Aloud Bible Stories* read the glossy cover. I figured I could use all the help I could get. I almost hated to do it, but I opened the cover and placed my foot on the rest of the book. I gently ripped the stiff, outer shell off its binding. It was a hard, flat, smooth surface. It was just what I needed. I did the same with the back cover and repeated the process with the other two books.

The carpet in our home was anything but plush. But there was just enough give under it that by angling the edge of the book cover under the bag and pushing down, I hoped to be able to slide it under the duffel. The first one slid under without incident, supporting nearly half of the bag. I slid another in from the other direction. There was still about a three-inch gap in the middle. Gritting my teeth, I took another cover and gently pushed the first one in farther until it met the other.

Then came the moment of truth. Hoping the coefficient of friction was less than the tolerance of whatever booby trap might have been set, I carefully grasped the corner of the bag, whispered a silent prayer, and pulled.

Chapter 32

This must be how they moved the pyramids, I thought as I placed another shiny book cover in front of the bag, which I had managed to move a grand total of three feet in ten minutes. But it was progress. The glossy surface allowed the bag to slide with very little vibration toward my goal of the kitchen phone. As the movement of the bag slid past another book cover, I would pick it up and place it in the front of the line.

When I had passed the radio by nearly two feet, I stopped and reassessed the situation. I had to leap frog the radio device over the duffel bag, and it then appeared that I would have enough slack to reach the phone. Gaining confidence, I picked it up and stretched the wires out and set it on the ground. Nothing to it.

Having moved the radio a total of about six feet closer, and having about 7 feet of slack between it and the clip, my wingspan was just enough to reach the phone on the kitchen counter. I picked it up, and with the knuckle of my still-closed and spasm-plagued hand holding the trigger device, I dialed Bryce's pager. I punched in my number and turned off the phone. And I sat.

Mercifully, the phone rang within minutes. "Help. I'm at home. Fast. Make sure you come in through the front door." It was all I could think to say. It was enough. He said he'd be right there.

I don't know where Bryce was coming from, so I wasn't sure how long it would be before he arrived. Through the window, I could see that it had begun to snow again outside, so I was prepared for a long wait.

The time gave me a chance to reevaluate my actions. I began to think I had been a little overcautious about moving the bag and radio as I had. Paranoid was actually the word that came to mind. When I first grabbed the clip out of the door, I was glad I had resisted my initial impulse to pull the wires out of the transmitter. Even though I didn't know about explosives, the door held the contacts on the inside of the clip *shut,* which meant that the triggering device wasn't looking for something to happen to *complete* an electrical circuit, it was instead looking for something to *interrupt* the circuit.

I was confident that pulling the wires out of the device would accomplish the same thing as just opening my hand.

But as for there being a booby trap on the explosives, I had just about convinced myself that was probably a product of my justifiably over-active imagination, when I heard the deep throaty rumble of a large vehicle come up the drive. Hudson. At least, I hoped it was. That didn't sound like his car.

I heard a door shut and the crunch of feet through the snow up to the front porch. The doorknob clicked and turned, and the door opened just a crack. I began to get anxious when nothing happened for about thirty seconds. I thought about calling out, but until I knew who was there, I remained silent.

I was just about to lose my mind when a voice behind me said, "Man, I can't leave you alone for a minute, can I?"

I whirled around. Bryce was standing behind me with a look of amusement on his face. "What are you doing *there*?" I said in exasperation. "I was expecting you to come though the front door."

"And if your call earlier to me was made with a gun held to your head, then that's where *they* would expect me to come in, as well." He assessed my situation. He was lucky I hadn't dropped the clip after being startled by his unexpected entrance.

He strode to look at the set up on the living room floor. "Interesting," he mumbled as he peered around the transmitter without touching it. He thought a moment, and said, "You wait right here and don't move. I'll be back."

"Oh, well, hey. I wasn't doing anything else. Take your time."

As he went out the front door, a gust of wind blew a fresh drift of snow into the room. Then it was silent.

True to his word, he returned about five minutes later, with a loaf-of-bread-sized package wrapped in black plastic tucked under his arm. He tossed it onto the sofa and turned his attention to my dilemma. He carefully unzipped the canvas bag. "My, my, Mr. Dunleavy. We have been a naughty boy now, haven't we?" With steady hands, he carefully reached inside the bag and fiddled with something I couldn't see. When his hands came out, each was cradling something. In his left, a short, pencil-like object attached to a couple of wires. The cylinder had a metallic cap on the end, with the rest of its body made up of what looked like dense cardboard.

But it was the object in his right hand that held most of my attention. It was a small electronic device of some sort, a mass of wires and metal, with a small, elongated capsule, looking like the glass in a carpenter's level, lying horizontally on top. A wire ran from each end of the glass, and inside was a shiny, liquid substance, half filling the glass chamber. Even in Bryce's steady hand, the shiny liquid quaked and trembled with every slight movement. "Is that...?"

"Mercury. A mercury switch, sensitive to anything but the slightest movement," Bryce explained. I resolved then and there if there was a home for old and destitute spy-novel writers, I was making a donation. A very large donation. Bryce went on. "It's a good thing you didn't try to lift the bag, because..." and then his hand seemed to slip on the device, tilting it slightly.

The pencil shaped device in his other hand popped loudly, and a blinding white light flashed at the metallic end.

I screamed and dove for the totally inadequate cover that the kitchen table would offer, sure the light was the last I would ever see.

The roar that I heard was not that of an explosion, but rather of Hudson's laughter. "Man, I love doing that," was all he could get out between guffaws.

In my frantic dive for safety, I had released the clip, which lay open on the floor. "I assume the thing is disarmed now," I said with no little annoyance at my friend's idea of entertainment.

"Yes. Completely. That flash you saw was the igniter. You should feel honored. It seems Mr. Dunleavy is only using the best for you." He held up the now-burned-out end of the igniter. "Pretty sophisticated blasting cap here. Only works with a special kind of explosive." He turned and hefted a flattened, brick-sized mass out of the duffel bag. "It's a highly modified plastic explosive, a derivative of Semtex. Semtex was a gift the Czechs gave to the terrorism industry. But this new stuff has the added bonus of allowing you to shape your charges. I'm afraid we can only blame our own military for coming up with this modification. If I understand this one right, Dunleavy shaped this so the explosive force would be almost entirely outward, instead of downward. Would have flattened the house pretty effectively."

"Why would he bother to do that?' I asked rhetorically.

He chuckled. "Because he is still trying to make it look like an accident. If there was a fifteen foot deep crater by the front door, the fire inspectors might look upon that as just a bit odd."

"Oh, sure. Whereas they wouldn't blink an eye if the house just blew up sideways, eh? I mean, what possible explanation...." I stopped myself. I looked at the package on the couch. "More plastic explosive?" I asked. He nodded. I remembered his tour around the house. "Propane tank?"

"Very good, ace. 300 gallons of propane going up can make quite a display. If my guess is right, here's how he set it up. The door opens, the clip falls out and opens. An interruption in the circuit causes this transmitter," he picked up the small radio like device, "to send a signal to the propane explosives. A few hundredths of a second later, it sets off the big bang here in the bag. It can't do it at the same time, because if the bomb here by the door goes up instantly, it might cut off the signal from the transmitter before it can torch off the propane tank." He looked at the set up admirably. "Quite ingenious, actually."

I groaned. "It ought to be. I gave him the idea."

He gave me a surprised look. "*You* gave him the idea?"

"The snow. The snow and propane tanks." I went on to explain how I've been warning my viewing audience about the dangers of snow building up around propane tanks. If the regulator valve coming out of the tanks isn't kept clear of snow, then the snow can melt and freeze inside the valve. Occasionally, this can cause the pressure from the tank that flows inside the house to increase, and far exceed the appliance's specs. Propane then starts leaking into the house. The next time the furnace kicks in... kablooey.

I thought. "He probably knew the snow was coming. For that matter, he probably heard *that* from me." I nearly drowned in the ocean of irony that created.

"Well, let's look on the bright side."

I looked up at him. "Bright side?"

"Yeah," he said, picking up the packages of explosives. "This stuff is hard to get. You never know when it might come in handy."

The rest of the day passed with a lot less excitement than that with which it had begun. I called Lauren and talked to the kids that night, telling her that I probably wouldn't be calling her the next night. I told her why.

"You are going where?" she asked, sounding worried.

"I'm convinced this is what I have to do, hon," I answered with a lot more confidence than I felt. "It's a way for us to go on the offensive. Or at least not just sit around and wait for something to happen to me. Don't worry, babe, I'll be alright." I knew she wasn't *that* gullible to feel a lot of comfort in that last statement, but it sounded good, and to her credit, she didn't try to talk me out of it.

I neglected to tell her about the adventure in the house. She had enough on her plate as it was.

The kids, as always, boosted my spirits to a higher level than they logically had any right to go. I think just knowing that I was fighting for them as well as myself added torque to the engine that was driving me.

Lauren came back on the line, and we made small talk. I had a hard time hanging up the phone. Just the sound of her voice was a connection that bridged the chasm that had been forced on us, but I realized I was just putting off the inevitable. "I'd better go," I finally forced myself to say. "You do know I love you."

"And you do know that I will be with you tomorrow," was her simple reply.

I thought about that. "Well then, sweetheart, it's time we go bell the cat."

Bryce drove. The loud engine I had heard outside my house the day before belonged to his new set of wheels. A full-sized four-wheel drive Ford Explorer. With oversized studded snow tires, it could probably climb trees if he had asked it to. And we might just ask a bit extra from the behemoth. As we left town mid-Saturday afternoon, a new storm was just reaching the mountains. I began to get anxious that we might get stalled on the pass. But the sight of the bright blue monster was reassuring.

When I asked where he got it, he was a bit evasive. "I rented it," was all the answer I could get out of him. I began to wonder where he got his financing. I then realized I should count my blessings, so I proceeded to think of other things, such as did I bring fresh batteries?

I knew we didn't have enough evidence to go to the authorities based on what we had gathered up to that point. But that didn't mean I wasn't going to try to get some. I brought along a small 8-mm video camera. I used it whenever I spoke at a school to take home movies of the kids so I could show them on the air later that night. The video quality of the camera wasn't up to the standard of the Betacams that the news crew used to shoot their stories, but that just added to the charm. And this particular camera had two advantages. One, it was small and easy to carry. Two, it shot in surprisingly low light. Both of those features would likely come in handy.

Skip rounded out the passenger manifesto on our little excursion. I had given up trying to talk him out of his involvement. "Nice, wheels, B," he told Bryce as he stretched out across the back seat. "This rig's almost big enough for me. I may have to get one of these things." He looked down at a small Japanese compact car as we passed it just before crossing the California State line. "Just be careful you don't run anybody over. You probably wouldn't feel it, and after a while if you let those Toyotas work their way into the tire treads, you'll have a devil of a time digging them out."

Bryce just smiled and cradled the padded steering wheel of his new toy. It was just beginning to snow as we passed Boca Reservoir on our way up the Truckee River Canyon. I looked ahead. The mountains were socked in, and it didn't look like conditions were likely to get any better. I settled in for a long drive.

When we got to the town of Truckee, we stopped briefly at the California Agricultural Inspection booth, better known as the bug station. The bored guard at the station asked us where we were from, and finding out we were somewhat local, let us pass without asking us if we had any fruit that might be carrying any unwanted larvae. If he had known what we *were* carrying, he might not have been so cavalier about letting us through.

Of course, if *I* had known at the time what we were carrying, my attitude might have been a bit different as well.

We traveled a grand total of perhaps 150 yards before we were stopped again, this time by the California Highway Patrol. I thought Bryce seemed a bit nervous, until he saw the officer was just checking to see if cars had chains on their tires. "You won't need them," I assured him. "You have a four-wheel drive with snow tires. They'll close the road before they make you chain up." This seemed to ease his mind, although looking at how the snow was coming down, I wouldn't have been surprised to see them close the road. It was going to get messy up there.

We smiled at the chain monkeys as we pulled out and started up the final 1,500-foot climb over Donner Pass, named after the ill-fated Donner Party, who were nearly wiped out back during the winter of 1846-47. The poorly-equipped group of immigrants from Illinois, trying to find a new life in California, arrived late to the Sierra and became stranded by early snows at what is now known as Donner Lake. A record snowfall that winter sealed their doom. Tales of intense suffering and cannibalism made them required reading in the history lessons of all California and Nevada school kids. It also seemed quite appropriate to have this mountain pass bear the Donner name. Even with state of the art snow removal equipment, winter storms in this area have been known to strand motorists on the pass for days at a time. Fortunately, even in the worst of the modern-day snowstorms, cannibalism seems to have been avoided. At least, none had ever been reported.

I turned around and looked at the yawning, reclining figure of my big friend in the back seat. Then I looked at the rapidly strengthening maelstrom of snowfall outside the car. I guessed it wouldn't hurt to check. "Skip," I asked. "Did you get enough to eat before we left Reno?"

"What?" he said sleepily.
"Never mind."

Chapter 33

We hadn't moved for over an hour and a half. Just over the top of Donner Summit, near the Boreal Ski Area exit, a semi had jackknifed about 300 yards ahead of us, completely closing down the roadway, and there was no telling how long it would be before they got the road opened up again. During our wait, it had snowed 4 more inches, so in all likelihood, even when they got the 18-wheeler out of the way, there would be more cars stuck where they had stopped. They had closed the interstate at the bug station shortly after they let us through, but with the cars that were already on it forming a twelve-mile-long parking lot, the plows couldn't get through to keep up with what snow was falling. It was nearly 6 PM, darkness had overtaken us, and I was beginning to wonder if we were going to make it to Bolinas in time for the drop. Bryce got out of the car and walked ahead to see if Cal Trans was having any luck at moving the roadblock out of the way. In order to keep from asphyxiating from carbon monoxide poisoning due to the snow buildup around the tailpipe, I turned off the car's engine. Now it was getting cold. I wasn't sure how things could get any worse.

"I'm hungry," said Skip from the backseat.

Need I have asked?

I tossed him my last slice of beef jerky, hoping it would stave off any primeval urges that might course through the big guy until we could get to a mini-mart. It seemed to do the trick.

A blast of cold wind and a spray of snowflakes accompanied Bryce as he opened the door and hastily jumped back into the car. "They finally have a couple of tow-trucks working on the semi," he reported. "They ought to have it cleared out in a half an hour or so."

"Even so, that's starting to cut it a little close, isn't it?" I asked worriedly. "Don't we want to get into position by midnight? Even if we get the truck up there out of the way, we still may be looking at 5 or 6 hours of travel time in these kinds of conditions."

"Don't worry, we'll make it, Greg. I've…*we've* …come too far to miss this appointment."

His response reminded me. "Well, since we are just passing time here, how about a little story?"

"Story?" he asked.

"Yeah. You never did tell me how you got from a back alley in Tejeda, to a snowbound Ford Explorer at 7,000' in the Sierra." I noticed a hesitation on his part to begin, and then kicked myself for my insensitivity. He would have to pick up the story right after his brother was killed, and no one would look forward to having to revisit that kind of horror.

"Hey, Bryce," I began. "I'm sorry. If you don't want…"

"No, that's OK. Now is as good a time as any."

Skip, in the back seat, possessed the good sense that eluded me, and kept his mouth shut.

Bryce worked his way into it. In a way, once he got going, it was almost cathartic.

"It was Jeff who saved me, you know. Even after taking a bullet through the back, he had just one spark of life left. Carillo," he spat out the name, "thought he had everything under control. As the life drained out of my brother, Carillo let him slide down in front of him to the ground. He just grinned and raised the gun and pointed it at me. Even under the best of circumstances, even if it wasn't my own brother I had seen gunned down before me, I don't think I could have had a chance at getting to my gun before Carillo put a half a dozen rounds into me. I'd had it. This was the end."

He closed his eyes as he recounted the next scene, an event that would change the course of his life. And by association, my life as well. "That black-hearted monster just smiled at me and said, 'I am sorry that we couldn't have done business together, Mr. Hudson. But I think I will just have to close this deal myself.' He laughed at his wit and began to pull the trigger.

"But Jeff wasn't dead yet." His voice caught, and then he went on. "An impartial observer might have assumed that he was just experiencing involuntary muscle spasms that can accompany death throes, but I know better. With his last conscious act, Jeff somehow managed to flop an arm up and hook a finger into the trigger guard of Carillo's handgun. Carillo got a shot off, but it went low and to the right. Jeff's finger remained tangled in the gun, and the shot going off jolted me into action. I dove for my gun, and, rolling, managed to get a quick shot off, purposely aiming high to try and avoid Jeff." He sighed. "It probably didn't matter. I think he was already dead."

Neither Skip nor I had any words that could help in the situation. I learned a lesson from him and didn't try to come up with any.

"I almost missed completely. But I did manage to graze him on the forehead," he said with his first hint of satisfaction. I recalled seeing the scar above Carillo's left eye. He went on. "I kept rolling and firing, missing Carillo each time, but I managed to take out one of his bodyguards."

He looked at me. "Do you remember when I said Carillo was a coward?" I nodded. "He could have stood his ground and easily gunned me down right then and there, but the nick on his forehead was a reminder that there was someone fighting back. Carillo immediately ran to get behind his remaining bodyguard, who was just drawing his gun. I managed to put two rounds into the bodyguard before I finally rolled behind some garbage cans on the side of the alley.

"When I looked up, I could hardly believe what I was seeing. The bodyguard I just hit was wounded, but still alive. Carillo was holding the guy up in front of himself and dragging him back to the doorway. I only had a couple of cartridges left, and I didn't want to waste them on anyone but Carillo, so I held my fire until I could get a clear shot. Carillo was shouting for help in Spanish. His wounded bodyguard began to struggle just a bit as they reached the door, and Carillo decided he was just too much of a liability to drag inside with him. So as he opened the door, he shot the bodyguard and ducked inside."

Bryce's eyes were still closed as he told the next part, the pain still raw like an open boil. "I didn't know if they would be back, but I didn't care. I ran over to Jeff." He paused. "But he was gone." He then looked at me, his eyes mirroring the agony that he must have felt. "Not a spark left."

"What did you do then, Bryce?" I asked gently. "If it had been me, I might have just stayed there and died."

"I nearly did," he answered. "I could hear Carillo shouting inside the building, getting reinforcements. If I had thought that there was a snowball's chance in Hades that Carillo himself might have come back for me, I would have stayed. But I could see the fear in his eyes when he was hiding behind his bodyguard, and I knew that he wouldn't be out until I was dead, and that he would let his men do the dirty work. So I made two decisions.

"I decided that I would live to see the day when Carillo would pay for what he did to my brother. To do that, I also resolved that I would live. So I left my brother, and I ran." That was the toughest part of the story for him to tell.

"That must have been hard to do," Skip said quietly. He wasn't baiting him. He was helping him.

"Hardest thing I've ever done in my life," he answered simply. "But I could almost hear him telling me to go. 'What's here is just a shell now, Bro,' he seemed to say. 'Leave now, and you'll carry me with you forever.' So I left." He looked at us both. "And here I am." His eyes burned, kindled with the spark of his brother's spirit. He looked ahead.

The lights of the cars ahead of us flickered on, as the wrecked semi was finally cleared, and the traffic began the painful process of trying to overcome inertia. "And now, gentlemen, we have a job to do."

For the first time, I began to believe that Jorge Carillo had something real to worry about.

At that time, though, I had a few worries of my own, not the least of which was whether we would make it to the California coast before the boat would. As I feared, even though Cal-Trans crews managed to get the semi pulled off of the road, the new snow accumulation made it tough for some of the smaller cars to get going again. Bryce seemed to ignore the roadway's existence a few times, taking detours around stuck cars that would have raised the hackles of the Highway Patrol, had any cruisers been around to begin with. After the third detour across a side hill… that I wouldn't have attempted in a snowmobile… I decided to just close my eyes and thank my lucky stars Hudson traded in his old Ford Taurus.

But the delays were tightening up our time schedule. When we finally passed Blue Canyon at the 5,200-foot level going down, it was nearly nine o'clock and the traffic was still bumper-to-bumper. The snow finally turned to rain at Colfax, and the roads cleared up, but the speed of the traffic was slow to respond to the improved conditions. At this point, the big blue monster we were driving became a liability, having a much tougher time weaving in and out of traffic lanes, but that didn't stop Bryce from trying.

The three of us were contrasts in demeanor. While not appearing tense, Bryce was totally focused on the task at hand, eyes boring through the rain-smeared windshield, looking for any opening that might save a few seconds of precious time.

Skip, on the other hand, when he wasn't napping, looked as if he were on a tour bus traveling through the Rocky Mountains, enjoying the scenery. It was too dark to see any scenery, but that didn't appear to matter to Skip. An impartial observer might think we were on our way to a 49'er football game by looking at him, and not just because he looked like one of their tight ends. If he was feeling tension, he hid it well.

Me, I just sat and worried.

It was still raining hard when we went through Auburn. Midnight. A trip that on good roads would have taken less than two hours had taken us over eight. We had three hours, maybe less, to get to Bolinas. "Are we going to make it?" I finally got up enough nerve to ask Bryce.

"We'll make it," was the terse reply.

That was good enough for me. I shut up and hung on. It was a good thing I did.

Our luck began to improve. Heading into the storm front all the way, we finally passed through the strongest part of it, and the rain began to lighten up and stopped altogether just before we hit the floor of the Sacramento Valley. Above I could see the moon begin to peer out from some breaks in the clouds. I willed the clearing trend to continue. Even with the low-light capability of the camera I had brought along, a full moon would improve the odds of anything discernible turning up on the tape.

Then the traffic thinned out just past Auburn, and Bryce picked up the pace significantly. We made it through Sacramento and all the way to Vallejo shortly after one a.m.. We turned off the interstate at Vallejo and headed west to cross the tide flats that skirt the northern edge of the San Francisco Bay. We hooked into Highway 101 and headed south, making good time on the nearly abandoned freeway all the way through San Raphael, only slowing down once when a small device on Bryce's dashboard chirped excitedly.

"Radar?" I asked.

He checked the readout on the device. "Actually, laser. These guys are getting pretty sophisticated these days. Used to be the Chips (California Highway Patrol) weren't allowed to even use radar. They had lost too many court cases, so all they could do was pace you. But it looks like they've outgrown that." He smiled and waved as he passed a Chips unit parked on an on-ramp. Our speedometer read exactly the 60 miles per hour posted limit.

1:45 a.m. We turned off on to Highway 1, the Pacific Coast Highway. Perfect if you want to observe some of the most beautiful scenery west of the Rocky Mountains. But the curvy two-lane highway was horrible if you wanted to make good time. There wasn't another straight stretch of road before we got to Bolinas. It took another half-hour to backtrack to the north up toward Pt. Reyes. Then another 10 minutes to find the turnoff to Bolinas. I heard Bryce make some interesting observations about the genealogy of the fair citizens of Bolinas as we turned around after missing the road the first time.

"What's that?" Skip asked, amused. "Why are you blaming the Bolinians for you getting lost?"

"They keep taking down the sign on the highway that marks the turnoff," Bryce commented acridly. "They don't like visitors."

"How do you know so much about them?" I asked.

"I did some field work on the peninsula years ago. A lot of pot was grown in the hills around here. There was no direct connection to Bolinas, but this is the only town within 20 miles of here, so I came in every once in a while to get supplies." He had to grin. "Townsfolk are actually pretty decent once you get to know them. But they don't encourage a lot of new people to come into the area. Here's the road. You'll see what I mean."

We got on a poorly maintained narrow road, overgrown with the lush brush that grew in abundance in the coastal region, and wove our way toward the tiny town. Even in the dark, without seeing anybody out at 2:40 in the morning, I felt like I had stepped into the Way-Back Machine and had been dumped out at Woodstock. If Volkswagen microbuses ever came back in vogue, they were sitting on a gold mine here. Macramé wind chimes, tie-dyed awnings, and painted school buses lined the streets in front of tiny houses, which hugged the steep hill as we descended into town.

"Wow," was all I could think to say. "They never left the sixties, did they?"

"Groovy," added Skip.

I thought it would be an interesting cultural exchange to visit the town during the daylight hours, but we had another job to do that night, and our once-generous timetable had shrunk to pretty meager proportions.

We had planned on arriving at midnight. I had suggested even earlier, during the daytime, but Bryce thought it would probably be better not to let any of the residents of the community see us. I wasn't sure why, since *we* weren't the ones doing anything illegal, but I wasn't going to argue the point.

With a midnight arrival, we still would have had at least three hours to scout out the area in order to determine the exact landing site, but now that had nearly all disappeared.

As the road dropped down into town, it made a large switchback, leveling out right down at water level, passing a grocery store and a couple of shops, before dumping out onto a gravel beach right at the mouth of Bolinas Lagoon. The inlet to the lagoon was very narrow, formed by a spit that stretched out about a mile and a half from the other side of the bay. A poorly defined road ran along the top of the spit and was nearly bare, save for a few pieces of driftwood and a ramshackle trailer hooked to a beat-up dark blue pickup truck that had obviously seen better days. Another relic of the sixties, but cut off from its brethren by the channel between the spit and the beach we were on. The opening of the lagoon was only a couple of hundred feet across, and the tidal current racing through on the rising tide was strong enough to form standing waves that I could see in the moonlight.

"Okay, here's the plan," Bryce told us as we parked the car by an old concrete wall at the edge of the beach. "We don't have enough time to scout this out properly. We'll have to split up and try to cover the possible landing locations individually.

"The way I see it, there are only a few places that make sense for them to drop their load. Right here is one of them, but I don't think they would want to try anything this close to where people might observe them. Just in case, Skip, I want you to wait here and watch the road and the opening to the lagoon. Make sure you stay out of sight, in case the pick up crew drives through here. Here, take this," he said as he handed Skip what looked like a small garage door opener. "This is a portable paging system. In the still night air, even the sound from a small walkie-talkie will carry a long way, and I don't want anybody to know we're here. When you push the button, it will vibrate the pager on my belt. If anybody drives or walks past where you are here, hit the button once. If you see any boat try to enter, or for that matter leave, the lagoon, hit the button twice. You got that?"

Skip smiled. "Sure. One if by land, two if by sea."

Bryce smiled. "Great. Stay out of sight and do your best to make yourself small."

"Hey, have you ever walked home through the hood in the middle of the night? You learn to be unnoticed."

Bryce turned to me. "You, come with me. From here on out, as little talking as possible. Ready?" We nodded. "Let's go."

"Let me grab the camera," I said as we began to get out of the car as quietly as possible.

"What?" Bryce said. "Oh, yeah. The camera. Okay." We got out of the car and before I knew it Skip had slipped up above the concrete bulkhead and into the bushes. I was amazed at how a man of his size could disappear so quickly and silently.

Bryce went around and opened the tailgate to the Explorer. He pulled out a knapsack and shrugged into the straps. Gently closing the rear door, he motioned for me to follow him.

The beach spread out before us, running out past the mouth of the lagoon before bending west after a couple of hundred yards and then ultimately swinging up to the north. The only access to the shoreline for a vehicle was from the direction we came, since ahead of us a steep and heavily vegetated slope bordered the beach. Bryce was looking intently toward the water as we carefully made our way away from the lagoon. I nudged him, pointed to the beach, and made a questioning motion with my hands as if to ask, "What are you looking for?"

He leaned over and whispered, "Tire tracks. However much they are bringing in, they probably need at least a small vehicle to tote it away." He looked worried. "But I don't see any sign of tracks." He thought for a bit. "The tide's coming in. They might have driven in earlier, at low tide, and the water's covered them up. Let's hope so."

As we turned away to go farther up the beach, a glint of light caught the corner of my eye. I swung back to look for it. Nothing. I was about to turn when I saw it again. Across the inlet. On the spit.

A flashlight. Coming from the trailer camped on the spit.

I tugged on Bryce's jacket and directed his attention to the trailer. The light had gone out again but returned after several seconds. It was just a single half-second flash of light, followed by about ten seconds of darkness. Then the pattern repeated itself.

"Oh, no," Bryce said. "No, no, *no!*" He didn't exactly shout the last "no," but it was uncomfortably loud in the silent night. "We're on the wrong side."

I understood what he meant. The owner of the trailer and pickup combination, while camouflaged nicely to fit into the local decor, was not a resident in fine standing of the borough of Bolinas. The owner was undoubtedly Jorge Carillo, or at least one of his minions. And even though we were separated by less than an eighth of a mile of water, it might as well have been ten miles, because that's how far we would have to drive back around the lagoon in order to get out on the spit. And even then, there would have been no way to approach without being seen.

Hudson cursed quietly. Like a dog straining at his leash, he rocked back and forth trying to come up with an idea.

I watched the constant on and off pattern of the light coming from the small window of the trailer. "Signaling?" I asked.

Bryce nodded in frustration. Then the small pager on his hip vibrated, stopped, and vibrated again. He looked out into the bay. I followed his gaze.

About a half a mile offshore, a single, dim light winked back. "The boat," he whispered.

Chapter 34

Bryce paused to think for a moment. Whatever it was he decided didn't take long. He looked at me, noticing again the camera in my hand. "You should be alright shooting that thing from this side. Does it have much of a telephoto lens?"

I shrugged my shoulders. "Not bad. Goes up to 15 power, I guess."

"Alright, then. Get back under cover behind the driftwood pile." He pointed back toward where we had come about 150 yards. "Stay out of sight, and no matter what happens, don't come out until I come back and get you. I'm going to go farther up the beach and set up a lookout in case they have anybody patrolling on this side of the channel." He unhooked the pager from his belt. "Here, take this. Either Skip or I can signal you if anyone's coming." He looked at the trailer across on the spit, and we could just barely make out three men coming out the door. "Happy shooting. Stay down." He started off farther up the beach.

I turned and scampered as quietly as I could and took up temporary residence behind a pile of logs that had washed up nearly to the tree line during a recent storm. I absentmindedly set the pager down on one of the logs and began to set up the camera. In the near darkness, I had to check all the focus and exposure settings by feel. A very faint beam of light from a lamp near the concrete bulkhead by the road cast a faint shadow that I hid in. In order to be sure I had the settings right, I leaned out over the logs and held out the camera to catch what little light the lamp afforded from that distance. Peering intently to make sure the auto focus was engaged, I didn't notice when I slightly pressed against the log upon which the pager sat. Soundlessly, it slid off into the sand. I didn't notice, and quite frankly forgot I even had it, so engrossed was I in what was unfolding across the channel.

By the time I put the camera to my eyes, two more men had mysteriously appeared around the trailer, bringing the total to five. The camera I was using was advertised to be able to shoot by the light of a single candle, perfect for those romantic occasions one wanted recorded for posterity. I was about to see if it lived up to its claim.

As I peered through the viewfinder, I was relieved to see that there was enough light from the lone lamp across the inlet combined with the now fully exposed full moon to at least make out general shapes and figures. The resolution was very grainy, and I doubted that it could ever be used for a positive identification of any of the parties. Perhaps with some digital refinement, but I wasn't going to hold my breath. But unless Carillo himself showed up, which was even beyond *my* ability to fantasize, the purpose of this little excursion wasn't to show faces, but to just confirm activity. And I was encouraged that as long as the moon stayed away from any clouds, there ought to be enough light to show a transfer of cargo from the boat to the trailer.

I swung the camera out toward the incoming boat. Even though it was running dark, the lights of San Francisco to the south created an eerie reflection off of the water, and the boat was framed nicely in the glare.

A small dark object ahead of the boat also interrupted the glare. At first I thought it was just a piece of driftwood. But then I noticed some movement from the object. My next impression was it must be a sea lion. The kaleidoscope of swirling colors of the lights reflecting off the water became almost hypnotizing as I strained my eyes to get a fix on the black object in the boat's path.

My guess that it was a sea lion was confirmed when I caught sight of its flipper slapping the water gently in a swimming motion.

I put the video camera to my eye and focused on the silhouetted outline of the boat. The dark contour of a man on the bow of the craft, casually cradling what appeared to be a rifle of some sort, was the only sign of life I could see, apart from the steady movement of the boat toward us. Backlit the way it was made it impossible to see the name of the boat or any other identification marks. I lowered the camera and decided to wait until it entered the opening of the channel.

With my field of vision broadened once again, I noticed the sea lion still hovered in front of the boat, seemingly unconcerned by the approaching vessel. "Cheeky devil," I thought. Out of curiosity, I turned the camera on the critter and zoomed in as far as it would go.

Water plays havoc with an automatic focus, so I switched it off as I tried to clean up the picture. Just as I brought the viewfinder into a crisp focus, the animal turned its head and gave me a nice profile against the shiny water. I expected to see a protruding snout and whiskers.

What I saw instead was the unmistakable outline of Bryce's face.

That wasn't a flipper I had seen, it was Bryce's arm. The idiot was *swimming!* Right in front of the boat. Had he lost his mind?

My concerns for his mental state of health suddenly became secondary to concern for his physical. I wondered if he knew about the man on the bow. He must. If I could see him from here, Bryce should be able to see him easily. But it also had to work the other way around. From my vantage point, Bryce could be easily seen in the water. Any second now, the lookout would have to spot him as the boat steadily bore down on him.

Without thinking, I started to get up to shout out a warning. Fortunately, my brain kicked into gear and put the brakes on any further action. I realized that I could see Hudson because the lights of the city were *behind* him. The man on the bow of the boat was looking into the lagoon, which was in almost total darkness. The water ahead of him would appear to be nothing but a sheet of black. Bryce must have known this. I then worried the men on the spit might also be able to see him, but their angle was different than mine, and I judged they would be seeing the boat with just open ocean behind them, with nothing to highlight the water.

I also noticed that Bryce wasn't completely stationary as well. The current flowing into the lagoon had very gradually drawn him toward the inlet. By the time the boat was upon him, both were traveling at a faster rate of speed.

I had almost forgotten my reason for being here. I raised the 8-mm to my eye and whispered to myself, "Lights, camera, action."

I was so entranced with the scene unfolding before me that I failed to notice the almost soundless hum of the pager, muffled now by its cushion of sand, as it gave a single vibration. Somewhere in the back of my mind I should have known that insects wouldn't be out this time of year.

Bryce timed it just right. Just as he and the craft entered the narrow channel, the boat began to pass him. He dipped under the surface, appearing again on the side of the boat away from the men on the gravel spit. He let the boat, engines barely idling, slide past him, and he reached up and took hold of the outside of the rear transom platform. As the vessel rounded the corner and turned back toward the inside of the spit, he remained shielded from both the crew on the boat and the men on the beach. He allowed himself to be dragged along until the boat nudged up against the shore. He then released his hold and disappeared out of my sight into the shadows of the far side of the vessel.

I didn't know what he had in mind, but I had a job of my own to do. I trained the camera on the happenings at the front of the boat.

Two men now stood on the bow, and the five men on the shore greeted them. A hatch was opened, and a portable off ramp was hauled out of the forward hold, and one end was hooked onto a slotted rail on the tip of the bow. The other end dropped onto the beach and two of the men on shore climbed on board. The other three, who I then could see were armed with rifles of their own, spread out onto the spit to keep watch. One of them came right out to the end of the spit, just across the inlet from me. Even with the aid of the telephoto lens, it was too dark to see his eyes, but he appeared to be looking right at me. I involuntarily shrunk down lower into the cover of the driftwood, although I knew there was no possible way I could be seen.

I forced myself to turn the camera back to the boat. One of the men had disappeared down the hatch, and I heard muffled voices of talk and quiet laughter. Something popped out of the opening and flopped on the deck. At first I thought it was a body, but that was a product of an imagination on steroids. Instead, I realized it was a fish.

A fish.

And then another.

My heart began to sink. Fish? I had visions of traveling all this way just to turn state's evidence so these men could be charged with two counts of cruelty to tuna. How could we have been mistaken? Could this really just be a fishing boat, unloading a few fish to some friends on the beach?

Not hardly. The fish were kicked over the side, and another item appeared out of the hold. This time, it appeared to be a burlap bag, tied off at the top. It was about the size used by the guy on the TV commercials to load the coffee beans on the back of his burro. The bag was placed on the deck and one of the men from shore approached it. Taking out a knife, he slid it into the bag, and withdrew it. He touched a residue on the tip of the blade, and touched the end of his finger to his tongue.

Apparently satisfied, he motioned for his two compatriots to begin the process of unloading.

My heart began to race. I was doing it. I was witnessing the landing of a multi-million dollar shipment of drugs and getting it all on tape. Somehow, this would be used to put these animals behind bars. I felt the first stirrings of triumph well up inside of me.

"Awful late for bird watching, dontcha think?" an unfamiliar voice came from behind me. The voice was accompanied by the sound of a loud click.

I froze. Which was just what the man pointing the AK-47 at my back wanted me to do. It would save him the trouble of unloading his clip of ammunition into me, which that particular brand of firearm could do very quickly, had I tried anything fancy.

"Why don't you just turn around very slowly, keeping your hands out in front of you where I can see them, eh?" I did what he asked. Never taking his eyes off me, he grabbed a button of some sort under the lapel of his jacket, squeezed and spoke into it, "Okay, Mitch. I've got him. Guy here with a camera by the looks of things. What do you want me to do with him?" He waited for a moment, apparently getting a reply through an earpiece. "Okay. He's on tach 2. Do you want me to call him?" He nodded. "Roger that. I'll get him over here, and then we'll bring him in."

He seemed to twist something under his jacket, apparently switching his radio to a different frequency. "Buck…Buck, you there?" He waited for a bit before repeating his call. "Buck, is that radio of yours acting up again? Listen, I can't hear you, but I assume you can hear me. I'm down the beach a couple of hundred yards from your location. I've picked up a snoop, and they want him secured. I'll wait here for you, and we'll take him in together." He clicked off, and then made some very disparaging remarks about his partner's radio, attributing some unsavory human characteristics to what was, after all, only a piece of electronics.

"You'd think they'd get us some decent equipment," the man grumbled. I found it hard to sympathize. He then smiled at me. "So what brings you out on such a fine night as this?" His eyes then turned cold. "I can guarantee you, before they get through with you, you'll wish you had stayed in bed." He seemed pleased at the thought.

"How did you…?" I stammered.

"Find you?" he chuckled. "It was easy. I just followed the little red eye."

At first I didn't understand. Then I groaned at my stupidity.

The tally light. I had forgotten to put a piece of tape over the little red light on the front of the camera that turns on whenever I pushed the record button. In the dark, it would have seemed like a searchlight. The lookout across the inlet must have seen it and radioed my new friend here to investigate. I sank into a pit of despair.

"I tell you what," my captor continued. "Why don't you just hand that little camera over to me. Very slowly. And don't try any tricks. I may look like a big lummox, but this finger here is very fast, and I never miss."

Defeated, I handed the video camera over to him. With a steady hand, he took it and popped the tape cartridge out. He slipped it into his shirt pocket. Then he looked casually around for his partner. "Now where is Buck, anyway?"

We waited for another minute before he finally said, "Stupid radios. He never heard me." He pondered for a moment, then decided. "Well, I imagine I ought to be able to handle bringing you in myself. You don't look too dangerous." If I was offended, I didn't show it.

He made me get up and turn around. After patting me down and failing to find a weapon on me, he said, "Put your hands behind your back, as if you are out for a casual stroll. And please don't try anything. These guns are really loud, and I feel a headache coming on."

The guy was a regular comedian.

As we began to climb over the logs, he patted the tape in his shirt pocket and said from behind me, "Interested in making movies, huh?" He chuckled. "Since I didn't find a badge, you must not be with the Feds. A freelancer? Thinking about selling the film to the highest bidder, huh? Well, I'm afraid you aren't going to make anything from this one. In fact, as movies go, I predict this one is going to be a real bomb."

At that instant, 150 yards away, accompanied by a brilliant flash and a cataclysmic roar, the boat erupted into a giant ball of flame.

Chapter 35

It was a cavalcade of sights, sounds and feelings. The force of the explosion nearly lifted me off my feet, and threw me back against my captor. The roar from the blast of the boat seemed muted in comparison to the sound of the rifle discharging next to my ear. Fortunately, the collision of our bodies diverted the muzzle of the gun away from my back, and I'm not sure if it was my imagination or not, but I could have sworn I heard the whoosh of the bullet skid past my ear buried within the cacophony.

Since I was between him and the blast, I was the recipient of the majority of the shock wave. That was evened out somewhat by the presence of his chin, which had the bad luck to play backstop to the back of my head. While it was painful to my head, I knew I had gotten the better of it when I felt/heard the awful crunching of his jawbone. Tie ball game.

Our momentum carried us backwards over the driftwood pile and plunged us into darkness, a darkness made even blacker since the bright flash destroyed what night vision either of us had built up to that point. We both lay dazed on the sand for a moment, fighting to regain our senses, much less our footing. I landed on my back, the wind knocked out of me. Staying perfectly still was tolerable. Moving hurt.

Even though the pain in his jaw must have been intense, my opponent staggered to his feet first, searching wildly around for his gun, which had been knocked from his grasp. Spying it to his right about ten feet away, its muzzle sticking into the sand like a lawn dart, he staggered toward it, only to catch his foot under a chunk of wood. This sent him sprawling, but at least sprawling in the right direction. He fell just short of the gun and began to belly crawl toward it.

At this point I had a decision to make. I could either find the motivation to move from my somewhat comfortable position, or I could die. The frantic and even somewhat crazed attitude of my foe left no doubt in my mind that capture was no longer his top priority, and the bullets from the AK-47 wouldn't be long in coming, and they wouldn't miss. After an internal debate that lasted longer than it should, I decided to try to fight back.

Finally reaching his weapon, he fumbled with the stock and swung it around toward me, trying to find me in the dark. When he spotted my indistinct shape, he realized I was out of his reach, which meant that he was out of my reach as well. He decided he could take a second and get me in his sights instead of firing wildly. With a look of triumph, he grinned crookedly in spite of his broken jaw and drew a bead on me.

I groped around looking for some kind of weapon, knowing I had no chance in making a rush at him. My hand found the only palm-sized object around. The camera. In a final act of desperation, I twisted and hurled the 8-mm at him, and watched in defeat as it bounced off his shoulder and fell harmlessly at his feet.

That's why I never pitched when I played ball. I could never hit the strike zone.

In the dark, he never saw it coming. Had my aim been on the mark, I might have had a chance, but to his credit, he didn't fire wildly as the camera glanced off his shoulder. Instead, knowing he had won, he simply said, "Night, Bub."

And then he pulled the trigger.

When the firing mechanism strikes the rear of a 122-grain Full Metal Jacket cartridge, the explosive mixture of chemicals in the shell casing ignites. The rapid expansion of gasses forces the bullet out the barrel, generating 1450 foot-pounds of energy. With an unobstructed flight out of the barrel of the rifle, it would propel the slug at a velocity of 2,350 feet per second, or 1,630 miles per hour, about twice the speed of sound. In this case, it was intended that the bullet would travel 1,630 miles per hour in a straight line, through my body and in all likelihood find its final resting place buried deep within the pile of driftwood behind me.

But only if its path is unobstructed.

If, perchance, the rifle were to have recently landed nose-down through a thin layer of sand and become imbedded in the mud below, and the mud was not cleared out of the end of the gun, then the preferred escape avenue for not only the bullet but also the rapidly expanding gasses would become blocked. Instead of blowing the obstruction out of the way, the force against the blockage would only serve to pack the damp, elastic mud into an impermeable plug in the end of the barrel. Without an easy avenue of escape, over 30,000 pounds per square inch of pressure must seek an alternate avenue of escape, and seek it very quickly. At that point, the easiest route for the pressure to vent itself was back through the firing mechanism and into the face of my unfortunate assailant.

I had really had enough explosions in my life by then, but in retrospect this one was nice to see. The stock of the rifle completely disintegrated in another loud roar, and when the smoke had cleared, he lay motionless on the ground. I don't know if he was alive or not. Frankly, my dear, I didn't give a rat's rear.

Painfully, I overcame an overwhelming urge to stay where I was, and I hauled myself to a sitting position. Turning, I got my first post-apocalyptic view of the aftermath of the explosion across the channel.

There wasn't much to see.

Small bits of debris smoldered on the beach, but anything large enough to sustain a fire had been blown either far out into the bay or back into the lagoon. There was no sign of the boat. The rear tail-gate of the pickup sticking up out of the water about 100 yards off shore was all that was left of either it or the trailer.

There was certainly no sign of life, from either the smugglers or Bryce.

Bryce. So that's what he'd carried in that knapsack. I figured it must have been the plastic explosives he'd taken from my house. I couldn't help think what would have happened if they had gone off when I tried to open my front door. I shuddered.

Feeling the first signs of shock begin to settle in, I stumbled back toward the car, trying unsuccessfully to get the bell choir to quit ringing in my ears. As I approached the vehicle, undamaged due to its position against the concrete bulkhead, I remembered there was another black hat out there. The unfortunate gunman back in the driftwood had called for his backup, and it was only due to a malfunctioning radio that he wasn't there to help in my demise when the blast occurred.

I approached the Explorer cautiously, wondering where Skip was. Trying to stay in the shadows, I crept up to the car and looked in. Nothing. I turned around and nearly ran into Skip, who seemed to have materialized out of thin air.

"Skip!" I heaved a sigh of relief. "Your ugly mug is a sight for sore eyes."

He viewed me curiously. "I'd hesitate making disparaging remarks about my visage if I were you, little brother. You ought to take a look at yourself. You look like death warmed over."

"At least I'm still warm," I replied. Then I turned serious. "Skip, we have to watch ourselves. There's another bad guy out here, patrolling. I don't know where he is, but we need keep an eye out."

"Oh, do you mean this little fellow here?" he asked. He walked to the edge of the roadway, and pulling away some brush, revealed a man, bound and gagged and quite incapable of causing us any harm in his present state of slumber. "Got this off of him," Skip said, pulling a Glock 21, 45-caliber handgun out of his ample waistband. "I somehow got the feeling he wasn't looking for ducks to shoot with this thing, so I, uh, sorta made a citizen's arrest."

I asked him if he had seen Bryce. He hadn't. I told him about his moonlight swim and about the explosives he must have brought along.

"I figured that he must have had something to do with that little fireworks display," Skip answered. Then he looked out at the spit, wiped clean of all life. "I just hope he was able to get out of there in time."

He was expressing the very thought that had begun to prod at the back of my mind. The force of the shock wave through the water probably killed every fish within the lagoon. "If he was in the water…" I began.

"Then I'd be feeding the crabs," Bryce said, as he stepped out from behind the bulkhead, still dripping wet. "What? You don't think I have enough sense to get out of the way of my own mischief?"

"Bryce!" we shouted in unison.

"Okay, okay, keep it down. Hugs and kisses to all later. I think it's time we get out of here. The folks around here tend to mind their own business, but with half the windows in town blown out, it won't be long before we have some visitors."

"The Marin County Sheriff's Department and an Emergency Management Crisis Team are on the scene of a massive explosion which occurred about an hour ago in the sleepy seaside community of Bolinas. According to witnesses, the explosion occurred at about 3:30 this morning. Fortunately the blast, which shattered windows throughout the small community south of Point Reyes, did not appear to have done any major damage to any structures in the town itself. At present, only one injury has been reported, although Sheriff's officials admit they may never know if there was anyone at or near the site of the blast. Early evidence seems to indicate the explosion centered on a gravel spit across Bolinas Lagoon, instead of in the town itself.

"When asked the cause of the explosion, a sheriff's spokesperson declined to say, although initial reports seem to point to a detonation of a methamphetamine lab. Witnesses report the presence of a small trailer earlier

in the day at approximately the same location where the blast occurred. Apparently, although there is very little evidence of any kind left at the site, a vehicle believed to be one that witnesses placed near the trailer was found in the water of Bolinas Bay, thrown there by the force of the detonation.

"An unidentified member of the County's Drug Task Force who was present told this reporter that the chemicals used in the cooking process of methamphetamine are highly volatile during certain phases of the production of the illegal drug.

"Police are not telling us if there were any casualties, although there appeared to be at least one injury of an unidentified man who was found unconscious along the beach near the blast site. And there are unconfirmed reports officials are holding another man for questioning.

"The investigation into this highly unusual event continues, and as we find out more, we'll pass it along to you. Reporting from the scene, this is Roger..."

Bryce leaned forward and clicked off the radio. "Perfect."

"Perfect?" I said. "Perfect? What do you mean, 'Perfect'? First of all, any chance of getting some good and hard evidence of Carillo's operation just went up in smoke." Skip choked on a swig of soda at the unintended pun. I didn't notice. "I had it all on tape, Bryce. The boat, the drugs coming out of the hold, everything. Now the tape, not to mention the camera, is gone. I've got nothing. Zip. Nada."

It was the first I'd said since we high-tailed it out of Bolinas. I was anxious when we passed a few of the townsfolk walking toward the beach to investigate what caused the disruption of a good night's sleep. But as far as I could tell, none of them seemed to pay any attention to us, so riveted was their attention to the gaping crater on the gravel spit. My anxiety grew when we passed the first of several Sheriff's and Emergency vehicles, which flew by us with lights flashing and sirens blaring after we had turned back onto Highway 1. But these ignored us as well. My fear of discovery didn't ease until we had returned to the relative anonymity of another early morning commuter on Highway 101. But the decrease in fear was replaced by an increase in depression.

I sighed dejectedly. "Now we're back to square one. We have to start all over again."

"Square one?" Bryce lifted an eyebrow. "Is that what Admiral Halsey said when they won the battle of Midway? My dear fellow, after getting your

204

booty kicked around so far in this war, you just had your first victory."

"What? How can you say that? We went to that bay with nothing, and as far as I can see, we've got nothing to show for our efforts now." I rubbed my temples. "Except a splitting headache and a ringing in my ears that makes the Bells at St. Petersburg sound like a door chime."

"It ain't what we're taking away that's valuable, Greg. It's what we've left them."

"And what's that?"

"Another chink in their armor."

I thought about that for a moment. Then I realized. "You never intended to use that video for evidence, did you?"

Bryce smiled sympathetically and shook his head. "Maybe eventually, but no, I knew it wouldn't do any good."

"You planned on blowing up that cargo from the start, didn't you?" He nodded. "Then why go through the charade?"

"Because you had to learn that you are in a different world now. All your life, all you've ever known is cops and robbers. Where there are bad guys, the robbers, you send the good guys, the cops, out after them. And for the most part, that arrangement works just fine. The cops catch the robbers. The cops turn them over to our justice system, and they are put in jail. For a long time, so they can't go on being robbers. It sounds somewhat Pollyannaish, but for most robbers, it works pretty well."

He glanced over at me. "But as I've tried to tell you, Greg, the rules that you've grown up with don't apply here. Even if we were to get some evidence that we could take to court, Carillo could hire the best legal talent in the country. We'd need a lot more than a grainy film of a drug shipment landing to ever put him behind bars." He looked at me again. "And who's going to testify?"

I knew where he was going. I wanted to say, "I would, of course," but I knew better. He'd already told me enough about Carillo to know that coming forward would not only sign my own death warrant, but in all likelihood my family's as well.

"He's like a rabid dog, Greg. You don't send a rabid dog to obedience school."

In a rare moment of self-appraisal, I realized that I knew all along that we weren't going to sink Carillo with the tape of the drug shipment. "But at least it felt like we were doing something proactive," I said to no one in particular.

Skip, who had been quiet throughout the exchange, said, "Greg, old buddy old pal, I believe our little excursion tonight just redefined proactive."

I had to smile, despite the growing conflict in me. But the more I dwelt on the problem, the more unavoidable the conclusion appeared to be. "Okay," I began, "so we have to play by Carillo's rules. But you said it yourself. I come from a different world. Even though he is an animal that this planet would be better off without, I still don't know if I can just walk up to the guy and shoot him."

Bryce said, "That's probably not going to be an option. For one thing, you'd never get close enough to him to do so. And even if you did, you'd end up being put away by the good guys, who might not have your perspective on Mr. Carillo's value to society."

"So how do we put him away?" I asked.

Bryce grinned. "If things keep going the way they are, *we* won't have to."

Chapter 36

I wasn't sure what to make of Bryce's comment. "*We* won't have to?" I asked. "I'm not sure where all this is going, but I assume you have a method to your madness?"

"Oh, yes I do. Do you remember when I told you the key to winning most wars is by crushing the enemy's morale before you go after his army?"

"I seem to recall you mentioning that."

"That's a true statement because most empires don't fall as a result of being conquered from the outside. At least not in the beginning. The beginning of the end comes from decay from within. You can see it throughout history, from the Babylonians to the Greeks, to the Romans and beyond. The first signs of weakness began to show themselves in times of relative peace and prosperity. It was internal dissentions and moral decay which weakened the very foundations of their power, and it usually happened with such subtlety that no one recognized it until it was too late.

"Take the Romans. Who did Caesar in? It wasn't some foreign enemy. It was his best friend. He was ready for any attack from outside his borders. But he wasn't watching his back when it counted."

I thought about his analogy. I had to admit it made sense. There was no way we were going to win in an all-out frontal assault against a man with the resources of Jorge Carillo. Heck, it was only dumb luck or providence that I had survived the attacks of Chance Dunleavy up to that point. So I was willing to do it Bryce's way. But there was still something that didn't make sense to me.

"Bryce," I began, "if we aren't going to try to take on Carillo directly, doesn't that kind of fly in the face of what we just did? Isn't blowing up 50 million of his dollars, give or take pocket change, sort of akin to charging the fort with a six-shooter? Seems like a pretty direct attack on his empire if you ask me."

"Ah, but it isn't," he answered.

"It isn't? How is that not a direct attack on Carillo?"

"Because," he answered with a Cheshire Cat smile, "it wasn't Carillo's 50 million dollars."

That little bit of information was met with dead silence in the car. Skip finally broke the ice. "Okay, I'll bite. If it wasn't Carillo's, whose was it?"

"If my information was correct, that little shipment belonged to Miguel Carerra. One of the five members in good standing of the Cali drug cartel."

"Another member of the cartel?" Skip and I asked in unison.

"That's right," Bryce continued. And then noticing the blank look on our faces, he said, "It looks like we need a little primer in cartel economics.

"Cartels are basically a way for competing factions in one industry, which have some common goals, to put their differences aside for a bit and combine forces to benefit all those involved. For instance, OPEC is an oil cartel. The oil-producing Arab nations decided a long time ago that instead of trying to compete with each other and allow a glut of oil on the world market to drive the prices down, it would be better if they could work together. They decided if they limit production of their oil, they could keep prices higher, and it would benefit them all in the long run. Even though there are other oil-producing countries out there, the Arabs have a large enough slice of the market that this has an awful strong bearing on the price of oil."

"Kinda sounds like price fixing to me," Skip said.

"It is, in a sense," Bryce answered. "It would be the same as if all the major auto makers all met in a room and unilaterally decided to double the price of all cars. Fortunately for us lowly drivers of said automobiles, our laws in this country frown upon that kind of thing. Without full participation from foreign and domestic carmakers, the whole thing would fall apart. Even if all the Japanese and European carmakers decided to form a cartel, if the American manufacturers weren't part of the deal, the Yanks would cut the price of their cars and drive the imports out of the market."

"So why does the OPEC cartel work if they don't have all the oil-producing countries participating?"

"Because, even though American oil-producing companies don't belong to OPEC, they still benefit, because anything that drives up oil prices is just fine and dandy with them. They don't have enough of the market to control prices themselves, and they don't have the kinds of reserves that will allow them to dump a lot of oil on the market just to get a bigger share. So it is a kind of a truce, but an uneasy truce at that."

"So how does this relate to the drug cartel?" I asked.

"Quite nicely, actually, in more than one way. First of all, the Colombians control the vast majority of the cocaine production in the world. But it isn't just one person or faction. It is several. The Cali cartel, which by the way is always changing, since drug lording isn't the most stable profession in the world, has five members in it at present. Originally, they all competed for a larger share of the cocaine market, but they decided they all might benefit from some form of cooperation." He smiled. "Someone probably introduced them to the game of Risk."

"Risk?" I asked. "That 'take over the world' game I used to play as a kid?"

"The very same. You know how it's played. You get a bunch of players together. Everybody has a number of armies and a certain number of countries, and you try to take over the world by attacking the armies of your opponent's countries until you possess it all."

"I was always terrible at that game," I mused.

"That's probably because you never formed the Parker Brother's equivalent of a cartel. You make a deal with one or two other players and agree to not attack them, and you just sit back and let all the other players beat each other up until they are so weakened, you can then go in and mop them up later in the game. The cartels work the same way. Forming an uneasy truce, they decide not to compete with each other, and in some cases even share resources."

"Sort of a conglomerate?" asked Skip.

"In a sense, yes. They hold secret meetings at very isolated and heavily guarded retreats in Colombia, and divvy up responsibilities so each can concentrate its resources more effectively. As we have found out, Jorge Carillo is basically the cartel's Vice-President in Charge of Importation. He's dreamed up this handy little scheme for getting the snow into the country right under the noses of the DEA. Someone else in the cartel is probably responsible for distribution, someone else for laundering, someone else for processing, and probably even someone for marketing."

"Marketing?"

"Sure. The larger a market there is for drugs, the more profit for the producers. Anybody from the pushers on the street trying to get your kids to try their first joint, to the lobbyists in government trying to keep the penalties for drug use from getting too stiff helps create a market for increased use.

"All combined, with the incredible resources at their disposal, they become a multi-billion dollar international conglomerate. They are organized, they are powerful, and they make their own rules."

My mind was reeling. I had always thought of the drug trade as a bunch of lone rangers out there dodging police and shooting each other. The thought of what we were really up against didn't exactly lift my spirits.

"So how does knowing this help us?" I asked.

"Because, as I said earlier, it is an *uneasy* alliance. Each and every one of the members of this, and probably every other drug cartel, would just as soon put a bullet through the head of the chap sitting next to him at that table in the mountain retreat. But you may have noticed none of the members is singularly responsible for muscle. Each member has his own fully equipped army standing nearby. That's because even though he realizes the benefits of working with the others, he would trust a Blue Tick Hound to ignore a raccoon before he would trust a fellow cartel member not to stab him in the back if he had a chance."

"So where does this Miguel...what's his name... come into play?" Skip queried.

"Carerra. He's another member of the cartel, and I believe it was his shipment that was spread all over Bolinas Bay this morning."

"What do you mean, 'his shipment'? Isn't it all the cartel's cocaine?" I put in.

"Nope. No more than any of Kuwait's oil belongs to Saudi Arabia. Each of the drug lords generates his own inventory of snow. Remember that they are each 'independent businessmen.' The cartel only serves to create a market environment that is beneficial to them all, and to consolidate some of the activities that each would have to do on its own otherwise. Each member's profits come from the eventual sale of its own cocaine supplies."

I felt a bit let down. After finally deciding that I was going to be St. George taking on the dragon, I felt my first arrow had landed in another serpent's hide. "So what you are telling me is we didn't really hurt Carillo at all tonight."

Bryce looked at me, still a little frustrated at how slow I was at understanding, and said patiently, "No, Greg, that's not what I'm saying. If it had been his own shipment, he would have been out money and some men. Men, he's got plenty of. Money, he's got even more of. Even when you are talking about a 50 million-dollar shipment, that won't hurt him in the long run. Might tick him off, but it won't damage him."

"But when it is another member's shipment?" I said, light finally beginning to dawn on me.

"Then what he loses isn't money, or men. What he loses is security." And then he added, "And it ain't what he loses that will worry him the most. It's what he gains."

"And what's that?"

"Enemies."

It all started to fall into place. Internal dissentions are the key to the undoing of a strong enemy. Creating suspicion amongst the cartel might just give Carillo enough to worry about to get him off of my back.

I realized that he was like a shark. In the water, a shark is only really at risk from one thing, and that's other sharks. Blue sharks, in particular, tended to hunt in packs, like a cartel. They could surround a large school of fish and attack at once. The spilled blood of the first victim then could set the pack off, creating a feeding frenzy more horrifying than anything else in all of nature.

But should one of the sharks get scraped and cut in the attack, then his previous partners would turn on him, and the predator would become the prey. He would soon be reduced to a bloody mass of entrails and cartilage.

Carillo probably knew this. He was so powerful it was doubtful he feared the law enforcement efforts of either my country or his own. And there was probably no single man alive who had the power to bring him down.

But what about the combined power of the cartel? Yes. That was likely to keep Carillo up at nights. He would only have one fear, and that was if they all turned on him at once.

I related my thought to my friends. They both thought the analogy of the sharks was an apt one.

Buoyed by the thought, I asked Bryce, "So what do we do now?"

He thought for a moment, and said with a glint in his eye, "I might just have a way that we can throw a little more chum into the water."

Bryce spent the next half-hour telling us of his idea. I liked it, but I couldn't resist asking, "Do you think it will be enough?"

He shrugged. "Who knows? Sharks are notorious for being unpredictable."

Skip added, "It sounds like a lot will depend on how good your information stream is coming out Colombia."

Bryce had to agree. "That's true. But I've still been able to maintain good lines of information through a couple of friends at the DEA. One thing they are pretty good at is developing information."

Skip asked something that he had been holding in for a while. "Bryce, my man," he began gently, "I know you had a rough time back there and took a big loss. But why aren't you still with the DEA? Wouldn't you be able to accomplish more with their resources?"

Bryce shook his head sadly. "Rules," was all he said.

"Rules?"

"Rules," he repeated. "The DEA's chock full of them. When I finally made my way back to the Agency, I spent a couple of days back in D.C. for a debriefing. I told them the whole story. I expected righteous indignation and a plan to go in and get Carillo and make him pay for what happened to Jeff…to one of their own agents. I got the indignation all right. What I didn't get was a plan.

"They put me on temporary assignment back at headquarters shuffling papers. After a month of my superiors saying they were still looking into how to respond to the 'Colombian incident,' as they put it, I finally walked into the office of Rick Jackson, the number-two man in the agency. Rick and I went through the academy together, and while I was never interested in moving up the administration ladder, Rick possesses all the right tools to one day take over the whole show. He has a lot more political savvy than I will ever have, which for most people is a license to lie to you while looking you in the eye, but he's a straight shooter.

"I walked into his office, sat down at his desk, and told him I didn't want to play any games. Were they going to respond in an aggressive way to bring Carillo to justice or not?

"I knew he wouldn't lie to me, and he knew I had him over a barrel. He looked straight at me and told the truth. 'No, Bryce,' he said, 'we can't.' I could tell it was tearing him up almost as much as me to be telling me this.

"I asked him why, and he told me the Agency has no way of going into a foreign country and trying to supercede the authority of the Colombian's justice system. To do so would create an international incident, and our administration wasn't about to go there. He even let on that some of the administration felt embarrassed about what had happened and really just wanted to sweep it all under the rug."

"Oh, and thank you all for your support," Skip offered.

Bryce nodded slowly. "I remember seeing what a foul taste that left in his mouth. Anyhow, I came back in thirty minutes later and placed my resignation on his desk. And I haven't been in the employ of the DEA since." He let that sink in for a moment, and then added, "At least, not *officially*."

He noticed our curious looks at his last statement. "I spent the following week sitting around and moping, trying to come up with a way to get back at

Carillo, when I got a call from Rick. 'Meet me at the wall, 2 AM tomorrow morning,' was all he said. It was cryptic enough to catch my interest, and seeing as how I had some time on my hands, I made my way to the Vietnam Veterans Memorial Wall in the middle of the night.

"Rick was there right on time. I felt like a player in a bad spy movie, but Rick had his reasons for secrecy. He told me that if this ever got out, he would deny it all, and he had the resources to make any denial stick. I told him I understood."

Bryce turned and looked at us. "I guess I should say the same thing to you," he said with a grin.

I held my right hand over my heart and gave him the Boy Scout Salute with my left. "Mum's the word," I intoned.

Skip made a zippering-shut motion across his mouth.

After what we had already been through together, it was as good as any signed and notarized secrecy agreement.

"What the heck. Who'd believe you anyhow?" Bryce went on. "Anyway, I knew from my last conversation with Rick that he was nearly as frustrated with the Agency's inability to act on Carillo as I was. But you don't get as high as he is in an organization like the DEA without being able to get around the rules once in a while. And the rules weren't just about to get bent; they were about to get rewritten.

" 'Bryce,' he started, 'I can only imagine what you must be going through. Your brother was not only a fine agent; he was a good friend as well. Unfortunately, there's not much *officially* the Agency can do.'

"I asked if that meant there was room for 'unofficially.' He smiled and told me about a little slush fund a few of the higher-ups in the agency had assembled, that not even Congress had gotten wind of. Since the DEA was only given law enforcement authorization domestically, all of its international operations were hampered by the same restrictions that Jeff and I were under as 'Country Attachés.' In other words, we could observe, we could accumulate intelligence, and we could swap stories with the locals, but if we really wanted to kick some booty, we had to leave that up to the host country. And as I saw, their motivation can be quite different than ours."

We passed the Applegate turnoff on I-80. The big Ford had to slow down as we began to get back into the snow left by the last night's storm. As we plowed through the slush on the road, Bryce returned to the fund by the same name.

"Apparently, the Administrator hand-picked a few of his key people, Rick being one of them, to put together a little task force. With a modest bit of funding, they could hire out 'consultants' having no direct connection to the DEA to create a little well-placed mischief. Some of these people are pure mercenaries. Others, such as yours truly, have other motivations."

Skip asked, "You said there is no straight line connection. Who directs your movements?"

"Rick is my contact. We coordinate on an irregular basis. But I have to get his approval if I need to get any equipment or intel. So far it has worked out pretty well."

"And if there comes a time when it doesn't work out well?"

Bryce smiled grimly. " 'Mr. Phelps, as always, if you or any of your Impossible Mission Force are caught or killed, the Agency will disavow any knowledge of your existence.' "

"Kinda sounds pretty one-sided to me," I suggested.

"Not really. I knew the score when I signed up."

It answered my questions regarding Bryce's funding. But I still had others. "So just how long a leash do these guys give you?"

"Just about as long as I need. It's almost a no-lose situation for them, and we are both trying to achieve the same goal. To put these slimeballs away. Since there's no paper trail back to them, if things go south, it will only be my butt on the line."

Skip smiled. "Correction. You have two more butts keeping yours company."

Chapter 37

The first place we put our respective butts by the time we got back over the pass and down into Nevada was into bed. The adrenaline had worn off by the time I hauled my bones back into The Ormsby House, my head meeting the pillow just prior to the little hand of the clock meeting noon. I know I dreamt, but even though I would awaken every hour or so, I couldn't recall what the dreams were.

I finally crawled out of the sack and into the shower at five, feeling no more refreshed than I had when I climbed in. It was a sadist's version of jet lag, and I knew I would just have to sweat it through.

I called Lauren and the kids. That was better than a weekend's worth of sleep. I went back and forth with myself trying to decide how much to tell her. I finally decided to give a somewhat watered-down version of the events of the previous night, if it was possible to water down the vaporization of 50 million dollars of drug trade. I didn't know whether to tell her that I was almost shot or to tell her that I was almost blown up, so I compromised and told her neither. I mostly tried to dwell on the fact that we were hitting back now and that we had a plan. It didn't sound like much, but it was more than we had when she left.

When she left. How long had it been? Less than a week? It already seemed like an eternity, and I once again cursed the fates that crossed my path with that of Jorge Carillo.

Lauren could feel my frustration. She asked me what I planned on doing the rest of the night. I told her I was going to meet Bryce at 9 PM. He had told me he had some work to do before we could go on to the next step.

"What will you do until then?" she asked.

"I don't know. Maybe get a bite to eat. Although I'm not very hungry. What I really need to do is clear my head. We have a lot of work to do in the next several days."

She gently suggested, "It's Sunday. Why don't you go to an evening service?"

My first reaction was to tell her that I didn't have the time or the energy. But the more I thought about it, the more I realized that was just what I needed to do. As usual, Lauren knew me better than I knew myself. There hadn't been too many safe havens for me lately, and I didn't know if there were ever going to be any again. Just for that night, I discovered I needed peace more than I needed food or sleep.

I knew I couldn't make it all the way to Reno and make the evening service at the church we usually attended, so I scanned the Carson City paper in their religion section. Only one Sunday evening service was listed late enough for me to attend. It was a small, non-denominational church, which met out in Jack's Valley, south of town, at 7 that evening. After a sandwich at the coffee shop, I arrived at their tiny sanctuary just as the music began.

There was nothing fancy at the church. No crystal palaces. No stained glass windows. Their parking lot wasn't even paved. But the small congregation welcomed me without being overbearing, they all sang the songs as if they really believed the words, and during a time of greeting, hugs replaced stiff handshakes. I began to feel a hint of the peace that had so effectively eluded me in the previous weeks.

But if I had any doubts that I was supposed to be there, they all disappeared when the pastor rose to speak and had us all turn to 1 Samuel, chapter 17. I pulled a Bible from the chair ahead of me and nearly doubled over when I read the heading above the chapter.

David and Goliath.

I confess I don't remember a lot about the pastor's teaching that night, although I'm sure it was very good. But I do recall one verse, which although written nearly 4,000 years earlier, must have been penned for me. *"Moreover David said, 'The Lord, who delivered me from the paw of the lion and from the paw of the bear, He will deliver me from the hand of this Philistine.'"*

Amen, Brother David.

On my way out of the service, I stooped in the gravel parking lot on the way to my car. I bent down and picked up five smooth stones. I put them in my pocket.

As I opened the door to my car, I glanced to the north, eyeing the lights of Carson City, and then beyond to the glowing halo reflecting off the clouds above Reno. Jorge Carillo was up there, somewhere, along with his prize warrior, Chance Dunleavy. I felt the stones in my pocket.

"Bring it on, you Philistines," I spoke to the darkness.

I got into the car and drove back into town to meet Bryce.

We had work to do.

Bryce arrived on time, and I answered the door in response to the coded knock. He hadn't even had the luxury of the few hours of sleep afforded to me, and he plopped into the chair at the desk with a deep sigh. But his eyes, dancing with excitement, belied the fatigue that he must have felt.

"Before we get started, do you want something to eat?" I asked him. "You look like you could use it."

"Sounds like a plan I can support," he answered. "I got so involved in writing code for Max that I didn't even bother with food."

I ordered up some sandwiches and a pot of coffee from room service, and then turned over the phone jack to my friend. He plugged in his laptop, and thanks to the back door he created earlier, quickly sent Max scooting back into the silicon wafers of the KOPP computer system. "Now let's hope their new General Manager isn't paying too much attention to what's going on inside their computer system." He put Max into position and pressed the enter button.

"If my information out of Colombia is correct, there is going to be a lot of activity real soon. Now all we have to do is wait until we hear from Max."

For once, luck was on our side. We didn't have to wait long. The next morning, shortly after 9 o'clock, Bryce's laptop beeped. Fortunately, the alarm on his computer was loud and insistent. It awakened me from a sleep so deep that it took several moments before I realized where I was. I focused blurry eyes on the computer's screen. There were two sets of numbers, nothing else.

Bryce had gone earlier and left me with a cell phone and instructions to page him should the alarm sound. I dialed his pager number, punched in the simple message of "* * * * * * *", and hung up. Less than a minute later, Bryce called me on the cell phone.

"So you heard back from Max, eh?" I could hear the glee in his voice.

"Yep," I answered. "So now what do I do?"

"Turn your radio on."

* * * * * * * * * * *

The music from the cabin of the *El Dorado* lazily wafted out over the swells of the Pacific Ocean. The captain of this vessel, similar in basic design

217

to the ill-fated fishing boat to make its last landfall in Bolinas Lagoon, sat perched on the bridge, half watching the seagulls hover above and half listening to the radio. The sun's reflection danced off the waves, creating an almost hypnotic effect, and his mind began to wander once again. He snapped to attention when the familiar voice of Barry Manilow began chanting the words of the key song.

"Awright," he grumbled. He then sat back, and with pen and paper waited on the next ten songs.

"Little Pico Creek it is then." The captain stepped back from the chart. "And they don't give us much time to get there, do they?" He turned and shouted back toward the galley. "Pablo? Tell Mr. Williams to get it in gear. We've got to make tracks, and fast."

A day and a half later, shortly after midnight on Wednesday morning, a pair of hard eyes stared out into the ocean, trying to pierce the darkness for any sign of life. They belonged to Judd Black, who was a veteran of many of these late-night excursions. A quick calculation reminded the man that of the fourteen previous shipments for Jorge Carillo, so far they had all gone off without a hitch. He planned on making the fifteenth job just as flawless. While the pay scale for what he was doing was beyond anything he could have ever hoped to achieve in his previous employment with the United States Navy, it would be hard to enjoy the fruits of his labor if something went wrong and he ended up behind bars.

The man had an unusually large contingent of helpers with him. He had heard of the fate of the shipment in Bolinas, and even though no one knew the cause of its demise, he wasn't a man to take chances.

Spread out along the beach, heavily-armed lookouts patrolled for any sign of life. All of these men were in constant radio contact with their leader and they checked in regularly with reports of nothing unusual. This seemed to satisfy the man, who was not easily appeased.

Even to the keen observer, not much could be seen from the highway which ran alongside the ocean shore just a couple of hundred yards away. An unmarked dirt road provided the only access to the shore where a HumVee and a U-Haul Trailer sat covered by the thick overgrowth so common along the Pacific Coast. Two men hidden on either side of the entrance guarded the road. Each was strategically placed so that neither would be in the crossfire should an unfortunate soul decide this might be a good time to take a moonlit stroll on a secluded beach. Fortunately for all involved, there were no sightseers that night.

The group leader looked at the illuminated dial of his watch and decided it was time. He took out a powerful flashlight, which was hooded so the beam couldn't be seen from the side. He pointed it out to the west and pressed the button.

"There it is." The captain of the *El Dorado* noticed at once the lone beam of light, standing out against the black background on the deserted shoreline like the beacon from a lighthouse. "Mr. Williams, return the signal."

The young, sparsely-bearded First Officer pointed the spotlight back toward the shore, switched it on for about a second, and then returned the vessel to its previous state of darkness.

The light on the shore returned, and then settled into a slow, but steady pattern of one second bursts, followed by ten seconds of darkness.

"Make course for the beacon, Mr. Williams." The captain settled back into his chair with a sigh of contentment. It would be good to get this trip over with. He had already decided this would be his last run for the cartel. With the profits from this trip, he could retire to a comfortable life with the girl he had met in Cabo. He pulled out the cigar he always lit at the conclusion of successful runs and struck a match on the bulkhead. "Ahead three quarters speed," he said between puffs. "Let's get this trip over with."

Following the slow but constant blinking of the beacon from shore, the shallow draft boat nudged its bow onto the sand forming a mini-delta at the mouth of Little Pico Creek. Located about ten miles up the coast from San Simeon, a couple of miles shy of the Hearst Castle Road, it was a perfect spot for a drop. Protected from view from the Coast Highway, the little inlet was screened from both the elements and from prying eyes.

The captain came out of the bridge and onto the bow. He carried a sidearm and had Mr. Williams at the ready behind him with an automatic. He peered into the near-total darkness until he could make out the vague shapes of four men materializing out of the gloom.

They approached the ship, and the man in front, who appeared to be the leader of the shore team, took a final look up and down the beach before speaking just loud enough to be heard over the idling engines. "Ahoy, captain. How was the fishing?"

The captain relaxed at the oft-used greeting, and even the usually high-strung Mr. Williams seemed to breathe a little easier. "The seas were quite generous to us, thank you," the captain replied. "Would you like to see our catch?"

"Indeed I would," replied the man on shore.

Two more crewmen from the boat came on deck and laid the boarding ramp down from the bow rail onto the shore. The men from shore climbed on board in a jovial mood, the hatch cover to the forward hold was popped, and the crewmen disappeared momentarily below.

"Any troubles on your voyage?" the shore leader asked.

"Nay, it was smooth sailin', me bucko," the captain answered in his best Blackbeard impersonation.

Their jocularity was interrupted by the sight and sound of a 25 pound yellowfin tuna, which appeared on deck as if it had leaped out on its own. The fish, which had obviously seen better days, was discolored, and due to a marked lack of maintenance in the hold's refrigeration unit, was beginning to assault the olfactory glands.

The man from shore wrinkled his nose, but still managed to say, "Nice fish. I hear they are hard to catch. What were you using for bait?"

The captain smiled. "So you'd like to see our bait, now? I think that can be arranged." He leaned over and shouted to the two crewmen inside. "Bring it up, boys."

A burlap coffee bag followed the fish up and out of the hold. The fish was kicked overboard, and the shore leader slid a thin blade into the bag. Even in the near total darkness, the snow-white powder that came out on his knife could be seen easily. He licked his fingers, touched the powder, and then tapped the end of his tongue. The acrid taste confirmed the ingredients. "That's some mighty powerful bait you've got there, Captain. Ought to be enough to keep our fishing stores supplied for a long time. Let's get this stuff unloaded."

The captain grinned and sent his two crewmen off with the landing party to get their trailer ready to load. He then dropped down the hatch with his first mate to begin the final job of hauling the 75-pound bags of addiction up through the forward hatch.

When the last of the bags was tossed up to the bow, he sent Mr. Williams up and paused to check and make sure none was left under the thin layer of fish used to hide the real catch. Satisfied he had off-loaded it all, he sighed deeply and looked around the hold, glad this was the last time he would be hip deep in fish glop at the end of one of these trips. Besides the money, he had originally signed on for the excitement he felt his life was missing and thought would appear during these midnight runs. But instead, he had come to discover that it was hours of mundane and routine work, followed by days of trying to get the fish smell out of his hair. "No," he said with a smile, "I won't be missing this in the least." He followed his first mate up the hatch.

The excitement that had eluded the captain those many lonely months at sea materialized before his eyes in the form of four semi-automatic rifles, each drawing a bead on the furrowed wrinkles between his eyes. Baffled, he looked around for aid, only to find Mr. Williams sitting dejectedly on the deck with his hands on top of his head. Another glance shoreward revealed his other two crewmen face down on the beach, their hands shackled behind their backs.

"Captain, it is my pleasure to inform you that you are under arrest," the leader of the shore party said with no small amount of satisfaction. "We haven't formally met. I'm Special Agent Patrick Mackelroy of the Drug Enforcement Administration, and we'd like you to be our guests for a while. Come out from that hatch please, but first, hand over your sidearm. I would recommend you not resist."

The captain looked forlornly around him, and with a shrug of resignation, handed the agent his pistol. "At least I can get off this blasted boat," he grunted.

"Agent Michaels, please read them their rights," Mackelroy said. He turned to the men on the shore. "Let's get this operation buttoned up. Tag the snow, and secure the boat." He shouted to a man nearest the truck near the dirt road leading onto the beach. "Gene, call HQ and report. Tell them we have a little present we'll be bringing in." He began to turn away, and then swung around and said, "And Gene, have them pass along a message to the Deputy Administrator. Tell Mr. Jackson that I don't know where he got his intel, but it was rock solid."

He turned to help with the clean-up operation. "Let's hope there's more where that came from," he said to no one in particular.

Forty miles to the north, on another lonely stretch of abandoned beach, Judd Black pushed the button on his lamp one last time. He stared out at the empty, black ocean, willing some kind of reply. But none came.

He checked again the dial of his watch. It was already more than an hour and a half beyond the scheduled time. He sighed resignedly and stood. He spoke into his mouthpiece, "All units, it looks like we have a no-show. Reconnoiter back at the pick-up point, and stay on the alert. Something's gone wrong."

Checking one last time for a light on the horizon and finding none, he stood and began to make his way back to the highway.

"Mr. Carillo's not going to like this," he muttered under his breath.

* * * * * * * * * * *

Chapter 38

"You're sure?" I asked when Bryce came breezing into the room with the news of the bust.

"Confirmed. Sealed and delivered. Several hundred kilos of pure, uncut cocaine. I just got off the phone with my contact. Apparently, they just drove the boat right up with a smile on their faces. Wish I could have seen the look when they found out it wasn't the reception party they were expecting. It isn't hurting my buddy's status over at the Agency either. As far as everyone down there is concerned, the guy ought to have his own 1-800-PSYCHIC phone line. He could put Miss Cleo out of business." Bryce allowed himself a moment's satisfaction. "And what makes it better is that as far as any of the bad guys are concerned, the boat just disappeared. They are keeping this under tight wraps."

"Why the need for secrecy?" Skip asked.

"Because it only adds to the confusion. And where there is confusion, suspicion is never very far behind."

We had all gathered at my new temporary home, the Silver Club in Sparks. Having felt I had used up all my luck at The Ormsby House, I decided it was time to pull up stakes again and make it a little harder for Chance Dunleavy to get a line on me.

"Okay, go over it all again for me," Skip requested. "I was missing when you sicced Max on the computer system at the radio station. Just what did he do?"

"It was really pretty simple, actually. Since all the computers are linked up in a network, I just had Max hang out until a new playlist that had ten songs from our code index was sent into the system. I assumed the coordinates, or perhaps even the playlist itself, is generated off location by Carillo. But it still has to get into the hands of the DJ. I knew their playlists were fed into their computer system to be read on a screen by the jock, thanks to what Greg told me."

I blushed modestly.

"I wrote Max's program to slightly modify the songs to change one of the latitude coordinates. I made the change as small as possible for a couple of reasons. First, I didn't want to send a boat from Mexican waters up to the Washington Coast if the original time frame only allowed for a one- or two-day trip to the Central California Coast. But even more importantly, I wanted the song list to be as close as possible to the original. I'm hoping that if anyone who knows what the playlist is supposed to be listens, he won't listen too hard to all ten songs. If we changed them all, Carillo would probably pick up on it immediately. But Max only has to change song number 7."

"Only song number 7?" Skip asked. "Why only that one?"

Bryce just grinned. "Think about it. Here's a 50-point toss-up question. Why do we only have to change song number 7?" He started to hum the Jeopardy countdown music.

I buzzed in. "Because song number seven corresponds to the first digit of the number of minutes for the latitude they are trying to convey." Bryce nodded. I went on. "A minute of latitude is equal to one nautical mile. If you change only the first digit of a two-digit number, you are changing the location by jumps of ten nautical miles each."

Bryce picked it up from there. "In this case, Max switched Chaka Kahn's 'I Feel For You' with Blondie's 'The Tide is High,' which seemed singularly appropriate, and voila! The boat comes in 40 miles south of where Carillo's men were waiting."

Speaking of Carillo's shore party, they were purposely left alone. I was concerned a bit about the possibility of bloodshed should the DEA agents try to take down a band of heavily armed men in the dark. I needn't have worried. There was never any intention of going after them. There was too great a risk of one of them escaping and tipping Carillo off that his operation was compromised. As it was, all Carillo knew was that another shipment of cocaine didn't get through. As far as he could tell the ship either sank at sea, or the captain decided to make a run for it and start his retirement with a little extra nest egg. If the second was true, that would be a decision that undoubtedly would cause an early retirement of another sort should Carillo ever catch up with him.

But at that point, all Carillo had was a mystery. And that wouldn't have been so bad if *he* was the only one faced with said mystery. But in this case, there was another interested party.

Jose Antigua, another member of the Cartel, and the owner of the El Dorado's cargo.

Skip laughed when told whom the drugs belonged to. "You don't suppose they might be getting just a wee bit peeved with our dear Mr. Carillo now, do you?"

Bryce looked at me. "We can only hope," I answered.

That night, Max buzzed us again.

Two nights later, on a lonely stretch of deserted beach south of Mendocino, Special Agents from the DEA made the second largest bust of a cocaine shipment in the history of enforcement efforts.

The media was not notified.

But Alejandro Dominguez was. And he was not happy.

Dominguez, another of the Cartel's five members, was the owner of that particular shipment.

It made for a wonderful Christmas present for us, although I doubt Señor Dominguez was filled with holiday cheer when he received the news. But for me, separated from my family, driven from my home, and pursued by a man bent on ending my life, the news provided me with a gift that was wonderfully similar to that which the shepherds received on the hill above Bethlehem on that first Christmas.

A gift of hope.

There was no way I was even close to being out of the woods. There were too many things that still had to go right, and even then there were no guarantees it would produce the results we were looking for.

But there was hope. And on that Christmas morning, it was all Santa had left in my stocking.

Skip insisted I come over and open presents with his family. I tried to refuse, but he wouldn't have any of it. His wife Roberta, whom I would have expected to be highly annoyed at me for taking her husband away so much lately, instead greeted me with a hug and a kiss at the door. She was a lovely and gracious woman who was a year older than Skip, but looked ten years younger. I told him he didn't deserve her, and he couldn't argue.

They had two girls about the same age as Christopher and Mary. When I arrived, they were hovering over the unopened presents like two buzzards watching a wildebeest take its last living breath. When they saw me, they squealed, "Hi, Uncle Greg!" and without missing a beat, turned to their father and said, "Okay, he's here. Can we open them now, puhleeeeeease????"

As much as I appreciated them opening up their home to me, in the end watching those two girls transform the wrapping paper and bows into instant confetti only served to make me painfully aware of two other children. In all likelihood, they were also destroying hours of meticulous gift-wrapping two time zones away. Without their Daddy.

But there was hope.

And for this Christmas, it was enough.

Max delivered another holiday gift ten minutes before Christmas ended. Another shipment. Apparently tired of losing deliveries in California, Carillo sent Judd Black and his crew to an isolated stretch of beach 15 miles south of the town of Yachats on the Central Oregon coast. A pickup was made. But it occurred 5 miles to the north of the town. Not only the cargo, but the boat and the crew was picked up as well. Your tax dollars hard at work.

Once again, Judd Black returned home empty-handed. And Antonio Javerez, the fifth and final member of the Cali Drug cartel, who owned the shipment, was left a very unhappy man.

Less than five hours after the Javerez shipment was seized, Max rang us up once again. "I told you things were going to get busy," Bryce commented. "But this is the most important one of all."

I noticed there was only one set of coordinates on the screen. "Wait a minute. Something's wrong. All the other notices had two sets of numbers."

"Right. The first was the intended destination, and the second was the 'New and Improved' location."

"Then why is there only one coordinate here?"

"Who do you suppose owns this particular shipment?"

The light went on above my head. "Jorge Carillo?"

"One and the same."

* * * * * * * * * * *

This time, Judd Black did not go home empty-handed. The shipment arrived right on time, and when he quizzed the skipper of the vessel, he found that the trip had gone smooth for him as well.

Anxious to finish the loading of the drugs and weary of the constant rain that fell that night on the beach south of Coos Bay, Black drove his men hard. Less than 20 minutes later, the boat was shoved off the beach, and without any running lights, quickly disappeared into the now-heavy downpour of the black night.

Black hopped into the cab of the nondescript brown pickup truck after briefly checking the hitch connection of the battered U-Haul trailer. The rain continued to pour down, making the windshield wipers work overtime. "No need to hurry now," Black reminded himself, relaxing for the first time. "We got what we came for."

It was a good thing he wasn't in too much of a rush. A mile and a half down the road, flares and flashing amber lights marked the presence of road crews working feverishly to remove a tree which had just fallen across the highway.

"The rains softened up the soil on the bank enough that the old fir just got undermined and came down," the road crew foreman told Black through the rolled down window of the pickup. "I don't think it will take long to get it cut up and out of the way. We'll have you on your way in about ten minutes." The sound of a chainsaw being fired up nearly drowned out his last words. He tipped the brim of his poncho hood, allowing a rill of water to stream down and splash off his nose, and walked back to help clear away the larger branches.

He was normally a man to have little patience with such delays, but Black's mood was softened with the relief that this delivery, unlike so many of the others, was secure. He sat back, turned on the radio, and waited.

When he was flagged through 15 minutes later, he smiled and even thanked the crew foreman, and drove away in an almost jovial mood.

His mood might have soured some had he been aware of the tiny device attached to the undercarriage of the trailer, placed there in the darkness by one of the road crew as he was hauling tree limbs away from the site. The device was a modified Global Positioning Satellite device, with an additional twist. It not only knew where it was at all times, but a satellite transmitter imbedded in the device assured that agents from the DEA were in on the secret.

Following its trail, agents were able to establish the location of one of the main distribution centers for the entire cartel's network. Over the next several months, by patient undercover work, over a third of the distribution routes were to be discovered.

But the members of the cartel knew none of that. They already had enough on their mind, and it centered on one Jorge Carillo.

The tension in the elaborately decorated meeting room, high in a heavily guarded mountain villa above the city of Cali, was palpable. The villa belonged to Antonio Javerez, who was the cartel's "head of marketing." A small, shrewd man, he possessed the political savvy, controlled disposition, and the total absence of conscience which made him a perfect candidate for high public office. Never having held an elective position before didn't sway him from his firm conviction that by that time next year, he would hold the position of Colombia's Deputy Foreign Minister. With his money and power, no one would have bet against him succeeding.

But the tight control the imperturbable Javerez generally exhibited was in danger of failing. Sitting slouched somewhat in his seat, already an unusual sign for a man whose posture never deviated from perfectly upright, he drummed his fingers impatiently on the table as he waited for the meeting to come to order.

But others in the room were far less reserved in their display of annoyance.

Miguel Carerra, the cartel's member in charge of the distribution of cocaine once it got into the borders of North America, was the largest man there, as well as the one with the quickest temper. An intensely suspicious man, he had once killed two of his cousins based on rumors they were skimming some of the cocaine in the distribution network and selling it for themselves on the side. At their funeral, which Carerra not only attended but at which he also gave the eulogy, he was notified that the real thieves had been caught, and that his cousins had had nothing to do with the missing snow.

"Really? Then I'd better make their eulogy a good one," was his only reply.

Carerra showed the same lack of restraint as he stormed into the meeting room. "Where is he?" he shouted. "He had better have a good explanation for this, or I'll hang his head from the wall of my hunting lodge."

"You'll have to fight me for it first," said Alejandro Dominguez, in charge of processing the cocaine for the cartel. "I lost over 65 million dollars to that fool, and I want to know where it is."

The only calm voice came from the former accountant, Jose Antigua, whose financial gifts made him the perfect choice to handle the money laundering for the cartel. Accountant might be an over- simplification. He received a doctorate in economics at Columbia University many years before, but to the rest of the cartel, he handled the money, and therefore was an accountant. "Gentlemen," he began, "before we make any rash decisions, let's wait until we hear from Jorge. I too lost a great deal of money last week, but before I open fire based on nothing more than suspicion," he eyed Carerra surreptitiously, "I want to make sure of who my enemy is." Of the five, Antigua probably most realized the value of keeping the cartel unified, and he was also acutely aware of how tenuous its stability was. He probably also was the one who knew that of the five members of the cartel, Carillo was certainly the most powerful, and as such, the hardest to bring down should it come to a shooting match.

"I don't care…" Carerra began, when the entrance of the final member of the cartel cut him off.

In the newly created silence, Jorge Carillo walked calmly to his position at the elegant, burlwood conference table. An aura of power and darkness surrounded him, which rendered even the bombastic Carerra temporarily impotent. He was impeccably dressed and groomed, as usual, and in total control of his movements and emotions. He strode to the table, sat down, and then fixed his black eyes on each of the members in turn, before saying with authority, "Shall we begin?"

The room was sealed. None but the five men present were granted entrance. Teams from each of the cartel's members had swept the room, each under the watchful eye of the others, in order to assure all there were no weapons or listening devices. Each member was searched before entering the room. If there were disputes to be solved, they wouldn't be solved with bloodshed. At least not in this room.

Carerra recovered and spoke first. "Yes, we shall begin," he said, standing up and leaning over the table, towering over Carillo. He continued in a menacing voice. "You can begin by telling us what happened to nearly a quarter of a billion dollars of product?"

If Carillo was intimidated by the big man's display, he didn't show it. He calmly replied, "It appears there has been a breach in our security."

The calmness in Carillo's voice belied the rage he felt when he discovered the irregularities in the playlists. Frantically searching for an explanation for four missing shipments, he crosschecked the radio station's playlist records with the one that he had supplied. When he found the discrepancy, he took his fury out on his new Station Manager, whose partially decomposed body was found weeks later washed up on the shores of Pyramid Lake.

Other members of the meeting shared his fury. "A breach in security?" shouted Alejandro Dominguez. "I should say so. It's an odd coincidence that the breach in *your security* didn't seem to affect your last shipment."

Carillo knew he was on shaky ground. As much as it would have cost him, he almost wished that his shipment had been intercepted as well. Predicting how this would appear to the other members of the cartel, he had come prepared with a response. "Because of the problems, I am dividing up the proceeds of my successful shipment and will make distributions to each of you in equal amounts."

That statement temporarily shocked the room into silence, but it didn't last. Carerra, predictably, countered, "So that's all well and good. That will only repay one fifth of what I lost. What about the rest?"

Recognizing that weakness here would only be an open invitation for destruction, Carillo had already conceded all he was going to. "Then what about my losses when one of your distribution lines is broken by agents of the DEA? Do I ask for a refund whenever one of your pushers is busted?"

He turned to the others at the table. "What happens when Congress passes a tougher drug law, Antonio, making it tougher to make any money on the street? That means your lobbyists failed. Do I ask you for a refund? And when money is skimmed off the top of the laundering, Jose?" looking at Antigua, and then turning his piercing gaze on Dominguez, "And Alejandro, what about when your yields aren't up to standards? Do we all come crying to you, asking for our money?

"This is a business with inherent risks. There are going to be losses incurred at times in each of our areas of responsibility. I have been quite generous with my proposal. I suggest we accept this little setback and go on with business." He rose to leave.

"But what about your 'breach of security'?" Dominguez asked.

"It has been discovered and will be taken care of. That I can assure you. Good day, gentlemen." Carillo strode out of the room.

The room remained in silence for nearly a minute before, predictably, Carerra broke it. He had never liked Carillo's smoothness, and he envied his good looks and feared his power. "I don't buy it," he spat out the words. "For his shipment to go through, and none of ours? It's crazy. It works out too well for him."

"How can it work out well for him?" Javerez asked. "You heard him…he is splitting up the proceeds of his shipment with the rest of us. He is allowing himself to suffer the same losses as we are."

Carerra snorted. "That's assuming the shipments really disappeared. Who's to say he doesn't have all of our shipments under lock and key in a hidden warehouse somewhere? I tell you, he's trying to weaken us to the point where he can step in and take over the cartel. I say we need to stop him."

"Gentlemen." Jose Antigua stood up. "Before we do anything rash, we need to have more than suspicions that something is amiss. We must have proof. I realize there is little in our chosen line of work that would encourage trust amongst one's associates, but for all of us to realize the benefits that this cartel affords us, we must not rush to judgment. The only thing we know right now is Jorge Carillo has volunteered to forego approximately 40 million dollars as a good faith gesture. I suggest we not look a gift horse in the mouth until we know the stink is because of his bad breath."

His words seemed to have a calming effect on the group, and it became apparent that no action would be taken against their associate…for the time being. "And if we should find any of the proof we are missing?" Carerra asked.

Antigua looked at each man before answering. "Then I think it is safe to assume we shall have to sever our relationship with Mr. Jorge Carillo."

As he was driven away from the mountain villa, accompanied by four bodyguards, Jorge Carillo was deep in thought. Rarely a man to worry about his position of power, he knew he had been walking on thin ice. But he felt sure that he had dodged a bullet by offering to split up his share of his shipment. Now he could turn his attention to repairing the holes punched in his importation machine. The first step would be to take care of some business closer to home.

Almost in response, the fax machine installed inside the limousine beeped, chirped, and gurgled before spitting out a two-page report from NimRod.

Realizing the breach must have occurred inside the computer system, Carillo had brought in an expert. Although only 28 years old, the thin, bespectacled man known to the eclectic computer community as NimRod74 was already a veteran of three arrests for computer hacking into financial organizations. Fortunately for Carillo's purposes, NimRod was much more adept at finding the tracks of other people's computer mischief than he was at covering his own.

Max continued to hide within the hard drives of the computer network and didn't rise to the bait when Carillo's expert tried to get him to show himself, so NimRod assumed that there must be a breach from the outside. Max generally swept his trail well enough so that it was very tough to track him backwards. But according to the report Carillo held in his hands, Max had apparently left just enough crumbs for NimRod to follow back through to the Internet ISP. By hacking his way into the phone company records, he was able, by means of a statistical comparison, to retrieve the caller IDs of the culprit. In each case, the calls into the Internet ISP, and thus into the

KOPP computer system, were made from different hotel rooms. But after a thorough investigation, aided by the liberal distribution of the portraits of dead presidents in high denominations, it was discovered that all the rooms had one thing in common.

They were all reportedly occupied by KRGX's Chief Meteorologist, Greg O'Brien.

"So Mr. O'Brien. You *have* decided to stick your nose into matters that are of no concern to you." His eyes darkened, and he said grimly, "That was your first mistake."

He leaned back into the padded back seat of the limousine, closed his eyes, and let out a deep sigh. "And it will be your last."

* * * * * * * * * * *

Chapter 39

"Uh oh, it looks like we've got trouble." They weren't the words I wanted to hear Bryce say.

I looked up apprehensively. "What's the problem?"

Bryce stared at the computer's screen and stroked his chin. "It looks like someone's been playing detective over at KOPP." He tapped the screen. "I built in some self-defense algorithms into Max's basic command set. As soon as he gets a hint that someone is sniffing around looking for him, he basically goes dormant, creates a series of hidden files, and tucks himself into bed. It looks like he's done that."

"Does that mean what I think it means?" I almost regretted asking the question.

"Yep, I'm afraid it does. They're on to us."

I sighed. "Well, at least we were able to get some mileage out of him. Do you think it was enough?"

Bryce tried to look hopeful, but I could tell he wasn't optimistic. "I don't know, Greg. I know we stirred up a hornet's nest. I got a report that the cartel just met back in Colombia, but the security is just too tight to know what was discussed. Carillo apparently walked out of the meeting before the rest of the members did, but the fact that he walked out at all isn't very encouraging for the good guys." He looked at me. "We'll have to wait and see."

I considered the news for a moment. "What about Max? Do you think we can still redirect some of the shipments?"

He shook his head. "I doubt it now. Carillo almost has to know how the shipments disappeared. I'm sure he will come up with a new code and install some new security measures before he tries to land another boatload." He tried to grin. "To be honest, we were pretty lucky to get as many shipments as we did. Fortunately, they came bunched together during the last week. There was so much activity, no one paid close enough attention to the modification of the playlists."

I tried to provide a little sunshine to the cloudy change that had come over the room. "Well, look on the bright side," I said with a smile, "at least he couldn't have figured out who was behind it all."

Bryce didn't say anything. My smile began to fade. "Lemme try that again, okay?" I said with a bit more urgency. "At least he couldn't have figured out who was behind this, *could he?*"

Bryce thought for a moment. "Well, Greg, I've got good news and I've got bad news."

I rolled my eyes. "Let's get the bad news out of the way first."

"If Carillo hired a good enough tracker, and I doubt he would hesitate to find the best money could buy, then there is some danger."

"Yeah, but he wouldn't be able to trace Max's origin to us, would he?" I asked with more confidence than I felt.

He shrugged. "Hard to say. Back in the old west, there used to be Indian trackers who could follow a coyote's trail across solid rock. There are a few computer hacks today with the same kind of innate skill."

"But I thought you said Max didn't leave a trail."

"Max doesn't leave *much* of a trail. Not enough for anybody to pick up on unless they were both really good and really motivated. Carillo's money could buy both."

"But how would that get back to us?" I asked. "All the calls were made from a hotel room. And different ones at that. How could they possibly connect anything to us?"

"Oh, they wouldn't connect us."

"I didn't think so."

"They would connect *you*."

I stared at him. "Me? How?"

He looked at me pityingly. "Greg, how do you think? Let's assume they were able to trace all the way back to each call's origin."

"That's what I mean. I paid cash for all the rooms. I didn't even use my real name on the registration. How would they know it was me?"

"Greg…" Bryce continued, "who isn't going to know it was you who stayed in those rooms?"

He was right, of course. Even a half-baked investigation would easily turn up folks who knew I was staying in those rooms, from cleaning ladies to bell hops. One of the disadvantages to having one's face broadcast into every household and plastered on billboards all over town.

I should have listened to my mom and become a doctor.

The thought that Carillo might be on to me gave me a cold feeling in my gut. I had to agree with Bryce; that qualified as bad news.

"So what's the good news?' I asked.

"I lied about the good news."

"Thanks."

* * * * * * * * * * *

There were few people alive who would have handled a phone call from an irate Jorge Carillo without being gripped with a paralyzing fear.

Chance Dunleavy was one of those.

"I didn't hire you to create a 'work of art,' Mr. Dunleavy," Carillo continued in a low, menacing voice. "I had patience with your methods before, because I didn't have any firm evidence that Greg O'Brien posed more than a distant threat to me. But that has changed now. I don't care if it looks like an accident or not. I want O'Brien eliminated, and I want it done fast. He knows too much."

Unaffected by the tone of Carillo's voice, Dunleavy calmly answered, "That's all the more reason you want to be careful, Jorge. Oy have it on good authority he's been to the police, and they didn't pay him no mind. But if he should end up outside his telly station with a bullet in his head, don't you think the coppers might just reevaluate his story and begin to pry into the matter a bit more?"

Carillo had to stop and consider this. "Has O'Brien told the police anything about me?"

Dunleavy shrugged his shoulders. "No way to tell. Oy've been able to git some information, but none of the details. All Oy know now is the cops aren't pursuing the matter now, and Oy don't think we ought to upset the apple cart."

Carillo, in spite of his anger and impatience, had to concede to Dunleavy's logic. But not completely. "You have four days, Mr. Dunleavy. If Mr. O'Brien isn't taken care of by the end of this week, I will bring someone else in who perhaps isn't as fastidious as you, but is more reliable."

Dunleavy chuckled. "Four days will be plenty of time, Jorge. Oy've got it all set up."

"Four days, Mr. Dunleavy," and the line went dead.

Chance Dunleavy shook his head as he put the phone back onto its cradle. "Bloke's been workin' too hard. Needs to take a holiday."

Pulling out a small pocket-sized electronic organizer, he switched it on and then tapped in a series of numbers and letters. The password encryption allowed him access to some names and phone numbers which high-level law enforcement officials throughout the globe would have willingly traded their pensions for. Finding the entry he sought, he picked the phone back up and dialed a long series of numbers. After a short wait, he made a connection. "*Guten tag*, Mate. It's all set up. Can you be here by Friday?"

* * * * * * * * * * *

I drove into the station with a heavy heart. I had let my expectations exceed reality. I had hoped that we could stir up enough suspicion and distrust within the cartel that a palace revolt might occur. Instead, all it appeared I had accomplished was to leave myself vulnerable to discovery by Carillo.

It had almost worked. The emergency meeting that Bryce had mentioned at least suggested there was some tension within the home ranks. But he didn't seem optimistic it was enough. You don't topple someone with Carillo's strength without some heavy firepower.

Or at least a well-placed charge.

A few years back, demolition crews brought down the aging Mapes Hotel in Downtown Reno. It was a huge structure, and I remember being surprised at how small the explosive charges were that caused the entire building to come crashing down in a pile of rubble. It made for quite a spectacle. When asked how this was accomplished, a demolition expert we interviewed said that it wasn't how much explosive was used, but rather where it was placed. Engineers find certain critical spots at the base of the structure, and instead of blowing up the whole building, you just blow up that critical spot. After that, it's gravity that destroys the building, not TNT.

I wondered if we had begun that process. Our scheme of intercepting Carillo's shipments likely undermined his foundation within the cartel, but it hadn't been enough. What I needed was one more stick of dynamite to place under Carillo's feet, and let the gravity-like force of suspicion within the cartel do the rest.

A great theory. The problem was when I looked in my arsenal I didn't even have a firecracker.

I had been moving around a lot. Renewed fear of Dunleavy tracking me down prompted me to switch hotels every day now. I was getting dizzy. As a result, I had forgotten about two commitments I had made weeks earlier.

Jeanne Marshal welcomed me when I came through the door with the following words, "So, do you have your skis waxed?"

I looked at her blankly. "Skis?" I asked.

She eyed me curiously. "Have you been having a tough week? Yes, skis. You are planning on upholding the honor of your place of employment this weekend, aren't you?"

Of course. How could I have forgotten? KRGX was the chief media sponsor for the annual "From Boards to the Boardroom Corporate Ski Challenge." The event was held every New Year's weekend up at the Mount Rose Ski Area. It involved dozens of different businesses in the area to compete in a ski race and raised a ton of money for the local Food Bank. We had been involved in it for years, and in addition to skiing in the race, I was tapped to be the emcee of the awards ceremony. Since it was a part of my job duties, I really couldn't get out of it.

"Uh, oh yeah. Sure. I remember. I'll be there." I hoped.

So did she. "I should hope so. And I expect you to bring home the gold once again."

I smiled. "We'll see what we can do, boss."

She slugged me on the shoulder, and I retired to my office.

The second of my forgotten commitments showed up at my office between newscasts. Twelve freshly scrubbed faces belonging to Brownie Troop 103 filed in about 10 minutes before the 6:30 newscast began. A somewhat harried mom with a "Troop Leader" insignia on her uniform eyed me nervously, apparently noticing the confused look on my face. "You...do remember our tour, don't you?" she stammered. "I called last month and set it up?"

"Of course!" I recovered quickly. I rose and said, "I'm so glad you could make it."

The leader heaved a sigh of relief and corralled her charges into my office. "They have been so excited about this trip. It's all they have been talking about during our last two meetings. This will help them all get their weather badges."

"Well, I'll bet they aren't as excited as I am," I answered. "Let's see... how many do we have tonight? Twelve Brownies and six parents? Okay, here's what we are going to do. We'll take a quick trip through the newsroom, and then we'll return to the studio here so you can watch the newscast live." My voice turned serious. "But I need your help with something."

"What's that?" a button-nosed brownie in blond curls asked.

"Well..." I began. "While we are broadcasting the news, it has to be very quiet in here. Now I've never had any problems with girls your age before, but I need your help to make sure you keep your parents under control. I'm going to hold you responsible to make sure they don't talk while we are on the air. That a deal?"

They giggled and promised solemnly that they would keep the adults under a tight rein. "And make sure they turn off their cell phones, as well," I added, grinning when three of the moms fumbled in their purses and tried to switch off their phones without me noticing.

After the newsroom tour, they all sat on risers at the back of the studio, and I introduced them to Mark and Sue Ann when they entered and sat down at the anchor desk. I would repeat the introductions for Skip when he came out later in the newscast.

I left them to watch the first block of the program as I crossed the studio and finalized my weather graphics. The show began, and true to their word, the girls made sure that nary a peep was heard from their folks.

When the first block of news ended, and the camera swung around to me to "tease" the weather block, I made my usual pithy comments sure to pique the viewing audience's interest in my upcoming forecast, and we went to break.

"So how do you like it so far?" I asked, as I crossed over next to them and stood in front of the blue Ulitmatte wall so the director could set the controls and calibrate, or "tune in" the Matte. "Do you have any questions?"

"Yeah," answered another of the moppets. "What are you doing now? Why are you standing in front of that blue wall?"

"Ah ha! You've discovered my secret," I said conspiratorially. "I'll bet when you watched me do this at home and you saw those big weather maps behind me, you thought there must be a big screen projection there, didn't you?" They all nodded their heads. I leaned forward, lowered my voice, and put my finger to my lips. "Shhhhh! Can you all keep a secret?" They nodded again. "I'm going to tell you how Superman flies."

Their eyes widened. This was turning out better than they thought.

"Do you see this blue wall behind me?" I asked. Another nod of the heads, in perfect unison. I pointed to the studio camera that was focusing on me. "We have a machine upstairs called an Ultimatte that this camera is plugged into. Whenever that machine sees this exact color of blue," I said, referring to the brightly painted blue wall behind me, "it will substitute another picture; in this case, the weather maps coming out of my computer. Do you follow me?" Most of the brown berets were staying with me.

"So wherever the camera sees me, as long as I am not wearing this bright blue color, you will see me on your TV as well. But behind me, where the camera sees the blue wall, at home it will look like you are seeing a giant computer map on a huge screen. It's a much cleaner picture since it's not really projected up on the wall, but instead is generated straight from the video source."

I was starting to lose them. I can tell that when their eyes begin to glaze over. I was saved by a question from a cute little Asian girl in the front. "But how do you know where to point? If all you have is a blank blue wall behind you, how can you point at the weather stuff?"

"Great question. I use these monitors." I referred to two television monitors on each side of the blue screen, each of which appeared to show me standing in front of a temperature map. "And in addition, I use the one on the camera." I pointed at the teleprompter mounted on the front of the studio camera lens.

The teleprompter was a small television monitor mounted face-up just below the lens of the studio camera. A sheet of glass over the lens, at a 45-degree angle, reflected the screen of the monitor directly toward the person in front of the camera. It acted just like a two-way mirror. The camera could see right through the glass to the person in front of it, but when the person looked at the camera, all he could see was the reflection of the monitor screen. Usually, the words of the scripts the news anchors read were scrolled electronically over the screen. This allowed the anchors to read the news stories while looking directly at their audience at home.

But since my weathercasts weren't scripted, I had a different need for the teleprompter. A switch on the side routed the on-air signal to the prompter, so I could see where I was just by looking into the camera, and seeing myself on the screen, with my weather graphics "behind" me.

"I always keep one of these monitors in my vision. If I want to turn and point to the temperature in Reno, for instance," I turned and pointed to a blank space on the wall, "from the camera's perspective, it looks like I am looking at where I am pointing. But from the side you may notice I am really glancing at this monitor, and if you look at the monitor, you can see I am pointing to what looks like Reno to the TV world."

"Coming out in 30 seconds," the floor director informed me.

I acknowledged the warning and turned to the kids. "Here we go. Watch carefully while I do my weathercast, and you'll see how it works."

I was given a 15 second warning, and hurried over to the anchor desk. When we came back from the break, after the obligatory small talk with

Mark and Sue Ann, I began the weathercast in earnest. I walked from the set to the blue wall and chatted about the sunny day we had enjoyed, while the director upstairs cut to some video of ducks walking on the ice at Virginia Lake. The director then switched to my camera, with me stepping in front of the blue wall, but continued to roll the video of the ducks for a bit.

It now appeared that I was out on the ice with the ducks. Having a little fun with the situation, I bent over, cupped my hand to my ear, and appeared to be listening to one of the ducks, which wonderfully chose that moment to turn toward me and start quacking. "Uh huh… Okay… yeah I got it." I stood up, and laughed, saying, "Great joke. That really quacked me up." I turned back to the duck and thanked him, after which he flew off.

The fortunate timing of the ducks' movements, combined with the incredible realism of the Ultimatted image, made up for what was in all likelihood the dumbest joke in the recorded history of broadcast news.

I continued with the weathercast. As I pointed out features in the satellite loop "behind" me, I couldn't help but notice twelve little heads snapping back and forth between the blue wall and the monitor, as if they were watching a frantic tennis match. After a while, they just settled their eyes on the monitor, which became more "real" to them than the blank blue wall I was actually pointing at.

I finished the weathercast and returned to the anchor desk. I turned it back over to Mark and Sue Ann, they teased some upcoming stories, the bumper music ran, the tally light on the camera went black, and we went to another commercial break.

I walked back to my troop of Brownies, who looked like they had just had a tour of Universal Studios. But one tiny hand shot up. "Yes?" I asked.

"You said you were going to tell us how Superman flies," she said with a pout.

"Ah, yes, I did, didn't I?" I grinned back. "Well, did you see how we could put any video, such as those ducks, behind me on the wall?" They did. "Well, with Superman, since he wears blue tights, they use a green wall that does the same thing as this blue one does. They bring out a green platform and place it in front of their green wall. Superman comes out, lies on his belly on the green platform, and they feed video of clouds zipping by. Then they get a fan and blow some wind into his face. The green platform disappears, and it looks like he's streaking through the clouds, floating on air. If you do it right, it looks real."

One of the moms piped in. "It sure looked like you were right there with those ducks. I was watching the television screen the whole time. I thought I was going to die when the one turned and started quacking into your ear. It looked so… well, so *real.*

I smiled. "Yep. Once for an April's Fools joke, I wore a blue jacket and filmed myself singing 'I Ain't Got Nobody,' and then played it back on the Ultimatte while I sang a duet with my disembodied head. You can make it look like you are anywhere, or with anyone, for that matter. It's the wonder of TV. If you do it right, you can make people believe anything."

I stopped. I stared out past the eager eyes of the pack of girls, oblivious to their presence. Slack- jawed, I remained silent for several seconds before repeating in a low voice, "If you do it right, you can make people believe anything."

It was only the seed of an idea, but it might just be the firecracker I could place at Jorge Carillo's feet.

Chapter 40

Back at the hotel du jour, I laid my idea out before Bryce and Skip. It was raw and needed some fine-tuning, but as we discussed the elements, I could feel their enthusiasm growing.

I had one major concern. "Can we get close enough to his house to make it work?" I asked Bryce.

He thought for a while. "No," he answered. Then he looked up with a glint in his eye. "But we won't have to."

"We won't?" Skip asked.

"Nope. Carillo is a creature of habit. He doesn't venture out very often, especially when it comes to any interaction with the radio station. He doesn't want to have his association with KOPP advertised."

"Gee, no kidding," I added unnecessarily.

"But he does allow himself one luxury on a regular basis. Twice a week, on Tuesdays and Thursdays, he has lunch at a small, run-down Mexican place called Miguels."

"Miguels?" Skip asked. "I know that place. I go there all the time. It's about the only place in town that serves real Mexican food, not this fake stuff that they try to pawn off on you at all the chain places. You can tell it's real. That's where all the Mexicans in town eat." He reveled for a moment at the thought of a plate of Miguel's chili rellenos.

"Carillo was born in Mexico, and didn't move to Colombia until his late twenties. Apparently, he gets a little homesick, and Miguel's has the closest thing he can find to the food he grew up on," Bryce finished. "Anyhow, I think we can make Miguel's work just fine for us. Skip, do you know the manager?"

Skip held up two crossed fingers. "*Esta mi amigo bueno!*"

"*Muy bien,*" Bryce smiled. I'll leave it up to you to set it up from that end." He turned to me. "Greg, what you are suggesting sounds like it will take some pretty fancy technical skills. Can you handle that end?"

"Not all of it myself," I said. "But I have just the guy in mind who can make Superman fly."

"Great. I'll make a phone call and set it up on my end." He looked at each of us, and his face cracked into a grin. "If we play our cards right, Mr. Jorge Carillo's favorite restaurant is about to give him a severe case of indigestion."

"Of course I know the man," Juan Carlos Batiste said. "He comes in twice a week and always insists on sitting at the table in the back. Although he always comes in accompanied by three other men, he eats alone." The manager of Miguel's restaurant thought for a while. He was an ebullient personality who had the ability to brighten the day of even the most morose individual. "I have always thought of him as somewhat of a strange man, but he paid well and has been one of my most faithful customers. So what can I help you with?"

Skip and I told him. As much as we thought he needed to know. We didn't see any way around it, and we decided that honesty was the best policy.

After hearing a brief curriculum vitae on his best customer, Juan Carlos pondered the information for a moment. "Miguel Ribera, who started this restaurant, God rest his soul," he crossed himself, "was very concerned for the fate of the young Latinos in this area. He was always trying to give them a shot at making it in an honest way in the world of business. He saw that the drugs and the gangs threatened to destroy the very foundation of his community." He smiled. "I think he would be very pleased to cooperate with you."

He then added, "And so will I."

Like clockwork, at 11:45 AM on Thursday, Jorge Carillo entered Miguel's Mexican restaurant and was greeted at the door by Juan Carlos Batiste. "Ah, *Señor*, welcome," the manager gushed. "I have your table ready. Can I get something for your associates?" he said, referring to the three bodyguards who accompanied him into the establishment.

"No, they are fine," Carillo said curtly. "Just show me to my table. I am hungry."

"A condition that we will once again strive to relieve you of before you leave, I assure you," Juan Carlos said affably as he led Carillo to the back of the small restaurant before seating him. "I will be back with your menu in a moment, *Señor*." He added as he left, "I hope this will be a memorable meal for you."

"How am I doing?" Juan Carlos asked Skip and me as he came into the kitchen.

"You're doing just great," I said. "Just be a little careful you don't lay it on too thick."

"Too thick?" he asked.

"Greg thinks you might be acting a bit too friendly, Juan Carlos," Skip said. He then turned to me. "Don't worry, Greg. This is the way he is to everyone. Anything else and Carillo might begin to get a little suspicious."

I smiled. "I'm sorry, Juan Carlos. You just keep being yourself."

Skip asked, "Now are you sure you know what to do?"

The effusive restaurant manager managed to look hurt and playful at the same time. "Yes, of course I know. Don't you worry. I'll have him eating out of my hands in no time."

"That's fine," I replied with a smile. "Just make sure you wash them afterwards."

A minute later, Juan Carlos returned to Carillo's table with two frosted bottles of Dos Equis beer. He placed one in front of Carillo, while he kept he other. "*Señor*!" he beamed. "I hope you will allow me the honor of serving you myself."

Carillo, who was becoming used to receiving special treatment, said in a dismissive tone, "Of course."

Juan Carlos took a small menu out of his pocket and showed it to Carillo. Carillo at first refused the item, saying, "I already know what I want. I don't need this."

"Ah, but *Señor*, please indulge me in this. We have some special items on the menu that I wish for you to consider," the manager said, setting the menu in front of him and further surprising Carillo by taking the chair opposite him at the table.

The restaurant had always invested its resources into its food as opposed to providing an elegant atmosphere, and the menu, like so many other things, was a testimony to that philosophy. It consisted of a simple typewritten sheet of paper with a limited number of entrees. This one differed from the rest in that it was notably cleaner than its grease-stained predecessors.

Carillo reluctantly took the menu and looked at it. He scanned it and scowled. "Where are the *huevos rancheros*?" he asked. "That is what I always have, and now it appears that you have removed it from your selections."

"We have?" Juan Carlos looked puzzled.

"Yes, you have. See?" Carillo turned the menu around and held it up to the manager.

Juan Carlos looked stricken, a response that seemed to please Carillo. "*Señor*, my most humble apologies. That was an oversight, I assure you. You are one of the few customers that order that selection, but we will be glad to specially prepare them for you."

Though put off by the fact that his favorite menu item should have been eliminated from the menu, Carillo seemed pleased that he alone would now be able to enjoy Miguel's *huevos rancheros* without having to share them with the public. "That will be fine then," he said, as he tossed the typewritten menu back on the table.

Seemingly relieved at avoiding a conflict with a valued customer, Juan Carlos picked up the menu and hesitated a moment before he decided to press his luck. "*Señor*, before I go, might I impose once more on your goodwill?"

Carillo looked up annoyed at the additional intrusion. "Yes, what is it?"

Juan Carlos saw the opening and dove in. "*Señor*, I know you are a generous man," he knew no such thing, " and I wish to tell you of a great need. Our restaurant's founder, God rest his soul, had a soft spot in his heart for the children in our area, as I am sure you do as well." Carillo *had* no soft spots in his heart, but that didn't sway Juan Carlos.

"What do you want?" Carillo asked, motivated more by a wish to rid himself of the intrusion than by any philanthropy.

"*Señor*," the manager continued on without missing a beat, "there is a park here in town that our founder helped build, and it is in great need of new playground equipment. Right now, it is not safe for them to play there, and I know you would want…"

Carillo reached into his suit pocket and removed a wad of bills. He peeled off ten hundred-dollar bills and laid them on the table in front of an opened-mouthed Juan Carlos. "There you are. That should be sufficient."

Jorge Carillo didn't care if it helped the children. Jorge Carillo was not a man who gave money away without expecting a return. But the minor financial investment was likely to pay back in two ways. One, Carillo expected it would buy him influence in the area's Hispanic community. You never knew when he might need to draw on some local resources.

But he had another and more immediate reason for the payment. He hoped it would buy him a quiet lunch. "Now please may I have my lunch and my privacy?"

Juan Carlos picked up the bills in his hand and then grinned at Carillo. "Of course, *Señor*." He then raised his own bottle of the Mexican beer, and toasted Carillo. "To you, *Señor*. *Salud*! You are a great man!"

Relieved to nearly see the end of the gregarious manager, Carillo absent-mindedly raised his bottle and tipped it to Juan Carlos in a return of the toasting gesture, and then turned back to the paper he was reading prior to the interruption.

Even Carillo couldn't help but smile to himself as he heard the manager's voice trailing off into the kitchen, "A great man...a great man!"

"Yes, I am," he muttered.

Twelve feet away, peering out from under a dirty dishrag on a cart filled with unwashed dishes and silverware, a small video camera continued to silently record a self-satisfied Jorge Carillo as he began to eat his plate of *huevos rancheros*.

"Ah, that's a nice touch," I said, seeing Carillo's half-hearted return toast to Juan Carlos.

"Cheers," Skip concurred.

We were reviewing the tape back at my home. Bryce had done me the favor of sweeping the house to see if Chance Dunleavy had left any more surprises. As far as he could tell, he hadn't, and we needed a VHS player to see what our little surveillance efforts had produced.

"What do you think?" I asked Bryce. "Have we got what we need?"

"That all depends on what kind of technical magic we can work at the studio. This has to be good enough to sell on the first offering. Is your guy there good?"

"He isn't good," I answered. "He's the best."

"Cool!"

It was one of Pete's favorite expressions.

"When do we start?"

Pete Potter, all 5'6" and 125 pounds, was the closest thing to a perpetual motion machine ever produced. His stringy, long blond hair, now just beginning to show hints of gray and tied back into a ponytail, constantly swept back and forth like a horse swatting flies as he looked alternately at Skip and Bryce and me. His hands were continuously occupied. If they weren't busy caressing the Grass Valley Switcher at the production control booth above the studio, then they were employed bending paper clips, wadding up paper balls, or ferrying an almost constant stream of M & M's to his mouth, to be mixed in with the omnipresent Bazooka Bubble gum, prior to being washed down by a can of high octane Mountain Dew. Diet, of course.

Sometimes I got a headache just looking at him. But he was the best technical director I had ever known, and a magician once you got his attention focused on a project.

"Well, Pete, I'd like to begin tonight, after the 11, if that won't keep you up too late."

"Naw, heck, it takes me a while to wind down after the late show anyway." Skip almost choked on that one. Neither of us had ever experienced a "wound down" Pete Potter. "I usually don't crawl into sack until 5 or 6. Let's start as soon as we can clear out the studio."

"That would be great, Pete." I was relieved that he didn't want to know any more about our reasons for needing his services, but I was not really surprised. Pete was driven by challenges, as well as a desperate need to avoid boredom in his life. If he wanted to know more in the future, I'd be glad to enlighten him. "I'll see you then."

"Cool!"

Later that evening, I called Bryce. "Has your man arrived yet?"

"I'm leaving in 5 minutes to pick him up at the airport."

"Okay. Do you remember where the back door into the studio is?"

"Sure."

"I'll meet you there at ten before midnight."

"Cool."

I rolled my eyes and hung up the phone.

The studio was abandoned and the lights were nearly all out, save for one spot and two fills lighting the blue Ulitmatte wall. Upstairs in the production booth, accompanied by the constant drumming of his fingers on the console, Pete Potter was reviewing the video taken at Miguel's. "You did a good job of setting up the camera," he said, peering intently at the scene. "The angle should be easy to reproduce if we just ped down the studio camera." He stared some more at the video. "Matching the lighting will be a challenge. It's pretty dark in there. I don't suppose you could have set up a couple of spots when you took this, huh?" he said with a grin.

"Uh, no, I'm afraid that wasn't an option," I answered.

"That's cool. I think we can run the studio cam through a filter that ought to match the tones up pretty well." He looked at the man that came with Bryce. "So is this the star of the show?"

"I'm just a supporting actor, actually," the man said good-naturedly. "The one we want to win the Oscar is already on the tape. Do you think you can pull this off?"

"Piece of cake," Pete said. "It may take a few tries, but by the time we're done, you'll think you were really there." He smiled at him. "So are you ready to get started?"

"Let's do it."

"Cool!"

"Alright, Pete, how's this angle?" I spoke into the headset attached to the studio camera.

"Ped down just a tad more, Greg," came the reply through my earphone.

I pushed the camera down into its hydraulically supported pedestal until it bottomed out. "That's all we got, Pete. Can't go any lower."

"That's cool. That's just about right. Rack in and get your focus."

I zoomed in on the man sitting in front of the Ultimatte wall. I focused the camera to a razor's sharpness, and then pulled back to frame him in the shot. He was in a chair we had borrowed from Juan Carlos. The same chair that was at Carillo's table earlier that day.

"Cool, Greg. Now tweak the focus so he's just a little fuzzy now."

"Huh?" I asked.

"We've got to be careful he doesn't look sharper than the other video. The focus on the VHS is okay, but it's never going to look as good as what we can get on these studio cams. So let's tweak it down a bit."

"Roger." I gently twisted the focus knob on the camera's handle until the subject in the studio appeared a little softer around the edges.

"Looks good," Pete's voice continued through the headsets. "Now let's get him framed up. Pan right a bit… a bit more… there. Now push in some… there. A little back to the left now…Bingo! Cool, Greg. Now lock it down. Look at the monitor and tell me what you think. Just for size and perspective. We'll fix the colors and drape him in a bit."

I looked at the monitor beside the wall. It appeared that the man was sitting inside the restaurant, opposite a frozen image of Jorge Carillo. He was the right size, and perspective looked perfect, but there were still a couple of problems. Even though the focus was a bit off on our studio subject, he still appeared much more vibrant than the lower quality of the VHS video. But as I stared at the monitor, that began to change. Pete adjusted the luminescence values of the studio camera, and subtly lowered the image quality. When it was almost right, I heard Pete say, "And now, *mes amis*, for zee *piéce de resistence!*"

All of the subtle differences between the "live" portion of the screen and the taped elementsdisappeared as the screen went from color to black and white. "That was brilliant, Pete," I said. "This is supposed to be a surveillance shot anyway. Losing the chroma is perfect. You're a genius."

"I know."

Pete added some grain to the whole picture, and apart from one thing, you couldn't tell they weren't both in the room at the same time.

The one thing was significant, though. It appeared the man was sitting in a chair in front of the table, instead of behind. We had to do one more thing to fix that. "Cool, now let's drape the table," Pete said.

In order to make the table from the restaurant video appear to be in front of our studio subject, we brought out a blue colored sheet and hung it on a frame in front of our guest. Under Pete's direction, we molded it to the shape of the table. When we were finished, I looked at the monitor. "Beautiful," I murmured to myself. I turned to the man seated behind the drape. "Appears to me you've been consorting with an unsavory character."

He smiled. "Let's not make this public, shall we?"

I grinned back. "Don't worry. This will be for a very select viewing audience."

"Cool," I heard Pete say through the headphones.

It took several hours of painstaking work. The timing of the movements was hard to get down, but even tougher was helping our subject with the subtle nuances of body posture and head tilt that made it all believable. Because he had to look at the monitor while he was "interacting" with Carillo, he had the usual tendency to get what I call "monitor lock," where he always appeared to be looking at the same spot. After a while, I was able to get him to change the angle of his head to appear to be looking up and down, while only his eyes drifted to the monitor. "I'll make you into a weatherman yet," I finally said with a smile.

"Not me," he said. "It's too dangerous."

"Ouch."

When we were done, just before the morning crew came in to take over the studio, we looked at the final product. To make Juan Carlos "disappear," Pete had split the screen and substituted video shot later when his half of the table was empty. When our guest in the studio came on the scene, Carillo looked up and appeared to be interacting with him, instead of the restaurant manager.

"You were lucky this was shot at such a low angle," Pete said. "And that you didn't pass the menu or the money directly from hand to hand. By setting it on the table, it disappears from view temporarily. It makes the transfer easy to fake. The only real challenge was the beer bottle, but that wasn't too hard to splice in."

We all viewed the tape once more, looking for any inconsistencies. Tapping his toes to the beat of a rhythm known only to him, when it was over, Pete asked, "Well?"

"It works for me," Bryce said.

"Awesome," added Skip.

"It's incredible," said our guest. "If I didn't know any better, I'd say I was there."

"You da man, Pete," I said in awe.

Pete smiled. "Cool."

Chapter 41

Bryce was left in charge of what to do with the end result of our late-night project. "I have a few contacts that can get this into the right hands without raising too many red flags," he mused. "Although I suspect with the mood of the cartel now, they probably won't be inclined to look too critically at its origins."

"Can you Fed-Ex it?" I asked, only half joking.

"When it absolutely, positively has to get there the next morning?" Skip added.

Bryce smiled through tired eyes. "I'll do you one better. I'm going to fly down there myself, and I'll be gone for a couple of days. For now, you just do your best to stay out of trouble."

Feeling emboldened by the results of our work, I said, "I will. So far, I've managed to stay a step ahead of Mr. Dunleavy."

Bryce glanced at me. "Well, yeah. But you won't have the same help."

"Help?" I asked.

He pulled a small metal object out of his pocket. "You are going to be without your guardian angel for a while, Greg. Watch yourself."

I warily eyed the object in his hand. "What's that?"

"It's a small tracking device I pulled off of your car last week. It's the third one I have found. I've been making it a habit to sweep your car on a regular basis."

I felt dumb. All this time, I had fooled myself into thinking I had avoided Dunleavy on my own, by constantly switching hotels. If I hadn't had Bryce babysitting me, Dunleavy would have drawn a bead on me a long time ago.

Now he was going to be out of the picture for a while. I suddenly felt vulnerable.

"Hurry back."

I stood and looked up from the base of the mountain, feeling the stirrings of a new beginning. New Year's Day always seemed to do that for me. The cloudless blue sky contrasting against the dark green of the pine trees and the brilliant white snow painted a picture that reflected the hope I felt for Bryce's Colombian excursion. All I had to do now was to keep out of Dunleavy's way and pray that our efforts worked.

Mt. Rose Ski Area seemed as good a place as any to stay out of Dunleavy's path. On the phone the night before, Lauren had expressed anxiety about me participating in the skiing event.

"Don't you think it would be better to just stay low and keep out of sight?" she asked.

"I thought about that, hon, but I would rather keep moving." I told her about the tracking devices Bryce had found on my car. "I'm checking the car now, but I don't have the expertise to do a sweep like he does. If Dunleavy is able to find me, I don't want to be holed up. I'd rather have some room to maneuver. And besides," I said with a grin, "I've been skiing most of my life. He's from Australia. I doubt he's had a lot of time on the slopes. It will be nice to feel like I'm on my home field for a while."

So after pulling my skis out of the garage early that morning, I drew a deep breath of the crisp mountain air and climbed onto the chairlift.

We couldn't have picked a more perfect day for the Corporate Ski Challenge. Early season snows had left the area with a healthy snowpack, and a brilliant sunshine was the perfect complement to the conditions. I knew I wouldn't have to shoulder the blame for "bringing such lousy weather" as happened the previous year, when a blizzard nearly canceled the event.

In fact, I might just try to take credit for this one.

The race wasn't scheduled to begin until one o'clock that afternoon. After a series of runs that morning, where I still found myself peering over my shoulder looking for any telltale sign of Chance Dunleavy, I finally began to relax and enjoy myself. It was the first opportunity I had to ski that season, and I could feel the rust beginning to wear away. The edges of the skis began to respond as instructed, and I felt the old form and confidence return.

It had been a long time since I had done any real serious skiing. I had raced competitively in high school and college, with only moderate success, but as race time approached, I could feel the old competitive juices begin to flow. This was just what I needed. I had won the event the previous two years, and I planned on making it a hat trick.

After a quick lunch, I made my way to the top of the course. There were several familiar faces there, both fellow KRGX employees, Skip included, as well as competitors from years past. I noted two others in particular who had come the closest to beating me the previous race, and we immediately began some good-natured trash talking.

Jacob Miller, a Vice President of the local phone company, started in on me first. "So they finally let you off the beginner's slope, eh, Greg?"

"Oh, hi, Jake. Yep. As soon as they told me that you took the training wheels off of your skis, it inspired me to better myself."

"Hey, Greg," this time from Mike Phillips, a power company executive. "When you make your run down the course, try to leave at least a few of the gates standing for the rest of us, will ya?"

I laughed. I was kind of known for taking the gates pretty close. "No problem, Mike. I hear they Super-Glued them in this time."

I skied the first of the two scheduled runs a little tentatively and was somewhat disappointed to find myself in second place, a quarter of a second behind Jake and only a tenth of a second ahead of Mike. I knew I could do better. Even though the race was mostly designed for fun, there were a few of us, Jake and Mike included, who still let our competitive natures get the best of us. This was for pride now, and for bragging rights all the next year.

And you thought the World Cup racers had pressure.

As silly as it was, my stomach still was in a bit of a knot as I slid my skis into the starting gate for my final run. Both Jake and Mike had made their second runs, and Jake still held a slim lead. But it was beatable if I put together a good run myself.

"Racer in the gate..." intoned the starter.

I felt the effects of the past month and a half begin to bubble up within me. I wanted to go fast. Real fast. Almost as if I was outrunning Chance Dunleavy and Jorge Carillo right here.

"Five... four..." the starter counted down.

I decided to go all out at the start. I remembered watching Jean Claude Killy in the 1968 Grenoble Olympics when I was a kid. He swept the alpine events partly because of a starting technique he developed. Instead of pushing his feet out through the trip wire first, he would hurl his body forward and kick his feet upward and backwards, then slam them through the gate. This almost gave him a running start, and made the difference in at least two of the three gold medals that he won. Ski racers ever since then have emulated this technique, and I was going to use it to blow away my competition right out of the gate.

"Three... two... one..."

Drawing on the strength that weeks of tension and anxiety had built, I exploded off of my skis, throwing my body forward and kicking my heels back and upward, waiting until the last possible moment before hurling them through the trip wire that would start the timer.

I was awesome. I was inspired. I was a sight to behold.

I was also somewhat heavier than the last time I had tried this maneuver.

As I leapt forward and kicked my heels back, both ski bindings protested and released. The gasps of awe from the crowd only moments before turned to tittering chuckles as I buried my face into the snow a mere four feet from the starting gate.

I thought about staying planted there until the next storm came and covered me up.

But as the muffled giggles from the crowd began to filter into my half-covered-with-snow ears, I felt the quakes of uncontrollable laughter begin to grip me. I rolled over slowly, wiped the snow from my face and began to bellow. This, of course, set off the crowd, and they joined in a roar of laughter.

With tears streaming down my eyes, I grabbed one of my now abandoned skis, sat on it, pointed it down the hill, and pushed off. Laughing maniacally, I sort of steered a course through the gates, picking most of them off in the process, until I arrived at the finish line at a higher rate of speed than prudence dictated. Fortunately there were several bales of hay strategically located as a backstop. Like a smart bomb drawing a bead on a munitions plant, my trip down the hill ended in an explosion of straw and snow.

As the dust settled, the first sight I saw was the beaming face of Skip Walker, who hovered over me. "Nice race, Tomba."

Still a little woozy, I asked, "How did I do?"

Skip, who had raced earlier, looked at the time and did a quick calculation. "Not bad. You just missed getting the gold by 34 seconds."

"Nuts."

Sometimes the ridiculous *is* sublime. My impromptu slide down the racecourse was just what the doctor ordered. I resolved to spend the rest of the day on the mountain enjoying myself. Tomorrow, and the accompanying dangers in the valley, would arrive soon enough. For the time being, I was going to allow the mountain to provide me with some much-needed escapism.

The awards ceremony and the banquet were scheduled to take place in the lodge that evening, so I had the luxury of skiing until they closed the lifts. After having acquitted myself in such a distinguished manner in the Giant Slalom race, I thought I would try to bust up a bit of the powder snow that was still left along the tree line above The Chutes.

The present Mt. Rose Ski Area originally started out as two separate areas, neither of which resided on the mountain that bears the name. The real Mt. Rose sits across a pass several miles to the north. The "Rose" side of the ski area lies on the north-facing slope of Slide Mountain, opposite Mt. Rose. The "Slide" side of the area covers the eastern slopes of the mountain. Separating these two bowls lays a deep, treacherous canyon called The Chutes, out of bounds to skiers because of its steep slopes, hidden rocks and severe avalanche danger. Ropes and signs along the edge of the canyon warned skiers of the hazards. But the edge of the drop-off also usually had some pretty decent powder snow still left on it long after the rest of the mountain had been skied off.

But before I got the chance to sample some of the untracked snow, I made a new friend. As I poled myself up to get on the chair lift, an accented voice cheerfully asked me if he could ride up with me.

"Certainly," I said. "Glad to have the company."

As we rode up the chair, I tried to place his accent. "German?" I asked.

He smiled. "Close. Austrian. Deiter Newhopf. Vacationing in your beautiful country. Are you from around here as well, or are you a visitor?"

"I live just down the road, Mr. Newhopf. In Reno."

"Please, call me Deiter. And what shall I call you?"

"My name's Greg, Greg O'Brien." We shook hands. "Welcome to Nevada, Deiter."

"Ach, thank you. I'm already enjoying myself. Perhaps we could ski a few runs together? I really don't know the mountain, and I would enjoy a local guide."

His friendliness was infectious enough that I put aside any reservations about whether he could keep up with me and welcomed him to join me. I also decided to put on hold my idea of skiing above The Chutes, until I saw at what level he skied.

As it turns out, I needn't have worried about his ability. He was a stereotypical Austrian, who probably owned his first pair of skis before he got his first pair of shoes. As we flew down the slopes, my perspective changed, and I was worried *I* was holding *him* up. "Not at all, Greg. You ski very well for an American," he added with a twinkle in his eye.

Wanting to make the day last as long as we could, we skied up and got on the chair lift just as they were closing it behind us. "Lucky us," I commented. "Looks like we may be the last ones off the mountain."

"Wonderful! That means we get our money's worth, eh? Where should we make our last run?"

The chair lift we were on took us to the top of the mountain on the far edge of the "Rose" side, right above The Chutes. I began to eye the still-untracked powder snow enviously. Up to that point, we had stayed on the groomed trails. "Do you like powder snow?" I asked.

"I thought you'd never ask."

At the top of the chair, Deiter stopped me and asked me to point out some of the landmarks around the area. The view from 9,700 feet of elevation can be breathtaking, and I showed him the lights of Reno, just now beginning to wink on in the shadows of the valley. Turning slowly to the south, Washoe Valley with its lake of the same name spread out before us, and with a short climb, I was able to point out Carson City farther to the south.

"This is quite a wonderful place you live in, Greg," Deiter exclaimed. "Such views." Coming from a man who was used to the Austrian Alps, this was high praise indeed. I realized I tended to take these views for granted. We stood in companionable silence for a while before turning to head back down the hill.

By the time we began our trek downward, the mountaintop was deserted. We skied under the now-empty chair lift, veered slightly off the easier slope, and began our descent down a run called Express, a difficult run even over the groomed portion, rated as one of the steepest on the mountain. Just before we disappeared from view, I warned Deiter to be careful about straying too close to the edge. Strong westerly winds had built up huge cornices that hung over the sides of The Chutes, and many an unsuspecting skier had fallen victim to the temptation of venturing out too far and having the snow break off from underneath him. If you broke through there, you likely wouldn't stop for over a thousand feet.

"Are you ready?" I asked.

"Indeed I am!" he answered exuberantly. He scanned the empty slopes ahead and said, "It seems we have the whole mountain to ourselves!"

I grinned. "I always wanted to be the last one off the hill."

He grinned back. "Looks like you will get your wish."

Deiter followed me down Express for about a hundred yards, before we veered to the right and got out on the edge of The Chutes. But after a long day of skiing, my exuberance wasn't matched by my stamina, and I caught an edge carving a turn around one of the pines which grew near the ledge. After the eruption of snow from my resulting fall settled, I picked myself up and began to brush the fresh powdery snow off my front.

Deiter skied up next to me, avoiding the pitfall that ensnared me, and stopped about 6 feet away. I smiled sheepishly and began to reach up my gloved hands to clear the snow out from under my goggles. My ski poles dangled from my wrists by leather straps and hung down on each side of my face. I noticed a quick movement out of the corner of my eye, just before something struck the thick plastic handgrip of my left ski pole, sharply knocking it against the side of my face.

"Ouch!" I said, momentarily stunned by the blow. I rubbed my face and neck to try and deaden the sting. I turned and focused on Deiter, who was peering intently at me, with his ski pole extended and pointed at me. It took me a moment to realize that he had attempted to jab me in the neck with his pole.

"What... who?" I stammered as I regained my balance. It was then that I felt something sticking out of the grip of my ski pole.

It was a small dart.

From the tip of my companion's ski pole.

My thoughts instantly flashed back to the paralysis drug that Chance Dunleavy had injected me with back in the steam room and with a shock realized that my new friend was no friend at all. Dunleavy had recruited some help...help that knew how to ski.

In the rapidly fading light, it was apparent that Deiter, or whatever his real name was, couldn't tell if the dart had found a home in my neck or not, and I could see him switching to grab his other pole, where a backup dart was undoubtedly stored.

I thought of trying to make a run for it, but he was too close, and any sudden movement would just cause him to stab me with the pole. Once the drug took hold, it would be an easy task to snap my neck and toss me over the edge into The Chutes, where even the most suspicious investigation would have to rule death by a skiing accident.

I had one of two options, and I needed to choose one of them fast. One, I could try to disarm him, perhaps by using my pole to parry his thrusts. But my childhood fear of being stabbed kept me from ever learning any of the rudimentary skills of fencing, and all he needed to do was to nick me with the tip of the pole and then sit back and wait.

I decided to try option two.

"Wha…waz happinin…?" I mumbled as I began to waver. "I…hmmm…wha…" My head lolled to one side, as I continued to sway back and forth, barely maintaining balance.

Deiter had been on the verge of trying to score with the second dart when, seeing my apparent drug-induced fog, relaxed his grip on his pole, straightened up, and smiled. "There you go friend, just relax now, and it will all be over with in a bit."

Weaving even more precariously now, I saw that my skis, which were temporarily at rest on a level spot, were about 4 feet from a short drop-off. If I tried to push off right away, the snow piled up around my feet, and the lack of slope would slow me down too much to get me out of Deiter's reach. I had to play for some time.

I groggily swung my head around to look at my attacker, hoping to convince him that I was on the verge of collapse. I let my eyes loll upwards toward the back of my head, and moaned a series of unintelligible sounds.

It seemed to work. He straightened up, smiled and planted his ski pole back into the snow.

I let one of my legs buckle and appear to slide out forward from under me, barely catching myself as I struggled to stand back up. With a great effort, I fought my way back to a semi-standing position. In the process, I had covered half the distance to the drop-off.

Deiter chuckled. "Herr Dunleavy said this stuff worked quick. He wasn't joking, was he?"

He noticed me wearily teetering toward the short ledge. He said, "You might as well quit fighting it. You aren't going anywhere."

It was just the response I wanted to hear. As the tips of my skis worked their way to the edge of the drop-off, I let out a final moan, and I appeared to buckle my knees and fall forward. As I did so, I brought up my poles, dug them into the snow, and, hoping to improve on the last time I wanted a quick start, lunged my body forward, kicked my heels outward, and prayed a fervent prayer my bindings would show a little more class this time.

They held.

Jean Claude would have been proud.

I flew off the short ledge so fast it took Deiter a moment to realize what was happening. Dodging trees, I frantically fought my way through the knee-deep snow in an effort to put as much distance between the two of us as I could.

I had a head start, but it wasn't much.

He reacted almost immediately, and as I brushed a branch out of my face, I could hear him gaining on me no more than twenty feet behind.

Nearing panic, I struggled to maintain balance as I careened off one bump to the other. Even in the deep snow, the steep slope we were on generated plenty of speed. Weaving in and out between trees, I wondered if my pursuer was having as much trouble staying on his skis as I was.

I needn't have wondered. As branches continued to slap at my face and sides, I heard a roar of laughter come out of the trees behind me. He was actually enjoying this. And was still gaining on me. I had to try another tack.

I swerved sharply left and burst out of the trees back onto the groomed portion of the ski run. Immediately, I realized I had made a mistake.

I had spent the afternoon getting my doors blown off by this guy when we skied these groomed runs, and as fast as I thought I could make it down the mountain, I knew he could make it faster. And it didn't matter if it was in the open or in the trees; there was no one around to witness what was going on. At least in the trees, it would be harder for him to jab me with his pole. Once he did that, it really would be over.

Deiter flew out of the trees right behind me, and making a couple of skating motions with his skis, began to gain some more. I had to do something, and I had to do it fast.

Turning sharply back to the right, I found a narrow crease in the trees. As I hit the soft snow, I leaned back slightly to keep the tips of my skis from digging in. I immediately had to veer a bit to the left to avoid another tree. This threw me off balance even more. And still he gained on me. In moments he would be close enough to reach out and plant the dart in my backside.

Things were not going well. I was out of control. I was out of time. And suddenly, I was out of room.

Several switchbacks were carved into side of the mountain to provide access to the lifts during the summer months. These sharply turned at each side of the run. With enough snow accumulation, the nearly vertical walls formed by the ends of the switchbacks are softened into steep ramps.

At my speed, there was only one place to go. I careened up the side of the impromptu ski jump and soared through the air, spread eagle.

There was only one problem.

On the other side of the ramp, in the direction I was now heading with nothing under my skis but thin air, the ground dropped away in a sheer cliff and fell over a hundred and fifty feet to a pile of broken rocks in The Chutes below.

Chapter 42

Seventy-five years ago, there was a fire.

It was not a large fire, as fires go. A four-acre blaze caused by a single lightning strike, which smoldered in the trunk of an old snag for nearly a week, before one afternoon winds fanned it into life. The fire spread to a small grove of Lodgepole pines, which were battered and worn by the harsh conditions on the exposed ridge.

Lodgepole pines are one of a small group of pine trees that reproduce only in the face of adversity. Their seeds sit dormant and idle within their cones, and are only released when triggered by the high heat of a forest fire.

One of these newly-released seeds was caught up in a rapidly spinning vortex of wind driven by the heat of the flames and carried beyond the reach of the fire. It found its resting place atop a boulder on the edge of a sharp precipice. Subsequent winds pushed the seed just beyond the edge of the cliff, where it nestled in between the cracks of a few rocks tenaciously clinging to the sides of the escarpment.

After the rains of another thunderstorm doused the original fire, the life-giving water from subsequent cloudbursts percolated down to the solitary seed, moistening the tiny bits of soil which had accumulated between the cracks in the rocks. Receiving a signal miraculously imprinted in its genetic code, the seed germinated, sending tiny roots downward to search out a foothold so necessary to its survival. Millimeter by millimeter, the roots grew, exposing and exploiting weaknesses in the rocks, until they found their way through to the dirt below.

As the roots began their migration downward, the tender shoots of the seedling above ground were protected from the harsh conditions by the rocks surrounding it. By the time the new growth of the seedling peeked out above the protection of the rocks, its roots had established themselves deep into the soil beneath its protective cradle.

As the years passed, the baby tree outgrew its cradle, and as the trunk grew and expanded, the rocks split apart, succumbed to the inevitable pull of gravity, and found their resting place atop the pile of talus over a hundred feet below.

But the tree prospered. Where once the rocks protected it from the elements, the cliff face on its western side shielded it from the harshest effects of the predominant winds. By the time it had grown the twenty feet needed to peer over the top of the ridge, it was strong enough to withstand the full onslaught of the storm track.

In the subsequent years, it had survived storms, pestilence, and other fires, and managed to grow another twenty-five feet above the top of the ridge.

Which was good, because by the time I hit the tree, I was about twenty feet above the ridge.

I have since found from first-hand experience there is no graceful way to use a tree to arrest one's passage through the air at forty miles per hour. But gracefulness was the furthest thing from my mind. As I struck the tree head-on, I found myself wrapped around the upper reaches of its narrowing truck, infinitely grateful that the top of the tree, at least, remained pliable enough to break my speed without breaking me.

Like a lightweight fishing rod that had just hooked a trophy-sized bass, the tree flexed and bent over double, and I struggled to maintain my grip. I continued being carried over by my momentum until I was just past horizontal, looking out over the precipice down at the rocks below and praying the tree was stout enough not to snap.

It didn't. But thanks to my arrival first on the scene, and my subsequent bending over of the tree's top, it also failed to serve as a catcher's mitt to the next object that came flying its way.

Deiter.

Apparently so intent on gaining on me and implanting Dunleavy's dart in my posterior, Deiter followed me right off the ramp and into the air. He might have hit the same tree as I, had I not bent the top of it down out of his reach.

As the tree stopped its forward motion, I sensed the streaking form of Deiter passing just over my head. I heard the beginnings of a cry of terror disappear down the canyon as I began to accelerate backward with the stiffening of the tree.

Like a catapult, the tree straightened. The snapping motion was too much for me to maintain my grip, and I flew back through the air from whence I came, landing unceremoniously on my backside in a snowdrift, barely five feet on the safe side of the cliff's edge.

I lay in stunned near-silence. A low rumble and a gentle vibration that I couldn't identify echoed out of The Chutes. I ignored it for the time being. I had my own internal rumblings to deal with. One does not land spread-eagle in a treetop, no matter how flexible said tree might be, without exposing certain unmentionable portions of one's anatomy to significant discomfort.

I waited a long time until the quakes, both external and internal, subsided, before getting to my knees and gingerly crawling to the edge. Both of my skis had released in the tree and were nowhere to be found. I peered over the edge to see if I could spot them, or my adversary.

There was no sign of either. Nor would either likely be found before spring.

The rumbling I heard was the sound of an avalanche, most likely triggered by Deiter's fall, which had released and roared down the slope. Deiter, along with my skis, was down there somewhere, buried under thirty feet of snow. Not that he would have ever known. The fall was certainly fatal.

It got dark fast in the mountains. Through the fading light, I turned and began to trudge through the snow, turning downward toward the lights of the lodge below.

Although I had survived another attack, I knew it wouldn't be the end. I fought to stave off a feeling of helplessness. I only had one hope.

"Hurry, Bryce," I muttered. "Hurry."

* * * * * * * * * * * *

The package lay on the finely crafted walnut desk of Jose Antigua. It had been screened for explosives and swept for bugs and pronounced clean. His chief of security assured him it was just what it appeared to be. A single VHS videotape.

Antigua stared at the tape for a while. Its origins were a mystery to him, and he was a man who did not like mysteries. It had been passed up through one of his lieutenants, but no one was able to trace it back further than that. It had just appeared.

But eventually, curiosity overcame reticence, and he took the tape over to an audio-visual center on the opposite wall. He slid the tape into the VHS player, sat down, and with a remote control unit, hit the play button.

He watched the tape without any apparent emotion. When it was over, he rewound it and watched it again, pausing in several places, and replaying portions as well.

As the tape went to snow after a third and final time, Antigua pointed the remote at the television, pushed a button, and watched the screen go black. Silently, he pondered what his next move might be. He thought about the implications.

The tape had two people on it.

He knew both people.

Finally coming to a decision, he crossed over to his desk and sat down. Deliberately, he picked up the phone and made three calls. They all contained the same message.

"We need to meet."

* * * * * * * * * * *

Apart from a scratch on my neck, there were no outward signs of my close encounter with the Lodgepole pine, and I decided I really didn't want to drive down the hill alone, so I went ahead and emceed the banquet. Skip looked me up and down when I stumbled in after the long walk/slide down the hill. "I was getting a little worried about you out there, little brother," he said, concern etched on his face. "What kept you so long? And what happened to your neck?"

"I got held up by a tree," I said. "I'll tell you about it later. For now, I just want to be surrounded by friendly people."

I spent the rest of the evening wondering. Wondering if Dunleavy had a back up plan in case his man failed to do me in. Wondering if there was a pair of eyes trained on me, watching and waiting for a slip-up. Wondering when this nightmare was going to end. Wondering when Bryce was going to get back.

Wondering if the videotape had a snowball's chance of making a difference.

* * * * * * * * * * *

There were four men seated around the burlwood table. One seat was conspicuously empty.

Without preamble, Jose Antigua pushed a button on a remote control, and the tape began to play.

To say he had a captive audience would have been a significant understatement.

The television screen sprang to life with a shot of Jorge Carillo being seated at a restaurant table by a man they assumed was the establishment's host. "So what is this?" Miguel Carerra spoke out. "So he's having lunch? I don't…"

The upraised hand of Jose Antigua silenced him. He pointed back at the screen and said simply, "Shut up and watch."

Carerra wasn't used to being talked to in that manner, but something in the smaller man's voice and attitude overcame his anger, and his eyes were drawn back to the screen.

The videotape appeared to be a black and white surveillance tape. Carillo was seated reading a paper, when a man carrying two bottles of beer approached him. In the initial shot, the men in the room could not see who the man was, but it seemed that Carillo, by his body language, was familiar with him. The man placed a bottle of beer in front of Carillo.

He remained standing for a moment, apparently engaging Carillo in conversation. The man then put his own bottle of beer down on the table, took a piece of paper out of his suit coat pocket, and placed it on the table for Carillo to pickup. He then slid around and sat down opposite Carillo. It was the first time the men in the room were able to get a good look at the man's face.

Expressions of shock emanated from each of them. If there was any lack of interest in what the tape showed before, that was gone now. Jose Antigua had their complete and undivided attention now.

Carillo picked up the piece of paper and scanned it. He scowled and appeared to be upset about something. He held the paper up and pointed at an item. The man held his hands up and looked as if he were offering an explanation.

"They are discussing the playlist," Antonio Javerez muttered in disgust.

Apparently appeased by the man's explanation, Carillo tossed the paper back on to the table, and the man retrieved it. He then spoke something else to Carillo, which appeared to temporarily annoy the Colombian. But after a bit, the druglord somewhat reluctantly reached into his pocket and pulled out a wad of bills. Peeling off a series of them, he placed them on the table in front of the man. He then dismissed him.

"I knew it," Carerra spat out the words. "It's a payoff."

Smiling broadly, the man retrieved the stack of bills and made to get up, but first raised his beer in a toast, which Carillo unenthusiastically returned.

"So here's to a long and profitable business relationship, eh, Jorge?" Alejandro Dominguez said sarcastically.

The man left the table. Carillo chuckled, and then smiled in a self-satisfying manner.

The screen went to snow.

The men sat for a moment in stunned silence. As their rage began to boil over, Carerra, of course, was the first to speak. "The black dog." He turned to the rest of the men in the room. "I assume you all know who that man was?"

"Of course we know, Miguel," Antigua answered. "It appears our associate Jorge has become drinking friends with the Deputy Administrator of the Drug Enforcement Administration, Rick Jackson."

"He sold us out," seethed Carerra. "No wonder his shipments were able to get through. He was in bed with a rogue from the DEA all the time." His face contorted in anger. "I'll rip his heart out."

"I'm afraid you might have some competition for that honor, Miguel," Antigua said. "Besides, I may have a better way." He looked at the three men. "So are we in agreement then?"

Each of the men at the table nodded.

Miguel Antigua reached for the phone and began dialing.

* * * * * * * * * * *

Chapter 43

Bryce paged me from the in-flight telephone when he was about an hour out of Reno and asked me if I could pick him up at the airport. When I met him, he looked about as worn out as I felt. "Well?" I asked hopefully.

He shrugged. "Only time will tell, Greg. I think I managed to get it into the right hands, but even if it does do the trick, Carillo is still going to be a pretty powerful guy to bring down." He looked at me and smiled hopefully. "We're just going to have to wait. In the meantime, let's try to keep you out of trouble." He punched me on the shoulder. "So... how was your weekend?"

I told him.

* * * * * * * * * * *

Chance Dunleavy had just hung up the phone when it rang again. "'Ellaugh?"

"Mr. Dunleavy," a cold voice spoke through the receiver.

Dunleavy smiled. "Oh, gidday, Mr. Carillo," he said cheerfully. He knew what was coming. He was almost looking forward to it.

"Mr. Dunleavy, have you fulfilled the terms of our agreement?"

"Well, here, it's like this, Mr. Carillo..." he began.

"I take it that means you haven't."

"Naw... he's a slippery bugger that one is. I even brought in some help, but Oy haven't heard back from him."

"Four days, Mr. Dunleavy. I gave you four days, five days ago."

"Oy know you did, Jorge. But he's been somewhat, how shall I say, *unpredictable*."

"It was your job to account for the unpredictable, Mr. Dunleavy."

"*Was* my job?" Dunleavy said with a grin.

"Correct, Mr. Dunleavy. *Was* your job. If you can't accomplish a simple task of removing an untrained opponent within a reasonable amount of time, I'm afraid I won't be requiring your services." Carillo paused to relish the moment. "You're fired. And I expect the return of the deposit."

"Ah, but Jorge, you can't fire me."

Carillo's voice turned even colder. "What do you mean I can't fire you?"

"Because five minutes ago, Oy quit."

Dunleavy hung up the phone.

Barely able to maintain his usual impeccable control, Carillo took great pains to hang up the phone without slamming it down. Although his body language appeared calm, venom poured out through his black eyes. "So you quit, do you, Mr. Dunleavy? Fine. I will get someone else who perhaps isn't so concerned about what the police think but will at least leave me a corpse." He went to his wall safe and dialed the combination. Upon opening it, he reached in and drew out a small black notebook.

He brought it back to his desk and opened it to a list of names and numbers. After a short consideration, he selected the name of a former member of the Contras who specialized in sniping. "Perfect," Carillo sighed, already beginning to feel better. "A bullet at night outside his television studio from the darkness will never get traced back to me." He then said to himself with an air of satisfaction, "And when he is finished with Greg O'Brien, I may have a bonus job for him. I've become quite weary of a certain smart-mouthed Australian."

He picked up the phone and began to dial a series of numbers.

He never finished.

At the same moment Carillo pressed the first button on his telephone, three miles away, another finger pressed another button on another phone. This particular phone was connected to a paging system, which sent a signal to the Galaxy 4-A satellite. This signal was routed back to earth, with a digitally encrypted code to assure only one pager would receive the message. The designated receiver picked up the radio signal and was prompted to begin vibrating to alert its owner that a message had been acquired.

Only this pager wasn't fastened to any person's belt. It was taped to the inside of a small satchel. The insides of the pager had been modified so that instead of sending the electrical signal to the vibration device, it was sent to an electronic switch. As the switch closed, it completed a circuit that sent a more powerful electronic current, supplied by a 6-volt battery, down a wire. The wire leads terminated in a pencil-like detonator buried deeply inside a 10-pound mass of refined Semtex.

At the end of the detonator, the electrical impulse caused a small amount of mercury fulminate to explode. This flash of thermal energy caused a sudden change in the stability of the plastic explosive. Electrons orbiting the molecules of the explosive suddenly jumped to a higher energy level and then fell back, releasing a tremendous amount of force. The violent release by those molecules caused a chain reaction by the surrounding molecules, until the entire ten pounds of explosive released its pent-up energy, all in the space of a couple of micro-seconds.

In other words, boom.

Big boom.

But the ten pounds of plastic explosive had help. The amount of potential energy stored up in a nearly full 500-gallon propane tank is designed to heat a large home for over a month's time when doled out gradually. When that energy is released in under a second, the shock wave created can flatten old-growth pine trees for a radius of over 100 yards. The resulting fireball of such a release would incinerate any flammable substance within that same perimeter. The satchel with the Semtex was inconspicuously attached to the backside of just such a propane tank.

In addition, as if that weren't enough, two other satchels of plastic explosive were placed nearby in strategic positions. Both had identical triggering devices.

One was located in a first floor closet of the elegant mansion, next to an outside, weight-bearing corner. The charge was shaped to direct much of the blast outward, undermining the foundational strength of the building.

The third and last charge was located inside an oil tank buried along side the estate. Heating oil is typically very stable and will only explode when exposed to extremes of heat and pressure. The kinds of extremes Semtex can provide.

Jorge Carillo's phone call never went through.

Before he could finish dialing, his 8,400 square foot mansion on Franktown road was reduced to a flaming pile of rubble.

* * * * * * * * * * *

Chapter 44

The snow was falling.

It had been falling almost continually for the hour and a half since I had arrived, and still the flames burned brightly. The fire, which shot out of the ground like a volcanic plume over the ruptured oil tanks, stubbornly refused to yield to the extinguishing efforts of Mother Nature. It was as equally unaffected by the constant stream of water that six pumper engines from the Truckee Meadows Fire Department poured on it.

What was once a beautiful, two-and-a-half million dollar estate lay in smoldering ruins.

I was in the newsroom when I heard the call come over our police and fire scanner, shortly after the end of the 6:30 newscast. "Four alarms," Chas Burton, our nightside assignment editor yelled, the excitement rising in his voice. "Truckee Meadows is sending everything they've got."

Large fires like this one were not completely unheard of, and I began to return to my office. Then I heard it.

"Franktown Road," Chas radioed to one of our photographers who was already in the field.

My head snapped around fast enough to nearly cause whiplash. I sped back to the assignment desk, and asked, "Where on Franktown?"

Chas looked at a note he had just made. "Don't have an exact address, but it's down on the south side, right next to the golf course. Huge place, apparently." He then looked at me with a crooked grin. "Might be time to do another propane safety package, Greg."

My mouth went dry. "Propane?"

"Yep. According to preliminary reports, it looks like they had a huge tank, and it coulda froze a valve and filled the whole house with the stuff before it was torched."

My knees felt weak. I grabbed my coat. "Maybe I had better check it out myself."

*

As the flames finally began to die out, I approached Stan Gardner, the Truckee Meadows Fire Chief. "What can you tell me, Chief?"

He whirled around. "Wha?" Then his eyes flashed recognition. "Oh, it's you, Greg. Well, we have a lot of sifting to go through, but it appears the propane was probably the source of the explosion." He turned and looked at the smoke rising from the rubble. "What made it even worse was the place had some old heating oil tanks buried next to it. They aren't supposed to keep them full if they've switched over to gas, but a lot of these guys do, to fill up any diesel autos they might have." He shook his head. "It must have been a heck of a blast to set that stuff off."

I almost hated to ask the next question. "Anybody inside?"

"Yeah, what's left of them," he said grimly. "The Medical Examiner is going to have a job on his hands trying to ID them, though. We've found five bodies so far."

"Any...survivors?" I asked with my heart in my throat.

"Nope. We still have a lot of looking around, but even if the blast and fire didn't take them out, the building just collapsed when the bottom of the house was blown. Anybody who was in that house was either blown up, burned up, or flattened." He turned away and set out to resume his grisly task.

As the Chief disappeared into the smoldering ruins, I sat down on a log and stared. Steam and smoke intermingled in whirling patterns, illuminated by a kaleidoscope of colored flashing lights from the fire units. The sight before me looked like something Dante would have dreamed up after withdrawal. The shouts of the firefighters, mixed in with the constant thrum of the generators and water pumps, eventually were filtered out of my brain so that all I could hear was the sound of my own breathing and the pounding of my heart.

I cried.

I really don't know why. I didn't feel sad. They weren't tears of joy, either. I didn't feel anything at all. I just sat there and felt the tears stream down my face and drip off my chin, mixing and freezing into the freshly fallen snow at my feet. Soon, rivulets formed by the snowflakes melting atop my uncovered head supplemented the tears. I ignored them, and just sat and stared.

"What a waste," I said, to no one in particular.

*

The firefighters were beginning to wrap up their hoses. Television crews were heading back to the their stations, tapes full of the aftermath of another disaster, but fully ignorant of the history behind their latest lead story.

Wisps of steam percolated up periodically from the ashes, but even those were giving way to the constant, cleansing onslaught of the snowfall. A thin layer of white was already covering up the rubble.

"Kind of ironic, ain't it?"

I whirled around to find Bryce standing there.

"How long have you been there?" I asked with a hoarse voice.

"A while," he said softly. He looked at my tear-stained face. "You okay?"

I shrugged. "I guess. I thought I'd feel more...I don't know, more..."

"Triumphant?" Bryce asked.

I tried to smile. "Yeah, I guess something like that. But all I feel is tired."

"You can never get it all back, Greg. You can only go on."

I looked at my friend. He had lost far more than I had. His brother was never coming back. "So how are you doing?" I asked.

He looked up at the flakes as they fell into the trees. "Revenge is a dish best served cold, my friend," he said. Then he looked at me. "But in the end, it's still leftovers." And in the fading light, I saw a tear.

We turned and looked at the rubble, standing together, but each in our own thoughts.

"What's ironic?" I suddenly said.

"Huh?" he muttered as he shook himself out of his reverie.

"What's ironic? A while ago you said it was kind of ironic."

He smiled. "It just seemed fitting, that's all."

"What's that?"

He bent down and formed a snowball and tossed it onto the now completely-covered ruins. "That Jorge Carillo's tomb should get buried in snow."

As we walked up to the cars, I asked Bryce, "What are you going to do now that it's over?"

He slid into the driver's seat. "Actually, it's not quite over. I still have one more little task to perform." He pulled a small Palm-Pilot computer out of his pocket. He hooked it up to the cell phone that was hanging on the dashboard. After punching in a series of commands, he looked at me and asked, "Care to do the honors?"

"Neutron bomb?" I asked. He nodded. I shook my head. "No. I think you need to do this one."

He nodded again, and with a small pointing device, pressed down on the small screen on the "enter" button. "Go for it, Max."

* * * * * * * * * * *

Listeners to KOPP Radio all across western Nevada reached for their dials to try and figure out why there was now dead air. After several frustrating minutes, all but the most diehard listeners had given up and switched the station to another channel.

Employees inside the radio station were even more frustrated. For no reason, every computer in the station, from the ones that controlled the transmission signal to the ones that held crucial sales and financial data and every one in between, suddenly ceased to operate.

Attempts to reboot the computers all had the same result. The reappearance of the same message that showed up on the screens when they quit functioning:

Jeffery Boyd Hudson
Special Agent DEA
1963-1995

"Greater love hath no man...
Than he lay down his life for a friend..."

* * * * * * * * * * *

Bryce shut off the miniature computer, opened his window, and tossed it out into a snowdrift. He started his car and turned to me. "That just about wraps up my work. How about you? Shouldn't you be getting back to the station?"

I smiled. "Yes, I suppose I should. But I've got a pretty important job to do first, as well."

He offered his hand. I took it. "Take it easy, Ace," he said. "Try to stay out of trouble." He then drove off into the falling snow.

I strode to my car and drove as quickly as I dared back to the highway, where the snowplows were just about in a tie ball game as they battled the drifts. I drove north for about a half a mile, before pulling into the parking lot of a small mini-mart. I walked up to the payphone outside and swung open the door.

I used my phone card. I dialed the number, shaking with anticipation.

It rang only once. Lauren's voice answered. "Greg?" she said anxiously.

"Yeah, babe. It's me."

She paused. "What is it?" she asked, breathlessly.

I said the words that I had barely dared to dream about.

"Come home."

Epilogue

I saw Bryce once more before he left town. We had lunch together. At Miguel's. On the house.

"It looks like your little venture into moviemaking is paying bigger dividends than either of us had expected," he began after we were served.

"How's that?" I asked, my curiosity piqued.

"Seems as if we have started a real live turf war back in Colombia. Miguel Carerra's body was found this morning. He'd put on a little weight."

"Weight?"

"Yeah. About 5 pounds of lead."

"That will teach him to ignore diet and exercise. What else?"

"Antonio Javerez has gone into hiding, and it seems his political aspirations have been put on hold for a while. Right now, it looks like a contest between Alejandro Dominguez and Jose Antigua to see who gets ultimate control of the cartel. Should make for a great show."

I looked at him closely. "You expected that to happen, didn't you?"

He shrugged his shoulders. "I wouldn't say I expected it to happen, but it doesn't surprise me. Anytime you upset an apple cart like one of the drug cartels, you are going to find some of the other apples looking for a way to climb to the top of the pile. There's a reason there's suspicion and distrust amongst cartel members. If you're in a cartel, you spend seventy-five percent of your time convinced the others are plotting to stab you in the back. That's because the other twenty-five percent of the time, *you* are plotting how to plant the dagger yourself."

"Takes one to know one, huh?"

Bryce grinned.

I changed the subject. "You've accomplished what you set out to do. Carillo's dead. So what are your plans now?"

"Now that St. George has slain the dragon? Well, I've been giving that some thought." He gazed off into the distance. "There are still a lot of bad guys out there. Rick Jackson asked me if I wanted to continue our 'informal' relationship. I told him I'd think about it, but I don't think there's that much to think about." He smiled at me. "I mean, after all, can you imagine me in business suit? What would I do? Start my own security company? I don't think so. Not enough excitement."

"You could always learn to be a weatherman."

"I'm not that brave," he answered.

I walked him out to his car. There was still one thing I needed to ask him, but wasn't sure I wanted answered. But I had to. "Bryce, is it really over?"

He looked at me squarely. "Dunleavy?"

I nodded.

He thought for a while. "There's no way to tell for sure, but I don't think he will bother you any more, Greg. He's a professional. He doesn't kill out of anger; he kills because it's his job. Even though…" He stopped.

I looked at him. "Even though?"

"Even though you were a first. From what I can find out, you're the first target that he hasn't brought down."

"Oh, great. I always wanted to be a first."

"I really wouldn't worry about it, though. Carillo's gone. If you cut off the head of a snake, the body might thrash around for a while, but it doesn't have fangs anymore."

I thought about that for a moment. "Just what does that mean?"

"I don't know, but I thought it sounded good."

Then he drove off.

After the early newscasts, I wandered into Skip's office on my way out.

"Hey there, Little Bro," Skip greeted me.

"Skip, I just wanted to say…"

"Don't mention it, Buddy."

"No, Skip, I mean it. I'm not sure how to say this…"

"Then don't." He smiled. "You'd have done the same for me."

He was right. I would.

He punched me in the shoulder. I was proud of the fact it stayed in joint. "Say, don't you have some folks to meet?" he asked.

I smiled through the pain. "Lauren and the kids arrive in a couple of hours. I'm going to pick them up at the airport, and God help Southwest Airlines if they are late." I looked at my watch. "I think I'll go and wait for them now."

"Give them all a kiss for me."

The night was crystal clear. It often did that after a good snow in Reno. The city sparkled, its neon lights trying to compete with the brilliant starlit sky. The neon put up a good fight but was hopelessly outclassed.

Since I knew I would probably drive the Southwest Airlines counterperson to drink if I tried waiting at the terminal, I decided to spend the next hour on Windy Hill. It's a small rise in an isolated part of town that overlooks the valley and the airport. I walked out to the edge of the bluff and sat down on the bench. I watched the jets come in, knowing that soon one of those planes would be bringing my life back.

It was good to be alone. I let my eyes drift off to the southeast, trying to peer through the hundreds of miles that still separated me from my family, willing my vision to see the strobe of their aircraft. I couldn't, of course. But it was good to know it was coming. It was good to know I could hold my family again. It was good to know that for the first time in over a month, we were finally safe.

"I have killed many men in my lifetime, but none have given me the pleasure I will feel when I kill you."

The words hit me like jolt of lightning. I spun around, unable to breathe, barely able to focus on the steady hand that held the Colt 45. As it was backlit by the distant street lamp, it took me a moment to recognize the face of the man who held the weapon, but recognize it I did, even though I had only seen it once in person.

Jorge Carillo.

Even in the poor light, I could see bruises, cuts and burns on his face. The hand that held the gun was wrapped in gauze. One eye was covered in a bandage. But his uncovered eye still seemed so dark as to suck even what little light there was from the surrounding area. The only brightness came from a splash from his teeth, as his lips peeled back in an evil grin. The black Phoenix had risen from the ashes.

My head spun. No! It couldn't be. "How…?" I sputtered.

His grin turned even more malicious. He slowly walked around me, beyond arm's length, until he backed me up to the bench. "How? How what? Do you mean 'How am I going to kill you?' The answer is 'Slowly, and with great pain.' Or do you mean, as I suppose you do, 'How did I escape the explosion?'

"I was in my basement study when your pitiful attempt to destroy me occurred. I was rendered unconscious, and when I awoke, the flames were beginning to work their way downward toward me. Fortunately, I had an underground passageway installed from my study to an outside entrance beyond the estate gates, in case I ever needed to get in or out unnoticed. This was one of those times. And all I have thought about since that time was this moment. I am glad I didn't have to wait long." He began to raise the gun.

I tried to stall for time. I knew pleading wouldn't get me anywhere. The man didn't have a merciful bone in his body. So I tried to get him angry. Not that it was hard. "But where can you go now? You're washed up, Carillo. Everything you have is gone."

He lowered the gun slightly and laughed. "Gone? You think everything I have is gone? I have lost but trifles. I have bank accounts even my associates don't know about. And I still have power. In fact, I may have more power when this is over than ever. I have heard of a disruption occurring within the ranks of my associates since my little mishap. When they are done fighting each other, it will be a perfect opportunity for me to go in and pick up the pieces." He looked at me and laughed. "I suppose I should give you the credit for that."

"Well, a simple thank you would be sufficient…"

"Shut up!" he snarled. "I have heard about your warped sense of humor, but I for one no longer find you amusing. You have become a nuisance, Mr. O'Brien. An irritation, like a buzzing gnat. And gnats don't last long around me before they get squashed." He raised the gun and lined it up on my forehead.

"Goodbye, Mr. O'Brien."

Without realizing it, my hands had drifted into my pockets, where I still carried the five smooth stones I had picked up in the church parking lot. I knew it was futile. At least David had a sling. Outraged at the thought I wasn't going to see my family again after all, I decided on one last desperate, though surely useless move. All it could do was to delay the inevitable. But at least I wouldn't give the demon the pleasure of seeing me go down without a fight.

As I sensed his finger pressing on the trigger, I dropped to the ground. I heard the roar of the gun discharge and was temporarily blinded by the muzzle flash. I felt a rush of air as the bullet zipped by my temple. I pulled one of the stones out of my pocket, and without having time to aim, hurled it toward him with all the strength and rage that the previous months had built up inside me.

I never saw if the rock found its mark, but I knew that even if it had, it was too small, and I was too defenseless. I rolled under the bench to try and find some cover from the inevitable bullet, but even that I knew would do me no good. The bench was so small it was like trying to hide behind a stop sign. I curled up into a fetal position, closed my eyes, thought of my children, and waited for the next bullet to tear into my flesh.

And I waited.

Two seconds under those circumstances seems like an eternity. Three eternities later, I cracked open an eye, and fearfully peered up at my attacker.

He stood staring, the gun still in his outstretched hand. He seemed to be looking toward me, but just above and to the right of where I then lay. His lips were still peeled back in that demonic grin of his. In a detached way, I tried to figure out why he didn't fire at me again.

And then I saw the blood.

There wasn't a lot of it, and it had already stopped flowing. Just above his patched eye, a small hole had appeared, and a tiny amount of blood had spilled out. Jorge Carillo stood staring…at nothing.

Even when balanced perfectly at the moment of death, gravity will still eventually triumph. Ever so slowly, Carillo's now lifeless body began to teeter backwards, gaining momentum, until it toppled off the bluff into the sagebrush below.

I stared at the empty place where Carillo had stood. Then I slowly withdrew another of the stones from my pocket and looked at it unbelievingly. Without a sling.

"Oy never did like that bloke. Bloody drongo he was."

I was already too much in shock to whirl around at the voice behind me. But even before I slowly rolled over, I knew the voice came from Chance Dunleavy.

As I looked up at him, he smiled back at me. He held a small caliber pistol with a silencer screwed onto the long, narrow barrel. A thin wisp of smoke curled lazily out of the end. He then pointed the gun at me.

Out of the frying pan and into the fire.

I rolled onto my back in a final gesture of resignation.

"You've been a bit of a burr under moy saddle, mate," Dunleavy said with a grin. "Can't remember when oy've had so much fun, though."

I didn't have anything left. "Spare me, please," I said, my mouth so dry that the words barely tumbled out. "Just get it over with."

Dunleavy looked curiously at me, and then down at the gun in his hand. He laughed. "Naw… ya got it all wrong. Oy'm off your case." He pointed at the spot where Carillo went over the edge. "Let's just say a better job offer came moy way. Oy was just fortunate to have made some initial preparations at his house earlier, just in case." He looked at me. "But as for you, mate…Like Oy said, it ayen't nothin' *personal*."

He slid the pistol into his jacket pocket. "Well, Oy'd better be getting off now. Thought Oy'd go on a bit of a walkabout. Maybe even try moy hand at that skiing of yours. Gidday." And as he turned and walked away, he began to whistle an unknown tune.

I stared at him, unbelievingly. He then stopped and turned. "Say, mate. What's the weather outlook, anyway? Oy wouldn't want to get snowed on up in them there mountains now, would Oy?"

Mechanically and without feeling or thought, I said, "Mostly sunny skies, light winds, highs in the 40's."

He nodded appreciatively. Then he smiled and winked at me, and said, "Oy hope your right. If you're not, you might just be hearing from me." And then he turned and disappeared into the night.

I have never wanted a forecast to be so right in all my life.

Printed in the United States
1499100006B/99